INSIDE

Death Row Chronicles Vol. 1

By Nicky James

Inside: Death Row Chronicles Vol 1

Copyright © 2020 by Nicky James

This is a work of fiction. Names, characters, businesses, places, events, and incidents are either the products of the author's imagination or used in a fictitious manner. Any resemblance to actual persons, living or dead, or actual events is purely coincidental.

Cover Artist:

Nicky James

Editing:

Boho Edits

Proofreading:

LesCourt Author Services

All rights reserved.

No part of this book may be reproduced or transmitted in any form or by any means without written permission of the author.

Trademarks are the property of their respective owners

All credit for the works and words of Edgar Allan Poe quoted in this document are given to him.

It is better that ten guilty persons escape than that one innocent suffer.
—*Sir William Blackstone*—

Chapter One

MAYBE THIS WHOLE transfer was nothing more than a big mistake. First the house, then the miscommunication with my start date, now the ever-growing mountain of guilt at abandoning my mother in Michigan. Guilt which grew heavier and more pronounced the more times she called, texted, or left messages. None of which I'd returned.

The collar on my black T-shirt stuck to my neck. Despite the goosebumps radiating down my arms and the constant chatter in my teeth, sweat trickled down my spine and beaded at my temples. My body was a conflicting ball of nerves. I'd rolled the window down on my Jeep Wrangler, and the whipping wind sent my dark hair flying in every direction. I breathed in the scents of freedom and change while absorbing the pre-dawn, seventy-degree temperature.

Texas. I'd run all the way to Texas. When my head stopped racing and a brief moment of respite wormed its way into my body, allowing me to think, I still couldn't believe I'd dropped everything and relocated my entire life to the other side of the country.

The US-190 was relatively quiet at this early hour, which was my one saving grace since I'd already missed my orientation meeting yesterday with the warden, and I was officially twenty-four hours late for my first day of work. I drove faster than the speed limit, one arm dangling out the window as the tires ate up the road. I was determined to be early today and save whatever reputation I had left. This wasn't how I wanted to start my new life.

Perspiration gathered on my palms, and they slid, slick with moisture on the wheel. Butterflies swarmed and swooped in my belly.

Inhale the good, exhale the bad, I told myself. Inhale. Exhale. Things would be different here. I'd make sure of it.

Firstly, the weather was already to my liking. The sun hadn't risen, and I could easily venture outside without a jacket. Huge plus. Back home, we'd be lucky to have spring temperatures in the low sixties. Nights still dipped close to freezing. Frost on the windshield in the morning wasn't unheard of in May. But not here.

This was heavenly.

I tipped my chin and let the current of air jetting through my window wash over me.

The past two months had tested my fragile resolve in more ways than I could count. Physically. Mentally. Emotionally. And that was before I'd made a life-changing decision to move across the country to work in a unit more complex than any I'd experienced in my life. Never mind buying a house on a whim after only a few brief conversations with a Realtor and seeing a half a dozen less than honest pictures of it online.

Not my smartest decision.

So I took small graces where I could find them. Namely, the balmy Texas weather.

The closer I got to the Allan B. Polunsky Unit, the sparser the landscape. A slim number of trees dotted the horizon on my left, their dark silhouettes reaching tall and barely visible against the indigo sky. Dawn was forty minutes out, the first signs of the coming day showing in the faint changing of color in the east.

It was a twenty-minute drive from my homestead in Onalaska to the prison. Twenty minutes of a mostly barren landscape. The signs dotting the side of the highway warned of the risks of picking up hitchhikers when in such close proximity to a high-security facility.

It wasn't like prison breaks were a frequent occurrence, but you never knew. The warnings were valid. Although, I hadn't heard of anything newsworthy happening in the area since the Texas 7 escaped the John B. Connally Unit in 2000.

That was almost twenty years ago. I was twelve years old at the time and had no idea that I would pursue a job as a corrections officer in the future.

Since I hadn't arrived in Onalaska until late last night, this was my first introduction to the Polunsky Unit. I saw the bright security lights in the distance long before I saw the tall, razor-wire topped fences and impenetrable concrete walls of my new home away from home. Those lights shone like the midday sun. There was no missing the looming building on the horizon and no disguising the horrors that lived within her walls. It screamed its presence and purpose loud and clear to anyone passing by. Guard towers stood out like beacons, set at intervals around the prison, manned with armed guards using A-15 assault rifles who were prepared to take action should it be necessary.

I pulled into the vast parking lot and found an empty spot about two dozen feet from the secured gates where I'd need to sort out my admission since I had yet to acquire my employee badge, uniform, or other belongings marking me as a corrections officer.

I killed the engine and collected my backpack with the few personal belongings I intended to keep in my locker, along with my lunch.

I exited my Jeep and scanned the colossal structure sitting sentient in the pre-dawn light. Encased in silence, it commanded respect of the highest order. A sense of rippling danger pulsed across the open land. According to my mom, it took a special person to do this job, and I knew for a fact, she wished I wasn't that person.

An eerie chill drew more goosebumps to the surface, prickling the hairs on my arms to rise. I rubbed them away, eradicating the unease as I noted all the similarities and differences from the last place I'd worked.

I'd been warned, transferring from a medium-security unit to a supermax prison would take some adjusting. At the time, the warnings hadn't affected me. I'd been dead set on change, no matter what. When a position working The Row came up, nothing could have dissuaded me from taking it. At the time, I wasn't convinced even Texas was far enough away from my problems.

I crossed the parking lot to the secured gates and guardhouse and was met by a uniformed officer with sagging jowls and a wide midsection. His face was pitted and scarred, likely from years of untreated acne as a teenager.

"G'day." He tipped his head and scanned my person. It was clear by the look in his eyes he'd pegged me for a worker and not some eager visitor showing up hours before visitations opened.

"Anson Miller. New employee. Corrections officer. I have a meeting scheduled with Warden Oberc at six."

Another scan and the guard pulled his radio from his shoulder holster and called it in, requesting an escort. Once he reclipped his radio to his shirt, he tucked his thumbs in the belt loops of his pants and rocked on his feet, puffing his chest out and keeping his chin high.

"New guy, huh? I'm Tully Wilkinson. Where they stickin' ya?"

"Not sure what block, but it'll be on The Row."

He whistled and nodded. I couldn't determine if he was impressed or thought me a sucker for taking such a job.

"Not surprised. They've been scrambling for staff for as long as I've been workin' 'ere."

"And how long has that been?"

"Oh, going on twenty years now. Wouldn't be caught dead on The Row, no sir. Not sure who's more troubled in the head after a few years behind them gates, the inmates or the poor sots who guard 'em."

That was reassuring. I'd learned the turnover rate for supermax prison officers was high. It was a risk I'd been willing to take, considering there weren't a whole lot of immediate options when it came to transfers after, what I liked to call, The Incident.

"Someone's gotta do it."

"Too true. Good luck to ya, lad. Don't let those boys in there mess with your head."

"Thanks, I won't."

We stood in awkward silence as I waited for my escort to take me to Warden Oberc's office. The sky was lighter in the east, a watercolor wash of indigo fading to azure, then to a pink-tinted sapphire. The dawning day was full of life and beauty that seemed out of place standing on the outskirts of a maximum-security prison. It would have been more fitting had there been storm clouds moving in or rain dotting the pavement.

I tipped my chin and closed my eyes, absorbing the gentle breeze as it washed over my face. "It's beautiful here. Can't imagine what summer must be like. It just stopped snowing back home."

"This here weather is about perfect. Summer tries to kill us more times than not. Blazing sun nearly cooks us where we stand. Where y'all from where there's snow?"

"Moved from Michigan. Was one of the most brutal winters I've seen in a lot of years. Freezing. Snowed right on through until Easter weekend. Was only just starting to thaw when I left."

In fact, it was a balmy forty-seven degrees the day I drove away.

Tully shuddered and shook his head. "Ha! No thank you. Y'all can keep that weather."

The noise of boots clipping on asphalt caught my attention. I turned in time to see a middle-aged African American guard saunter down the path from within the prison walls. He wasn't in a hurry, that much was apparent. His chest was wide, and his scowl turned the age lines on his face into deep craters.

"This here's Clarence." Tully clapped my shoulder and gestured. "Clarence, we got another newbie on our hands. Name's Anson..." He fumbled with his memory, waving a hand as though it might conjure the missing name.

"Miller," I provided.

"Right. Anson Miller with an appointment to meet with the warden."

"Nice to meet you." I held out my hand to shake, but Clarence stared at it with hard eyes and a stone-cold expression. There was a void beyond their depths that was unnerving.

I retracted my hand and gave a tight smile, shifting my backpack on my shoulder and standing taller, injecting my own authority into my stance to show I wasn't a pushover. I was a shade over six feet, and unlike my old coworkers back at the Ionia Correctional Facility, or the I-Max for short, I spent all my free time working off my daily stresses in the gym instead of drinking them away at a local pub.

"This way," Clarence mumbled.

I kept a close clip behind him, matching his slow stride as we headed to the main building. Before we disappeared within her walls, I took one last look at the coming day before I was locked inside with the rest of them.

Clarence remained unspeaking as we weaved down a few drab corridors. The fluorescent lights overhead were harsh against the once-white concrete walls. They were dingy and bland now, sucking the life out of everyone who passed them by.

The jingle of keys and the clang of metal stopped my roaming perusal of the hallway. Clarence guided me into another section of the facility and stopped short at one of the few doors that held any life. A small plaque marked our final destination. It read, Warden Pearson Oberc.

"He ain't in yet. Not until six every day. You'll wait here."

Clarence shoved the door open and tipped his chin, indicating for me to head inside. There was a large, metal-framed desk, a few chairs, notable framed certificates hanging on the walls, and a dying fern in the corner that looked in desperate need of a drink and some sunlight. There were no windows. No extras. Nothing to alleviate the weighted somberness that hung over the entire facility. It was a functional office, nothing more. The scent of stale coffee and mildew hung in the air.

I thanked Clarence, who didn't acknowledge me, and let myself into the room. Dropping my backpack on the ground, I sat on the edge of a steel-framed chair, fanning my shirt again as I looked around. My nervous state had me perspiring like a damn pig. It didn't help that the circulation in the building was shitty, and the air in the room sat stagnant and stale.

I wasn't alone for long, but it was enough time for the past to creep back in, and I caught myself massaging an invisible ache on my left side below my ribs. It was a reminder of why I'd broken my mother's heart and jumped ship, running across the country to get as far away from everything as I could.

I dropped my hand and stretched the afflicted side, wondering if the sensation of pulling skin was real or imagined. Before I could lift my T-shirt and examine the remaining scar, the door behind me opened.

I shot to my feet and turned to greet my new boss but was met with a confused scowl on a weathered face that stopped my words in my throat.

"Who are you?"

No hi or hello or where were you yesterday. The barked question carried a hint of irritation like I should be ashamed for bringing a hiccup into this man's scheduled day.

He was sturdy and tall, broad-shouldered, thick-waisted, and wearing a suit that was wrinkled like one might expect to see at the end of a shift, not the beginning.

Pearson Oberc had warm brown skin, dotted with many scars and age marks, hair that was cropped short and more white than its original black. Deep wrinkles surrounded his eyes and mouth, lines that spoke of a hard life that came from managing a place like Polunsky.

I offered my hand. "Anson Miller. Transfer from Ionia in Michigan. I'm sorry, there was a miscommunication, and I think you were expecting me yesterday."

Unlike Clarence, the warden slapped his giant callused mitt into mine and shook with a firmness I expected from a man in his position. "Ionia?"

"Yes, sir."

He released my hand and sucked his teeth as he scanned me, a deep V between his brows.

"Sit down. To be honest, it's been such a shit show around here, I ain't got a clue who you are."

I found my seat as he circled the desk, relieving himself of his suit jacket and tossing it over another chair. He tugged a thick loop of keys from his belt and unlocked the top drawer on the filing cabinet in the corner, yanking it open with a drag of rusty metal that resonated in my teeth.

"What'd you say your name was again?"

"Anson. Anson Miller, sir."

He flipped through a few files and slammed the drawer, opening the one underneath it with the same whine of metal. Whatever he was looking for wasn't there either. He paused his search, leaning his arm over the open cabinet as he scanned his desk. It was piled high with loose papers, brown folders, manila envelopes, and a handful of dirty coffee mugs.

Abandoning his search in the filing cabinet, he dropped onto his chair and rifled through the stacks of papers on his desk until he found a folder that interested him. He tugged it loose, opened it, and squinted at the pages inside as he held it a distance from his face. His frown deepened.

"You're late. You were supposed to report in yesterday."

"Yes, sir. The paperwork Warden Eakens gave me stated I should be here on the eleventh, not the tenth. I apologize." I tugged the forms

I'd been given for my transfer from my backpack and handed them over.

Warden Oberc snatched them and read them over once before thrusting them back into my hand.

"Left hand don't know what the right hand's doing, ain't that always how it goes?"

"Yes, sir."

Warden Oberc scrubbed a hand over his face and wet his lips as the phone on his desk rang. He leaned back in his chair, looking exasperated, and yanked it off its holder.

"What?"

He pinched the bridge of his nose as he listened to the person on the other end of the line.

"What time was that at? Uh-huh... Where's Ray? Oh. Okay... You need extra hands?" He blew out a breath. "I'll be down in a few."

He hung up but lifted the receiver right away and punched a few numbers. When the call connected, he said, "Send Ray down after briefing; I got his new guy here and no time to take him through the ropes."

He slammed down the receiver and studied me. "Raymond McCarthy is the Director of Commissions for 12-Building. He'll get you set up with a uniform, take you through our daily documentation process, give you the grand tour, assign you a block, highlight our rules and regulations—which you'll find are very different than what you might be used to—and lastly, he will pair you with another officer for a few days until he feels you're ready to be fit into the schedule. Any questions, he's your man. He's your superior officer. You take your shit to him and don't bring it to my feet unless you feel it's absolutely necessary. Do I make myself clear?"

"Yes, sir."

Warden Oberc pushed away from his desk and retrieved his suit jacket, punching his arms through the holes and tugging it straight over his wide chest.

"Welcome to the Polunsky Unit. If you'll excuse me, I have a riot brewing in F that needs my attention."

With that, he was gone.

I sat motionless, jaw tight, muscles clenched as I wondered again whether this move was for the best. The warden's short fuse could be blamed on many things, including staff shortages, long hours, or too many years of exposure to the darker side of life. The truth was, working in such an environment inevitably sucked the spark of life out of a person. Based on the credentials on the wall, Warden Oberc had been at it for almost as many years as I'd been alive.

It was nearing six thirty before the Director of Commissions came to find me. I rose from my seat when the door opened, and I came face to face with a redheaded man in his late forties wearing an ash-gray uniform with darker navy stripes running down the sides of both legs and across the top of his shoulders. He had a radio clipped to his thick utility belt along with multiple closed pouches containing treasures such as a flashlight, handcuffs, keys, tear-resistant gloves, first aid kit, pepper spray, and other useful tools to make our job easier and safer.

It was commonly believed corrections officers were armed, but that wasn't the case. The last thing we needed was an inmate who had nothing to lose to gain the upper hand and relieve us of our weapons.

Raymond's pale cheeks were heavily freckled, and his green-blue eyes glimmered with the first smile I'd seen since I left my Jeep.

"You'd be the long-lost Anson Miller, I presume."

His handshake was equally firm as his stature. He wasn't a small man and filled out his uniform nicely, matching my height.

"That'd be me. Mix-up on paperwork. I apologize for the tardiness."

"No worries. I'm just glad you didn't jump ship before you started. It's happened."

I quirked a brow. "That's not reassuring at all."

"Bah, you'll be fine. It ain't as bad as they make it sound. Name's Raymond McCarthy, but everyone calls me Ray. Follow me, and I'll take you into the belly of the beast."

I snagged my backpack off the floor, and we headed into another section of the facility, then up two flights of stairs until we were on the top floor.

"I'll assign you a locker, get you a uniform, and show you where we take care of morning briefings. I'll also get you a passcode for the computers so you can log your daily reports. You've worked in the system before, correct?"

"I have. Worked ten years at I-Max in Michigan."

"Medium-security?"

"Yup."

"This will be a whole different dance for you."

"That's what I'm hoping."

"Bad experience? I haven't had a chance to read your file yet."

"It was fine." I didn't want to get into the nitty-gritty of why I'd left Ionia. That was the point of walking away. A fresh start where no one knew me or the secrets that should have stayed hidden. Ray would learn all he needed to know from my file, but I trusted it to remain confidential. "Just needed a shakeup."

"All right. Well, you'll see we do things a bit different here. You ever been in a death row unit before?"

"No, not directly. I did some reading before coming so I'd know what to expect, but the information varies."

"It does." We arrived at a bland metal door, and Ray scanned a card before it buzzed and clicked. He held it open and followed me inside. "What you'll learn about death row in Texas is we ain't nothin' like everyone else. We're the badass motherfuckers with the strictest rules going. Privileges are something our guys don't see a lot of. Just how it is, and there ain't no changin' it. Them rules come from up top."

"Gotcha."

We'd entered into what looked like a common staffroom, which doubled as a conference room and workstation. There were lockers along one wall, long metal tables, plenty of chairs similar to the one I'd sat on in the warden's office, and a row of windows with heavy, crisscrossing bars over them that made a tiny diamond pattern. The windows overlooked a fenced-in yard below that was unoccupied at the moment. Old coffee grew stale in a pot on a table, there was a small fridge, and more dying plants that I assumed were a failed effort at making the area homier.

"You'll see security cameras everywhere you go." Ray pointed to one in the corner by the ceiling. "After some bullshit in 2008, we got funding to install some video surveillance. There are over a thousand cameras spread all over our nineteen buildings. Don't get all weirded out thinking there are eyes on your back at all times. Unless you work in the hotspots of general population, we don't have a manned surveillance station watching everyone twenty-four seven. Too many man hours, not enough dollars. We have a small crew who focus strictly on six troubled areas in GP. That's it. The cameras here and throughout the rest of the facility record and hold up to two weeks of video, so if we have an incident, we can roll it back and check things out. If we suspect suspicious behavior, we can check that out too. That kind of thing."

"Sounds good. We had something similar at I-Max."

Ray crossed the room and fiddled with a lock on one of the lockers in the bottom corner before he succeeded at yanking it open. Inside was a tall stack of plastic-wrapped uniforms, the same as the one he wore. "Come pick your size and grab two of each. If you want more than two fresh uniforms, it'll come out of your own budget. I'll get your belt."

I fished through the pile of shirts and pants until I found two suitable sets. Ray fiddled with a utility belt he'd laid out on the table as he ensured all the pouches contained the correct items. He talked me through each piece of equipment, and I listened attentively even though it was identical to the setup we had at Ionia.

Ray nodded at a set of doors along the opposite wall. "Bathrooms, showers, change rooms. We have a staff gym on premises, too, if that's your thing. I can show you later. For now, head on in there and get yourself dressed. I'll find your passcodes, and we'll do a quick computer orientation before I take you on the grand tour."

I didn't waste any time getting dressed, and by the time I was done, Ray had a locker set up for me. I tucked my lunch in the staff fridge and shoved the rest of my belongings in my new locker.

Ray had me sit beside him at one of the many computer stations set up along one wall and showed me where to find all the basic forms I might need on any given day. Daily log forms, incident reporting, and so forth. It was all similar enough to my old job, I didn't have too many questions.

"We do a mass debriefing every day before your shift starts where you'll learn of any incidences around the compound, be it pertaining to your section or not. When you meet with the guard you're relieving, they'll go through the details more specific to your area and share if there've been notable issues with any of your charges."

Once I was clear on the basic administrative procedures, Ray announced it was time to head to the dungeon.

He took me back down to the main level, and we followed numerous lifeless corridors with the same dark blue jagged stripe along the middle of the wall. It stood out against the bland white behind it and drew my eye as we walked. It jumped and dipped in uneven patterns, some larger than others.

"12-Building will be your new home," Ray said as we walked. "It houses all our death row inmates and those sentenced to administrative segregation, or Ad Seg as we like to call it, also known as solitary confinement. There are six pods in 12-Building, and each pod consists of eighty-four cells divided among six sections. Each section is broken down into fourteen cells each. Two guards cover two sections. So you'll have twenty-eight charges on your watch with one coworker.

"At present, we have 287 men on The Row along with forty-six guys in solitary. We keep those guys in F-Pod, and if you haven't been warned, they are the crazy fuckers you need to watch out for. They'll keep you on your toes."

"Really? I thought it'd be the other way around."

"Common misconception. Although the guys on The Row don't have anything to lose, they're the ones battling appeals left and right. A judge won't look kindly on a troublemaker. Mostly our guys cross their t's and dot their i's. Whereas the guys doing stints in Ad Seg, they don't give a fuck."

We approached the first of what looked like many crash gates which separated each hallway and section of the unit. Ray slowed and stood with his hands on his hips, looking beyond the blue barred door.

"Welcome to death row, my friend. Before I walk us through, a word from the wise. I've been Director of Commissions for just over seven years. Officer like yourself before that. If there's one thing I learned working at this level, it was not to take a macho attitude to work with me every day. Ever heard the saying, you attract more bees with honey than with vinegar? That applies here. From my experience, you'll get on better with the men behind these doors with a drop of understanding and a touch of kindness than you will throwing your muscles and authority around. They are human beings. It don't matter what they did to get here, your job is to keep them safe, from themselves and others. Of course, you can ignore me and go in all tough guy, but I promise you, you won't be doing yourself any favors. This isn't the same work you did in general population medium-security. This is hard time. This is the end of the line."

Ray studied me while I absorbed his words. It made sense and gave me a strange sense of hope that this was going to be a better fit for me than back home. I peered through the first crash gate and down the long corridor beyond. The same white walls that we'd followed thus far continued, along with the same dark blue line I'd been admiring. Except, the line was no longer jumping and jagged. It was straight, running horizontally at about waist height for as far as the eye could see.

I turned and looked back from where we'd come, noting the jagged, uneven rhythm of the same blue line behind us. Frowning, I flipped my gaze back beyond the gates.

"You see it, don't you?" Ray said.

"Tell me I'm wrong."

Ray chuckled and rubbed a hand over his close-cropped red hair. "Wish I could. Although, I'm sure the government body that decided on this design would deny it until the end of time."

I walked to the wall and placed my hand over the last spike of blue as it shot up a shorter way than the rest before returning to waist-level before the crash gate. From that point on, the line remained flat.

"It's a heart monitor," I said. "And the pulsing beats stop here. That's…"

"Morbid?"

I nodded. "A disgusting joke. That's not creative or funny at all. This is horrible."

"Agreed."

We stood, staring at the blue line along the wall for a minute more. The uneasy chill I'd felt in the parking lot returned, and I was glad my uniform was long-sleeved and hid the raised hairs on my arms. It didn't matter how many years a person worked in this field, no one was unaffected by death row—even me, who'd never been inside the unit before.

"Shall we?"

I swallowed my disgust with the blue line and met Ray at the gate. He radioed control for entry, and we were through the first of many gates, the metal crashing closed behind us with an aura of finality that was disconcerting

The belly of the beast, Ray had called it. The ominousness of our destination weighed heavy on my shoulders the farther in we strode. One thing I knew, once inside a place like 12-Building, if shit when down, you were stuck there.

Chapter Two

"THIS HERE'S A-POD," Ray announced as we approached the first long corridor of cells. "Section A and B are designated as deathwatch. Twenty-eight cells total, and it includes this row of cells right here, the ones directly above, the hall adjacent to this one, and the one above it. It's rare they're all filled at once. Deathwatch—"

Before Ray could go on to explain, I jumped in and filled in the blank as we faced the long line of numbered cells. "When the Criminal District Court Judge signs the Warrant of Execution, prisoners come here for their final weeks."

"Correct. This is their last home before they get moved to Huntsville or Death House as we call it. Guards are doubled in these sections, and it will be part of your rotation on occasion, although I do ask for volunteers most of the time because it can be heavy and trying. These fellas here are the most apt to try suicide by whatever means possible. Their numbers are up, and their dates are set. It's our job to ensure that doesn't happen. Mostly, they want to purge and talk. You'll hear a lot of uncomfortable stuff working here. Be prepared for that."

I noted the guards present. They'd made brief eye contact when we'd come onto the floor, but they were busy with their daily routine and hadn't bothered with a second glance in our direction.

Ray clapped my shoulder and aimed me toward an open steel staircase leading to another level. "Up we go. We'll move right on through to B-Pod to give you a general idea of how we're all set up down here. These are all single person, sixty-square-foot cells. The inmates get a slit window, about two inches high and two feet long.

That's all the exposure to sunlight they get. They have a bed with a thin mattress and a toilet and sink combo. Nothing more. That's what they are provided outside a standard-issue jumpsuit. Whatever else they have in their cells was bought at commissary, and they earn the right to keep those possessions. It can be extra clothing, extra food items, art supplies, fans because it's hot as fuck in there, books, stuff like that. Unlike other death row units, we don't allow TVs, only radios are permitted if purchased."

We made it to the upper level, and Ray guided me down various halls and through another crash gate until we entered a different pod.

"The days at Polunsky begin at three-thirty in the morning when breakfast is served. After breakfast is eaten and medication is administered to certain inmates who require it, the men are responsible for tidying their cells while we go around and find out who's going to rec and showers for the day."

"Everyone gets that option?"

We stopped in front of a bank of cells, white steel doors with thin rectangular windows on both sides—no more than three inches wide—if that—and reinforced with the same crisscrossing diamond-barred pattern inside the glass as I'd seen in the staff area. They had black painted numbers to identify each and locking chute-style doors midway down where food trays could be delivered and inmate's hands cuffed before transfers.

Ray turned to me. "Nope. Shower and rec privileges depend on what level class they're currently in. We work on a three-tier system based on good behavior. In level one, they are getting the best of what they can hope for." Ray ticked off on his fingers. "They have their property, commissary accessibility every fourteen days, visitation rights for two hours once a week, and shower and rec time for two hours, five days a week.

"Downgrading to level two or three happens if an officer has to file a report for poor behavior. When that goes down, restrictions come into effect. They can't return to a level one until ninety days of cooperation have been noted. In level two, inmates are restricted from having personal property, have reduced rec and shower time, commissary is strictly hygiene items, no library requests, and reduced visitation rights to twice a month. Level three is pretty close to the same as two, less visitation again—one a month—fewer dollars toward commissary, longer wait time to rise back to one. No extras."

"Gotcha."

As Ray gave me the rundown of levels, another officer made his way down the long row of cells. We'd stopped on the upper level of section B in B-Pod. The man banged on each door and peeked in the cell window before moving to the next. The noise traveled and bounced off the ceiling, echoing off the walls.

"We are anything but soundproofed around here. Just because the doors are well sealed doesn't mean we can't hear every goddamn thing that goes on inside them. These men fart, we hear it. They shit loud, all I can say is, enjoy." Ray chuckled as I made a face.

"Lovely."

"Some guys complain of headaches because the noise gets to them, but you get used to it. It's echoey and worse in the daytime when everyone is awake."

My attention returned to the officer checking cells. After squinting through the slim window at door B17, the officer banged a second time. "Give me something, Ricky, or I'll clang and bang all fucking day." He must have got what he needed. The guard chuckled as he moved to the next cell. "Fuck you too, buddy."

"We do checks every hour," Ray continued, gesturing to the officer. "Make sure everyone's still alive and well. If inmates are sleeping, look for breathing patterns. If they're covered up and you can't tell if they're alive or not, you do what Javier did and request a response. The guys are pretty good about it. No one wants the response team called for an in-cell check. That gets messy. Hey, Javier," Ray called to the squat man banging on cells. "I want you to meet Anson, our newest recruit."

Abandoning his checks, the man Ray called Javier wandered over, shoulders back and chin tipped high—perhaps an effort to make himself look bigger. Javier couldn't have been more than five foot six tops, but for all his lack of height, he had the breadth of a linebacker and the confident swagger of a man twice his size. His biceps strained his uniform shirt, and his thighs were like tree trunks. He had russet skin, black hair cut short, a goatee, sharp eyes, and a flat nose. I couldn't determine his heritage but guessed on a glance that he had both Mexican and possibly Native American blood running through his veins.

"This here is Javier Chavis. Javi, this is Anson Miller, Michigan native joining the team."

Javier clasped my outstretched hand and shook. "Nice to have you on board. Does this mean I can go home once in a while?" he asked Ray with a shit-eating grin.

"Fuck no. I'm gonna give you your own cell."

"Might as well, man. Not sure when's the last time I saw the sun."

The men chuckled before Ray nodded at the line of cells. "I was giving Anson the grand tour and laying out the basics. Thought you two would make a good pair for a couple days while he learns the ropes. You up for some training?"

"Sure thing. You want to jump in right now?" Javier asked me. "I was completing a check before I joined up with Mason downstairs and we put the next lot in the showers."

"I'm in."

Ray smacked Javier on the shoulder. "This here is one of my best guys. He'll take you through everything. Meet up with me on your lunch break, and we'll go over the finer points of the scheduling and whatnot. Any questions?"

"Nope. It all sounds good." I held out my hand to shake. "Thanks for taking me this far."

Before Ray could walk away, Javier piped up. "What's shakin' on F? I hear they had some trouble last night. Fires again?"

Ray tipped his head to the ceiling and blew out a long breath. "Same shit, different day. It's contained. Called in Marx and Angelo as extra hands. Warden is down there now, wrapping it up with the nightshift. Everything is back in order."

Javier nodded but didn't seem particularly fazed by what had taken place. Almost like the trouble they'd encountered was routine.

"I'm heading there now. You two need anything, radio me." Ray headed back to the steel staircase, his boots clanging as he descended to the first level.

"So, Anson Miller from Michigan. What brings you to Texas and The Row?"

"Needed a change of scenery."

"Hell of a distance to travel for a change of scenery."

I shrugged and concentrated on the line of cells instead of making eye contact with my curious coworker. Airing my past wasn't something I cared to do with a guy I'd known five minutes.

"It's all good, man. You had your reasons. Come on, I'll take you through a day in the life of death row. I was midway through an hourly check, so let's finish that off and we'll go through the basics for our showering procedure and move on to rec."

"Do these guys spend much time outside?" I gestured to the row of doors.

"Depends where they go for rec. There is a dayroom, which is a thirty-by-twenty-foot cage with a table, toilet, and pull-up bar, or there is a similar sized outdoor rec area with a basketball net. They go alone. Unlike other death row units, our guys don't get to spend their time with anyone else. Strictly solitary. One hundred percent no contact."

"Gotcha."

I followed Javier as he approached the window of cell eighteen. He peeked inside, then encouraged me to do the same. The man behind the door was hunched over, doing something I couldn't see. His back was to the door, and his head was bowed.

"That's Desmond. He's always writing."

"Letters to family?"

"Nah, creative stories. Says it keeps his mind active. He buys paper every time from commissary and fills it just as quickly. He let me read some once." Javier cringed and lowered his voice. "Penmanship of a grade-schooler. Literary skills aren't much better, but it keeps him busy and out of trouble."

We left Desmond's door and walked to the next. "Basically, during hourly checks, we're ensuring everyone is breathing. No need to make a racket unless it's needed."

"Like with Ricky." I thumbed toward cell seventeen.

"Yup, and that earned me a middle finger salute, but that's typical. The guy was curled up under his blanket."

At door nineteen, I peered in first, noting the man inside was lying on his bed with his feet up the wall. There was a radio playing, low enough I couldn't make out the tune. My appearance at the window caught his attention, and he rolled his head toward me. When our eyes locked, he scowled and called out. "Hiring more fucking white boys? Figures. Hi, white boy. You must be Ray Ray's friend." His grin was toothy and borderline sadistic. I didn't let it faze me. He wasn't the first inmate to call me names or try to intimidate me. This job required thick skin.

"That's Jeffery," Javier said, chuckling.

"It's Jeff, asshole."

"Sorry, my bad. That's Jeff. He's a mouthpiece at times. Gotta know when to brush that shit off. You're new, you're white, so you'll be his new target. He's gonna spin you tales like you wouldn't believe. Creative imagination that one. All bullshit."

"Is he mentally unstable?" I asked as we checked door twenty. It was an honest question. There was a large percentage of people in the system whose mental health was questionable. Often times, they got thrown into prison instead of into a facility where they'd have received better care.

"Bah, everyone in here has a certain level of instability. It comes with the amount of time they've spent behind bars. You can't spend a decade or more confined to a cell like this for twenty-two hours a day and not have it affect you on some level."

"Truth."

"But no, Jeff isn't diagnosed with anything specific. He's your run of the mill death row headcase. Certified sociopath."

"I heard that."

"You were meant to, Jeffery. Why don't you get your ass naked? We're coming around for showers soon. Maybe I'll collect you first if you're ready."

We checked the next cell—whose occupant was asleep—before approaching the last one on the end, the black paint on the door read, B21. Javier peeked inside and lingered longer than before. By the time he leaned back again, I was curious.

He side-eyed me and quirked a brow. "This here's Bishop. We call him the brooding giant or the silent giant. Never says much but somehow comes across as intimidating. Most guards feel uncomfortable around him. Something about the strong silent type that gives off a permanent sense of unease. You never know what he's thinking, and those dark eyes of his pierce right through to your core.

"With the lippy ones, you never have to worry what's going on in their head. They're vocal enough to tell you. This one keeps you guessing."

Javier stepped aside, and I took a turn looking beyond the cell window. The man inside seemed ill-fitted to a room that size. Even sitting on his bed in the corner, I could tell he would surpass my height by leaps and bounds. Six and a half feet, if I had to guess.

He had one leg stretched across his bed, and the other foot rested on the floor. In his hands was a small tattered book. The white T-shirt he wore was a sharp contrast against his deep brown skin. His head was bowed as he read.

How did a man that big sleep on such a tiny bed? If he were to lie across it, his legs would dangle off the end. Although his muscle depletion was what one would expect from a long-term inmate, he did not lack tone or definition. I would guess this man used his rec time well.

I was so taken by the sheer size of the man Javier had called Bishop that I didn't immediately notice the other aspects of his cell that set it apart from the other inmates' in the row. Every inch of wall space was covered in art. Not hanging pictures but charcoal sketches made directly onto the concrete.

And they were brilliant.

"Jesus," I whispered under my breath. "Did he draw those?"

"Every one of them. The first time he did it, they made him clean it off. Wrote him up, and he spent ninety days with no privileges at a level two. The minute he went back to a level one and they returned his art supplies, he did it again. He starts on the wall we can't see, so by the time he fills it and moves on to the next, it's been a month or so. Then he got busted on it again. Same deal. Rinse repeat. After the fifth or sixth time, Ray took it to the warden. Warden said, let it go. He's not hurting anybody. So there you have it."

"Wow."

"Man's got talent. Too bad it's hidden behind a prison wall."

It was hard to take it all in when the crisscrossing bars in the window restricted my view, but what I could see took my breath away. There were birds and flowers, butterflies and trees, buildings with sidewalks and cars, people young and old. A world that didn't exist to Bishop any longer.

When the hairs on the back of my neck rose, I shifted my gaze to the man on the bed. Eyes as dark as pitch stared back at me. Bishop had a shaved head, a square face, and wide lips on a generous mouth. But it was the depth of his attention that threw me off my guard. *Piercing* didn't begin to describe his stare. It was like he was looking right into my soul, and my heart tripped faster, but I couldn't determine if it was fear of this silent giant or something else that had caused it.

I pulled away and blew out a breath to hide my discomfort as I peered back the way we'd come. "So, showers next?"

"Yup. Give me a second." Javier pressed the button on the radio attached to his shoulder and spoke, calling in his count before changing channels and speaking a second time. "Mason, are you available?"

The radio crackled a minute before a voice came on the line. "On my way."

Javier paced back toward cell nineteen, the one with the guy named Jeffery. I knew from experience, you never made promises to inmates unless you intended to follow through on them. The best way to earn disrespect was to go back on your word. So I knew we'd be starting showering procedure with him.

"Mason and I are covering sections A and B of this pod. Twenty-eight cages in total. Fourteen up here. This hallway and the next one over. Fourteen below, same setup. We split counts between us and will monitor cells separately, but all transfers are two-man. No exceptions. When we take these men to shower, to rec, to visitations, the barber, anywhere, we do it together. I'll have you observe the first few."

I nodded as a clip of boots on concrete sounded behind me. Mason approached from the open stairs at the far end of the row with a grin on his face. He had blond hair, spiked with gel, silver-blue eyes, and a clean-shaven face. He was a few inches shorter than me, five ten at most. He wasn't bulky with muscles, but it was clear he took care of himself.

"Training up a new guy," Javier said, waving in my direction.

Mason thrust his hand out, and we shook. "Another white boy. Jeffery will be so pleased. I'm Mason."

I grinned and returned the firm handshake. "Anson Miller, and yes, he's already vocalized his excitement in that matter."

"I bet. Nice to meet you, Anson. I take it we're walking you through the routine all day today?"

"Seems like. I'm not fresh out of school, so I know the basics. First time on The Row. Worked ten years at I-Max in Michigan."

"Good. So maybe your foundation is a little more solid than the last one we trained up. He lasted ... what? Six, seven weeks?" Mason's eyes turned up and to the right as he did the math.

"Just under seven weeks," Javier said.

"Right. Okay, so—" Mason clapped his hands and rubbed them. "—who's up first?"

"Me if you girls are done with your little teatime social," Jeffery said from behind his door.

I chuckled as Mason's grin took over his face. "Oh, Jeff, my man, you're gonna let two white boys handle your care today?"

"Ain't got no choice now, do I? If I want my damn shower, I gotta suffer with your two punk asses and the Mexican."

"That you do," Javier told him before turning to me. "Okay, so we'll do a full walkthrough of procedure. This isn't like general population where you open the door and let 'em head to showers or rec time on their own. Any time a man leaves his cell, he's strip-searched, cuffed—wrists and ankles—and escorted to his destination by two officers. Any time a man is brought back to his cell, we repeat the process in reverse. We search and cuff them coming *and* going."

Javier approached one of the slit windows and Mason the other. "And our boy is already naked and ready for us," Mason said.

"I told you, I'm first," Jeff said through the door.

"Normally, we'd instruct them to get naked. Jeff here saved us a step," Javier said over his shoulder. "Okay, Jeff, let's see it." Javier didn't take his eyes off the window as he continued explaining. "Mostly, they all know the drill and don't need to be instructed. They need to show us that all their creases, crevices, and cavities are bare. Armpits, ass crack, inside their mouth. If you don't get a good enough look, you ask them to do it again. Two sets of eyes. Always."

I peered over Javier's shoulder as he explained, noting the way Jeffery willingly opened his mouth, pulled his cheeks aside, and flicked his tongue up and down. Then he lifted his arms, spun, and gave us a proper inspection of his ass crack and under his dangling bits.

"Once we're clear, they'll dress in their inspected, prison-issued jumpsuit. Okay, Jeff, let's see it."

Mason undid the locking mechanism on the small chute below waist-level and lowered the door.

Jeffery passed his jumpsuit through the chute, and Javier—wearing his tear-resistant gloves—went over the garment while Mason ensured Jeffery stayed standing in the middle of his cell. Once Javier deemed it clean, he passed it back to Jeffery through the slot.

"Dress."

All three of us watched as Jeffery donned his inspected clothing. Once he was dressed, Mason kept his eyes on Jeff as Javier turned to me and continued with instructions. "Next, Jeff is going to back up to the chute with his arms behind his back."

"Let's go, Jeff. Show the new guy what a pro you are," Mason said as he unclipped handcuffs from his belt.

"Jeff will fit his hands through the chute," Javier explained as Jeff complied, "and Mason is gonna cuff him."

When two hands appeared, Mason made quick work of fitting the cuffs on each wrist. There was limited space between them, which restricted Jeffery's movements significantly.

"Move to the middle of the room," Mason said as he closed and relocked the chute, his eyes never straying from the window.

"Now, we unlock the door and have him back out of the cell so we can add the ankle restraints."

I stood back and watched the two men take Jeff from his cell. Once they cleared the secured door, they placed him facing the wall as they instructed him to lift one leg at a time behind him as they finished their process. Once the man was cuffed—legs bound, wrists bound, and a chain running between the two—and his cell door closed again, Mason took one arm and Javier the other, aiming him down the hall.

"And now we head to the showers."

Jeffery grinned that same sardonic smile at me the entire time. It was meant to throw me off my game, but it had zero effect. I was used to shit like that, and it bounced off my thick skin.

"That's not too bad. I can manage that," I said, following the three down the row.

The showers were closed-in concrete stalls, approximately three feet by five feet with the same secured door as the cells. The process was reversed. Jeff's ankle restraints were removed, and he was closed into the stall where he fit his cuffed hands out the chute for Mason to undo. Once the chute was locked, we left him there to shower.

"Ordinarily, we give 'em about fifteen or twenty minutes. If we get caught up taking other guys to rec or doing an escort with a chaplain or nurse who might have been called onto The Row, they might get stuck in there longer." Javier aimed us back the way we'd come. "Now, we'll fill up a few more showers, and by then, we can get the lower level moving toward rec. They showered earlier, after breakfast. We try to keep a rotation going. Some days, we have guys with visitors. Then we call in for an escort team. When you're on the pod, you stay on the pod. If the inmates have to leave for medical or such, you call for an escort. If we have to use rec cages outside our area, the escort team is responsible for the move."

"Got it."

We made it back to the same row, and Javier and Mason completed the process of taking men to the showers again and again until the stalls were filled. I watched the process carefully, keeping a distance but taking mental notes. It was different than my old job. Far more secure, in a way, but nothing I couldn't handle.

There were a few men left who needed a turn, but they had to wait to be rotated in. One of those men was the daunting giant in B21 named Bishop.

Afterward, we headed down to the lower level and organized those men for their rec time. It was all orderly and precise. None of the inmates caused issues, and they all complied when asked to strip and be cuffed. It was a normal, daily routine for them. They were used to it. If they wanted their few precious hours out of their cell, they didn't cause problems. For most of them, it was the highlight of their day.

We stayed busy on the lower level for a bit before Javier waved a hand for me to follow him to the second level. "Think you can handle a transfer with me?"

"No problem."

"Good, we'll leave Mason to do the headcount for this hour, and we'll rotate the guys in the shower back to their cells. Then, we can get the last bunch in and do our own count on the upper level."

I followed Javier to the line of secured shower stalls, and he pounded on the first door. "Time's up. Pass me your jumpsuit and stand in the middle of the stall for inspection."

He unlocked the chute and accepted the jumpsuit from the man inside. A man named Syed from B16. Javier told me to glove up, and once I'd pulled them on, he handed me Syed's outfit. I spent a second shaking it out and inspecting it for hidden contraband. When I deemed it clean, we spent a few minutes inspecting a naked Syed through the window. Despite the process being the same as before, Javier instructed me through each step.

Once Syed's strip search was complete, I fed his jumpsuit back through the chute, and he dressed before turning and backing to the door, feeding his hands through so Javier could cuff him.

It all went smooth, and we added his ankle restraints once he was on the outside of the shower stall, and then we took him back to his cell without an issue. We completed the same process with the rest of the showered men and got them back in their cells too. Jeffery was the only one who had anything to say during the transport.

As Javier and I clutched both his arms and guided him along toward his cell, he pinned me with that devious grin from earlier and wouldn't look away.

"Got a name, white boy?"

To show I wasn't intimidated, I answered his question coolly and without emotions on the surface that he might pick apart or use against me.

"Anson. Do you plan on giving me a hard time, Jeff?"

"No, sir. I ain't no troublemaker. Tell him, Javi. I'm one of the good ones."

Javier snorted. "When it suits you."

"Come on, man. That's not fair. I do good."

"You do. Mostly. Come on. Against the wall."

Jeff leaned his forehead against the wall while we uncuffed his legs and got his cell unlocked. Once he was inside, he fit his cuffed hands through the slot, and Javier removed those chains as well.

"All right. Let's take the rest down and get them in the showers, check in with Mason, and see what's shaking."

It was cell B21 where Javier headed next, and an odd sense of unease rippled across my skin. When I closed my eyes, I could still see Bishop's dark, penetrating stare from earlier. Like his focused attention was a physical entity, I still felt it thrum through my bones. Although I wouldn't admit it out loud, the man had thrown me off-balance. A commanding presence seemed to pulse out of him, invisible through the air. Was that what spooked off the last new guy? Was it Bishop or this place in general? Every one of them was here for a reason. I wasn't stupid.

Burying the restless unease, I approached the second window beside Javier and peered in. There he was. In the same position as earlier. Sitting on his bed with his head lowered to a book. Nothing about his posture should have been intimidating, yet it was.

Maybe it was knowing what *could* be going on inside his head. How did I know he wasn't imagining gutting me? Many of these guys were sociopaths. I wouldn't put it past him.

"How about you do the talking this time. I'll fill in if you miss anything."

I met Javier's gaze and nodded.

It's just another day at the office, I told myself. *This man is no different than the rest.*

Except something deep inside me told me I was wrong.

This man was *nothing* like the rest of them.

Chapter Three

I BANGED ON THE DOOR to grab Bishop's attention, ignoring the sweat gathering under my pits.

Bishop raised his head, and those same obsidian eyes reached out and hooked onto me in a near physical manner.

I choked on my nerve and was glad when my voice came out sounding authoritative, hiding my trepidation. "Shower time. Strip down and pass your jumpsuit out for inspection."

They were the same words Javier had used repeatedly all morning, yet their effect on this giant man wasn't at all the same. All of the other inmates complied without question, almost eager to stretch their legs outside their cells for a few minutes. Bishop didn't react. He didn't move or hop off his bed to follow my orders. Instead, he remained sitting, his focus on my face spellbinding.

He didn't blink.

He didn't move.

There was a world of mystery behind those eyes. They were steady and arresting with a dash of danger on their surface and more than a little evasiveness clouding Bishop's true nature. The emotions they stirred were conflicting, and I couldn't decide if Bishop was dangerous or misunderstood. It was always safer to err on the side of caution. These men were hardened criminals of the worse degree.

"Get going, Bishop," Javier said when the stare down continued. "Don't give Anson here a hard time on his first day."

Bishop's gaze slipped to Javier's in the other window. He seemed to contemplate the order for another half a minute before sliding his laser focus back to me. In no rush, with slow, deliberate movements,

Bishop closed the book he'd been reading and set it down on the mattress. He dropped his legs to the ground and shifted to stand.

I hadn't been wrong. The man cleared six and a half feet easily, and the sheer presence of his large body almost made me step back despite the steel door separating us.

Bishop's gaze skewered me as he snagged something from the floor and held it up, letting it dangle from his giant fist. It was his jumpsuit.

Javier unlocked the chute and slid it open as Bishop crossed the short distance to the door. As he pushed the material through, not once did his laser focus leave my face. I wouldn't step back. I wouldn't give him a response or show that he intimidated me. It was what he wanted, no doubt. To make me second-guess myself or to instill fear.

I held my ground.

Javier grabbed the jumpsuit, and while he inspected it, I kept watch on Bishop as he backed up to the middle of his cell. He reached his long arms overhead and removed his ratty white T-shirt, tossing it on the bed with his book. Next, he tugged his black sweatpants down and off, adding them to the pile. The last thing he removed was his underwear.

He stood naked, a looming obsidian statue in the middle of his cell.

For as long as I'd worked as a corrections officer, I'd been unfazed by nudity. It was common to strip search inmates—less common at I-Max, but not unheard of. It was part of the job. Routine. Clinical. Like a doctor or a nurse, working in prisons meant you saw naked bodies from time to time. If you'd seen one, you'd seen them all. They came in all different sizes, shapes, and colors. But a naked man was essentially a naked man. No big deal.

Bishop was *not* just a naked man.

My tongue stuck to the roof of my mouth, and despite the sharp reprimand I'd issued myself earlier, I couldn't hold his stare any longer. It was too much. Bishop was long and lean, with enough angles and edges to remind a person he used that pull-up bar in the dayroom and that he likely dropped to the cement floor of his cell multiple times a day and sweat through a hundred or more push-ups and crunches.

His skin was taut and satiny smooth. There was evidence of a scar on the inside of his left forearm, but it was old, and the years had faded it away. It was almost invisible. Apart from a dark patch of hair around his genitals, his body was hairless. A dark map of perfection my eyes couldn't help but explore.

It was impossible not to take note of Bishop's impressive cock as it hung long and thick and flaccid between his thighs. It was after that extended and unprofessional perusal when I darted my gaze up and away, a warm rush of heat blooming over my skin. I shuffled and fisted my slacks as I fought to center myself again.

"Arms up. Fingers spread wide," I croaked, trying to cover my shaken foundation. "Spin around slowly."

I felt the heat of Bishop's gaze as he pivoted, then faced the other side of the cell. My heart calmed a fraction without those dark eyes invading my soul. Without being told, Bishop continued with his part in the strip search, allowing us to check all parts of his large frame.

Once he faced us again, that unease slipped right back in place. The only reason I didn't look away was because I wasn't allowed to. We inspected the inside of his mouth before Javier handed him back his jumpsuit. Bishop dressed, then it was time to let him out.

I unhooked the cuffs from my belt. "Turn around and back toward the door. Fit your hands out the slot."

Bishop held my stare for an extra beat before complying. Once his hands came into view, I made quick work of fitting the cuffs around his wrists, but not without noting the heat radiating off his skin and the sheer size of his fingers and palms. He had hands that could easily overpower a man like me if I wasn't careful and fingers long enough they could curl around a frail neck and take a life without effort.

Had they already?

I swallowed a tight lump as Bishop stepped back to the middle of his cell, arms bound behind his back.

The worst thing a corrections officer could do was let their guard down or allow their imaginations to get away with them. This had never happened before, and I was rattled to the point I wasn't sure I hid it.

"Go ahead and unlock the door and we can back him out," Javier said.

I followed each step as I'd seen Javier and Mason do.

Bishop backed out of the room, and we pressed him face-first to the wall. Without issue, he lifted one leg, then the other behind him as I added his leg restraints.

I took his right arm, and Javier took his left, and we walked in silence toward the showers. The entire way, I told myself not to let Bishop's size intimidate me. I reminded myself that we had the upper hand and the control. Every procedural step was for our safety.

Nothing would happen. But if it did, I was trained and prepared.

The entire journey, I was aware of his mass and the heat radiating off his body, carrying his unique scent to my nose. The entire time, my heart thrashed.

Nothing happened.

We got Bishop into a shower stall without issues, and once the lock on the chute was reengaged, I stood and stared at the large steel door to the shower room. I heard the water turn on inside and saw Bishop strip from his jumpsuit. I stepped back and away but couldn't seem to make my feet follow after Javier who'd gone several steps ahead.

"What's up, Miller?"

I vanquished the unsettling feelings overtaking me and turned from the shower room. Once I'd caught up with Javier, I paused again, looking back. "What'd he do? Why's he here?"

For the most part, knowing what put these men behind bars wasn't something officers concerned themselves over. We didn't get handed files on these men to read about their crimes because it didn't matter. We weren't judge or jury. All we needed to know was they were dangerous men and to heed caution.

Javier quirked a brow and followed my gaze. "No clue, to be honest. Never bothered to look him up. Some of these guys share their stories if you ask, but not Bishop. He rarely talks to anyone. Mostly just his grandma when she visits."

I'd never looked up the crimes of the men in my care before either. Never cared and always believed ignorance was bliss. Knowing the truth was nightmare-inducing. It was easy enough to find out why they were behind bars if a person cared to find out. Often times, prisoners loved to tell you their tales—along with how wrongfully accused they were.

Always innocent.

Listening to them talk, a person might suspect our criminal justice system was broken with the number of *mistakes* they made.

"Everything all right?" Javier had picked up on my agitation.

I pulled my shoulders back and stood straighter, doing all I could to shake off the odd feelings Bishop's presence stirred.

"Yeah. I'm good. He just ... gives off a weird vibe, you know? I don't know how to describe it."

Javier chuckled and slapped my shoulder. "That's Bishop. His silence gets under your skin. It's happened to all of us at some point. I think he likes making everyone squirm. You get used to it. I can tell you, the man has never made threatening remarks or advances on any of the officers in all the time he's been here. The only time he gets written up on behavior is when he refuses to comply with stuff like the drawings on his walls or refusing to leave the visitation booth after his grandma comes, and that only happened once."

I absorbed that and tried to fit that image into the man I'd escorted to the showers. "How long has he been in?"

Javier whistled and shook his head. "No idea. I wanna say plus ten because he's been here longer than me, but I don't know how many past it's been."

Anything more than ten years was a lifetime in itself. I wanted to ask, *"How old is he?" "What is he like with his grandma?" "Does anyone else visit him?" "Does he glare with those dark eyes at everyone or only the new guys or was it reserved for me alone?"*

But I knew better than to push. Bishop was just another inmate. He was B21. The more I knew, the worse off I'd be. It was best to let sleeping dogs lie and not worry myself over one man whose presence had thrown me off guard for the first time in my career. And I'd seen some intense and downright terrifying individuals at I-Max.

I chalked it up to first day jitters and followed Javier.

For the rest of my shift, I didn't allow myself to stew over the unsettling reaction I'd had to Bishop. When it came time to return him to his cell, I remained detached and refused to meet his penetrating gaze. Like Javier had pointed out, he was compliant and didn't cause a ruckus.

However, once he was in his cell and I was heading off with Javier to our next task, the hairs on the back of my neck prickled. I didn't need to look to know Bishop watched me through the small window on his cell.

Javier took me through all the standard day-to-day procedures. How to call in the transfer team for escorts when an inmate had to go for a visitation or meeting with a lawyer or public defender. What the protocol was for taking the chaplain or nurses through the unit. How to deliver lunch, do counts—ensuring they got reported in every hour—and at the end of our shift, how to properly write up logs or incidences.

Ray touched base with me once while I was on lunch and explained I'd have one more day working side by side with Javier before I'd be placed into the rotation.

It was a full day and a lot to absorb. By the time I made it to my Jeep, it was after three in the afternoon, and the temperature was in the mideighties. After a day working in a closed-off building with only recirculated air, it was hot. Sweat gathered along my spine and dripped from my temples as I fumbled with my key fob and unlocked the door. I didn't miss the cooler weather from back home, but I was starting to wonder what summer would be like if it was this hot at midday in May.

I'd be glad to get home and find something cooler to put on.

Then, I remembered the endless stacks of boxes waiting to greet me in my new house. The previous night, after arriving far later than I'd anticipated, I'd unpacked enough to find a fitted sheet for my mattress and clothes to wear this morning. That was it.

I was heading home to a disaster, and I wasn't sure I had the energy to deal with it.

I let the engine run long enough I could do a search on my phone and find the closest place to grab a case of beer. I noticed I had two more missed calls from my mother, both back-to-back, both around noon. Making a mental note to call her back later before she sent out a search team, I sorted out the GPS to take me to the liquor store and threw the Jeep in gear.

Pulling out of the parking lot, I took one last look in my rearview mirror at the tall, concrete walls surrounding my new job. It looked less daunting and ominous in the light of day, but I knew what lived within those high, razor-topped fences. I'd met the men behind the high-security doors and crash gates. I'd been in the belly of the beast as Ray had called it.

Polunsky *was* daunting and *was* ominous. Sunlight and blue skies, green fields and bird's songs—those things were the illusion. They painted a pretty picture while trying to mask the truth. I knew better. There was a sense of relief that overcame me as I drove away. A release of pressure that I hadn't noticed had been sitting on my chest all day.

I took a deep breath and let it out slowly through puffed cheeks.

It'd been a long day. Not to mention the stress of those weeks and months leading up to my relocation. It was time to settle into this new life.

Start fresh.

STANDING IN MY LIVING room, dressed in a pair of cut-off sweatpants and an old T-shirt, lost among dozens of boxes, I cracked a beer as I tried to decide where to begin. The moving guys had dumped everything I owned in the front room. They'd been behind schedule, and I wasn't willing to pay them for the extra time it would have taken them to sort out where everything went.

Besides, yesterday was the first time I'd stepped foot inside the house, and I didn't know where I wanted things to go anyhow.

While I studied the arrangement of boxes stacked six and seven high and three deep against the far wall, the peeling paint and missing framework around the windows caught my eye. The hardwood floors were in desperate need of sanding and varnishing, and the musty scent in the air told me I had mold growing somewhere.

It was a project, I reminded myself. The listing had called it "An affordable starter home, with charisma and plenty of character." The pictures accompanying the listing had been a tad deceiving. Character and charisma were fancy words for rundown and falling apart. At least it'd been cheap. The previous owners had taken my first offer, and I'd lowballed them big-time, so I couldn't complain.

I chugged half my beer and set it down on top of a box marked Kitchen. There was no way I'd have enough things unpacked in time to sort out dinner, so I would be relying on takeout this evening. I left those boxes where they sat and aimed for a stack marked Bedroom.

It took ten trips up the creaking wooden staircase to move all those boxes. By the time I was ready to move the pieces of my disassembled bed, I was soaked in sweat and on my third beer. Stripping from my T-shirt, I took two pieces of the frame together and hauled them over my shoulder before climbing the stairs. Next came the dresser—sans drawers, since that was awkward—then two overly large bookcases that would have been easier to move if I'd had help. Unfortunately, being new to town, there was not a single soul I could call. So, I did it all on my own.

It was another hour before my bed was assembled, my dresser was filled with clothes, and a few boxes of my favorite hardcovers were carefully arranged on the bookshelf. That was about all I was going to manage for one day. My body had protested the last few trips I'd made up the stairs, and my stomach growled.

I called to have pizza delivered and hopped in a cold shower before it arrived. My muscles ached, and I was bone-tired. I needed a good meal, a good book, and my bed so I could sleep before I had to be back at work the following morning. My five o'clock alarm would feel early, and it was getting late.

I ate the pizza right out of the box instead of trying to locate a plate among the disaster downstairs. And since my bedroom was the only place looking half-put-together, that was where I dined, smack dab in the middle of my bed. The only person who would complain about crumbs between the sheets was me.

With the pizza box beside me, I thumbed through a tattered copy of *1984* by George Orwell. I'd read it so many times, I knew large sections of it by heart. The pages were thinning and fraying. The binding was so creased, the title was hard to read, but it was loved.

I was too exhausted to start a new book, so I'd grabbed an old favorite to peck at while I ate. Something I knew well enough, I didn't have to think too hard.

I'd been mocked many times for my eclectic collection of novels. Unlike most people, I didn't have a favorite genre or author, I simply read whatever I could get my hands on. From true crime to horror, fantasy to paranormal, sci-fi to historical, classical literature to poetry, I loved it all.

My mom and I had grown up without a lot of money, so the best source of entertainment I had as a child was our weekly trips to the local library. It was there where I'd first discovered what real adventures were. Maybe we hadn't been able to afford to vacation like other families, but through fiction, I felt as though I'd lived a thousand lives and traveled to a thousand places. In my opinion, Disney had nothing on *Treasure Island*.

With my third piece of pizza consumed to the crust, I turned another page as my phone buzzed on the bed beside me. My mom's smiling face lit up the screen.

"Shit." I'd forgotten to call her back.

I dropped the crust into the box and wiped my saucy fingers on a napkin before snagging my phone.

"Hey, Mom."

"Well it's a good thing you decided to answer this time. My next call was to the local sheriff's department to tell them my son had gone missing. I thought you'd died in a ditch on the side of the road between Michigan and Texas. Are you trying to give your old mother a heart attack?"

Warmth bloomed in my chest hearing her voice, and I smiled. "No. I'm sorry. I didn't get here until late last night and didn't want to wake you. Then I had to be at work before six in the morning. I was working when you called earlier."

"And the three days before that? I haven't heard from you since you pulled out of my driveway on Saturday morning. A message would have sufficed. Something to let your mother know you hadn't been kidnapped or killed. You know I worry."

"I'm sorry. It's been crazy. My head's a mess."

She sighed, and her voice softened when she continued. "I know. I wish you'd have thought more about this rather than jumping and running. How are you? How's the new house?"

I glanced around my bedroom, noting the dull beige walls that were in dire need of a fresh coat of paint and the thick layer of scum over the undraped window which clouded my view.

"It's ... not exactly what I hoped for. The house. It needs work, but I'll take care of it. It will give me something to keep me busy when I'm not working. Something to focus on."

"And the job?"

There was a tone to her voice, a wariness. She didn't approve that I'd taken a job on death row, never mind that it was on the other side of the country.

"It wasn't too bad. More secure, which I figured. A lot more details and procedures when it comes to handling the inmates, but it's all good. I think I'm gonna be okay here. The guy showing me the ropes today was nice."

"Anson—"

"Mom, it's safe. I'm fine."

"That's what you told me about I-Max, and look what happened there. Anson, those men weren't living on death row."

"It's not the same. I promise. These guys have no free rein. They get escorted in cuffs everywhere they go."

"Because they are ten times more dangerous."

"Mom, it's my job. We've been over this. What happened at I-Max was... It was bad luck on my part. It shouldn't have happened at all. I've learned, and I'm moving forward. I won't let it hold me back from doing what I love."

A heavy sigh came through the phone. "I worry about you."

"I know, but I'm a big boy, and this is what I do for a living. These guys don't scare me. Death row or not, I know what I'm doing."

Bishop's dark eyes flashed through my mind. The invasive way they'd stripped me down and rooted inside me. He was likely trying to instill fear, and it had worked, but there was no way in hell I was telling my mother I'd been intimidated by a prisoner on my first day.

"I hate how far away you are. I'm going to miss our Saturday morning brunch."

"I know. But we can make a new tradition. How about a Saturday morning chat or something? I can teach you how to work Skype. I'll visit as often as I can once I'm settled, okay? I had to do this, Mom. I needed space."

"I know." Her voice was small.

For all my life, it'd been just the two of us. I never knew my father. He'd taken off long before I was born and never looked back.

"I'll call you this weekend, okay? I'm going to be busy this week between working and getting unpacked. I don't want to promise phone calls and forget to make them."

"Saturday is fine."

"Around ten?"

"Perfect."

"I love you, Mom."

"Please be careful."

"I will."

"I love you too."

We hung up, and I leaned my head back against the wall with my eyes closed. The worst part of my life-changing decision was leaving Mom behind. No amount of pleading had worked to convince her to come with me. Michigan was her home, and Michigan was where she wanted to stay.

Done with my dinner, I took the box of pizza down to the kitchen and fit it into the fridge. Then I shut down the house and checked that all the doors and windows were locked. Back in bed, I flipped through my book, contemplating if I wanted to read more or turn off the lights. I was tired, but my head was spinning with residual energy from my day.

My thoughts turned to work, and I wondered what tomorrow might bring. I thought of Jeff and his sardonic smile, his light quips and chill attitude. The way he'd teased and called me white boy. There was an air of comradery in his tone when we'd met, like he was simply making friends. It was all so chilling.

And wrong.

He was a criminal. Most men on death row were there for capital murder charges. Him included.

Bishop included.

Not for the first time, I wondered what Bishop's crime was. There was something about him that got under my skin, and I couldn't seem to shake it off. Maybe if I researched some and learned more about him, it would take away the mystery and help my head settle. Sometimes, knowledge was power. Even when that knowledge showed you the vile truth behind a person's nature. If I knew Bishop's secrets, then those looks he gave me would make sense. Maybe they wouldn't haunt me the same.

Or maybe I'd make it worse.

My laptop was buried in a box downstairs, so I grabbed my phone and was typing in a Google search, seeking a list of inmates' names at Polunsky, when I realized what I was doing.

My fingers froze over the screen.

It was never a good idea to get invested in the inmates. Rule number one. I knew that. Keep a professional distance. Some corrections officers loved knowing the gruesome stories of the men behind bars, but that had *never* been me. Why was I doing this now? The pull driving me to know more about Bishop was unsettling.

Instead of losing myself down that rabbit hole, I shoved my phone away and headed to the bathroom to get ready for bed.

"Enough is enough," I told myself as I smeared paste on my toothbrush. "Leave work at work."

Chapter Four

THERE WAS CHARCOAL residue on his hands when they came through the chute this time, and I knew he'd been drawing more. I cuffed his wrists, and his fingers twitched almost like he wanted to make fists but refrained.

Once he felt the second lock in place, he pulled his hands back through the hole and moved to the center of his cell.

Javier had encouraged me to help with every transfer on my second day and put me in charge of counts and reporting and all the decision-making to ensure I'd be functional on the floor. None of it was hard. The duties were straightforward and textbook.

It was shy of noon, and because I was also going to be part of the escort team on occasion, Javier had suggested I mirror them while they took some of our guys for visitations and the rec rooms outside our area.

B-Pod was full to capacity, so we often used other area's rec cages for our men. Blocks D and E were less populated. When you were scheduled on a pod, or block as some called it, you didn't leave that pod, so Mason and Javier were restricted to the bank of rows they were assigned. All outside transfers were conducted by a separate team of two officers who came when called to take the men where they needed to go.

The officers handling our escorts today were Jin and Doug, and I'd been working with them to take inmates to rec. It was almost my lunch break, and Bishop was the last one heading down for his two hours of yard time. It was nothing more than a slightly larger cell on a cement pad outside. Entirely contained with no direct access to other people.

Since the inmate was essentially the responsibility of the escort team, they were the ones who performed the strip search and cuffing, but since I was shadowing, it was my job. Jin was beside me as we got Bishop from his cell, not Javier.

Once I unlocked Bishop's steel door, I called out, "Back up slowly."

His steps were precise and unrushed. Once he'd cleared the cell, I took him by the arm and directed him to face the wall. I kept one hand planted in the middle of his shoulder blades while Jin closed the door.

The heat of Bishop's skin radiated through his thin jumpsuit, and I noted the calm rise and fall of each consecutive breath he drew into his lungs—much steadier than my own.

I was better working around Bishop today, but no less intimidated, which pissed me off because it wasn't something I'd ever experienced around an inmate before. Allowing them to intimidate you gave them power, and I *never* wanted to give a dangerous man power.

His morning transfer to the shower and back had been uneventful, and I'd refused to allow that piercing stare of his to distract me.

Jin handled the ankle cuffs while I remained in position, knowing full-well Bishop possessed more strength than me and could shove me off if he wanted to. He wouldn't because it wouldn't get him anywhere except written up and disciplined for behavior.

Bound, Jin and I guided him down the hallway with Doug trailing behind. The outdoor rec rooms were essentially steel cages. This wasn't like general population where the individual was allowed yard time. This was pure isolation. There was no grass underfoot, no wide-open field to walk around on and stretch your legs. It was a tiny, twenty-by-thirty-foot cage like Javier had described the previous day. The only accommodation was a basketball hoop, a ball, and a toilet.

Lions at the zoo had more freedom and fewer restrictions.

The door on the cage had a similar chute, so once we'd removed Bishop's ankle cuffs and maneuvered him inside, he slipped his hands through the hole so we could take off the wrist restraints as well.

"That's the bulk of it," Jin said, handing me my cuffs so I could clip them back on my belt. "We leave him here for his two hours, then take him back. He's guarded now by those guys." Jin pointed to a pair of officers a few dozen feet away. "They take care of this area of rec cages. We'll show you the visitation room and walk you through that this afternoon. Why don't you grab a lunch break and meet up with us when you're done?"

"Sounds good. Thank you."

I clasped hands with the two men before they wandered off.

Doug and Jin headed back the way we'd come, scheduled to bring more men down for their rec time in separate contained cells. I spied the two officers and gave them a wave. They looked busy with an angry inmate in a cage a few down. It was purely vocal, and they weren't exhibiting signs of distress or like they needed a hand, so I figured they knew what they were doing just fine.

I was about to head in the opposite direction and the doorway leading to the staffing area outside The Row when I felt eyes on me. A searing, piercing, soul-stripping gaze. My skin prickled right up my spine and over my scalp. Bishop watched me. I could feel it as I shuffled around.

I wasn't wrong. Two mysterious onyx spheres stared back at me. Bishop stood in the middle of the cage, holding the basketball in one giant mitt. I swore his fingers covered half the ball. I was about to turn away, refusing him that power and control he sought with just his eyes when he spoke for the first time, his voice a deep baritone and silky smooth like liquid honey with a hint of a Texas drawl.

"Can I get some air in the ball, boss? Can't play with it like this." He made to bounce the ball, but it splatted against the cement and didn't rebound, indenting on the bottom and staying there. It was deflated.

It took me a second to get over the fact that he'd talked to me and to absorb the way his voice resonated through my bones. It was kind-sounding and not anything like I'd imagined in my head. I'd expected Bishop's voice to be as threatening and dominating as his presence, but it wasn't.

I peered toward the two officers, but they were still engaged.

"They keep a pump in the supply room there." Bishop pointed behind me with one of his thick fingers. "You don't gotta take my word for it, boss. Ask 'em if you ain't sure. They won't mind."

I glanced at the door behind me and back at the officers, then to Bishop. His attention never left my face for a moment, and I studied the look in his eyes for a beat before nodding. "Of course. Give me a minute."

I didn't know the protocol for stuff like this. In general population, I'd taken care of similar issues in the yard many times, but rules were different here. It wasn't like I could ask Bishop to pass the ball through the chute or hand him the pump. For one, the ball wouldn't fit through the hole.

The two officers saw me approach, and the one held a hand up to the arguing inmate inside the cage. "Cool it for a fucking second, Jerry." Then he tipped his chin in my direction. "Hey, what's up?"

I thumbed over my shoulder. "The ball has no air. Any way I can remedy that for him?"

The officer I'd addressed sighed and shook his head as he fished around on his belt, removing a set of keys. "I swear to fucking God, we spend half our days filling these balls."

A glance at the cage beside me told me he wasn't joking. A basketball sat in the corner of Jerry's cage, looking equally depleted of air.

The officer shoved keys in my hand and gestured to the same door Bishop had pointed out. "In there. The nozzle fits through the little holes in the cage—barely, but it does. Bring it down here when you're done. You'll want that ball when you're finished with your bitchfest, right, Jerry?"

"Fuck you." Jerry spat through the cage, and it landed less than a foot from my boot.

"I guess Jerry wants a flat ball today. Never mind." The officer waved me off and turned back to his coworker.

I didn't hang around and ask questions. Whatever was being discussed with Jerry wasn't my business, and the guy was clearly upset about something.

At the storage room, I shuffled around inside until I came up with a standard bicycle pump. There were other balls in the room, but they didn't look like they were in any better shape than the one in Bishop's cage. When this was the one source of entertainment and exercise these men got, I'd have thought they'd have come up with enough funding to replace equipment that was in such bad shape, but I knew from experience, that was never the case. The Department of Criminal Justice always claimed there weren't extra funds for stuff like that, nor did these guys deserve more.

I took the pump and headed for Bishop's cage. When he saw me coming, he picked up the ball and crossed toward me. We stood close. Only a steel, diamond-patterned cage wall separated us. He loomed over me, his shadow swallowing me whole. Heat radiated off his frame, and I could have sworn I felt it, but then I told myself it was my imagination, and there was no way.

The holes in the cage were big enough for a finger to poke through, but not two. The pump head was a tight fit. I had to wiggle and shove and force it to make it go through.

Unspeaking, without lifting my gaze, I managed to get the nozzle in the little hole and watched Bishop's oversized hand catch it on the other side. Even as he fit the pin into the ball, I couldn't meet his eyes. I kept my focus on his hands.

When the pin was in place, I worked the pump over and over, watching the ball inflate. Neither of us spoke, but I knew without looking that Bishop's attention was not on the ball. When it seemed full to capacity, I asked, "How's it feel?"

Bishop didn't answer. I tipped my chin higher, slowly seeking those eyes that had haunted my dreams last night. Like I'd suspected, I was his sole focus.

"You ain't gotta be afraid of me, boss." Those few simple words came out on a whisper, their tone as deep and arresting as the first time he'd spoken.

And troublesome because he'd seen through me. He knew.

I didn't want to acknowledge my fears or discomfort one way or the other, because their presence pissed me off, so I ignored the comment and pointed at the ball, asking again, my words steadier than my racing heart, "How's it feel?"

"About perfect."

Bishop removed the pin and wiggled the nozzle end back through the cage. I didn't know what to say, and I didn't like how accurately he'd picked up on my emotional unrest, so I stood straighter, kept my shoulders back and chin high, refusing my unease any power. Refusing to let him see.

"Enjoy your time." Then I nodded and left him so I could return the pump.

Once I'd relocked the supply room and returned the keys to Officer What's-his-Name—I'd never bothered finding out—I headed to the hallway that led out of 12-Building. Before I cleared the doorway, Bishop called out. "Hey, boss?"

My feet rooted in place, and I took a breath before spinning around to face him. With all the stoicism I could manage, keeping my features tight and expressionless, I said, "Yeah?"

Bishop held up the ball. "Thank you. I appreciate your kindness." Then he turned and bounced it around his cage, no longer watching me, no longer dissecting my soul with that heavy gaze.

"You're welcome," I whispered under my breath.

It was another two or three minutes before I could convince my feet to move. I watched Bishop sink a few baskets and jog around the small cage. His body moved with the fluidity of water, each action gliding into the next. He was an enigma. The more I was around him, the more complex the mystery became.

THE FOLLOWING WEEKS passed in a blur of work and getting settled in my new house. Ray had given me a schedule and informed me my rotation would include escort duties at some point and would eventually encompass all rows and sections of B-Pod. He explained how the warden was trying something new and wanted to see the officers working rotations within the same block all the time rather than being thrown all over 12-Building. He thought familiarity with inmates and behaviors would help things run smoother. It was an experiment, Ray had explained. They'd been trying it since January and people seemed to like it.

The only exception to the rule was when he scheduled officers to work on F-Pod. Everyone had a string of days dedicated to F. It was the only pod without a set staff. No one enjoyed working with the Ad Seg guys. They were brutal and unpredictable, and it was unfair to expect the same group of officers to work solely in that area without a break. It was burnout waiting to happen.

I'd experienced many sections and rows of B-Pod and met a number of other officers. They were friendly enough—save for one or two whose welcomes were less than genuine and who made me feel like an outsider.

I was on the escort crew for the following few days, working with a guy named Ezra Atterbury. He had yet to say more than ten words to me and walked around with a permanent chip on his shoulder and snarl in his lip. At first, I thought it was because he'd been stuck with the new guy; then I decided it was just who he was. A certified dick with a perpetual sneer. He wasn't winning any brownie points from me.

He was rougher when handling inmates than anyone else I'd seen. I wasn't fond of being paired with him and hence winding up guilty by association if trouble arose.

Since I was on the bottom of the totem pole, Ezra had taken charge of our day, radioing command to find out where we were needed and when. I was lucky if he shared information with me and found myself chasing him down more times than not when he took off without a word.

"We have sign-ins for Sabel in B04 and Ndiaye in B21." The voice over the radio crackled and cut out.

Ezra's furrow deepened before he depressed the button on his end and answered. "Roger. Heading down right now."

"Visitations?" I asked when he walked away without so much as an explanation.

"Yup."

Ezra didn't stop his forward march toward B-Pod, once again taking off without any communication. Zero explanations about where we were going or what we were doing. I was very quickly becoming done with him.

Once I'd chased him onto B, Ezra stopped in front of cell B04 on the main level and spoke with the patrolling officers, informing them of the visitation. They too had received a call and knew we were coming.

It was a textbook process getting John Sabel from B-Pod to the visitation room. From strip search to cuffs to sitting him in front of a thick, plexiglass window, separating him from a man in a suit who I could only assume was legal representation of some kind.

Inmates on death row had zero contact visits, which meant they sat with a thick bulletproof and soundproof wall between them and their guests. They spoke through phones on the walls. The inmates remained in their four-point restraint the entire time and were chained to an eyehook in the concrete floor below their chairs. They were limited to a maximum of two hours of talk-time. They were permitted visitations once a week, provided they weren't under disciplinary restrictions.

Once John Sabel was settled, we returned to B-Pod for the next transfer. It wasn't until we ended up in front of B21 that I realized it was Bishop's cell. I hadn't recognized his last name because I'd never heard it mentioned before.

I hadn't seen Bishop since my second day on the job, but it didn't mean I hadn't thought endlessly about our small exchange with the basketball and the way he'd ensured to thank me before I walked away.

Something about that moment had stuck with me and had changed the way I viewed the giant man in B21.

Ezra pounded a fist against Bishop's cell door and barked, "Visitation. Get your ass up and undress."

I eyed the snarling guard but held my tongue, tamping down the urge to tell him to chill out. Instead, I stood by the second window of Bishop's cell and peered inside, ready for the strip search inspection. Bishop had been reading—again. The booklover in me wanted to see what kind of literature interested a man like him. But we weren't there for a midday chat, and Ezra was quick to remind me of that.

"Move your ass, Bishop. We ain't got all day."

Bishop pulled his large body to standing and faced the door. Our eyes hooked and held for a beat, a silent hello passing between us before that sturdy gaze I remembered from my first week shifted to Ezra. It was dark and menacing. Chilling in a way.

Bishop snagged his folded jumpsuit off the ground and approached. I opened the chute and accepted the clothing, making quick work of inspecting it inside and out.

"Clear."

Hearing my declaration, Bishop shed his clothes and followed Ezra's commands as he walked Bishop through the search of his person.

"Bend the fuck over and show me your asshole, asshole." Ezra snickered at his own idiocy, and I barely stopped myself from punching the guy.

Once suited in his jumpsuit, we cuffed Bishop—wrists in front for visitations so he could use the phone—and removed him from his cell. I didn't miss the way Ezra used a little extra force, slamming Bishop's head against the wall.

"Hold still, ya big imp. Everything has to be a fucking slow ass game with you."

I bit the inside of my cheek and worked Bishop's ankle cuffs on. Then Ezra jerked his arm when it was time to walk, and Bishop grunted at the awkward strain. I wouldn't have been surprised if Ezra's grip was forceful enough to leave Bishop bruised.

But the silent giant remained impassive, never once objecting or complaining about Ezra's handling. His gaze no longer pierced either of us. Instead, he peered ahead to middle space, a deadened look in his eyes. I couldn't help but think that this absent expression was more disturbing than everything I'd seen from Bishop to date. It was like he'd drawn into himself, shrank away to a deep, dark recessed place in his own mind. A place, I imagined, was full of nightmares.

He kept pace as we guided him to the visitation room. The entire way Bishop kept his chin lowered to his chest. We sat him on the hard metal chair at the plexiglass window and attached him to the eyehook in the floor.

Ezra slapped my shoulder and shot past me. "Gotta piss. Hang out here for a bit, and I'll figure out where we're headed next once I'm back."

I watched him walk away and shook my head as the mounting irritation he drew from me grew.

"He doesn't like me much."

I turned and saw Bishop watching Ezra's retreat as well. The empty look from earlier was gone, and in its place was the soulful mystery I was becoming more and more intrigued with.

"Not sure he likes anyone much, to be honest. He's a miserable fuck, and the way he handled you was uncalled for."

Bishop didn't respond. He studied my face like he was searching for something under the surface. Whatever it was, he must have found it, but when he opened his mouth to speak, movement beyond the window caught both our eyes.

A small, African American woman with tight corkscrew curls in a shining silver color shuffled up to the window. She was hunched over and had an obvious tremble in both her frail hands—one clung to a cane and kept her leaning frame balanced. At a guess, I'd have pegged her to be in her mideighties or older.

She had a colorful silk scarf around her neck and a knitted sweater over a navy floral dress. Her stockings were bunched and twisted around her knees, and her slip-on loafers were tan with a chunky sole.

She squinted beyond the glass as she approached, and when she caught Bishop's eyes, her entire face lit up like the midday sun.

There was a palpable wave of relief that rippled through the man at my side, and he shuffled forward on the chair and reached for the receiver, whatever unspoken words he was about to share with me long forgotten.

I gave him privacy and moved to the doorway. Ezra hadn't returned yet, so I watched Bishop's exchange with this old woman who I assumed was a relative of some sort. The grandmother Javier had talked about, if I had to guess.

Bishop's entire demeanor changed. His shoulders relaxed, his eyes shone, and there was a hint of a smile on his lips for the first time since I'd met him. The harsh angles and invasive presence were gone. Before me was a man who looked out of place within the walls of this prison. It was impossible to envision Bishop with blood on his hands when I watched the interactions between him and the old woman.

Straining, I tried to listen in on Bishop's side of the conversation, knowing it was rude but unable to stop myself. His tone was soft, gentle. His words a low hum that soothed and caressed. I couldn't make out what he was saying but felt the power behind it. Whoever this woman was, he loved her very much.

The woman on the other side of the glass kept one bony hand on the window, and Bishop did the same, his bound hands smoothing over hers, seeking the connection while the phone remained balanced between his shoulder and ear. Joined, save for a three-inch-thick piece of plexiglass.

The woman's eyes sparkled as her lips moved in response to whatever Bishop said, words I couldn't hear. Bishop nodded, moving his fingers on the glass like he wished he could grasp her tiny hand and hold on. It was heartbreaking.

"You can't miss your appointments, Maw Maw." Bishop's voice rose, loud enough I caught the statement and concern behind it. "It's important."

The woman spoke, her head tilting to the side, and I could imagine her placating the giant man and promising she was fine.

"Hey!" I startled and flipped around to face Ezra, who'd snuck up behind me. "Been told Sabel will be done with his lawyer in about ten, so we can hang out and take him back in a few. I'm grabbing a Coke from the machine in the staffroom. You want anything?"

I was shocked he'd bothered asking. "Nah, I'm good. I'll hang out here."

He was walking away before I finished talking. Yeah, Ezra was not my favorite person, and I hoped I wouldn't be paired with him too often.

I turned my attention back to Bishop and the woman he'd called Maw Maw. His voice had dropped back to a level I couldn't make out, but bearing witness to their interactions was enlightening in itself. Maw Maw, which I guessed was a nickname for grandma or mother—but probably grandma since the woman look too old to be his mother—took pictures out of a small plastic baggy I hadn't noticed she'd brought into the room. Security was tighter here than I-Max, so I wouldn't be surprised if her purse and other belongings were being held elsewhere during her visit.

One by one, she pressed photographs to the window. The distance and angle were too great to make out what the images were, but they evoked a strong reaction from Bishop. He touched every one of them through the glass. Large fingers moving over their surface and tracing lines I couldn't see. She let him take his time viewing each before setting it aside and showing him another. This process continued. There had to be over twenty pictures, and Bishop took in each like they were precious.

It was during his examination of the tenth or twelfth picture that I caught sight of a single tear as it trailed down his cheek and fell from his chin. He didn't wipe it away. It was the first of many. Through the rest of the pictures, he cried silent tears.

When he'd seen the last one, the woman put them back into the plastic baggy and pressed her shaking fingers along the top to seal it. Bishop took that moment to close his eyes and scrub his face. He blew out a breath and shook off whatever emotions those photographs had caused, but in the process, he turned his head and caught me watching him.

Our gazes locked for a fraction of a second. It was enough time to see the raw vulnerability behind this man who I'd spent my first week fearing. It wasn't often incarcerated criminals allowed you to see the human being beneath the surface, the unguarded part of themselves they did their best to hide on a daily basis.

If Bishop was upset that I'd seen those emotions, I couldn't tell. He swallowed thickly, straightened his shoulders, and shifted back to the woman behind the window.

I'd lingered long enough and bore witness to something personal I had no right to see. With a stone of guilt sitting heavy in my belly, I looked around, wishing Ezra would hurry up so we could get on with other duties.

Chapter Five

ON THE FRIDAY BEFORE my weekend off, while I was grabbing my backpack from my locker at the end of my shift, Javier found me. I hadn't worked with him since that first week over a month ago, which was disappointing because he was a decent guy I wouldn't mind knowing. We'd seen each other plenty in passing, which was something at least.

"Hey, man, you got anything going on this weekend?"

I threw my bag over my shoulder and slammed my locker door before securing the lock. "Not much. Thought I'd fire up the grill and maybe get the last of my boxes unpacked. If I feel ambitious, I'll do some painting."

"Still unpacking?"

I chuckled. "Yeah. I got the important shit put away, but I've been procrastinating with the rest."

"Well, if you want a hand, I don't mind. Not sure I'm great with a paintbrush, but I can try. I was gonna see if you wanted to come hang out at mine for a few beers, but if you want to fire up a grill, I won't say no to barbecued anything. I can bring the beer your way just as easily."

"That would be great. I'd love the company. You don't have to help me paint, though. I won't ask you to do that."

We exchanged numbers and walked out to the parking lot together.

"So how's it been going? Sorting everything out okay? Liking the job?"

"For the most part. No real issues. No complaints. The guys have been decent and helpful." *Except for Ezra,* I wanted to say but thought it wise I didn't start bashing coworkers before I knew them better. Maybe Ezra had been having a rough week or had personal shit going on. I didn't want to judge someone on a first meeting.

"They're all pretty good guys. There are a few..." Javier trailed off and shrugged.

"But aren't there with any job?"

"You know it."

"This is me." I gestured at my Jeep. "So, tomorrow night? How's five sound?"

"That'd be perfect. Text me your address, and I'll be there with some cold ones."

We knocked fists, and Javier headed to his truck.

My drive home was becoming familiar, which also meant I didn't need to pay as much attention to where I was going and was free to think about my day and week and all that had taken place.

Ezra's behavior had bothered me every day I'd worked with him. He wasn't the first officer I'd seen get a little rough with inmates, but it didn't mean I agreed with it or liked it. Thoughts of Ezra quickly turned to thoughts of Bishop and his visit the other day with his Maw Maw.

I wondered what those pictures had been. The ones that had made the big man cry. I wondered about his relationship with the woman. Lastly, and not for the first time, I wondered what had landed him on death row.

My curiosity and interest in this man were starting to concern me.

As many times as I'd told myself I didn't need to investigate his history, part of me thought I should. Without meaning to, I'd grown a soft spot for this inmate and no longer saw him as fearful or intimidating, which was a huge problem. I needed to remind myself he was a dangerous criminal deep down inside and not allow myself to get fooled by the gentle, soft-spoken person I'd seen shed tears while conversing with an elderly woman.

Some corrections officers got attached or befriended inmates. It was never a good idea, but when you spent day in and day out beside these prisoners, it was sometimes inevitable. Especially if they latched onto you, chatted, or shared more about their pasts. Their true nature got buried under a false façade, and sympathy was a human emotion that was hard to shut down in most people. I'd always considered myself pretty good at detaching. For whatever reason, Bishop had dug under my skin, which was odd because our interactions had been minimal. There was something about him.

When I got home, I stripped from my uniform and showered, the old pipes rattling and groaning inside the walls. The oppressive end-of-June heat was overwhelming, and the house's central air unit did a piss-poor job of keeping up. I'd decided earlier this week I might need to get a guy in to look at it. As much as I'd adored the warmer weather when I'd first arrived, it was heating up a lot faster than I expected. A lot faster than back home.

Dressed in gym shorts and a T-shirt, I dug an icy can of Coke from the fridge and found my laptop in the living room. Flopping down on the couch, I scanned the mess surrounding me. Paint cans, trays, and old sheets lined the wall by the front window, waiting for me to get energetic enough to give the house a fresh look. Thus far, I'd been too exhausted to bother. Buying the supplies was as far as I'd got.

Several boxes still lined the inside wall adjacent to the kitchen door. The entertainment unit was mostly bare except for the ancient stereo system I'd been carting around since high school. It worked, so why get rid of it? There were no personal touches yet—no photos on the walls, no plants—the lighting was poor, and the uncovered bay window was grungy.

I decided I'd make more of an effort this weekend.

I flicked on the TV for background noise and propped my feet on the old wobbly coffee table that used to belong to my grandparents. I shuffled my laptop onto my lap and logged on.

Finding out the reasons behind an inmate's incarceration was an easy process if a person cared to take a minute to look. The Texas Criminal Department of Justice had a site that listed all the convicts, their crimes, the date they were arrested, and the date of their arrival on The Row at Polunsky, along with a list of the person's past offenses, if any. No excessive details were provided, but with those pertinent pieces of information, it didn't take much to run a Google search and find out more.

The first thing I did was pull up the list of men serving time on Polunsky's death row. Some of the names were familiar. Since I worked exclusively on B-Pod, that left a large chunk of inmates I hadn't met.

Although it shouldn't have come as a surprise, when I found Bishop's name on the long list and clicked to expand for more information, the words on the screen shot a chill up and down my spine. It read:

Name: Bishop Ndiaye #787239
Prior Occupation: Unknown
Prior Arrests: Aggravated assault. B&E
Summary of incident: On April 13th, 2001, killed his ex-girlfriend and her 5yr old son.
Codefendant: Isaiah Gordon
Race and Gender of Victims: Black Female and Black Male

For a long time, all I could do was stare at the words on the screen. I knew before I'd looked that Bishop's crime would likely involve a murder charge—it was a given since he sat on death row—but the facts, written clear as day on my computer screen, wouldn't compute. I *couldn't* cast him in the role of murderer no matter how hard I tried.

Killed his ex-girlfriend and her 5yr old son.

My stomach churned.

According to this small bit of information, Bishop was arrested on April 13th as well, the same day as the incident. He either hadn't run and tried to hide, or he'd willingly turned himself in. His sentence wasn't handed down for four more years, which was typical of our slow penal system. He wasn't entered into Polunsky's death row until 2005, which meant he'd been in that cell in 12-Building for fifteen years. Twenty-one years old at the time of his arrest and forty years old today. That was almost half his life behind bars.

I let all of that information sink in.

It was hard to imagine anyone being capable of such atrocities, and I'd been working alongside murderers and rapists and thieves for my whole career. It took me a full minute before I could find the strength to jot down those little pieces of information before I drew up a new search window. My fingers hovered over the keyboard as I considered how important details were. Did I need or want to know more? Wasn't that enough? I had my answers. I should shut my computer down and walk away.

I closed my eyes and saw the frail old woman again, saw the tears as they'd rolled down Bishop's dark cheeks. Despite knowing it was a bad idea, my fingers typed of their own accord, adding Bishop's full name, the date of the murders, and the word *Texas* into the search parameters.

I paused over the enter key.

This would be a sure-fire way of shutting down my inexplicable sympathetic attitude. I knew that, and it was what drove me to hit the key. In a flash, the screen filled with links to article after article of the horrific events that had transpired on April 13th, 2001 with headlines such as *Man Mercilessly Stabs his Ex-Girlfriend and her Child to Death* and *Ex-Boyfriend's Jealous Rage Ends in Double Murder* followed by *Remorseless Killer Arrested at Crime Scene*.

It went on and on for pages and pages. I shoved my Coke aside and went and found a beer in the fridge instead. A bone-deep chill had settled inside me, and it was uncomfortable. I needed to move around, shake it off. If I was going to read any of those articles, I needed to relax and put up my defensive walls again.

After drinking half my beer and staring at the long list of links on the laptop screen, my nerves were settled enough to keep going. I clicked the third article down: *Remorseless Killer Arrested at Crime Scene*. The fact that Bishop had been taken into custody at the scene of the crime struck me as odd. If this was considered a capital murder charge—which it would be if he was on death row—then it was hard to believe he would have waited around for the cops to show up, unless he was caught in the act.

The article was lengthy and showed a picture of a young Bishop and the woman and child he was accused of murdering. In short, it explained how the police had been called after the upstairs neighbor at the apartment complex had overheard a man and woman arguing. The neighbor claimed there was loud crashing that sounded like furniture being upturned or broken and constant crying from the woman's young boy. The neighbor also explained to reporters how this was a frequent occurrence and not the first time she'd called the police because of it.

That day, when the police had arrived on the scene, Bishop was found sitting in the middle of a destroyed living room with his victims splayed out in a pool of blood on the floor. Bishop was covered in their blood as well, and he was holding a utility knife that had been taken from a knife block in the kitchen. The woman, twenty-one-year-old Ayanna Williams, and her son, five-year-old Keon Williams, were dead when the police and emergency medical services had arrived on the scene. Both had been stabbed multiple times.

The article claimed Bishop had not resisted arrest, nor had he spoken with authorities about what had happened. Neighbors claimed when he was removed from the scene, he looked almost catatonic.

It went on for a few more paragraphs and included an interview with the upstairs neighbor, explaining how the police had been at Ayanna's apartment multiple times in the past for calls about domestic violence and how Bishop was a regular visitor, unable to let his failed relationship go.

I closed the article and drew up another and another after that. They all told a variation of the same story. Later articles talked of Bishop's trial and how he'd pleaded not guilty. Based on what I read, Bishop didn't have a leg to stand on. The evidence spoke for itself. The weapon was clutched in his hand, and the next-door neighbor testified to ongoing violence and threats against Ayanna. She claimed she'd witnessed Bishop losing his temper with her many times and making threats that he would *do something about it* if she didn't start listening to him. The codefendant, Isaiah, was never mentioned, so I didn't know who he was or how he fit into the story.

Three hours into my research, I slammed my laptop closed and collapsed back on the couch. My eyes stung and head throbbed. I stared at the ceiling as I absorbed all I'd read. Spinning through my head were visions of blood and violence, the images of a small boy and a young woman whose lives had been taken far too soon. Then I saw Bishop, a single tear trailing down his cheek, a hand fruitlessly trying to grasp a frail old woman's through three inches of plexiglass. Words of thanks given in a tone so gentle and grateful, I couldn't imagine him ever raising his voice in anger. All because I'd put air in a basketball.

I was a fool.

Based on every single article I'd read, the case was cut and dry. There was no reason to believe anyone else was guilty of the two murders. Bishop and Ayanna had dated. It ended. He couldn't seem to let it go and had harassed her on a daily basis. Threats were made, and eventually, he'd had enough. Two people were dead.

Bishop had stabbed them both to death.

I pinched the bridge of my nose and squeezed my eyes closed. Regardless, the whole thing sat uncomfortably in my gut. It left doubt when it shouldn't. None of the articles told Bishop's side of the story. He'd pleaded not guilty. Where was his account of what had happened? Who was this Isaiah man? Why was it all missing? Had they dismissed him so fast, it didn't make the papers? Was it so implausible that anyone else could have committed the crime that they'd laughed the notion out of the courtroom? What was Bishop's story, and why was it missing?

With a growl, I launched off the couch and grabbed the accumulated collection of empty beer cans from the coffee table. "What the fuck is wrong with you? It doesn't matter."

I stormed to the kitchen and banged around, looking for something to eat since I'd long ago missed dinner. I didn't like how deeply Bishop had rooted under my skin. I never should have looked him up. Instead of feeling disgusted and justifiably horrified by his crimes, I was enraged. And the rage wasn't because of what he'd supposedly done.

"Not supposedly," I yelled at myself. "He murdered two people. Two. Fucking. People." I slammed a hand on the counter with each word for emphasis. "Stabbed them to death. Jesus, listen to yourself."

Except reading the articles didn't petrify my heart toward Bishop; it had the opposite effect. It stirred doubt. Doubt, which I refused to give any more of my attention or time. The day I questioned our justice system was the day I should walk away from my job. Forgetting what kind of people I dealt with every day was dangerous beyond belief. This all needed to stop right now. I'd spent three hours trying to convince myself Bishop was wrongfully accused because his crimes didn't fit the personality of the man I'd seen a mere handful of times behind bars.

"Enough of this. He is a monster like the rest of them. Stabbed a woman and child to death. He is not gentle or kind, he is dangerous."

After my little pep talk, I focused all my energy on finding something for dinner. Moving across the country and starting a new job had taken a toll on my mind and body. That was the simplest explanation. Once I settled in, this sympathetic obsession would go away.

I opened and closed cupboard doors, stared into the fridge, and checked the pantry. Nothing appealed to me. My stomach was knotted, and any appetite I might have come home with was long gone. I considered painting or unpacking to work off some energy but couldn't bring myself to focus on either task.

Instead, I threw on some running gear and took to the streets. Pounding the pavement for an hour cleared my mind like nothing else. It was hot, but I didn't care. I pushed myself beyond my limits and ran hard and fast, learning the streets of my new little town.

By the time I got home, I was drenched in sweat and my chest burned from exertion. I showered again and decided to call it a night. I crawled into bed with a new book, hoping it would be enough of a distraction to chase away the lingering images my mind had created of crime scenes and murder. My body was tired, but my mind was as active as ever, and I feared I was going to have a rough night.

AFTER A RESTLESS SLEEP, I woke and decided to make a dent on painting the living room before Javier arrived that afternoon. If I could tape, cut in, and get the first coat up this weekend, I'd consider myself accomplished. But first, I wanted to take care of meal prep for that evening.

I spent the first two hours of my morning running to the grocery store, making a salad, and fixing the homemade patties for the grill that evening. Once that was ready to go, I dressed in ratty clothes and faced the living room and the painting chore.

With floor fans running on high and all the windows open on the main level to air out the fumes, I set to work taping, then cutting in around the windows and doorways with the ash-gray color I'd chosen.

The heat was stifling, and I shed my T-shirt by noon. Each time I stepped down from the step ladder to reposition myself, the plastic covering the floors crinkled underfoot. It was a methodical process that required a lot of concentration, and it worked well to keep my mind from wandering to the research I'd done the previous day. The last thing I wanted was to think more about Bishop and his crimes.

Classic rock blared from the small speakers on my entertainment unit, and I sang along to a little AC/DC while I worked, not caring that I was off-key and fudging up the lyrics.

I worked all morning and into the afternoon, stopping on occasion to guzzle water and once to stuff a peanut-butter-and-banana sandwich down my gullet. I'd long ago lost track of the time, so while I was applying the final touches of the first coat of paint to the wall and Javier called into the house, I startled to discover how late it was.

"Hello? Knock knock?"

"In here." I swiped a paint-covered hand over my sweaty brow and jumped down off my step stool as Javier entered the room.

He carried a case of beer, was wearing cargo shorts and a T-shirt, and had sunglasses perched on top of his head. It was the most casual I'd seen him. He whistled as he glanced around, admiring the new paint. "Nice. You've been busy."

I dropped the roller in the pan and wiped my hands on my discarded T-shirt before checking the time on my phone. "I have. Shit, is it seriously five?"

"It is."

"I lost track of time. I didn't mean for you to walk into a mess."

"Not a big deal. Do you need a hand?"

"Nah." I spun, admiring the day's effort. "I'm done for the day. I wanted the first coat up. Cutting in took forever. I didn't anticipate that."

"Always does."

"I'm sorry. Let me clean this up and have a quick shower. The kitchen is through there. Feel free to throw the beer in the fridge. I'll fire up the grill once I'm done. The back porch is shady this time of day, so it should be nice to sit outside. Sorry it's so hot in here. The central air barely works, and I shut it down to open the windows and air the place out. I'll be back."

"No rush. I'm good at making myself at home."

Javier carried the case of beer through to the kitchen, where I heard him unloading it into the fridge. I made quick work of clean-up, leaving the brushes and rollers to soak, and folding up the plastic drop cloths to use again another day. Then I hustled upstairs for a quick shower.

In no time, clean and dressed in a pair of shorts and a T-shirt, I rubbed some gel through my hair and hustled back downstairs. Javier had turned up the music, and some good old Led Zeppelin filled the house.

I snagged a beer from the fridge and joined him on the back deck, collapsing on the Adirondack chair opposite him. Javier had his feet propped up on the railing, his shades covering his eyes. He appeared relaxed as he reclined on his chair, staring up at the blue sky.

My yard wasn't huge, but it was private and quiet with a high fence all around and a few red oaks that offered plenty of shade from the hot Texas sun.

"Nice place you've got here."

I snorted. "Did you walk through the house with your eyes closed?"

Javier's grin split his face. "Needs some work, but you're already making a difference. The location is nice." He waved a hand at the quiet yard.

"It isn't too bad, considering I bought it blind. It has potential."

"Blind?"

"Yeah. The real estate agent sent me pictures and answered my questions, but I didn't see it firsthand before purchasing it. I didn't have time to dick around, so I took the risk."

"I think you did all right. You could do with a hot tub back here. Nice big deck like this."

"Perhaps in the future."

We fell silent as we sipped our beers and took in the serenity of the backyard. I didn't know Javier all that well, so fishing for topics of conversation was tricky. I wasn't some social recluse, and I was decent at making friends, but it'd been a while since I'd needed to start fresh.

"Do you live around here?" I asked, realizing I had no clue how far he'd come to visit me this evening.

"I have a small house in Livingston. A stone's throw from work. I bought it last year with the girlfriend. It's okay. We should have found something a little bigger since the woman has all these plans of marriage and about a dozen children in our future."

I chuckled and sipped my beer, avoiding eye contact, fearing the direction of the conversation and how I'd respond. Conversations about relationships would inevitably turn into confessions about my sexuality. It wasn't that I was against sharing, but my recent past had left me a little more leery.

"Have you been together long?" I asked, keeping the attention off me for a bit longer.

"Three years. She's a nurse at St. Luke's. Sweet girl. I was under her spell from the moment I laid eyes on her. Mama loves her, too, so what can a guy do?"

"Sounds like your future is planned."

"That it is." Javier chuckled and held up his beer bottle so we could clink them together. "But I'm happy with it. Melanie's a great girl." He shuffled and sat more upright, elbows on knees as he peered across the lawn. "When she found out I was coming over tonight and that you were new to the area, she got all excited. She's a self-proclaimed matchmaker. I'm warning you. I'll hold her off as long as I can, but her determination will prevail. She'll have you on a blind date by next weekend if you give her the go-ahead."

And there it was. The inescapable turn of conversation that led to talking about my love life. I laughed at his comment even though my blood pressure spiked. Biding time, I guzzled my beer dry and stood, gesturing inside the house. "I'm gonna grab a couple more. Do you want me to put the burgers on now? Are you hungry?"

"I could eat." Javier stood too. "Let me give you a hand."

Together, we went inside. I passed Javier a fresh beer before digging the patties out of the fridge as well as the containers of toppings I'd made for our burgers earlier that morning before I'd started painting. I also found the salad, condiments, and a couple of plates and napkins.

Javier helped carry stuff to the table outside and leaned against the railing, sipping his fresh beer as I started up the grill. I considered the pros and cons of telling Javier I was gay. If his girlfriend felt the need to set me up, it'd have to be with a guy, or I wasn't interested.

I wasn't closeted—per se—but I'd always been a little more private about my personal life than some people. When word got around I-Max that I was gay, my work life went in the shitter overnight. Convicts weren't the most accepting bunch of people, especially when they had something to prove to their fellow inmates. They were macho men doing all they could to gain a position of status in their self-made community. If that meant harassing and assaulting guards and other prisoners because of their sexuality, race, religion, or size, they didn't care.

"You all right, man?"

I tore from my thoughts and realized I'd been staring at the grill with the cleaning brush in my hand doing nothing. I blinked and blew out a breath. "Sorry. My mind was elsewhere."

I scrubbed the grill clean and set the brush aside before laying the patties over the heat. Closing the lid, I took my beer and sat back on the Adirondack chair. Javier didn't move from his spot against the railing, but I felt his heavy, curious gaze follow me.

Did I trust him? Would I shoot myself in the foot if I opened my mouth? I didn't get the sense Javier was a bad guy, and I'd told myself a hundred times since the incident back home that I wouldn't go back in the closet because of it. It would be best if my personal life stayed away from the prison, but I was entitled to make friends, and if Javier and I were going in that direction, it was something he needed to know about me. Sooner rather than later. I wouldn't pretend to be someone I wasn't.

"Might as well say it, whatever it is." Javier lifted his shades off his face and studied me.

The meat sizzled under the barbecue lid, cutting through the heavy silence, and the smells of charred beef lingered in the air. Birds chirped from the trees in the yard, and I knew it was now or never.

"All right. Your girl's a matchmaker, huh?"

He beamed, and his shoulders relaxed. "That she is. Why? Are you interested? She'll be thrilled."

I sipped my beer, giving myself a moment. "I don't know. Maybe. I haven't dated in a while."

"That's not a problem. Tell me your type, and I'll pass it along. It will save you getting the third degree over the phone because, believe me, she'd do it. We can go on a double date or something, take the pressure off. What do you say?"

"Um… Okay. Type. Let's see. Tall. Athletic. Someone who likes to read. Intelligent."

"Ass or tit man?"

A shot of laughter burst from my chest. "Definitely ass."

"Blondes, brunettes, redheads?"

I carded my fingers through my hair and fought the urge to jump up and check the burgers. "Dark hair, I guess. But, most importantly, when it comes to my type, you should know, I prefer men."

Silence hung between us for a long time, and I was afraid to meet Javier's eyes. It was stupid how nerve-racking revealing my sexuality could be in a new friendship. People were unpredictable, and I'd come across my fair share of close-minded individuals.

I was about to open my mouth and say something—anything—when Javier spoke. "Well, that narrows down the choices somewhat, but I'm sure she can manage it."

Certain I'd heard him wrong, I lifted my chin and studied the smirk on his face.

"What?" Javier said. "Just because we're in the South, did you expect everyone to be a homophobic twat?"

"Wouldn't have shocked me."

"I'm not like that. But, I'm not sure I'd be gloating around work if I were you. We hire some real pieces of shit at that place. Their attitudes toward homosexuality leave much to be desired, and those are our fellow corrections officers I'm talking about. If the guys behind bars found out—"

I couldn't shake my head fast enough. "No! No, I had no plans of people there finding out. Ever. Bad scene. Been there, done that, have the souvenir scars to prove it."

Javier's gaze shifted to my side and the scar hidden under my T-shirt. I instinctively reached for the old wound. How did he know it was there?

"Is that what happened?" When I rose a brow in question, he added, "I saw it when I came in and you were painting."

Right, I'd been shirtless.

"Yeah." I rubbed the spot, even though it didn't pain me anymore. Habit. The residual ache was all in my head and ailed me at random. I got up to check the burgers, keeping my back to Javier. "Got attacked by three inmates at I-Max. They ganged up on me. Put me in the hospital and into surgery. Stabbed me with a switchblade someone managed to get their hands on, and they nicked my kidney. The doctor said I was lucky it wasn't worse."

"Because they found out you were gay?"

I nodded, moving the burgers on the grill for something to do and not because they needed to be shifted around. "A few guys I worked with knew. We were friends, so it wasn't a big deal. I trusted them. I came out in college, so I wasn't closeted or anything. All it took was an overheard conversation for the wrong person to find out, and the harassment started. First it was here and there and just among my colleagues. Random rude remarks. Name-calling. I brushed it off. You can't let that shit get to you. But it didn't take long for the news to travel to general population. When the whispers started among those men, I knew I was in trouble."

"Shit."

"Long story short, after a running month of problems, I was working the yard one afternoon. Me and a few other officers. It was time to go in, and we'd cleared the last few inmates from the yard, rounded up the stragglers, and sent them in. I was responsible for the final sweep that day, and because counts were still taking place as they filed inside, we didn't know yet we had three guys missing. It'd happened before. They hide out on the field, thinking they'll pull a fast one on us. It never amounts to anything.

"Anyhow, while I was doing a walk around, they came out of nowhere and took me down. Blindsided me. I didn't have time to react. They'd planned it well because my backup was inside the doors doing counts, and they didn't see what happened until it was too late. One of those hiccups in your routine you don't realize is there until something bad happens. I shouldn't have been alone. Those three inmates had enough time to beat the fuck out of me, and they stabbed me twice before they were taken into custody."

"Twice?"

I flipped my arm over, showing Javier the backside where a long pink scar was hidden among the dark hairs of my forearm. It had been stitched together with six stitches at one time. "Defensive wound, that one. I blocked their first attempt to stab me, but I was no match for all three of them. It happened so fast, I'm still a little fuzzy on details. I remember fighting back, but they knocked me around good, and I couldn't get my bearings. They... I remember them saying some cruel shit about my being gay. Told me they would kill me because they didn't want no fucking faggots in their domain."

"Jesus."

"Yup." I shook my head, trying to dispel the memory. "I'm sorry. I hate that word. I don't even like repeating it. Anyhow, I got to spend some time in the hospital. Stab wounds, one which required surgery, a fractured cheekbone, two black eyes, broken nose, stitches here on my lip, and bruised ribs. The list goes on and on. Enough injuries to keep me immobile for a while. When I was well enough to return to work, the warden pulled me into his office and suggested a transfer. 'Unsafe working environment,' he said. Although he didn't have a problem with my sexuality, he feared for my life and couldn't promise I wouldn't be attacked again. As many safety measures as we had in place—"

"Anything can happen," Javier finished. "Yeah, I've seen it. As locked up as our Ad Seg guys are, they are the ones who've been known to attack us when they get the chance. General population would be worse. They're given a lot more freedom. Those fuckers are dangerous."

"Exactly, and that's where I worked at I-Max. GP."

"So you took the transfer."

"Yup."

"But why Texas? There had to be somewhere closer to home."

"There was, but the incident at work resurfaced other issues. I'd been having ongoing problems with an ex before I was stabbed. Ironically, he hated my job and told me it was too dangerous. Wished I would quit. I left him but spent months dealing with him showing up at random and trying to convince me we could work shit out. Everything was dying off nicely. I thought he'd finally gotten the picture. Eight months apart and the phone calls and random visits were almost non-existent.

"Then he caught wind of what happened at the prison, and it all started again. Tenfold. He spent every waking hour at my hospital bedside moaning about my job and how he'd warned me this would happen. He loved me and maybe I would listen now. Anyhow, I couldn't stick around and deal with him anymore. So when the warden gave me a list of possible transfers, I took the farthest one from home there was. I didn't give two shits it was on The Row. I needed out and far away from people who knew me."

I lifted my beer to my lips only to find I'd drained it without realizing it. Javier removed the empty from my grasp and fit the burger flipper back into my hand since I'd put it down at some point. "I think another beer is in order. Check the burgers before they burn, and I'll hook us up."

The burgers were ready to come off. I slid them onto a plate and added them to the table with the rest of the dinner. When Javier came back out, we made our plates and sat back on the Adirondack chairs to eat. For a long time, we enjoyed our meals in silence. I hadn't meant to dump my history all over Javier our first time spending time together outside of work; it just fell out of my mouth.

Javier finished eating and set his plate aside before raising his beer to me. "To new beginnings. Welcome to Texas, to Polunsky, and The Row. I'm gonna hold Melanie off for your sake while you get adjusted. Being set up on a blind date is the last thing you need, by the sounds of it."

I chuckled and clinked our bottles together. "Thanks. You're probably right."

We spent the following few hours sharing beer and light conversation while the sun set and the temperature cooled to something more tolerable. We talked sports, where Javier tried to convince me my move to Texas made me an automatic Cowboys fan, like it or not. We talked about the differences between living in the North and the South. We talked about music, TV shows, movies, books, and Javier's future plans with his girlfriend. We touched a bit on family, too, but in the end, we veered into talk about work because it was common ground for both of us.

"Have you worked with Ezra yet?" Javier asked, removing his sunglasses and setting them aside. The sun was almost down, and he didn't need them any longer.

"This past week. We worked escorting together."

"And?" Javier quirked a brow.

I chuckled. "And this is a trap, isn't it?"

"Piece of work, isn't he?"

"So it wasn't just me?"

"No way. He's had more complaints filed against him than anyone I know. It's a wonder he still has a job. If we weren't so short-staffed, I think Ray would can him."

"Not gonna lie, his handling of prisoners bothered me."

"And you're new, so he'll test you and see how far he can push before you'll say anything."

"I almost did. More than once. The guy is lucky he doesn't get spit on more."

Javier laughed out loud. "It's happened. If anyone is going to push our guys to react, it's Ezra."

"That guy pisses me off."

"You aren't the first. A word of advice, he is one you definitely don't want to find out you're gay. He'll make your life hell. You think he's a dick with the inmates, just wait."

"Noted. I'll be keeping my mouth shut at work. Believe me. No reason for anyone to know."

We drifted back into a comfortable silence as the sky darkened and the bats took flight in the faraway distance. My thoughts drifted to the coming week. I was scheduled for my first stint on F with the guys in solitary, and I wasn't looking forward to it. There had been more and more tales shared about that pod since I'd started, and each one was consecutively worse than the one before it.

I was about to query Javier about what I could expect when he cut in. "I meant to ask you something."

"What's up?"

"I'm scheduled on nights next week, and Melanie booked us for this couples' thing Tuesday and Thursday evening without telling me. Any chance you'd be interested in switching for the week? I'd say just those days but that'd be hell on my sleep schedule flipping back and forth."

"I'll happily switch, but you should know, I'm on F all week."

Javier groaned and tilted his head back, staring at the dark sky. "It would figure."

"I'm sure someone else would switch with you."

"Not likely. These guys all hate working midnights about as much as they hate F." He groaned again and roughed a hand over his hair.

I chuckled at his dilemma. "Well, like I said, you can take my rotation, and I'll gladly work yours."

"You don't mind the nights?"

"Based on the rumors I've heard, I'll take straight nights over that pod. What sections are you in?"

"A and B. Same rows we worked on your first week. You got the golden area, my friend. Definitely the better end of this deal. Those guys are a cake-walk compared to F."

I refused to acknowledge the twinge in my chest when I realized I'd be working in Bishop's area again. No matter how much I'd tried to ignore thoughts of his case and crimes, they rolled around my head on a loop, and I had this strange urge to see him and study him and find the criminal behind the gentle façade he portrayed. My intrigue into this man and his story hadn't lessened in the least. I was playing with fire, but I couldn't help wanting to know more.

"You've got a deal."

Javier offered his fist to bump. "I owe you, man."

"No problem."

I considered bringing up my recent quest looking into Bishop's case, thought about asking Javier if he'd ever questioned an inmate's guilt or innocence or what his opinion was on certain men behind bars, but I knew it was a topic best left untouched. He'd already told me once, he wasn't one of those people who dug for information.

Except, neither was I until I'd met Bishop.

Chapter Six

"HEY, WHITE BOY. COME 'ERE."

"Hold up, Jeffie. Gotta report my count and check in with Davis downstairs. Give me five."

An exaggerated sigh came from within cell B19, and I chuckled. One thing I'd learned working this section was Jeff's impatience and the way he flapped his gums without a care in the world to express his indignation.

"Don't call me Jeffie, man. Fucking hate that shit."

"Don't call me white boy."

"Fucker." But the insult was followed by a laugh, so I knew it was just Jeff being a mouthpiece, like usual.

I unclipped my radio as I headed toward the staircase leading down to the next row. "Anson Miller, ID 26903, reporting for B-Pod section B, rows one and two. All's good here."

There was a burst of static before, "Copy 26903, thank you."

I clomped down the steel staircase, my boots resonating and echoing off the concrete walls. Jin Davis, my partner that night, met me at the bottom of the stairs. He was a short Asian man in his midforties. He had a contagious smile when it broke free and an intimidating posture for someone who barely stood as high as my shoulders. I'd met him once before when learning the ropes doing escorts, but this was the first time we'd officially worked together. I got a good vibe from him, unlike the one I'd gotten from Ezra.

"Did you call in your count?" he asked.

"Yup. All's quiet."

"Perfect. Call lights-out at eleven sharp and kill the breaker on the far wall. They mostly all have alternate lighting sources and will be up later. It's of no consequence so long as they stay quiet. Nights are easy, man. Mostly counts every hour and pacing until your feet get sore. Don't fall asleep, or it's a one-way ticket out the door."

"Understood. We take a section each and meet up here after counts for check-in?"

"That's how I work things. Some other guys spend half the night chatting on the stairs, but if Ray catches us doing that, he gets pissed."

"Fair enough."

"But if you have a problem, shout or radio in. It's rare, but it happens. We got a good section for nights, to be honest. Not much happens here."

"Sounds good. I'll call if there's a problem." I knocked on the metal railing, making it clang. "I'll touch back in an hour."

"All righty."

We both went our separate ways. I returned to Jeff's cell since I'd promised to find out what he wanted once I was done with my count. Checking my watch, I saw there were still twenty-five minutes until lights-out so I had plenty of time to listen to his woeful story, whatever it might be.

At B19, I peeked through one of the side windows and saw Jeff sitting on his bed, feet kicked up, and arms folded behind his head.

"What's up, Jeff?" I called after knocking once.

He bounced up and approached the door to his cell. "You have to get our commissary slips. We didn't get 'em filled out today, and commissary comes tomorrow afternoon. That's not fair, man. We didn't do nothin' to deserve missing commissary."

"What are you talking about? Why didn't you get them?"

Commissary happened every fourteen days and was an important part of these guy's schedule so long as they weren't living with restrictions due to bad behavior. It was an opportunity for them to purchase toiletries, stamps for their mail, extra food items, and all kinds of stuff from art supplies to spare underwear. They received forms to fill out the day before, checked off the items they wanted to purchase—within a specific budget—and those forms were collected and sent in to be processed.

"We didn't get 'em because Officer Asshole was working, and he thinks it's funny to forget shit like that. He knows if them papers ain't filed, we ain't getting shit this time 'round."

"Let me look into it. Who's Officer Asshole?" I had a hunch but didn't want to assume.

"Come on, man. Asshole Atterbury. The guy's always trying to make our lives more hellish than they already are."

Ezra Atterbury. Why was I not surprised?

"Give me a few minutes to see what I can find out. I can't make promises, Jeff, so don't get your hopes up. But if he purposefully ignored his duties, I will ensure the higher-ups are informed."

Jeff gave a sharp nod and returned to his bed, his face a picture of pissed off—rightfully, if he'd been denied commissary for no reason.
I blew out a breath and decided to investigate the matter on my level first to see if anyone else said the same thing.

I stopped at B20 and rapped on the door. Armando, who was already under his covers, waved a hand at me, thinking I was doing checks and couldn't tell if he was alive or not.

"Not a check, buddy. Did you get your commissary slip today?"

He flung his blankets off and glared daggers at the window. "Fuck no. That fucker wouldn't give 'em out."

I held up a hand in a peaceful, calm-down gesture. "I'm looking into it. I wanted to see if it was contained to certain people or the whole row here."

"I ain't got mine. None of us did. That asshole better hope he ain't working tomorrow 'cause I'll fuck him up."

"All right, calm down and don't make problems for yourself. I'm gonna see what I can do about fixing this. Hang tight, okay?"

Armando flopped back down under his covers and muttered what I assumed was cursing in a different language.

And that right there was a fine example of why you didn't go around pissing these guys off. Ezra had a lot of balls and no brains. He was asking for trouble.

I glanced at the next door. B21. Bishop's cell. Approaching, I took a second to peek in his window before calling for his attention. He was drawing on his wall with a nub of charcoal that was so small it barely fit in his giant hand, filling the space above his bed with what looked like a portrait of a woman. My angle from the window wasn't ideal for making out the finer details, but it was unmistakably the woman he'd called Maw Maw. The soft curls of her hair, the frailty and gauntness of her cheeks, the way her eyes glimmered with such love and life when she'd spied Bishop through the window.

He was an incredible artist and had captured her likeness.

Bishop must have sensed my appearance. When I looked from the art to the man responsible, those dark eyes were fixed on me. Where I'd once considered his attention to be invasive and almost threatening, I now saw it another way. It still felt like he was able to strip me bare and see into my soul, but it was different. It was almost like he was studying me, trying to understand where I sat in the hierarchy of corrections officers. Was I a threat? A friend? Someone he could trust? An enemy like Ezra?

"You've captured her beauty," I said, not taking my eyes off him. "It's stunning."

His attention shifted back to his drawing. He stared so intently, it was almost like he was looking through the concrete wall to the past. To a time when he'd been with that woman outside of a prison cell. It was subtle, but a wistfulness crossed his face, and a glimmer sparkled in his eyes. Longing. Hurt. Sadness.

Bishop pressed his lips together and swallowed a tight enough lump, I saw the movement in his throat.

It was obvious the giant man wasn't going to share or talk about his art, so I cleared my throat and asked what I'd come to ask. "There's a complaint that this row didn't get their commissary slips today. Did you get one?"

Bishop blinked and examined his drawing for another beat before tipping his head and peering at me sidelong. "No I did not, boss. None of us did. Sure would have liked to buy more art supplies." He fiddled with the nub of charcoal, rolling it between his fingers, and I could see it wouldn't last him another two weeks. He'd be lucky to get another day from it.

"Okay. I'm looking into it. No promises, but I'll see what I can do."

He tipped his chin in a clipped nod. "Thank you, boss." Then he turned back to his portrait and immersed himself in his work.

I checked the time and found it was five to eleven. After lights-out, I'd check in with Jin and see what he suggested and ask if his group downstairs had received their slips or not.

I waited the five minutes and killed the breaker, which shut down all the overhead lights in the row of cells. "Lights-out, gentlemen," I called, loud enough for them to all hear.

Individual lights clicked on in a few cells, and the murmur of voices floated like a rippling wave along the hall. Once I was sure everyone was settled, I moved to the second hallway and the second bank of rows and did the same. After, I headed to the stairs. At the bottom, I whistled for Jin, who came and met me with a questioning look on his face.

"Problems?"

"Yes and no. Everything is fine, but I've got some complaints that commissary slips weren't handed out today. It seems to cover both rows upstairs. Suggestions? They aren't too happy. I said I'd look into it."

Jin sighed and wiped a hand over his short black hair. "Not the first time, and I can guess who's responsible. Have them write their requests on whatever paper they have. Take the forms and their ID cards and clip them together on their doors. We can send them down with mail collection in the morning and explain the delay. Shouldn't be a problem. I'll check and see if it affected my guys here too."

"Thanks, and what about the officer responsible?"

Jin pursed his lips. "Add it to your shift report. Ray reads them every day, and he'll take care of it."

"Will do. Thanks."

"No problem."

We headed in opposite directions. At the top of the stairs, I worked my way down both rows, informing the guys what they could do if they wanted their commissary this time around.

"I like you, white boy," Jeff said when I knocked on his door and let him know the verdict.

"Yeah, yeah, today you do."

There was more commotion than there should have been for after lights-out, but I let it go. At half-past the hour, I did my routine check of each cell and called in my report. After meeting with Jin again—

who informed me the missing slips didn't affect his rows—I headed back up to collect papers and ID cards.

Each ID card contained a magnetic strip that, when swiped, held all the inmate's information from medical history, classification within the prison, to financial account holdings. It was used when they made purchases at commissary, and their money was directly withdrawn from their holdings.

I started at the far end of the row, B16, Syed's cell. The man was stoned-faced, expressing no emotion whatsoever as I unlocked the chute to accept his list and ID card. Dead eyes watched my every move, and although it should have rattled me, it didn't. *That* was the kind of expression I expected from the men behind bars. Looking at Syed, I could picture him responsible for horrific crimes like the ones I'd read about this past weekend.

Once I had his commissary requests in hand, I locked the chute and clipped the paper and ID card to the outside of the door. Before I walked away, I took one last look inside Syed's cell. Same beady eyes. Same blank expression. I hated to stereotype, but he had the look of a psychotic killer. I wouldn't have been shocked if he was dismembering me in his mind at that exact moment despite the good deed I was doing for them all. A deed I could have ignored.

I moved along to the next cell and the one after that, repeating the process over and over again, collecting papers and cards. Desmond, or the manic smiling man as I remembered him, lived up to his name. He leered through the thick window, twitchy and edgy as he waited for me to unlock his chute. His eyes were bloodshot, and I noticed the tremors in his hands, making his paper shiver as he held it tight. The whole impression pinged trouble on my radar. Instead of questioning him, I noted all the little indicators of what could have been a drug high and sighed, knowing my report later would induce a shakedown on this row.

"You da man, Miller. I got all kinds of respect for you," Jeff said when I approached his cell.

"At least you got my name right this time."

"They gonna deal with that asshole?"

"Not up to me, but the report will go in."

I took Jeff's list through the slot and folded it around his card, clipping it to the door. Once the chute was locked up tight, I rapped twice. "Have a good night, Jeffie."

He grumbled something about not calling him Jeffie as I walked away with a grin.

Armando was ready with his list, and he seemed a degree less pissed off than he had when I'd inquired about the missing slips earlier. Once I'd cleared his cell, I was at the end of the row, B21. Bishop was waiting, list in hand. He didn't offer words, waiting silently as I unlocked the chute. Eyes always watching. His large hand appeared, smudged with black charcoal again, and it left residue on the page where he'd written his commissary list. I ran my finger over the black spot where his thumbprint remained and turned my attention to the window.

Our gazes locked and held. His eyes were dark and attentive. With him so close, a mere few feet and a window away, his features were as clear as I'd ever seen them. Sharp jaw, velvety dark skin, pronounced lips, and a wide nose. But it was the fierce attention that snagged me every time. I couldn't look away. Caught in his barbed grasp, I searched for the man I'd read about online. With everything I had, I dug and dug and tried to unearth the murderer behind the gentle giant. Tried to find the person who'd stabbed a helpless woman and her child to death.

But I couldn't see him. Nowhere behind those curious, intense eyes could I find the person responsible for such a crime.

I paused, holding the paper and his card, the chute open while we stood and watched each other. He was as glued to me as I was to him, and I wondered what he saw when he looked at me.

Shaking off the invisible thread tying us together, I broke eye contact and stepped back. I locked the chute and clipped his papers to the door. Reluctantly, I peered back in the window, anticipating he'd walked away. But Bishop hadn't moved.

I could have left. I could have continued with my duties and ignored our strange connection, but for some reason, I opened my mouth and spoke in a soft enough tone, none of the other men would hear me. "Is she your grandmother?"

Bishop flinched. It was almost imperceptible, but I caught it. His lips pressed a fraction tighter before he nodded once. "Yes. She's also the woman who raised me and my brother, so you best not have a single bad thing to say about her, boss."

I shook my head, my heart knocking a little faster at his defensive tone. "I would never."

"She's the best person I know."

"You seem close."

Nothing. No response.

"Does she visit you often?"

Bishop looked uncertain, like he wasn't sure if he wanted to answer or talk to me about something so personal. More hesitation ensued before, "Every week since the day they locked me up."

I absorbed that, shuffling my feet, knowing I should leave it there and walk away. I had so many questions on the tip of my tongue, yet my conscience was screaming for me to let it go. Where was his brother? Did he visit too? What did his family think about his incarceration?

"Best you don't ask them questions. I can see them swirling around in your head all the way from here. A word from the wise, be careful, boss. Us guys on this side of the bars shouldn't be trusted. It's too easy for people to hide their true nature, and if you get yourself invested or you start to care too much, it will only lead to no good. I've seen it. We ain't worth your compassion."

"I don't believe that. You're still human beings."

"That's where you're wrong. We're just monsters in cages waiting to die."

His comment made my gut twinge, and I didn't know what to say.

"Don't get lost in the storm that is death row, boss. You let it overtake you, you won't make it out alive. At least not with this in one piece." Bishop tapped his temple.

He turned his back and rolled the charcoal between his fingers as he returned to his bed and knelt, examining the portrait of his Maw Maw.

"Bishop?" His body stilled, and he cocked an ear, not turning his head, so I continued. "You said people hide their true nature, and I believe you. This isn't my first job in a prison. I've seen it. Guys in here wear masks all the time. They want you to believe they aren't capable of the crimes that put them here. I see that. I know. But let me tell you what else I see." I paused. He hadn't moved, but I knew he was listening. "Can you look at me? Please."

Bishop tipped his head, pools of onyx as deep and dark as outer space and just as mysterious landed on me. When I knew I had his full attention and that strange and unsettling connection bound us once more, I continued.

"A person's soul can't lie. Whatever mask they wear, whatever reality they want you to believe will only be on the surface. The truth is in a person's eyes. They are gateways into your soul. If you look hard enough, deep enough, then you'll see what's real and what's not. You'll see their true nature. You'll see the truth. And you're not a monster, Bishop Ndiaye."

"You don't know what you're talking about."

"Not always. I've made plenty of mistakes in my day, but I've never felt more conviction about something than I do right now. Maybe that makes me an idiot. Only you would know for sure."

The charcoal fell from Bishop's hand, and he was off the bed, stalking to the doorway once again. He had a half a head on me, and when he stopped, I had to tip my chin to maintain eye contact.

"Do you know why I'm here, boss?" Bishop's voice was barely loud enough to penetrate the steel door.

"Yes. I looked you up. I read every article."

He placed his large palm against the three-inch-thick window and leaned in so his forehead touched as well. "Then you know what kind of monster I am."

The husky edge of his voice prickled the hairs on my nape. I traced the contour of his large palm with my eyes, noticing a faded scar that slashed through the middle. I lifted my hand and placed it over his, the reinforced glass and diamond bars the only thing separating us. In my mind, I imagined the heat leaching off Bishop and seeping through the window into my palm. I thought of what it'd be like to touch him. I wasn't afraid.

I lifted my gaze once again and studied his face, those dark pits of his eyes, and shook my head. "I don't believe it. Monsters don't cry," I whispered.

For an extended beat, neither of us moved or breathed. Then, a wave of emotion and confusion pummeled me, and the spell was broken. I dropped my hand, stepped away, and shot my gaze down the row in both directions. Without looking back, I walked away, needing relief—*something*—from the unexpected exchange.

The remainder of my shift, I avoided conversation with everyone behind locked doors. When I did my hourly counts, I peered through the windows only long enough to ensure I saw the occupant and movement. I was grateful to find most men sleeping by one in the morning, so my tension lessened. Bishop, however, remained awake until long into the early morning. He read. Whenever I checked his cell, he didn't lift his head from his book, and I was grateful.

Without a doubt, he knew I was there each and every time.

Breakfast came at three-thirty, and mail pick-up happened at five. The missed commissary slips were collected and taken down to be filled.

I was grateful for the end of my shift at six. Jin and I met up with our relieving officers and went through a rundown of our night. My insides buzzed, and little bursts of adrenaline wouldn't stop flooding my system. I needed to sleep and shake off the whole exchange I'd had with Bishop. It'd unsettled me all night.

When our debriefing was complete, I headed to the staffroom to write my reports for the night shift. Despite how groggy and tired I was, my mind was restless. I planned a long run when I got home. Then I'd collapse in bed and hope the following night went smoother.

My main rule had been shattered, and I didn't know how to scrape up the pieces and put them back together. My first mistake was looking up an inmate's backstory. My second was believing my gut when it told me what I'd read was wrong.

I was so far beyond fucked, and I needed to pull back or I'd get lost in the storm like Bishop had warned.

Chapter Seven

I SLEPT LIKE SHIT. The conversation I'd had with Bishop spun on a loop in my head. Every word. Every look. I saw it all again and again. I heard the tone of his voice, the conviction when he'd told me he was nothing more than a monster.

But it was the tiny twinge of emotion that had surfaced when he'd spoke of his grandmother. The way he'd looked beyond the portrait he'd drawn on the wall. The way he'd called her Maw Maw.

The storm was all around me.

I gave up on sleep around six in the evening. My eyes felt full of dust and burned with irritation that was due to not enough shut-eye. I splashed water over my face and stared at my reflection. Two days' worth of dark stubble covered my chin and neck, and I rasped a hand over it while I convinced myself to shave.

I needed a haircut too. My mud-puddle brown mop was getting long enough to show the unmanageable curls I always tried to keep at bay. Tugging my last reserve of energy up from the bottom of the barrel, I worked at putting myself together so I didn't appear as pale or troubled.

After devouring a bowl of cereal, I checked my phone and saw a recent message from Ray, asking me to give him a call as soon as possible. Unsure what it might be about, I dropped my dishes in the sink and hit the call back button.

"Anson. How's it going?"

"Not bad. Just getting up. Something wrong?"

"Actually, I was wondering if you could come in a couple of hours earlier tonight. Got our hands full in your area and could use some extra bodies."

Hands full? I couldn't fathom what kind of problem they were having.

"Is something the matter?"

I knew Ezra was still on the afternoon rotation, and I remembered Armando's threats from the day before because they'd been denied their rights. Had something happened? Did he make good on those threats of fucking Ezra up? His comments had been included in my report, but I hadn't taken them to heart. The guy was upset, but I'd ensured the problem was corrected, so I didn't believe he would act.

"Shakedown, Miller. You reported suspicions of drug use. They moved in this afternoon."

"Shit." I rubbed a hand over my hair, wrecking all the effort I'd made with gel earlier. "I forgot about that."

"It's routine. It happens frequently, but it takes up a lot of the day and messes with regular procedural stuff. Any chance you can give us a few more hours?"

"Yeah, no problem. What time did you want me there?"

"Can you be here by eight?"

Considering I didn't have much going on, it wasn't an issue.

Since I was coming on shift at an odd time, there was no 12-Building briefing and no exchange with another officer. When I checked Ray's office to let him know I'd arrived, he wasn't there. Some inquiries later, I learned he was down in B helping out. So that was where I headed.

It didn't take long to see that a shakedown on a death row unit was far different than anything I'd experienced in the past. The inmates were moved from their cell into a large cage located in the main death row hallway. And if a strip search in their cell or in the rec cages weren't humiliating enough, the prisoners were then asked to strip in this central location and surrender their clothing for a thorough inspection. Once naked and cleared, a piss test was collected, right there in the open where there was no chance of games or shifty behavior.

While two officers took care of the convict, two other men went through his cell, inch by inch, checking and confiscating anything that they weren't allowed to have. It was meticulous and organized. Everyone had a job and a place.

Unsure where I was needed, I found Ray, who was supervising the men in the process of tearing apart Armando's cell.

"Evening, Ray. Where do you want me?"

"Oh, hey. Thanks a lot for coming in. Some of these guys missed their lunch. How about you jump in here and help out. I'll send Doug off for a fifteen minute break at least. I know it ain't much, but I'd rather get this done."

"No problem."

I snapped on my tear-resistant gloves and entered Armando's cell as Ray called over my shoulder, telling Doug to take off for fifteen. It was enlightening seeing a cell from the inside. The air was more stagnant and heavier than I expected with various unpleasant smells that we didn't experience on the outside. Body odor and unclean toilets. It figured since these men spent twenty-two hours of their day in a small room where they ate, slept, and shat.

There was mold growing up the walls and bare concrete patches over the bed where the paint had long ago peeled away. The clutter of junk and garbage was thick. An officer I knew only as Angelo tipped his head in greeting as he pulled the thin mattress off the bed and did a visual inspection, checking every inch.

"You ever done one of these?"

"In GP back at I-Max. Not here."

"Not too different when it comes to inspection, except for some minor stuff." He dragged the mattress into the hallway, and it was then I noticed the machine at the end of the row. "Gets X-rayed. It's not unlike the shit they have at the airport when you go through security. Once it clears, we put it back. We go through every inch of the room, looking for contraband. Be respectful with belongings. That's it. We don't worry about putting it back in order. Once they come back to their cell, they can take care of it on their own. You start trashing the joint, you'll get on someone's shit list, I guarantee it."

So we took apart Armando's cell bit by bit. Searching through his belongings and making piles in the middle of the cell as we went so we didn't miss anything. Once we'd deemed it clean, Angelo called an all-clear out to Ray.

"All right, let them know they can bring Armando back and move along to the next. I have to jump out for a few. They're having issues on F, surprise, surprise." Ray gave a wave as he walked toward the staircase. "Call me if you need me."

"I'll go let them know we're good for Armando to return," I said.

Angelo nodded as he left the cell and leaned against the wall, stripping his gloves and scrubbing at his face. He looked like he'd had a long day and could use a minute, which was why I'd not bothered radioing the other team.

I heard commotion before I turned the corner into the main hall area where Armando was being held. Raised voices and tempers pierced the air.

"You're a fucking piece of shit. I swear to God, if I get my hands on you one time, you fucking little punk, I'll break your neck."

"Back down, Armando. You don't want to do this."

"Yes I fucking do. This asshole gets away with too fucking much, and I'm sick of it. If no one wants to deal with him, I will."

There was a pause. Whispers drifted through the air, but the words were too low to discern. I picked up my pace and turned the corner. The cage sat dead center in the hallway. A naked Armando faced off with a cocky and arrogant Ezra who had a smirk on his face a mile wide. Even I wanted to punch it off. There were mere inches separating them, and I had no doubt if Armando wasn't inside the locked cage, he'd have made good on his promises.

Ezra had a hand on his coworker's chest, holding him back as he spoke words to Armando in a hushed tone. The coworker looked uncomfortable. He held Armando's jumpsuit in one hand, shoes in the other.

Armando's lip hooked in a snarl as he stared Ezra down.

"What's going on?" I yelled.

My distraction snapped the taut tension between them, and everything exploded. Armando launched his body at the cage wall, hocking a thick loogie right through the tiny holes and onto Ezra's face. Ezra whipped a canister of spray from his utility belt and doused Armando in the face.

I ran.

The other officer grabbed Ezra and pulled him back as he shouted objections.

Armando screamed and collapsed to his knees as he grabbed his face.

"I'll call the fucking CERT, and they can take care of you," Ezra roared. "How do you like that, Armando?"

Ezra tore his radio from his shoulder clip as I reached him. I helped the other officer restrain him as I got in his face. "What the fuck is your problem? What are you doing?"

"Get out of my face, newbie." Armando's spittle dripped down Ezra's cheek, and he glowed with his anger. The burning residue of pepper spray filled the air and stung my eyes. I'd walked into the aftermath. I couldn't imagine what Armando was feeling.

"Why are you antagonizing him? To be a dick? To wave your authority around?"

"He threatened me. You weren't here, so fuck off."

"Yeah? Did he threaten you before or after you pushed his buttons?" Instead of waiting for an answer from Ezra, I turned my attention to the quiet officer holding Ezra's arms back.

The man didn't respond with words, maybe because Ezra was as big a threat to his coworkers as he was to the inmates, but he nodded, confirming my belief.

"How about you take a walk, cool off, and come back when you have your head on straight?" I said to Ezra.

"How about you mind your own business? That man made threats to my person, and I have every right to call in CERT to take care of him."

CERT was a five-man, correctional emergency response team who were called in the event of prison riots, cell extractions, mass searches when an inmate was non-compliant, or violence against a guard. They came in full riot gear with a ranking officer in command.

"CERT isn't needed if you step away. There is bad blood between you two, and we can take care of it without you." I gestured to his coworker, still not sure of his name. "Armando?" I called to the gasping, whimpering man behind me.

"What?" he snapped, his anger barely restrained.

"How do you feel about Ezra taking a hike and me and—"

"Philip."

"Philip taking care of your transport back to your cell? It's all clear."

"You get rid of that fucker because if I get my hands on him—"

"Curb the threats, my man. I know he pissed you off, but you'll get your ass in deep shit if you keep this up. I'm on your side right now, and I suggest you recognize that."

"I'm reporting this," Ezra said, his voice caustic and full of rage.

"Yeah, so am I, and Philip here doesn't look impressed with your process, either, so I'm sure he'll have his own report to make."

Philip didn't say anything but watched on, still not releasing Ezra's arms. I saw the disgust in his eyes and didn't need verbal confirmation to know how he felt.

"Now, are you gonna walk away and give yourself a break, or do I need to call Ray back from F? I promise you, he won't be happy."

Ezra tore from Philip's hold and pulled himself straighter, aiming to intimidate me, but I matched his puffed-out chest with my own and didn't break eye contact until he turned on his heels and stormed away.

"Fucking dickhead," Armando grumbled.

Once Ezra cleared the nearest crash gate, I peered down at Armando. His skin was flaming red with irritation, and he continuously rubbed at his eyes. I doubted at this point he could see anything at all. Pepper spray to the face was all kinds of horrible.

"Are his clothes cleared?" I asked Philip.

"Yeah." He collected them from where he'd dropped them on the floor during the commotion. "Ezra wouldn't let me give them back."

Figured.

"Piss collected?"

"Yeah, he's good to transport."

"You ready to move, Armando."

"I'm fucking blind. Damn, that shit burns."

"I bet. On your feet. Philip will give you your clothes back. Once you're in your cell, flush with lots of water. Next time, don't take the bait and keep your mouth shut. He wanted to do that and was waiting for you to give him a reason."

Armando squinted up at me, his lips in that hooked snarl again. "Yeah, but he was—"

"But he was nothing. I know he was being a dick, but you made threats against an officer. That could get you dinged, and you know it.

I'll make an honest report, and maybe Ray will ignore your part in this and deal with Ezra, but that's not up to me."

Armando relented and pulled himself to his feet using the cage wall for support. Philip used the chute to return Armando's clothes, and we waited while he dressed. He submitted to his wrist and ankle restraints without issue, and while Philip and I took him back to his cell, he turned his head and studied me through squinting, bloodshot eyes.

"You're all right, Miller. Wish they was all like you."

Once Armando was back in his cell, Angelo quirked a brow and dropped his voice. "What the fuck happened? Why was he sprayed?"

"Ezra, and he's taking a break, if he knows what's good for him. Who's next?"

Angelo tipped his head to Desmond's cell, the culprit whose behavior and appearance were what had tipped this whole thing into motion. Doug was back, which was a good thing since we were down a man again. Unfortunately, that also meant no one else was getting a break.

"Give me five seconds. I'm gonna radio Ray and let him know what happened. If I were him, I'd be telling Ezra to call it a day. He's too hot right now, and his shift is almost over."

Ray was less than pleased and informed us he'd deal with the situation.

The rest of the shakedown went smooth, apart from the baggie of coke found in Desmond's cell. It was always a wonder how prisoners managed to get their hands on stuff like that when our security measures were so stringent. Desmond got written up and knocked down to a ninety-day level two. His possessions were confiscated, as per protocol, and the paperwork was filled out.

The last check was B21, Bishop. I avoided direct eye contact and maintained a professional attitude the entire time. More than once, I felt the heat of those onyx eyes on me. He didn't speak, and he didn't argue. As always, he was complacent and agreeable.

Ray pulled me off the floor to write a report about Ezra, and it was after eleven when I relieved Angelo. By that point, I felt like I'd already put a whole shift under my belt. I did a personal count since I was coming on the floor. Most of the guys were asleep, with the exception of Armando, who sat folded in half on his bed, fingers pressed into his eye sockets, and Bishop, who once again was reading.

"You all right in there, Armando?" I asked, pausing by his window on my next pass.

"Fuckin' eyes are still on fire."

"Did you flush them?"

"Yeah, I flushed them," he snapped. "You think I'm an idiot?"

"Just a question."

His anger hadn't simmered much, so I left him alone, not interested in getting stung by a pissed-off prisoner.

It was a quiet night, and I was grateful. It was after my 2:00 a.m. count as I was on my way back up the steel staircase after checking in with Jin when Bishop's soft baritone caught my ear. I stilled and listened. His voice carried more with how quiet it was.

The words weren't clear, so I approached his cell and leaned an ear against the door, out of sight of his window. The heart-wrenching emotion of his words washed over me.

"And neither the angels in heaven above,
Nor the demons down under the sea,
Can ever dissever my soul from the soul..."

"*'Of the beautiful Annabel Lee,'*" I whispered.

I closed my eyes, recognizing the poem at once. I mouthed each stanza that followed, feeling the woeful words by Edgar Allan Poe pierce my heart. It was made all the more sorrowful coming from the man inside the cell.

When Bishop fell silent, I spoke without thought, loud enough he'd hear. "'Annabel Lee' by Edgar Allan Poe. He's among my favorites." I pushed off the wall and made myself visible at the window. Bishop watched. "When I was in high school, they assigned us a famous author for an independent study project. I had to write five thousand words about him and his work. It was my first introduction to Edgar Allan Poe. I never looked back. There was something haunting about his poems and stories that called to me. I couldn't get enough. Gobbled them up one after another. Memorized them. From 'The Fall of the House of Usher' to 'The Cask of Amontillado.' 'The Raven,' 'The Black Cat.' All of them."

Bishop closed the small book in his lap and waved it at me once before setting it down. "Borrowed it about a hundred times now. Know it by heart."

"You like to read." It was a statement based on observation, not a question.

"Not much else to do 'round here. It's easier to escape into the written word than to think about a future I no longer have. Not all these guys have that luxury. They don't read well and can't discipline themselves enough to learn."

"But not you."

"No. Not me. Maw Maw taught me to read when I was a boy. We didn't have a lot of money growing up, and she told us, you didn't need money to get lost in a book. The library—"

"Was a gateway to adventures beyond your wildest imagination."

Bishop tipped his head, his forehead creasing with wonder.

"My mother told me the same thing," I said. "It was like a second home to me growing up. Introduced me to a means of escape. A place I could go when the real world got to be too much."

"What do you gotta escape from, boss?"

I bit the inside of my cheek and glanced down the row at the other cells. There was no way I was about to share how I'd grown up confused and scared of my own sexuality, unsure how or if I could fit in with the other boys my age when we were so different.

All was quiet in the row. It was the middle of the night. Although I wasn't prepared to answer his question, I didn't want to walk away yet either. "Do you have favorites?" I asked, instead. "Books, not Poe. Favorite books?"

Bishop pushed himself up and slid to the side of his small bed, his legs resting on the floor. He retrieved the one he'd been reading and studied the cover. It had seen better days. "I like the older stuff, mostly. Not that we get many choices. Probably a thousand books in this here prison library. I've read them all a few times over. Not sure I have a favorite. It all depends on how I feel. Went through a Charles Dickens phase a few years back. They have four titles available. *A Tale of Two Cities, Great Expectations, Oliver Twist,* and *A Christmas Carol.* Read them all a half a dozen times each. Until I knew every word."

He paused, smoothed his thumb down the cover of the old tattered Poe collection before meeting my eyes.

"Sometimes I feel like a Mark Twain kinda adventure; other times, it's the darker stuff I crave, like this here Poe." He shook the book and set it down again before shrugging.

"I love Dickens, and I made my mom read *The Adventures of Huckleberry Finn* to me long before I was old enough to read it myself. Those are good choices."

A spark of interest lit up Bishop's face, and a faint upturn in his lip hinted at a smile. God, I wanted to see that smile—which was an enigma in itself I wasn't prepared to explore.

"What else do you like, boss?"

I leaned against the steel door, keeping myself visible while I considered. It was rare to find someone who would talk books with me. Most of my friends back home rolled their eyes at the idea that I'd rather read some nights than go out to a club.

"As a young teenager, I remember reading *The Catcher in the Rye* by Salinger. When my mom found out, she was pretty angry. She thought it wasn't suitable for a fourteen-year-old kid. I didn't care. It made me seek more books she might deem as inappropriate. God, I've read so much, it's hard to remember them all."

"The old stuff. Tell me 'bout that."

I racked my brain. "I don't know. I've read lots of Brontë, *The Count of Monte Cristo* by Dumas was good, *Gulliver's Travels* by Swift, *Robinson Crusoe*—"

"Defoe. I read that one. They have it here."

"Have you read George Orwell?"

Bishop shook his head.

"Really? *1984?* Have you heard of it?"

"Can't say I have."

"A shame. That's my current favorite. I get in these fits where I read the same book over and over for comfort. Especially when I'm stressed out. It's been that book for about a year now. So good. Makes you think."

"Like me and Dickens."

"Yeah. I guess so."

"Why've you been stressed out?"

The personal question asked so nonchalantly knocked sense into me. What was I doing getting personal with an inmate? I straightened, and rubbed the back of my neck, checking again down the hall with a sudden burst of nerves, like my lackadaisical conversation with Bishop was being observed. There was nothing wrong with chatting up an inmate, but it was the feelings Bishop stirred in me that knocked me off-balance.

No one was there. Not that I expected to see anyone. Jin was down below, doing his thing, and all my guys were long ago in dreamland.

I checked the time instead of answering. It wasn't time for a count, and nothing else needed doing.

"You don't gotta answer that, boss. Not my business. I shouldn't have asked. Been a long time since I talked to someone who treated me with respect. Not that I deserve respect, I guess. Bein' here and all."

The urge to flee evaporated, and a rock of irritation settled in my gut. I disagreed. Recalling how Ezra had treated Bishop, I wondered how many times in fifteen years he'd experienced similar treatment. How many times had he been the bigger man and clenched his jaw against a retort?

Yes, these men were criminals of the highest order, but they'd all been tried and punished for their crimes. Because they were living out their last days behind thick steel doors didn't mean they no longer deserved respect. Even their deaths would be treated with respect when their time came.

Since I was halfway down the road to insanity already when it came to Bishop, I stayed my feet and resumed my comfortable lean against the outside of Bishop's door.

"So where are you from? Originally."

Bishop peered from his seat on the edge of his bed, as surprised by my question as I was of my decision to stay and ask it. He stood and approached the other side of the steel barrier, leaning in much the same way.

"North of Austin. Williamson County. A little place called Georgetown. You heard of it?"

I shook my head. "I'm new to the state. Only been here for a month. I know Austin, not what's around it. That's a distance from here, isn't it?"

"'Bout three and a half hours give or take."

"Is that where your grandmother comes from to visit you?"

Bishop paused, pressing his lips together until they tinted white. He was as reluctant to share personal details as I was, it seemed.

"Yeah. My brother, Jalen, drives her every week."

"He doesn't come in and visit?"

"No." The clipped way he delivered the single word warned me not to ask further questions about him.

"Does she know you draw?"

Bishop's gaze drifted to the portrait over his bed. "Yes. That's why she brings me pictures. So I can remember and give this here room some life."

"What are the pictures of?"

"Back home. Places we used to go. The old neighborhood. Her garden. Sometimes the house. Whatever she finds important each week. She takes her camera with her everywhere, and the day before she comes to visit me, she gets them all printed off. They're a lot of the same thing lately. Her mind isn't what it was, and she forgets she already took pictures of the new community center or that she already showed me her dying rose bush three visits in a row. Doesn't matter. She's been doin' it since they locked me up. She says she does it for me, but I think it helps her cope, in a way."

"You recreate those pictures on the walls?"

"Yeah. Some of them. It's more abstract, so I can fit it all in, but that's the idea. It gives me a sense of home."

There was a wistful longing in his tone, and my heart clenched. His gaze wandered the multitudes of charcoal-drawn pictures, his thoughts far away. I let him have his moment and took that stolen time to observe him. His jaw was scruffy with thick black stubble, and I knew it would soon be time for these guys to go to the barber. No beards were currently allowed in 12-Building. Stupid, ever-changing rules.

When Bishop lifted his hands and rubbed the old scar slashed through his palm, I frowned. I knew his body well. I'd seen him naked numerous times, and guiltily, I'd memorized it. He was undeniably attractive, and that secret part of myself that couldn't ignore a magnificent male figure had noted every curve, angle, and mark across his skin.

He had two scars. Both faded to near non-existence. One on his arm, one on his palm. My own scars twitched in sympathy, making me want to rub them, and touch them, and remember what had caused them.

"What happened?" I asked, unable to break my focus from the faded slash.

Bishop stilled. His large body tensed, but he didn't answer my question.

Something niggled at the back of my mind as we both continued to stare at his marked palm. Like a beacon I couldn't quite see, an idea I couldn't quite process, I squinted and tugged that thread inside my head, trying to bring it forward. Whatever lingered on the outskirts of my memory was too foggy, too distorted to see.

The crackle of my radio launched my heart right into my throat.

"Looking for ID 26903. We're missing a count for B-Pod, section B, rows one and two. Please report."

I scrambled backward as I checked my watch. Where had the time gone? How could it be this late? I fumbled with my radio and clicked the button. "Roger. Give me a second. Almost done."

Bishop's eyes were on me, our gazes clashed. Held. Something passed between us, but I didn't have time to study or analyze it further. Nothing more was said. The interruption tore us out of our friendly little bubble, and I could have kicked myself for getting so lost in conversation and forgetting my duties.

I shot down the hall, checking each window as I passed. No one else had stirred in the time I'd been talking to Bishop. The row was quiet and asleep. Soon, breakfast would arrive, and the world inside 12-Building would come alive again.

I felt as though I'd been transported away over the last hour to a different plane of existence. There were no steel doors, no locks or chains, no crash gates, or razor-topped fences. It was just the two of us and a feeling deep in my chest I wasn't willing to face or admit.

I knew as I scrambled to get my count done, that no amount of purging would eliminate Bishop from my system. He'd rooted deeper over the past hour. The only place I could go from here was forward and hope I'd chosen the right path.

Chapter Eight

WHEN I GOT HOME that morning, I collapsed on the couch and buried my face in my hands, going over the entire conversation I'd had with Bishop again and again. Every detail stuck in my head, every reaction and inflection in his voice. The tiny hints of emotion that showed on his face, especially when he'd discussed his favorite books and spoken of his grandmother.

I had a hundred questions and as many excuses why I should never voice them. For the first time in my career, I'd bonded with an inmate, and I didn't know if I should be terrified or roll with it.

And then there were the unmentionable twisting vines of feelings growing through my chest. I did everything possible not to look at them directly because—

My phone buzzed on the coffee table.

Reaching for it blindly, I drew it above my face and opened the text. My blood ran cold when I saw it was from Travis, my ex. The guy I'd broken up with almost a year ago who couldn't get it through his head we were over.

Travis: You moved to Texas? WTH? Why am I just hearing about this? When did you leave? Why didn't you call?

It buzzed in my hands again before I could process the barrage of questions and know how to respond.

Travis: DEATH ROW?!? Did you learn nothing? Are you insane?

I chucked my phone aside and listened to it clatter to the ground when it slid off the other end of the table. Pinching the bridge of my nose, I worked on leveling out my breathing and shoving away old anxieties from that other life. My long-healed injury ached with the injection of Travis into my day. Apparently, a thousand miles wasn't far enough away.

I clutched my side, digging fingers into the flesh over the scar until it cramped, and the old zing of pain throbbed with my heartbeat. I wasn't a masochist, but a reminder from time to time of why I'd run was sometimes needed.

I rolled off the couch and went to my bedroom to change into running clothes. In the back of my head, I heard Travis's preachy warnings about safety and being openly gay while working in the system. His constant pleas that I find different work so he could sleep at night joined the mix.

I didn't want to hear it anymore. We'd gone round and round about it enough times, I was sick of it. I refused to live in a bubble because I was gay.

It took five miles of a steady jog to eliminate that voice from my head. Five miles of stomping pavement before I felt half human. By the time I got home, I was exhausted and soaked with sweat. Running midday during a Texas summer heatwave was a horrible idea.

In the kitchen, I guzzled water and mopped at my brow before escaping upstairs to shower. I stood under ice-cold water for a long time before tugging on a pair of boxers and collapsing in bed.

My dark blinds blocked most of the daylight, so I clicked on my bedside lamp and fumbled for the book I'd left on my nightstand, tugging it down onto my chest. Seeing the title, the battered dusk jacket, and worn pages, I was instantly reminded of Bishop and our conversation about literature.

"Probably a thousand books in this here prison library. I've read them all a few times over."

Fifteen years on death row, almost twenty behind bars. What else was there to do? A thousand books didn't go far. It sounded like a lot, but to someone like Bishop, it was crumbs. Barely enough to keep his brain active. Unreasonable irritation grew as I considered his confined life and those severe limitations.

He's a criminal. A murderer, my brain whispered.

But I no longer believed it.

An idea formed as I leafed through the beat-up copy of my current favorite book. Before I could second-guess or change my mind, I set the alarm on my phone so I wouldn't sleep too late. Then I turned off the light and kicked my blankets to the end of the bed. It was too hot for covers.

MY SMALL TOWN WAS lacking in used bookstores. I'd searched online and come up with a few in the general area, but they required me traveling to other towns nearby. It was a small store called Tales Once Told where I wound up.

A dying overhead fan groaned and struggled to spin, doing nothing to dispel the stale air in the crowded single-room store. The shelves reached the ceiling, and the scent of musty books lingered thick all around me.

I squeezed through the aisles, stepping over stacks of books that looked like they'd been lying dormant on the floor since the dawn of time, entombed in cobwebs and a thick layer of dust. An old woman with silver hair and spectacles tended the ancient cash register upfront. The sign on the door warned customers that it was a Cash Only establishment.

There was no order, no rhyme or reason to the rows of books. Non-fiction was mixed with fiction, sci-fi was beside self-help, recipe books shared shelf space with do-it-yourself home improvements. It went on and on. For a person who had a distinct manner of organizing his shelves, it was enough to make my skin crawl.

Luckily, I'd given myself enough time to wander and shop.

An hour later, I left with a plastic sack of books hanging over my arm and a smile on my face. There was nothing more stress-relieving than being surrounded by books. I could never walk away empty-handed.

Back at home, I lined my new purchases up on the coffee table. There were three for me and five for Bishop. I refused to consider the appropriateness of what I planned to do. In my search, I'd scored him a copy of *1984* by George Orwell, *The Old Curiosity Shop* and *David Copperfield* by Charles Dickens, *Of Mice and Men* by John Steinbeck, and *For Whom the Bell Tolls* by Ernest Hemingway. The last two I couldn't be sure if he'd read or not, but I took a chance since they were classics.

I wrote a simple note on a small piece of paper and stuck it inside the cover of *1984*. It read, *When you're done with this one, we have to talk about it.* I left my name off and wrapped all five books in brown paper. On the front, I wrote the prison's address—as per the instructions I found online—and included Bishop's ID number and area in 12-Building so it went to the right inmate. I didn't bother with a return address because I didn't want it traced back to me. I knew the package would be opened and subjected to a full inspection before it was delivered, so the anonymity suited me.

THERE WAS AN OMINOUS weight, a ripple of tension that surrounded me the minute I passed through the crash gates and entered B-Pod. Not the usual sensations I got from having entered 12-Building, but something different. There was a change in the air, and I didn't know what had caused it. My general briefing a few minutes ago hadn't raised any flags, so I was cautious and hesitant when I found Ezra for our shift exchange.

Even he was more subdued than normal. Maybe Ray had given him a warning about his behavior the day before. He deserved to be let go, but I wasn't in charge, and I knew our staffing situation was the only thing saving his ass.

He caught my eye when I landed on the second level and wandered over, his ever-present sneer contorting his face.

"Same shit, different day, Miller. No noise to report with this lot except the District Judge signed off on buddy boy in nineteen. He's been moved to A."

I flinched and darted my eyes to the row of cells. Nineteen? A quick search in my memory told me that it was Jeff's cell.

"Wait, what happened?"

"Boy in nineteen. He's toast. End of the line. Moved him to deathwatch this afternoon."

"Jeffery's Warrant of Execution was signed? Is that what you're saying?"

"Do you not speak English?"

I clenched my fists and took an extra breath so I wouldn't react to Ezra's indignant attitude. "Jeffery got moved to deathwatch? Clarify that for me."

"Yes." Ezra spoke slow, enunciating every word like I was hearing impaired or stupid. "Lippy guy from nineteen is finally gonna be shut up for good."

"You're an asshole, you know that?"

"Fuck you. These guys aren't worth the shit on the bottom of my shoe. They made their choices. If you ask me, they should fry them up the minute the judge calls them guilty."

"Go home, Ezra."

"Gladly."

He shoved past me, knocking my shoulder, and clomped down the steel staircase at the end of the hall. I closed my eyes and filled my lungs, once, twice, and a third time before I opened them again, focusing on my job.

Jeffery's date was set. Jeffery had been moved to A-Pod, to deathwatch. His days were numbered.

With my head clouded and buzzing with that new information, I made my way down the length of the row and mindlessly took count. At Bishop's window, I was met with dark eyes as they peered up from behind his book. Faltering in my step, I lingered an extra minute before tipping my head in acknowledgment and walking away.

Jin met me at the bottom of the stairs, somber and without a smile today.

"You heard?"

"Yup. It always leaves a weird vibe in the air when shit like that happens," Jin explained. "Sometimes these guys live on death row so long, we forget there's a next step."

"You ever worked deathwatch?"

"A few times. Ray normally asks for volunteers, but I'm not sure we have enough staff for that luxury nowadays. Fifteen warrants were delivered today. All guys from other pods except for Jeff. Don't be surprised if you're booked to work down there next week."

"Thanks for the heads up. I haven't seen the schedule yet."

"Ray said it'd be up before he left. Check on your lunch break."

"I will."

We went our separate ways, and I wandered with little enthusiasm to the top level. It wasn't sympathy for Jeffery that sat heavy on my chest, it was more the fragility of life and how it was shoved in our faces sometimes out of the blue. A reminder that we *all* had an expiration date. No one was promised tomorrow. Most of these guys would die by the hand of the law because of the choices they'd made in their past, but I could easily be hit by a truck on my way home and perish before every one of them. The ambiguity of death applied to us all.

I shivered and ejected those morbid thoughts from my head.

There was a quiet buzz of noise drifting from each cell. Radios, shuffling, men talking to themselves—which was so common in solitary, it didn't register as bizarre anymore. Among the steady hum, I easily picked out Bishop's voice. He was reading aloud again. I slowed my pace as I went past his door and listened.

It wasn't lyrical poetry today but a passage from a familiar book I couldn't put my finger on. I smiled, enjoying the rise and fall of his tone as he injected emotion into his reading.

Lights-out came and went. I performed another hourly count and fought the urge to linger near Bishop's cell to listen to him read. More than once, I told myself that what had happened the day before could have gotten me in serious trouble. It couldn't happen again.

By one in the morning, the majority of my row was asleep, and my self-made rule evaporated.

I lingered out of sight.

It was like an invisible thread bound us together. When the midnight hour encased us, the mood in the air changed, and I no longer remembered why I was so adamant about keeping a distance. A bone-deep craving overtook my body, and I wanted to know more about him.

It was *The Odyssey* by Homer. That's what he was reading. It took a solid five minutes of leaning against the wall beside his cell for me to place the story. I'd read it a few times years ago, so it was familiar, and it wasn't. The emotions he infused into each sentence gave me the urge to read it again.

"You don't need to hide from me, boss. I know you're there."

I rolled, using my shoulder to leverage me off the wall until I stood in front of his window and smiled into his cell. "I was enjoying the live audio version of that book. Been a lot of years. You read well out loud. I never could. Used to sink as low as possible in my desk at school so the teacher wouldn't pick me."

Bishop closed the book and met me at the door, keeping his voice low. "It ain't so bad. Sometimes the solitude gets to me. Reading out loud makes me feel less alone."

"I get it. Not saying I know what that feels like, but I can see how it would help." There was a gravity-like pull to his attention tonight. It drew me in, lured me under his spell, and for a beat, we shared a peaceful, silent hello of locked gazes and tentative smiles. "Did you get any sleep today? I kept you up all night last night."

He shrugged and studied the frame around the window, dragging his finger over the cocked edge against the steel frame. "I got nowhere else to be apart from a fifteen-minute shower and two hours in a rec cell. The rest of the day, I stare at these four walls. I sleep when I'm tired, read when I'm not, draw when I need something different to do."

"Did you get new books today?"

"Nah, they only let us exchange them once a week. I have four out right now."

I nodded and licked my lips, grasping for something to say, something to talk about. Whereas I hadn't wanted to approach his cell a short while ago, now I didn't want to leave.

"How was your day today, boss?"

Relieved he'd jumped in and given me an excuse to stay a few more minutes, I scratched the back of my neck while I considered. "Well, my nights and days are all mixed up. I went home and ran about five miles to make myself tired. I don't recommend exercise under a Texas heatwave, that's for sure. I crashed for a few hours, did some errands, made some food, and came to work. I live a boring life. Not much to tell." The minute the words fell from my lips, I wished I could pull them back. Who was I to act like I had a boring or mundane life?

"Sure do miss the sun shining on my face." My guilt expanded and grew. "That there window gives me a glimpse sometimes, but it's not the same."

The two-inch slit in the wall gave him nothing.

Nor did the outdoor rec cages. Just because they were technically *outside* the building didn't mean these prisoners had any exposure to grass and sunlight. They were steel cages with solid roofs stuck on a concrete slab built into a section of 12-Building. The prison surrounded them on all sides, providing nothing but shade and long shadows. Even there, the sun was out of reach.

"I'm sorry. That statement was insensitive."

"Don't you dare. I asked. I can't live that life no more, but it doesn't mean I can't find joy from what other people experience. That's why Maw Maw brings me those pictures."

I didn't respond. I didn't know how.

"Tell me about your dinner. What's on the menu tonight?" He licked his lips at the mere thought of good food. Without thinking, I watched his tongue's journey, admiring the glistening trail it left behind. My insides stirred.

Bishop turned his head to look at me, and I jerked my gaze away before I was caught with a telling look on my face.

"Chicken. Um… Barbecued chicken, rice, and steamed broccoli." I bit my lip before I added "Nothing special" to the end of that statement.

A wistful smile crossed Bishop's face, and I held my breath at the sight.

"I remember my granddaddy used to barbecue a lot in the summertime. The smells were like nothing else. The sizzling meat as it dripped juices on the flames. He taught me how to make a steak just right."

"Medium-rare?"

"Nope, medium-well."

I shook my head, and we shared a laugh. "I like it with the right amount of pink in the middle."

"Jalen, my brother, he does too. Or did. I guess I don't know anymore. I used to tease him and tell him he was part vampire because he liked his meat running with blood still. He'd run crying to Maw Maw and get me in trouble."

"Are you close in age?"

Bishop paused, and when I didn't think he was going to talk more about his brother, he shrugged. "He's six years younger than me. Enough to be a brat when we were kids."

"Did you get along?"

A cloud crossed through Bishop's dark eyes, and his chin dipped with his frown. "That kid worshipped the ground I walked on, but I never gave him the time of day." Bishop rattled his head and let out an exhausted breath. "Damn, I can still remember the way stuff tasted when it came off the grill. Ain't nothing like it. It might be the one food I miss the most. That and Pizza Hut's deep-dish pepperoni and mushroom pizza. Maw Maw used to order it on the last day of every month when she got her pension check. The one day of the month Jalen and I made sure to get along."

"Did she threaten to not order pizza if you fought?"

"Darn right she did, and it happened more than once before we learned how serious she was."

It was an odd conversation, and I didn't know how to proceed. It wasn't like there was a future where I could promise Bishop he would taste those things again. Saying sorry about his situation seemed trite. The chance of Bishop experiencing barbecued meat or Pizza Hut pizza again was slim to nil.

Even if his journey ended at the death house in Huntsville, last meals weren't like they showed in the movies. Prisoners couldn't order anything under the sun and have it served on a silver platter before they took their last walk to the death chamber. Last meals were regulated and restricted to tight budgets and a chef's limited menu plan.

Somberness leaked in and clotted the air between us. Bishop cleared his throat and motioned to my wristwatch. "Best not forget about your count, boss. Don't want to see you getting in any kind of trouble because of me."

"Right." I checked the time and had five minutes before I had to report in. Not knowing how to say goodbye or if it was necessary, I gave Bishop a half-hearted wave and broken smile and wandered away to the end of the row.

I didn't return afterward. Battling with the right and wrong of our conversations, I wandered for the following few hours, thinking. Sometime later, I found myself outside Jeffery's empty cell while an uneasy tremble rocked my core. This would be Bishop's fate one day. He'd occupied a cell on death row for fifteen years. How long until his number was up? How long until I came to work my shift only to discover *he'd* been moved to deathwatch?

From two cells down came a deep, steady voice that slipped up my spine and wrapped all around me like a warm hug on a cold day. "You pull yourself together out there, boss. Ain't a single person here who doesn't deserve the fate they've been given. You best not be feeling sorry for any of us."

"Even you? Do you deserve the fate you've been given?"

My stomach clenched, and I held myself rigid, desperately wanting to hear him say no.

"You read them articles about me. You know why they put me here. What do you think?"

I marched over to his window, angry at his deflection. He was on the other side looking out, towering several inches above me, so I lifted my chin to meet his eyes. "That's not what I asked. Yes, I read those articles. Yes, I know why they locked you up, but were they wrong? Did you do those things? Did you murder a helpless woman and her defenseless child in cold blood? Did you?"

So many emotions stormed in the dark pits of his eyes. Rage, hurt, shame, guilt, but above all, sadness. A deep well of sadness I couldn't even begin to process. Why, dammit?

We stood, challenging each other through a thick steel door, neither of us backing down.

"Tell me," I whispered. "Did you kill them?"

Bishop deflated a fraction; his gaze flicked away and back. Sorrow made his face sag. "It don't matter if I did or if I didn't. Fifteen years ago, a jury of my peers found me guilty. That's the bottom line. I've appealed it to death and to no avail. Last month, they denied hearing my newest petition. It's only a matter of time before I follow Jeff. Once they decide to stop hearing your appeals, it's the end of the line. Do you understand? My fate has been decided. My path in life is set. The end is closer every day. The truth doesn't matter anymore. I'll make my peace with the big man upstairs when my day comes." His head bowed, and his shoulders drooped. "If you'll excuse me, boss. I don't wanna talk no more."

He turned his back and wandered toward his bed, defeat making his feet drag.

"Bishop?"

He paused but didn't turn around.

"It matters to me. Maybe your path in life is fixed. Maybe there is nothing that can be done to change it, but it doesn't mean your truth isn't valid."

Time hung suspended for a minute. I wanted to unlock his door and force him to turn around and look at me. I wanted to hold his face and beg him to spill his wounded soul at my feet, but I couldn't do any of that. If Bishop wanted to take his truth to the grave, he would, and I couldn't stop him.

I was about to walk away when his voice floated to my ears, soft enough I had to strain to hear it.

"I didn't kill them. I was too late. I was always too late. Ayanna was..." He choked on the next word, shook his head, then lifted his scarred palm, massaging it absently. "I loved her, but it wasn't... If only I could have..."

He turned, his cheeks pale and eyes haunted. He wasn't seeing me but a horrific scene from his past. "I couldn't be who she needed. I wanted to be. I tried. I couldn't love her like she did me. She went off and... I tried to protect her. Both of them." He shook his head, and his gaze jumped about the small cell. "I didn't kill them, but I deserve this punishment because I should have spoken up. I should have done more. I knew they were in trouble. I just..." He trailed off again.

An internal tremble made his big body shake and his teeth chatter. He tried to hold his frame strong against it but failed.

My heart constricted, and I couldn't process the wave of emotions rolling over me, but I wanted to reach out and touch him, comfort him, take him into my arms and tell him everything would be okay.

Was I crazy? Possibly.

Probably.

If Bishop knew he evoked these feelings in me, he might never talk to me again.

I lifted my hand to the window and pressed my palm to the reinforced glass. It was a small gesture of unity. Me offering to be there and stand with him.

"I believe you," I whispered.

Bishop studied me for a long time, dissecting my honesty perhaps—or challenging it.

Without another word, he turned back to his bed and lay facing the wall.

Chapter Nine

THE FOLLOWING WEEK'S schedule wasn't up until the next morning when my shift ended. I'd debriefed my relieving officer about my night and escaped to the staffroom as Ray was walking out.

"New schedule is posted, if you were looking for it."

"Thanks."

His boots screeched on the floor as he ground to a halt and spun, catching my attention. "Oh, I'll be taking a couple of weeks' vacation before the summer is out. I'm gonna do up about a month's worth of scheduling ahead of time since the warden will be keeping an eye on y'all. I wanted to give you a heads up since I won't be around after next Wednesday."

"All right. Sounds good. Have fun, wherever you're going."

"Will do. Taking the wife and kid into the mountains to do some camping. Can't wait to get away from here for a bit."

"You deserve it. Try not to think of us while you're gone."

"Oh, I won't."

We shared a chuckle, and Ray continued on while I headed inside the staffroom.

A few of the nightshift guys were at their lockers, shuffling around with slow, methodical movements. A recognizable end-of-shift lag we all got after so many hours on the floor. I grabbed my backpack from my locker and slung it over my shoulder before slamming the door again with a clang and attaching the lock. Before racing out the door and heading home, I pulled up the next rotation on the nearest computer and scanned for my name. A-Pod. Jin was right,

I'd been stuck on deathwatch the following week. That promised to be an experience.

I closed the program and aimed for the door, considering how I felt about that. Knowing deathwatch was one step before death's door made the idea of working on that pod a little more daunting. I'd see Jeff again—for the last time. Would he call me white boy? Would he tease, as was his nature? Or would he have lost that edge that made him poke fun at his guards? I had the sneaking suspicion he would be a different man by next week. Someone I didn't recognize.

The sun was already up and baking the town by the time I got home. Sweat gathered under my uniform, and I immediately aimed for the fridge and a cold beer. It was too hot to run this morning despite my knotted head and straying thoughts.

I collapsed on the couch and kicked my feet up as I replayed Bishop's words over and over again in my head.

"I didn't kill them. I was too late. I was always too late."

What did that mean? Was he there when whoever it was murdered his ex-girlfriend and her child? Did he arrive for the aftermath? But he was found covered in blood with the weapon in hand. How? Why?

I brought my laptop onto my lap and pulled up the dozens and dozens of articles I'd read before. I scrutinized them, twisting and turning the stories around to see other angles, to find Bishop's innocence and understand how he could have been mistaken as the killer. None of it made sense. His guilt seemed so evident, but the reporters and their opinion pieces made sure to paint him in a negative light. Where was the truth in all the gory mess?

I knew he was innocent. I believed him, no matter how foolish it made me sound, but what had happened that day to put him at the heart of such a vicious murder scene? What was it about the crime that had left the jury doubtless? And why had he spent fifteen years on death row if he was innocent?

I'd told myself, hearing his confession would be enough. I would know the truth, and I could move on. Knowing would silent the nagging wonder that kept pulling me back to the giant, soft-spoken man.

The truth did not set me free in this case.

I wanted—*no, needed*—the whole story. What was Bishop's truth? Why was an innocent man going to die? Why wasn't his lawyer winning his appeals?

Anger bubbled in the pit of my stomach when I considered the horrific possibility that Bishop had been locked away for half his life for no reason. He was going to die, like Jeff, and soon if the appellate courts had stopped listening.

A wave of nausea overcame me, so I drained my beer and found another. This whole reality made me sick. It was a known fact that a small percentage of convicted criminals were innocent. Plenty of men had died at the hands of our penal system before they could be exonerated for their crimes.

Was Bishop within that statistic? Would he die like those guiltless men before him?

I shoved my laptop aside and sank lower on the couch, clutching my beer as I rolled all these thoughts around my head. Why did I feel so strongly about this one man and his story? Why couldn't I let it go and do my job?

I scrubbed a hand over my face and groaned, still unable to face the truth I'd buried deep inside. A truth that made my heart beat a little faster when in Bishop's presence. A truth that flowed heavy in my veins when he spoke in that deep baritone or gifted me with a hint of a smile.

I was screwed.

THAT EVENING, I ARRIVED at work and did my job robotically. Performed counts as required, called in reports, checked with Jin, and ensured lights-out happened on time. I avoided lingering at Bishop's cell until I knew the rest of the men nearby were sleeping. I had so many questions but wanted to ensure some element of privacy when I asked them.

There was a restlessness in the air that evening. Men stayed up later, fidgeted and moved around their cells as though trying to dispel an excess amount of energy they'd accumulated throughout the day. Ricky in B17 had some sort of random, manic episode at half-past eleven where he yelled and spat curses at the concrete wall of his cell. He punched the steel door a few times, and I warned him to calm down. By midnight, he settled, sputtering under his breath but winding down.

Juan, in B15, hung by the window of his cell and watched me pace, a deadened look in his eyes that was unsettling. Every time I got closer to his end of the hall, he tinkled his fingers on the window to grab my attention, then muttered something in Spanish that was both monotone and threatening.

It made me wonder if it was a full moon with the way everyone was acting.

Things quieted closer to one. Juan had given up trying to get a rise out of me and had moved to his bed. Ricky had fallen asleep after exhausting himself with his rant, while Desmond remained hunched over a notebook, scribbling nonsense stories Javier had told me were impossible to read.

Not everyone was asleep, but I couldn't hold back any longer. The mountain of questions I had for Bishop had been eating at me since our talk the day before. My hourly count was approaching. After, I'd see if the man was willing to open up about his past.

Starting at the far end of the row, I peeked in every cell, rapping on the windows of those who slept so deeply it was impossible to make out movement. They were used to the constant interruption and waved in their sleep when I knocked.

Bishop was awake, lying in bed with a book. He caught my eye when I glanced in his cell but ducked his chin again almost right away.

Heading to the staircase, I met up with Jin, and we chatted for fifteen minutes about random nonsense. Nights had a tendency to be boring, and we both enjoyed the small reprieve every hour.

"I've worked deathwatch a few times. It's heavy. Leaves your head in a bit of a blunder when you go home at night. Try not to let it get to you."

"Leave work at work."

"Exactly. Don't forget, these guys deserve what they've been given. They're killers, all of them. Seeing them day in and day out and listening to them talk and share stories can make us more sympathetic, but it's an illusion. Out there in the real world, they are animals. Ruthless. They deserve to be put down."

There were a lot of opinions about the death penalty floating around. It was clear Jin was pro, and I respected his views. I didn't know where I sat with the whole thing and hated getting tangled in a debate with anyone about right and wrong, so I kept my mouth shut.

When I left Jin to his rows and landed back on the second level, a faint—yet familiar—noise drifted through the air. Heavy breathing. Stifled grunts. The distinct sound of a hand moving rapidly over swollen flesh. It wasn't the first time I'd listened to men jerking off in their cells.

There was no privacy in prison. Urges arose, and these men took care of them. Dignity had long ago gone out the window.

But it was where those noises originated that had my steps faltering. I knew the sounds were coming from B21.

All the saliva in my mouth dried, and my heart canted hard enough, blood whooshed and pulsed in my ears. I squeezed my eyes closed and reached for the wall for balance as I tried to bury the rush of desire that swamped my system when I recognized the muffled voice. I didn't know what was wrong with me.

Was it simply a physical attraction? Bishop was a good-looking man, and I'd have to be dead or blind not to notice. It'd been a long time since Travis, and there'd been only one guy after who'd lasted all of two weeks. It wasn't like I sought hookups or was present and active in the dating scene, especially since the incident at I-Max.

Of all places, work—*the prison*—was not where I wanted my sexual frustrations to surface.

I pinched the bridge of my nose and told myself to walk back down the stairs, find Jin, and chat for a bit longer. Ignore the panting breaths emanating from within Bishop's cell.

My body refused to listen. Inching forward, my feet moved of their own free will until I stood across from his door. Far enough away to avoid being seen, yet close enough I could steal a glimpse in his window.

Movement.

On the bed.

Swallowing a lump of budding desire, I edged closer, sneaking like a child to the cookie jar in the middle of the night. Desperate for the prize. Yearning for that one sinful glimpse I could sear into my memory.

Blankets moved with his fist as he jerked himself out of sight. He had one knee drawn up, but it had fallen lazily to the side, giving him a vulnerable posture my imagination ran with. The long dark stretch of his throat was exposed, Adam's apple aimed at the ceiling. I watched as Bishop's lips parted, and more muted moans rolled to my ears.

His hand sped up.

Sweat gathered along my spine. I stepped closer, my breathing equally erratic, my insides shivering.

I fisted the fabric of my pants, suppressing the urge to touch myself, feeling the swell of arousal in my boxers.

Then it happened. Bishop's back arched off the bed, and his hand stilled under the covers, large body trembling. A silent cry of pleasure filled the air. He emitted not a single noise, but I heard it all. In my mind, he screamed my name as his release poured hot between our bodies. His deep baritone penetrated my soul and seeped through my veins. I squeezed my eyes closed when my own cock throbbed sympathetically.

I was so fucked. So, so, so fucked.

Racing to pull my shit together, knowing I needed to escape, I tore my eyes open and stopped dead when dark pools of onyx stared back at me. My heart seized. The truth was written all over my face—how could it not be? My cheeks flushed with my guilt, and I stumbled backward a step, unsure of what to do. I'd been caught. God only knew what Bishop would surmise of the situation.

It felt like I-Max all over again, and my old scar itched and throbbed. If Bishop discovered I was gay, if he thought for one second I'd watched him jerk off and enjoyed it, I was a dead man. It didn't matter how much security surrounded these prisoners, they'd find a way. A broken nose, black eyes, and pierced kidneys would be the least of my problems.

With my thoughts and emotions in a blender, I scrambled away, unsure what had gotten into me.

Maybe it was fear or guilt, but I could have sworn Bishop's penetrating gaze followed me.

In retrospect, I should have come up with a smart-ass remark or comment, acted like it wasn't a big deal, or pretended to be disgusted.

It would have absolved me of looking guilty or turned on. But I'd panicked and ruined the opportunity.

As it stood, I was twenty minutes from doing another count, and I knew I needed to make a presence at Bishop's cell again. I prayed his orgasm put him to sleep.

A short time later, when I couldn't avoid it any longer because I had to perform my duties, I approached Bishop's cell, palms slick, and mouth desert dry. I peeked in his window and found his bed empty. Frowning, I scanned the room and nearly jumped out of my skin when he appeared like an apparition from the wall beside the door where he'd been standing out of sight.

I stumbled back, but his husky voice rooted my feet to the ground.

"Stop."

Our eyes locked, and I couldn't read his stoic features. Was he angry? Murderous? Forgiving? *Please be forgiving. Please don't deduce the truth from this small mistake.*

My side ached, and I gritted my teeth to refrain from clutching it and massaging my old wound.

"Come here."

A chill shivered through me, and I stepped back, increasing our distance. It was stupid. He was locked up. There was a steel barrier between us. *Walk away*, I told myself. *Report your count and get through your shift.*

"Need to report in," I mumbled like he was deserving of an explanation. Like it explained my thundering heart.

Before I could pivot and run, he spoke again. "I got something to say to you, and you sure as hell don't want me raising my voice for others to hear. It won't take long, then you can run off and make your report. Cower from me, if that's what you want."

I swallowed a tight lump and firmed my shoulders as I walked forward, hoping the air surrounding me didn't stink of fear. All these years working in the system and I'd never been afraid of the men behind bars. My bad luck at I-Max had done a number on me—more than I was willing to admit. Wouldn't Travis rub this in my face?

At Bishop's window, I stilled and waited, swimming in two pools of multifaceted black diamonds as they studied every inch of my face.

If I wasn't so off-balance, I'd have clung to their beauty. Instead, I struggled not to look away.

Bishop lowered his voice to a shade above a whisper, enough for it to carry through the steel door, and he leaned his forehead against the slim window. He peered down at me like a giant panther waiting to pounce. His sheer size and presence held me motionless.

"It ain't no one's business what you like and what you don't. You understand? They ain't never gonna hear it from me. I promise you that. If you think for one minute I didn't know you were standing there the whole time, you're wrong, boss." He paused, holding me in a vice with just his words. "I feel you in my bones whenever you're near me. I knew. I always know."

I moved my lips, trying to force words to the surface, but nothing came. With my indecision, Bishop raised a hand and pressed it to the glass. Instinctively, I did the same. Palm to palm, save a three-inch slab of safety glass.

"I'm sorry." It was the only thing I could think to say.

The corner of his lip twitched. "I'm not."

He curled his fingers against the glass. The same motion he'd made that day with his grandmother, like he was trying to grasp hold of my hand.

"You know, no one except Maw Maw has ever believed me before. Not even Jalen. No one. When you're a punk-ass black kid with no parents and a record for getting in trouble, they assume you're guilty before you even try to defend yourself. I never stood a chance. But you—"

"I believe you didn't do it."

His eyes warmed and lingered. We shared an intense moment, drawn together, our tether pulling us closer.

What the fuck was happening? A whirlwind of words and thoughts and feelings pummeled me. I heard statements he'd made the previous evening in a new light. *"I couldn't love her like she did me."* What did it mean? Was I contorting his words and hearing what I wanted to hear, or was Bishop trying to tell me something? He'd known I was standing there while he jerked off. He'd let me watch and—

"Anson."

My name on his lips in that deep baritone with the faint hint of a Texas drawl shooed the storm away. My head fell silent, and I watched him. Waited.

"I told you," he whispered, fingers curling over mine again as he devoured me with his dark gaze. "You don't have to be afraid of me. I mean it."

Without thought, I pressed my forehead to his on the glass and closed my eyes. Together we breathed. The silence between us like a blanket, hiding us from reality and the world.

I could have stayed like that for the rest of the night, but Bishop—who had more sense than me—spoke. "You best report that count before they come looking for it."

"Yeah." I pushed back from the door and straightened, peering down the row in both directions.

When I met Bishop's stare again, something had changed between us. It was subtle, but it was there. The corner of his mouth edged up into a smile, and he winked before returning to his bed.

Yup, I was fucked.

Somehow, I'd been dragged under by a beautiful, dark angel on death row.

WE DIDN'T GET TO TALK any more that week. The following night was chaos. A guy on Jin's row tried to off himself with a makeshift clothesline when no one was looking. We had to call in the CERT team for an in-cell intervention. It was violent and ugly. Once inside, we determined the guy was out of his head on drugs. Pepper spray was required, and we went into an instant section A/B shakedown because of it. Every cell was searched. Every guy was required to piss in a jar. *Again*. It was a whole night affair, and Ray came in a shade past midnight to offer a hand since Jin and I couldn't handle it on our own and it wasn't part of CERT's duties.

Because the ordeal lasted well into the morning, I ended up working a double, and my final night shift was canceled.

I had a few days off before my stint on deathwatch, which meant no more time with Bishop in the foreseeable future and no means of getting answers to my endless questions any time soon.

With all I'd seen and learned in the past few days, I was antsy and confused. I second-guessed everything he'd said and questioned if I wasn't transferring my feelings and twisting his words to what I wanted to hear.

Was he gay? Sympathetic to the gay community? A supporter? Was he straight? Bi?

Did it matter?

He was untouchable, regardless.

No amount of yearning or wishful thinking would change that. Allowing even the slightest fantasy freedom would only hurt me in the end.

Monday morning, I pulled into the parking lot at the same time as Javier. He waited outside his Dodge Ram, smiling from behind his shades as I collected my backpack from the back seat of my Jeep.

"Anson, my man. How did that string of nights treat ya?"

"Piece of cake. Never mind me, you're the one who was on F. Thanks again, by the way."

"I should thank you. I was the one who needed the switch."

"True, but we both know I got the better end of that deal."

We wandered to the guardhouse and entrance and flashed our IDs over the reader, waving at Tully as we passed through the whining gate.

"I hear Jeffie got his papers." Javier shook his head. "We all knew it was coming. Even he did."

"I'll be seeing him today. Not sure what you say to a man facing his death in a few weeks."

Javier's brows winged up. "Ray put you on watch?"

"Yup."

"Did he ask first?"

"Nope. Got scheduled in."

Javier whistled. "We must be working tight. He always takes volunteers first. That shit's hard. The only thing harder is when they use you for the transport to the death house in Huntsville."

"Let's hope I don't get roped into that. Got any advice?"

"Sure. Number one, listen. Now's when it all hits them. Those guys will want to purge their souls. You don't need to give opinions or agree with anything that comes from their mouths. Be an ear. Let 'em talk."

Javier held the door for me once we got to the main entrance. We swiped our cards to get through to the restricted access doors and headed to the employee area and staffroom.

"Be prepared for some gruesome tales, my friend. Now's the time when most of these guys will come clean about their past. I can count on one hand how many men have had appeals go through after their death warrants were signed."

"How many?"

He made a zero with his thumb and pointer finger. "Nil. It's happened before, but not in the ten years I've been here."

"It sounds like a shitty place to be working this week."

"Not gonna lie, glad it's you and not me."

"Where'd they put you?"

"Escorting with Angelo."

I half wished Javier held a different opinion about deathwatch because I'd have suggested a switch in a heartbeat. It may not have offered a private opportunity to chat with Bishop, but I'd have at least seen him if I was doing escorts.

After our morning briefing, Javier and I parted ways with promises to meet up on the weekend for beers.

Deathwatch was double staffed. Twice as many eyes on the prisoners meant less chance they would do something stupid. Now was when suicide attempts were highest. These guys were facing the end, and they'd rather take their own lives than have the law do it for them. Unfortunately, that luxury was not allowed, and we had to be vigilant to ensure it didn't happen.

On deathwatch, a prisoner's life became even more restricted, much like being at a level three. They didn't get any extras, had the minimal amount of shower time offered per week, no commissary, no rec. It was four confined walls from now until the end. Counts happened every fifteen minutes rather than once an hour.

Because our transfer duties were limited and there were so many of us assigned to the floor, I understood what Javier meant when he said I'd be listening to confessions and stories. When the Polunsky reverend was busy with other inmates, some men sought us out, needing to talk. Others sat motionless in the corner of their cells, lost in their heads. I could only imagine where their thoughts strayed.

Jeffery was one of them.

I stopped at his window and examined the vulnerable form of the man curled in a tight ball, face buried in his drawn-up knees. As much as I didn't want to hear horror stories, I felt drawn to help these men transition from fear to acceptance when it came to their deaths.

"Hey, Jeffie. Wanna talk?"

For a moment, I didn't think he was going to respond, then he muttered something into his knees. As much as sound traveled and bounced off these concrete walls, I almost missed the words.

"What'd I tell you about calling me Jeffie, white boy."

I chuckled. "Yeah, yeah. I bet your mama called you Jeffie when you were a kid."

"No."

I could see it was going to be like pulling teeth to get him to unfold and open up, but I had nowhere else to be. "Was awfully quiet without you on B last week."

"Better get used to it."

His stubborn silence made me shuffle. "Come on, Jeff. I'm reaching out. I know I can't get you out of there, but I'm willing to listen, which is more than half these guys on this side of the cell are willing to do. Believe me."

More silence.

I sighed, and my shoulders fell. "All right. I'll be around this week. If you change your mind, give me a shout."

It was Thursday, four days into my stint on deathwatch before Jeff broke down. It needed to happen. The guys in the cells surrounding him had cracked and cried and screamed and yelled and begged and pleaded, but he'd done none of it.

Thursday afternoon, after I'd returned from a lunch break, he waited by his window, eyes nothing more than dark bruises, sclera bloodshot. My bet was he hadn't slept much since they'd moved him here.

"Miller?" His voice hitched but caught my attention as I passed by his cell.

I stalled and approached. "How you doing, Jeff?"

"Why do you treat us all so good? I don't get it. Don't you realize who we are? What we've done?"

"I know. I'm not stupid."

"So why?"

"It's not my job to judge you or punish you. I'm here to ensure the safety of people inside and outside the prison. That's all."

"Man, I shot five people at a bank. Point blank. In the head." He made his hand into the shape of a gun and aimed it at me out the window. Then he pulled the trigger and made the sound of a gun firing. No emotion crossed his face. "Just like that. Watched their brains splatter the walls behind them. And you know what?"

I firmed my muscles and maintained steady eye contact even as my stomach churned. "What?"

"I felt nothing." He shook his head and laughed a little. "Not a fucking thing."

"Why'd you do it?"

"I was pissed the fuck off. They'd denied my loan, and I was heading toward bankruptcy. No one gave a shit about me and the fact that I was getting buried in debt. I was always an outsider. My job sucked, and my boss was a fucking prick. I should have shot that motherfucker in the head too." Jeff smiled at the thought, a leering, sadistic smile made worse by the tired look in his eyes.

"Do you regret your actions?"

Jeff snapped out of the fantasy and regarded me with humored curiosity. "Would my repenting help you sleep at night, white boy?"

"I don't give a shit if you repent or not. It was a question. It's not me who's gotta lay on that stainless steel table a few weeks from now, knowing it's the end of the line. They're your sins, not mine. At the end of the day, I get to go home. I have my freedom."

He didn't expect me to stand up to him, and it earned me a sick sort of admiration I wasn't sure I wanted.

"You're all right, Miller. I'm not afraid to die. I know what I did was wrong, and the fact that I sit here night after night and don't feel any sense of remorse tells me I don't deserve to ever be set free. I'm the boogeyman. Society don't like guys like me."

"You have a lot of awareness."

"I've had a lot of time to think. I know who I am. I know *what* I am. This fucking world and their morals and rules is stupid. I ain't got time for that shit. They can all suck my dick."

"Have you had a chance to talk with the reverend?"

"Nah, I don't believe in God. Don't need him praying over me and muttering all that nonsense about saving my soul. Fuck that shit. I don't have a soul, and if I do, it's black as midnight. I wish they'd get this over with. All the waiting is a pain in my ass."

I wondered if his position on God would change. Long ago, my grandfather used to tell me stories about his time in the war. Then he'd tell me stories about his father before him and how he'd fought in World War I. He used to say, there were no atheists in a bomb-targeted trench. Every man who was about to die prayed. Every. Man. It seemed fitting that whenever someone's life hung in the balance, there was always that sliver of uncertainty. That question of *what if?* Maybe Jeff would change his mind when he lay on a cold, stainless steel table in a few weeks, but I suspected the only person who would ever know was him.

"Did they really notice I was gone on B?"

"Of course they did. Those men are no different than you, Jeff. It brought reality to the forefront. The entire mood changed that day. Not one man didn't feel it."

Jeff leaned his back against the door to his cell and peered wistfully about his small room.

"Wanna talk, Jeff?"

"Yeah. Wanna listen?"

"Of course."

So we chatted for hours. I had to interrupt a few times to perform my duties, but I returned to his cell and lent an ear as Jeff told me about his dysfunctional childhood, his broken family, his education, and his multiple failed attempts at making friends. He spoke a lot of isolation—one of his own making—and the eventual downfall that had landed him on death row.

As a teenager, he'd recognized in himself a sense of separation, a lack of emotional connection with the world and the people around him. An inability to empathize and a feeling of superiority. He'd been called cold-hearted by the kids at school. He couldn't hold a job or his tongue. But Jeff wasn't a stupid man and had pinpointed and diagnosed himself as having sociopathic tendencies long before he'd committed major crimes. "It was inevitable," he told me. "A curious part of me wanted to make other people suffer just for the pleasure and control. To bask in the power I had over such insignificant, inferior beings. People are so fucking stupid, it's a wonder how they survive. I wanted to watch them die, for kicks, you know? 'Cause I could. Watch them tremble with fear because they finally recognized I was above them and could end them without blinking an eye."

Javier was right. It was heavy and intense working deathwatch. More than once, I thought of Bishop and lost my stomach when I considered him occupying Jeff's cell someday, his hourglass running out.

At the end of my shift on the same day Jeffery spilled his life story at my feet, I drew up the new schedule Ray had posted before he'd taken off on vacation.

Not a single week over the following month was on Bishop's row, nor was there an escort in my rotation. It bothered me to my bones.

I clicked the plunger of a pen that I'd found lying on the table beside me as I studied the chart of shifts and thought. The draw to see Bishop was stronger than my good sense. There had to be a way. Javier had swapped shifts with me once, maybe others would be equally willing.

Nights were among people's least favorite shifts—after F-Pod—and those would be the most ideal if I wanted to talk and learn more about him. My rotation wasn't anywhere extreme. If I could exchange my weeks with the men working nights on Bishop's row, it'd give me time to learn his story.

I did a quick scan of the staffroom and saw Doug, one of the guys scheduled to work midnights on Bishop's row the week after next.

"Hey, Doug, my man. Got a minute?"

He'd come from the bathroom wearing workout clothes, headphones dangling around his neck. I assumed he was heading for the gym.

"Yeah. What's up?"

"Any chance you wanna switch weeks with me here?" I pointed at the screen, drawing a finger over his week of nights.

"You want my nights? Are you serious?"

"Yeah. If you don't mind a stint in C and D."

"Hell no. I hate nights. Write it up. I'll take that deal."

"Thank you. I appreciate it."

"No problem."

Before he could get away, I pointed at Mason's name. "Any chance you have Mason's number so I can get a hold of him?"

Doug slapped his hands over the pockets on his sports pants and found his phone. "Yeah, here." He fumbled with the display and turned it toward me so I could write it down.

If I could work out the next couple of weeks, I'd worry about the others when the time came. "Thanks, man."

Chapter Ten

"WHEN ARE YOU COMING HOME TO VISIT?"

"Mom, it's summer, and I haven't been here that long. I'm not entitled to any sort of vacation for a long time, and I'm the last person getting approved for time off when everyone wants to get away for a week this time of year."

Killing the engine on the Jeep, I scanned the vast parking lot outside of Polunsky. Even though the sun had gone down, it was stifling.

Mom sighed. "I know. I miss you."

"I miss you too."

We'd missed our Saturday Skype session since I'd spent the day at Javier's house, helping build his girlfriend a rock garden. Melanie was sweet—and persistent, asking me if I'd consider a double date with this male nurse she worked with.

I'd tactfully turned her down and squirmed under the attention, much to Javier's amusement.

"Travis called me."

My attention snapped back to the present. "And you told him I moved to Texas to work on death row, didn't you? Mom, I wish you would stop feeding him information about my life."

"He cares about your safety. Like I do."

"My safety is fine, and he's an ex. Please stop friending him."

"I'm sorry." There was a pause. "Have you met anyone?"

She didn't mean friends or colleagues, and I knew that. "No. No one like that. Still getting settled. I'm not looking right now." Which was a lie because every time I closed my eyes, all I saw was six and a half feet of gorgeous dark skin and a coy hint of a smile. "Mom, I gotta go, or I'll be late for the debriefing."

"Fine. We'll talk again on Saturday?"

"Yes. Count on it. I have no plans this time."

"I love you, sweetie."

"Love you too, Mom."

Anxious to see Bishop again, I snatched my backpack from the backseat and hightailed it inside.

It was ten on the nose when I made it to my section of B-pod and debriefed with the officers on duty. That night, I was working with a guy named Derrick who'd recently transferred from general population. He was a sturdy, six-foot-tall African American kid who didn't look a day older than twenty with his youthful, bright eyes and devil-may-care attitude. Death row had yet to dig her claws into him.

"You wanna split up for the night?" I suggested, using Jin's philosophy. "We can check in with each other every hour and radio if there is a problem?"

"Sure, man, that's cool. You want up or down?"

"I'll take up."

We parted ways, and I paced myself as I climbed the steel staircase to the top level, refusing to acknowledge my increased heart rate or clammy hands. As was standard practice, I wandered down both rows and acknowledged all the men under my care that evening so they knew who was on duty.

At B21, I peered in the window and wasn't surprised to find Bishop lying on his bed, propped against the wall with a book in hand. I rapped on the door to catch his attention. Bishop's gaze flicked my way, and he flinched with surprise before a light shone in his dark eyes.

"What are you doing here, boss?"

"Man's gotta work. You still hanging around this joint?"

A smile bloomed across his face, and he ducked his head as I caught the gleam of white teeth. "Ah, you know. Ain't nowhere else to go."

"How was your week last week? You stay out of trouble?"

The smile didn't break from his face, but he struggled to meet my eyes—which was a first. He shuffled, tucked the book he'd been reading under his arm, and approached the window. Only then did he meet my eyes again.

"Got mail last week. Some mysterious, unknown person sent me some new books, like this here one." He pulled the book from under his arm and waved it at me. *1984.*

"Well look at that. That there is one of my favorites. Whoever sent those books has good taste in literature, if I do say so myself."

Roaming my face, smile ever-present, Bishop lowered his voice again. "Thank you, boss. I don't even know how to express my gratitude."

"You just did. You're welcome. How far did you get?"

He opened to the marked page and showed me. "Just started it. I read through those two Dickens books first. Couldn't help myself. I didn't know when I'd see you again, so I was saving this one so it was fresher in my mind so we could talk about it like you wanted."

"I look forward to that chat."

"Me too."

I peered down the row and checked the time. "Got to take care of some stuff, but maybe if you're awake later, we can visit some."

"I'd like that."

"Me too."

That tether was there again, pulling strong and tying us to one another. Whatever was behind it, whatever it might mean, I knew I needed to be careful. This wasn't the place for emotions or feelings or attachments.

The men in this section were familiar with me at this point. Their taunts and sneers had lessened since my first day. I walked the rows, made my count, called lights-out at the appropriate time, and checked in with Derrick downstairs.

All the while, there lived a steady buzz, an itch under my skin that drew me toward Bishop's cell. Fighting against it proved harder than I anticipated. It was closing in on one in the morning before enough of the men were asleep for me to feel comfortable lingering by his cell.

He was waiting for me. Our comfort level had grown by leaps and bounds. His smiles came easier, and those dark eyes of his shone with a hint of life when they found me at his window.

"Did your grandmother visit last week?" I asked by way of opening the conversation. I was hoping to veer us toward his more personal past and find out what had happened that night his ex and her son were killed.

"Every week."

"Did she have new pictures for you?"

"A few." Bishop leaned close to the door, head tilted forward so we could keep our conversation more private. "I get the feeling she's not doing so well."

"What makes you say that?"

"She complains about doctor's appointments and pills more than before. When I ask about them, she refuses to talk about it."

"Does she have anyone taking care of her or looking out for her?"

"Jalen, I assume. I hope. We don't talk about him neither."

Not for the first time, I got the sense there was bad blood between Bishop and his brother. The question was, did I push for information, or let it slide?

Bishop saw through me. "Go on. I can see all those thoughts rolling around your head. Say whatever it is on your mind and quit stewing."

"You're entitled to privacy. Just because I have a curious mind doesn't mean you need to entertain it."

"I'm locked up in this here cell. If I get the privilege of your company from time to time, what will it hurt if I give away a little piece of myself?"

And I craved more and more of Bishop every day. If all he gave was one tiny morsel at a time, I would take those pieces, collect them, and savor them.

"Okay. I'll take the bait. Why do I get the feeling you and Jalen don't get along?"

Bishop nodded like he knew that was what I was going to ask. He scanned his cell and scratched his chin. It was clean-shaven today, so I assumed they'd had the barber in sometime in the past two days.

"Jalen testified against me in court. They subpoenaed him and forced him to take the stand, even though he was underage. Jalen never knew the whole story, and he twisted his own reality into what he believed to be the truth. He was angry, and he didn't know how hard they were going to come down on me. He tried to make amends, afterward, when I was first locked in here, but I couldn't look at him. I refused to see him every time he returned until he stopped coming."

I took that in and rolled it around my head. Bishop's own brother testified against him. Was he partly responsible for Bishop's death sentence? How? Why? Where was the truth in all of this?

"Go on. Ask it. It's been eating at you since you first questioned me."

Our eyes met. He emitted no anger or accusation, even when he saw my doubts surface. Patient as always, he waited.

"What happened that day? I've read so many articles about it, but I can't figure out the truth. Why are you here if you didn't kill them? Where is the person responsible?"

Bishop continued to study me, his features unchanging. "Can I trust you, boss?"

I flinched. "Of course."

"There are parts of this I haven't shared with anyone. Not my lawyer, and not my Maw Maw. Things I don't want just anyone knowing about. It could be dangerous for me. However, I get the sense you might understand more than most."

"You can trust me."

He swiped a large hand over his mouth and paced away from the door like he was gathering his thoughts. When he returned to the window, he rested his forehead against the glass and spoke so low, his voice barely carried to my side.

"Ayanna and I went to high school together. I met her freshman year. She was real pretty, and lots of the boys wanted to date her, but she was shy and turned them down when they asked. Her and I bonded, became good friends. Unlike those other boys, I never asked her for a date, but it turned out, I was the one she wished would. She told me that after we'd been friends for the better part of a year. So that's what we did. We dated each other. I'd never dated no one before, and I liked her well enough, but I learned quickly that I preferred our chats and hanging out. When she wanted to kiss and touch and do all those things boyfriends and girlfriends did, it was awkward for me. Like trying to write with your left hand when you've only ever done it with your right or vice versa. No matter how hard I tried, I couldn't make it feel right. I couldn't make it work."

My heart thundered as the implications behind Bishop's story became clear. I wasn't misreading him. If what he was saying was true, Bishop was gay.

"I was embarrassed, certain I was the only fifteen-year-old kid who didn't like this dating thing. It took a long time before I was brave enough to share it with her. She was angry at first. Thought it meant I didn't like her, but that wasn't it at all. I liked her a whole lot. We went our separate ways. Didn't talk for a while. Then, on a cold night in January, Ayanna showed up at my house. She was crying and didn't look so good. Her clothes were all messed up. Wrinkled. Torn. Her pretty makeup ran down her cheeks with her tears, and she had bruises on her face and arms.

"I didn't want Maw Maw to see her and ask questions, so I took her to my room. Tried to calm her down because she was hysterical. Long story short, a guy at school took advantage of her. He was older. A senior, she said. They'd been dating a short time, I guess, and he wanted more than she was willing to give. He got tired of waiting, so he took it. Raped her. Beat her. Threatened her if she told anyone what happened."

"Jesus."

Bishop, who'd been lost in the past, refocused on my face, his jaw tight. "Yeah. I can't even describe the level of anger I felt that day. She was so small and trembling in my arms when I held her."

"Did she tell you who did it?"

"Not for a long time. She spent the night in my room, cuddled right up beside me and wouldn't let go all night. I got in a world of trouble for it the following day when my granddaddy found out. Ayanna went home and lied to her parents about the bruises and where she'd been that night, but that was when the rumors started. Jalen knew she'd spent the night with me, and 'cause no one saw the state of her when she went into my room, and he'd heard all the crying and such, there were a lot of people figured I did that to her. I hurt her and gave her those marks."

"She corrected them, didn't she?"

Bishop shrugged, and my own rage simmered to life.

"Are you telling me she let everyone believe you'd hurt her?"

"She was afraid of the guy who'd done it. We both knew the truth, so I didn't worry about it at the time. Figured it was kids being kids, and it would all go away in its own time. They'd see we were friends, and those rumors would die off."

"But they didn't."

Bishop didn't confirm or deny my statement, but he didn't have to. "She found out she was pregnant a couple of months later. Again, she showed up at my house in tears, unsure of what to do. Scared. I was so angry because she wouldn't tell me who'd hurt her. We argued, and I got to yelling. Maw Maw and my granddaddy weren't home that time, but Jalen was. He made sure to tell the court verbatim that I said, 'Who is he? When I find out, I'll fucking kill him.' And 'You stay away from him, do you hear me?'"

"Shit."

"Yup. Didn't look good on me. That and she was audibly crying and arguing back, and Jalen heard all of it without knowing what was really going on. It was a month later when she told me who was responsible. Her guardedness made sense after that. Isaiah Gordon was the son of a local Texas Ranger. His daddy was a captain and held a lot of power in the community, never mind his connections all across the state. Ayanna knew if she spoke up, she'd never be believed. Law enforcers have a knack for protecting their own, and Ranger Gordon was an upstanding citizen who was involved in all kinds of local charity functions. His wife sat on the council, and his son was going to follow in his footsteps someday."

"The fucker."

"So Ayanna kept quiet. Begged me to do the same. For a long time, people thought that baby was mine because we were always together. That bothered me, and I insisted she correct that rumor. She did, but Isaiah's name never surfaced either. He made sure of that. Smacked her around for good measure a few times to ensure she didn't tell no one."

My mind reeled with all this new information. They'd been kids. Fifteen. I couldn't fathom the kind of secrets they'd carried with them out of fear. This Isaiah asshole knew how to manipulate her young mind too. If I'd been in Bishop's position, I'd have struggled not to react, not to step in and do what I could to get justice for her. But, yet, I understood why he hadn't.

"Best do your count, boss. We've been chatting a while now."

I glanced at my watch and couldn't believe the time. "Shit, yeah, I gotta do that." I met Bishop's eyes and didn't know what to say.

"Go on. I ain't goin' nowhere."

Reluctant to leave, I pressed a hand to the window and lingered. Bishop laid his over mine. It was becoming our thing. A way of connecting without being able to touch.

"I'll be back."

A load of somber information sat heavy on my shoulders as I checked each cell. Juan was awake, muttering to himself as he lay curled up on his bed, facing the wall. He didn't notice me peeking in his window. Everyone else was sleeping. I radioed in my report and jogged down the stairs to meet up with Derrick.

"Nights suck," he announced when he saw me.

I chuckled. "Yeah, they're pretty quiet compared to the day shifts. Should be thankful."

"Did I hear you worked deathwatch last week?"

"I did."

"What's that like?" He crossed his arms and leaned on the wall nearby, looking far too comfortable like he was ready for a long chat to kill time.

The last thing I wanted was to linger. Bishop was talking, and I needed to know the rest of his story.

"It was depressing, to be honest."

"Did people talk? Did you hear their gruesome tales? Their confessions?"

Derrick was far too eager to absorb other people's nightmares, and I wasn't willing to share.

"Not my place to say, man. Sorry."

His shoulders fell, but he laughed it off. "No worries. I'm sure I'll get to work their soon enough. So, where are you from? I heard you transferred not that long ago from somewhere up north?"

I peered up the stairs and back at Derrick. "You know, I'd love to chat, but I was midway into dealing with an issue upstairs, and I kinda need to get back."

"Oh." Derrick straightened and glanced in the direction of the second level. "Something wrong? Did you need a hand?"

"It's all good. Nothing major."

Disappointment crossed Derrick's face as he nodded. "All right. Well, I'll catch you soon."

"Yup."

I waited until he walked away before aiming back up the stairs toward Bishop's cell. He sat on the edge of his bed, leafing through the book I'd sent him.

"If you'd rather read, I can stop bugging you."

He lifted his chin as a smile penetrated his face. "I can read anytime, but it's not often I get the pleasure of talking to good company."

He approached the door again and peered past me down the row as far as he could see. "The rest of them asleep?"

"Mostly. Juan, on the far end, isn't, but he can't hear us."

Bishop nodded and wet his lips, his gaze turning inward as he drifted to the past. "You sure you wanna hear all this, boss? It ain't a pretty story."

"I'm sure."

He nodded and continued. "Ayanna never had it easy. Her parents kicked her out once the baby was born, and that left her strapped for cash and living in shithole apartments while she tried to make a few bucks working at the local supermarket. I didn't have money either, so I couldn't help. When the struggle became too much, she did what she thought was right for her and her baby, even when I warned her not to. Begged her not to. She went to Isaiah and threatened to have a paternity test done and tell everyone what had happened the night he raped her if he didn't step up and help her and his son out."

"Why do I get the feeling that was a bad idea?"

"'Cause it was. Blackmailing the blackmailer would only bite her in the ass. I told her as much. Isaiah didn't take kindly to those threats. By calling him, she brought his abuse back into her life. Oh, he paid up and helped her out for a time, but it came with a price. He knocked her around, gave her more bruises, and although she never owned up to it, I'm pretty sure he took advantage of her again and again. She was never the same after that. Always had this vacant look in her eyes.

"I'd get phone calls from her, crying and scared. She was important to me. As much as I couldn't be in a relationship with her like that, I loved her, and it broke my heart to see what was happening. I felt so helpless. I thought I could protect her. I should have gone to the cops, but I was almost as scared as she was."

Bishop blew out a breath and rubbed a hand over his shaved head. "It came to a point when I started fighting back. She'd call me because he was there or on his way over, and I couldn't take it anymore. Isaiah and I went toe to toe a few times. I'm not ashamed to admit I gave him a taste of his own medicine. Messed him up real good. But... Daddy was a Ranger, and Isaiah had my ass arrested a few times."

"You were charged with aggravated assault. I read that on your record."

"Yup. Ended up doing five months. It should have been two years, but I'd only just turned eighteen, so the judge took pity on me and cut it way back."

"You didn't tell them the truth? You didn't say why you'd attacked him?"

Bishop narrowed his eyes and pinned me with a hardened stare. "Darn right I did, and who do you think they believed? A parentless black kid from a poverty-stricken area who had a reputation for leaving bruises on his *girlfriend,* or the biracial kid whose *white* daddy was a Texas Ranger and whose mama sat on the council?"

I pinched my lips closed because I knew how our system worked, and I knew the injustice people like Bishop faced every day because of the color of his skin or the lack of money in his family's bank account.

When I said nothing, he nodded. "Exactly. Didn't matter what I said. While I was inside, my granddaddy ended up with stage-four liver cancer and died, Jalen started acting out at school, and Maw Maw grieved her husband's loss on her own. Things got worse, and by the time I got out, Ayanna was so withdrawn and scared, I didn't know how to help her. I couldn't be there for her like I wanted to be. I visited when I could and talked to her on the phone. She was at the end of her rope. I saw it. She started to hang threats over Isaiah again."

"Dammit."

"He got tired of her milking him for money and hanging Keon over his head. Isaiah was in college, studying law enforcement. His life was on track except for her constantly digging under his skin.

"One night, Isaiah showed up at Ayanna's apartment, and they fought. He gave her some real good bruises on her face and arms that night. She managed to escape to the bathroom and called me. I wanted to call the cops. I wanted them to go to her apartment and see the truth right then and there, but I also knew I couldn't leave her alone another minute with Isaiah in the house. So I did both. I placed a call to the authorities, and I ran to her house as fast as my legs would carry me. She didn't live far, and when I got there, I heard the yelling inside. The door was locked, so I busted it open before the cops got there. I grabbed Isaiah, threw him against the wall, and laid into him really good while Ayanna cried in the corner. Broke his nose. Busted up a few of his teeth."

The pieces clicked into place. "And they arrested you for B and E."

"Yup. Plus they tacked on more assault charges. I had a record now, and there was no explaining my way out of it. No one would listen. It was a one-way ticket back to jail."

"Ayanna didn't speak up?"

"She tried at first, but she was hysterical. It's funny how the authorities can spin things when they want to. She wasn't in the right headspace after being attacked and was therefore confusing the truth. Isaiah stepped in and played the hero, flipping the whole story on its head. Said I was the one who'd given Ayanna those bruises."

"Bullshit."

"It was a huge 'he said, she said' debacle. In the end, I was the one at fault. They issued me a restraining order against them both and told me I couldn't go near her anymore."

"And what about Isaiah? What did he say was his reason for being there?"

Bishop laughed, but it was humorless. "He told his daddy, Ayanna was his new girlfriend and I was the pissed-off abusive ex who couldn't let her go. He said I wanted her all to myself."

"And let me guess, Ayanna corroborated."

"Battered woman syndrome. She was too scared to fight for me and retracted her original story. Isaiah was more and more violent every day. She feared for her life."

I knew where this story was going, and I knew who'd been responsible for those two murders all those years ago. My stomach clenched as I watched the emotions play out on Bishop's face. "He killed them, didn't he?"

Bishop's Adam's apple rose and fell with a thick swallow. He blinked hard a few times before nodding. "I couldn't stop him. I was too late."

He brought a fist to his mouth and took a minute to find his voice again. "Maw Maw paid my bail money. My case hadn't even gone to trial yet, but I wasn't allowed to be near Ayanna or Isaiah. One night, she called me in hysterics. Said she was going to put her foot down with Isaiah because she was done jumping through his hoops, and it wasn't fair what he'd done to me. I'd heard it all before. For years she'd been telling me the same thing. He was the one responsible for ruining our friendship, he was the reason I was heading back to jail, and so I told her I didn't believe her.

"She stammered apologies over the phone, promising she'd make it better. She told me she loved me and then she hung up. She called him after that and told him this was it: she was coming clean about everything and she was sending his ass to jail. As you can surmise, their phone call didn't go over well. Why she felt the need to tell him, I will never know. Whatever words were exchanged put her on alert. She knew right away she'd made a mistake. She knew he was coming over, and she didn't know what to do. Did she take Keon and run? Did she call the cops and hope they got there on time? No. She called me. Stupid woman. I told her immediately to call the cops and lock her door.

"Except he burst into her apartment right then when we were talking on the phone. All I heard was him yelling and her screaming and crying. Furniture crashed and she dropped the phone. I heard it clatter to the ground. Keon cried out for his mama and there was this shrill sound next that I can't describe. It tipped me over the edge." Bishop shook his head. "I knew I was on parole. I knew I had orders to stay away from her. But... I ran. I ran so fucking hard because I knew... I knew. But I wasn't fast enough."

A single tear slid down his cheek, and he batted it away with his building anger.

"I was too goddamn late, and when I got there, he was..." Bishop's bottom lip trembled, and he washed a rough hand over his face. "There was blood everywhere. Pooled on the carpet, on the furniture. Jesus, it was awful. He kept stabbing her over and over.

"I didn't think twice about my own safety. I launched forward and attacked him. We fought. Eventually, I got the upper hand and took the knife, but he ran. I was so mixed up after that. Did I chase him down or take care of Ayanna? I think I was in shock because my whole world tipped upside down. Ayanna and Keon weren't moving, and there was so much blood. So, so much. Little Keon he... I tried to wake them up. I tried to stop Ayanna from bleeding all over. Told her she couldn't die on me. My whole body shook and trembled, and I could barely see straight. I ... knew it was too late. I knew they were both gone. That's when I heard the sirens coming." He drifted off, seeing the day clear in his mind. He was a stone statue, rigid and trying hard to remain unmoving, except he trembled much like he'd done on the day he described.

"Bishop?" My voice carried through the door, but he didn't respond, didn't blink. He was lost in that long-ago moment. Stuck in a horror-filled past. "Bishop, look at me."

He couldn't. I wasn't certain he heard me through the chaos of the storm inside his head. He opened his hands and stared at his palms. The left one slashed with an old scar. It was then when I understood how he'd gotten it.

Defensive wound.

"I didn't even know I was still holding the knife when the Austin police got there. They kept yelling at me, *'Drop the weapon. Drop the weapon.'* When I saw it there in my hand... When I realized what the police saw, how it all looked, I knew."

His large hands quaked, and fat teardrops landed on them with increased frequency as this giant, broken man fell apart.

I didn't think of consequences. Knowing only that I needed to comfort and pull Bishop away from the ledge, I fumbled with my keyring until I found the key to unlock the chute on the door. Glancing once in both directions, I drew the small door open and reached inside, taking Bishop's scarred hand in my own and holding on for dear life, instilling as much strength and compassion into the connection as I could. It was all I could offer, and it was enough to lose my job if I wasn't careful.

But I didn't care.

The minute I made contact, Bishop startled and sucked in a breath. He didn't pull away but stared at where we were joined for a long minute before his fingers folded over mine. Another minute passed before Bishop's stormy gaze rose.

"You can't do this, boss. You can't—"

"Shut up and come here." I leaned my head against the glass, imploring him to listen with just my eyes.

He came. His forehead joining mine on the cool window. Our gazes connected. Our souls intertwined.

"I believe you, do you hear me? I know you tried to help her. I know you didn't hurt her or her son." I squeezed his hand tighter. "You aren't alone."

He hardened his grip as well, and for the longest time, we simply watched one another. Our tether growing stronger. Our bond solidifying.

Bishop's lips moved around words, but nothing came out. He squeezed his eyes closed, opened them, and tried again, his voice so hushed and raw, I strained to listen. "I loved her, but I wasn't in love with her."

"I know."

"I... I don't like girls in that way, do you understand what I'm saying?"

"I do. Me neither."

His hand clung desperately to mine, like I was the only thing giving him strength enough to confess his deepest, darkest secrets.

"I've never told no one before."

"You keep my secrets, I'll keep yours. Deal?"

"Deal."

Chapter Eleven

THE WALLS PRESSED IN from all sides as I sat forward on my couch, clutching the back of my head. I'd been home for an hour and didn't know where to put myself. It was too hot to run, and I was too anxious to sleep. A million thoughts pummeled my brain at once, and I was convinced if I didn't hold my head together, it would explode.

Between Bishop's gruesome story, his confessions about his sexuality, my actions—opening his chute to touch him—and our growing bond, I didn't know what to do. Nothing like this had ever happened to me before. I was so far out in left field, I didn't see the bases anymore.

With my thoughts bouncing between Bishop's innocence and my rising feelings toward him, I shot off the couch with a growl and paced my living room. What the hell had I gotten myself into? Why had I let this get so out of hand? I never should have looked him up. Never should have asked questions.

In the kitchen, I stood with the fridge door open, staring at the shelves, unseeing, and drifting back to our conversation. I saw his tears, felt the tremors in his hands again, the crash of emotions as they'd poured out of him and into me. My heart ached when I recalled his desperation as he'd clung to me.

I never should have unlocked that chute.
I never should have touched him like that.
Regret was a funny thing. Jeff didn't feel it, and neither did I.
Slamming the fridge door, I paced some more, carding my fingers through my hair, over and over until it stood up on end. My

heart slammed double time, and I clutched my chest at one point, willing it to calm.

Tugging my phone from my pants, I leaned against the counter and studied it, thinking and deciding who I could talk to who might understand. I wasn't the type of person who stewed alone. The only way to get the anxiety out was to purge. Unfortunately, I'd left my therapist back in Michigan with high hopes that I'd overcome the incident that landed me here.

I could call Mom. She'd listen. She always had, no matter what, but she would worry. The last thing I wanted to do was tell her I was falling for a man on death row.

My friends back home had drifted away after the incident. I'd been uptight and anxious. Angry. I'd placed blame where I shouldn't have and lost friends because of it. The few that had stuck by me hadn't contacted me since I'd left the state. To be fair, I hadn't contacted them either with my adamancy to start fresh.

That left Javier.

Hesitating, I put my phone down on the counter and leaned my head against the sliding doors that overlooked the backyard. It was gearing up to be another hot summer day in Texas. Birds chirped high in the trees, and the blue sky was bright and cloudless. The glass was warm against my forehead, and I closed my eyes, remembering the connection Bishop and I shared through the small window of his cell.

I fisted my hands, wanting to punch something if only to expel the trapped energy inside. Spinning, I glared at my phone on the counter and cracked my knuckles. Thinking. Thinking.

Javier was at work. Even if he was a person I could talk to, he wasn't available.

Except, I was going to go crazy if I didn't do something.

Not allowing myself a chance to further consider, I snapped my phone off the counter and typed him a message.

Anson: Meet me in the parking lot on your lunch break?

Sweat beaded my forehead when I hit enter. My insides jittered. I tossed my phone down and dug a beer from the fridge, twisted off the cap, and drained half of it in one go.

It wasn't like I was going to be able to sleep anyhow.

It was half-past twelve when I pulled into the parking lot at Polunsky. I knew for a fact Javier religiously checked his phone on his lunch break. Since they'd put up cellphone blocking devices at the prison a few years back, it wasn't uncommon for officers to scurry outside on their breaks to check their messages or text their friends.

For privacy, I chose a spot in the back corner of the lot, farthest away from the guardhouse and gate. Because the sun was scorching the earth, I left it running with the air conditioning on full blast.

Javier appeared a short time later and spotted me as he crossed the lot. His shades covered his eyes, and he strutted toward me with a shit-eating grin and all kinds of arrogance. He dropped onto the seat beside me and slammed the door.

"Holy fuck, it's hot out there." He removed his sunglasses and wiped the sweat from the bridge of his nose before aiming a vent on his face. "Why the hell aren't you sleeping? You're gonna have a shit night at this rate."

"Don't think I could if I wanted to."

He kept his shades off and shifted sideways in the seat to face me. When the radio on his shoulder crackled, he turned it off. "Something's up. What's going on? I could tell from your text you weren't all right."

I ran my tongue along my teeth and studied the cars in the parking lot, unsure where to start and what all was safe to share.

"I've got myself in over my head, and I don't know what to do."

"In over your head how?"

Hesitating, I rubbed my unshaven jaw and bounced my knee. "Have you ever worked with an inmate who you knew was innocent?"

Javier didn't speak at first. Then he shuffled and rattled his head as though he didn't hear me right. "What are you talking about?"

"Have you?"

"I told you, I don't get involved. I don't look shit up, and even when some sorry sod talks and tells me stories, I leave that all behind when I go home. Anson, these guys will tell you anything you wanna hear. Not a single man inside those concrete walls will admit they're guilty of the crime that put them there. We house a whole fuck-of-a-lot of innocent men."

"I know, but some of them *are* innocent. The statistics say that a small percentage of incarcerated people are doing time for crimes they didn't commit. And another smaller percent will die for those crimes."

"What the hell did Jeff say to you?"

I shook my head and stared at the horizon. "Not Jeff. He was very forthcoming about his crimes. He didn't pull his punches or bullshit me. He's made peace with his death."

"Then who?"

A single bird soared across the sky in the distance, his wingspan vast. My avian knowledge was non-existent, so I didn't know what kind of bird it was, but I watched it swoop and circle and dive at the field before dipping out of sight behind Polunsky.

"Bishop," I mumbled, my voice low as though part of me wanted to hold him close and protect him against other people's harsh opinions.

Again, Javier paused for a long time before he spoke. "He talked to you?" There was an edge of disbelief in his tone. Bishop didn't talk to anyone. It was why he'd inherited the nickname Silent Giant by some. His secrets were locked up tight, and no one in the past had been able to encourage him to share.

Until me.

"We've ... had a number of conversations." Unable to meet Javier's analytical gaze, lest he see the truth in my eyes, I flicked my attention to the prison. The high noon sun reflected off the fencing and distant windows like shimmering diamonds. "I looked him up. Read all I could find. He told me—"

"He is lying to you if he told you he didn't do it."

"He's not." Those two words came out with such conviction, Javier touched my arm to draw my attention to him. There was worry on my friend's face.

"What's going on? You don't strike me as the gullible type."

Even though no one was around, I lowered my voice like my shame and vulnerability could travel. "We've been talking a lot. Getting to know each other. He's not who he appears to be." Fisting my hands in my lap, I shrugged. "We ... have a lot in common, and his company has been—"

"Jesus, Anson, what are you telling me?"

"I'm telling you I believe him. He shouldn't be here. Everything I read. Everything he told me. He got the raw end of the deal. He was trying to help." I was rambling, and I was sure Javier couldn't make sense of a story he knew nothing about, but I couldn't stop. "Ayanna didn't stand up for him. All those times he tried to help her, she let him take the fall over and over. Do you know how angry that makes me? Fuck me, he shouldn't be here. He's kind and gentle, and he has an old soul that rolls out of him when you get to know him. He likes classic literature and—"

Javier tugged my shoulder around again because I'd turned away, and he got right in my face. "Did getting your ass handed to you at I-Max not teach you anything?" he hissed. "Do you have a death wish? If Bishop had any idea you were mooning over him, he'd find a way to have you gutted."

Tearing from his hold, I scowled. "I never said I was mooning over him. And who the fuck says mooning?"

"You didn't have to say it. Listen to yourself. I can read between the lines, and the look on your face says everything. What is wrong with you? You know what can happen if those guys in there find out you're gay."

"Bishop already knows."

"*What*? You told him? Have you lost your mind? You can't trust those men, Anson. They are dangerous."

"I trust him. He's innocent. I'd bet my life on it. And ... I'm pretty sure his feelings are returned."

The air vibrated as I waited for Javier to respond. He collapsed back in his seat and pressed his fingers into his eyes sockets like he was battling a headache. "Shit," he whispered. "Shit, shit, shit."

That about summed it up.

I let him process while I stared out the window, replaying Bishop's story over and over again in my head. The feel of his warm skin was imprinted on my mind. His strong grip, holding me for dear life. It'd been so hard to let go and lock that chute afterward. Harder yet to walk away and finish my duties.

We'd both accepted the heaviness of what he'd shared, and there was an unspoken understanding that I needed time to process.

"Is he why you switched up your shifts for the next couple of weeks?"

"Yeah."

"That's gonna ping on Ray's radar."

"Ray isn't here."

Javier blew out a long breath, and the sharp edge disappeared from his voice. "You know his last appeal was shut down, right? Bishop will be walking the mile soon. His time is fast running out."

"I know."

"Anson, what are you doing?"

I pinched my lips together and threaded fingers through my hair for the hundredth time. "I have no idea. I'm so fucked."

"You're smarter than this. I know you are. Why are you so sure he's innocent? He could be taking you for a ride. With all of it. You might have put yourself in a lot of danger telling him you're gay."

"I feel it right here." I tapped my chest over my heart. "I know I'm right. I know. I trust him."

"I honestly don't know what to tell you. Be careful. I'm serious."

"You won't tell anyone?"

"Are you kidding? No way."

"Thanks."

"What are you gonna do?"

"I... I don't know yet."

Talking to Javier didn't solve my problems, but it lifted a great weight off my chest and allowed me to relax when I got home. I managed to get a few hours of sleep before I had to get up and get ready for work. He'd left me a text sometime in the middle of the afternoon. A simple, *Don't do anything stupid.*

I didn't respond because I couldn't make any promises at that point. I'd already crossed a line. No matter how much I'd revealed to him earlier, there was no way I could admit to breaking protocol and opening Bishop's chute. Sure, we did that a number of times in a day. To cuff men for transfers or to pass commissary sheets, items, library requests, and books, and mail back and forth. But each of those times was recorded and, when possible, there were always two officers present.

Opening the hatch to offer comfort and share a touch was over the line. *Way* over the line. These men lived under strict *no contact* rules. Even visitors weren't permitted to touch their loved ones. No exceptions.

The first half of my shift, I avoided hanging out at Bishop's cell, despite feeling the weight of his attention pulling me closer each time I performed a count.

Because he was eager and new to 12-Building, I indulged Derrick in conversation for larger chunks of time—refusing to admit it was solely to absolve my guilt from the night before.

At 1:30 a.m. my resistance vanished. I radioed in my count and wavered on my feet. Like he sensed my indecision, Bishop's face appeared at his cell window, and he looked out at me, so many mysteries and unspoken words bleeding through his dark gaze.

"You avoiding me, boss?"

I was a few cells down and cut my eyes in both directions to ensure no one else was by their cell windows. Wetting my lips, I approached with a measured pace. "No. Just ... processing."

He said nothing, studying me with that intense glare. I let him, no longer bothered by his soul-stripping analysis. "You're unsettled."

"Among many things."

"Did you sleep when you went home?"

"No. Not well."

"I can tell. You have shadows under your eyes."

I touched the fragile skin in question and frowned.

"Are you angry, boss? You seem a bit on edge. Tense."

"A bit."

"How come?"

I gnawed my lip, scowling at the floor as I rolled the mountain of information around my head, pinpointing the exact cause of my annoyance. "*She* did this to you. *She* refused to speak up or have your back, yet you were the first person she called when she was in trouble, and you ran to her aid every time. You did time before this because of her." I pressed my lips together as a rumble vibrated in my chest. I was angrier than I realized. "Yet you stick up for her even now," I spat. "Why?"

I had no idea how much that small piece of information bothered me until Bishop asked.

"I played the blame game for a lot of years. Went through a time when I was angry too. At her. At my choices. At life for not giving me a fair shot and coming down on me so hard when all I wanted to do was help a friend." A deep V in the middle of Bishop's brow grew more prominent as he thought.

"But you moved past it? How?"

"Had to. What good does being angry do? It doesn't change what happened. It won't bring Ayanna or Keon back. And it certainly won't get me outta this here cell." He smacked the steel door once for emphasis. "I don't blame her anymore. Ayanna was doing all she could to protect herself and her son. She had her own guilt a mile high for what happened to me. You see, I left those good days we shared outta my story. Just told you the hard stuff. The stuff surrounding this." He waved a hand around his small cell. "Ayanna and me, we were as close as two people could be without being intimate, you know? She always wished for more. I just… I guess you could say she was like the sister I never had. Wouldn't you do all you could to protect your sister, even if it bit you in the ass?"

"If I had a sister, I'd like to believe I would."

"She was a victim. I'm not angry at her, and I don't blame her. I don't blame anyone for me being here."

"That's not true. You blame yourself. I see it." Our eyes clashed, and I saw the truth before he confirmed it.

"Every day." He laughed, but there was no humor behind it. "I've played the *what-if* game for almost twenty years, since long before I was locked up here. *What if* I'd tried harder to love her like she wanted? We could have stayed a couple. She would never have met Isaiah. *What if* I'd gone to the police the day she told me she was raped? *What if* I'd been faster that day Isaiah killed her?"

"But *what if* doesn't change the past."

"That's right."

"What happened to Isaiah? You told the police the truth when they arrested you. You pled not guilty, I read that. He must have been brought to trial."

"He was, but between my county appointed public defender and his fancy lawyer, his daddy's Ranger status, my police record, and the fact that I was on parole with a restraining order at the time, the evidence all had a way of pointing directly at me. All the other evidence? Anything that came close to incriminating Isaiah? That stuff had a nasty habit of disappearing or getting dismissed due to procedural errors. They buried his connection as deep as they could."

"And your appeals?"

Bishop sighed. "I can't afford a big fancy lawyer. The ones they appoint give half-hearted attempts at making a judge listen, but they aren't ever gonna change people's minds. In the end, no one is willing to work very hard for a poor black man who looks far more guilty than he does innocent."

I closed my eyes and shook my head in irritation. "But they can't have buried everything. What about his fingerprints on the knife. His DNA had to have been all over that room. Keon was his son, and that must have come out. The neighbors must have seen more. Why didn't—"

"Anson." My rarely used name stopped me in my tracks. "I've been to hell and back with this case, believe me. Unless I can get a lawyer who gives half a damn about me, there is nothing that is gonna stop me from following Jeff's footsteps to deathwatch and then the chamber."

"But there has to be—"

He held up his large palm, stilling me. Without a word, he walked into his cell and rooted around in a pile of stuff he collected beside his bed. When he returned, he waved a file folder at me.

"This here contains everything about my case, including the umpteen appeals that have been filed over the years. I've studied it inside and out. Noted all the inconsistencies. My lawyer has pushed different angles here and there. Does she work hard for me? I don't think so. Does she give two shits about my life? Not likely. Do I think there's stuff being ignored or buried? Absolutely. But people won't listen to me." He nodded at the chute. "Take it, if you want. Make a copy for yourself. You have my permission. Read it. It will answer all your questions. You'll see."

The folder was well over two inches thick and spilling papers out the sides. They were bent and frayed and well-read. The folder itself was on the verge of disintegrating it was so old. The binding was split and worn.

It was tempting.

"Take it," he said again. "Better you get your answers here than ask me to relive it again and again. I like talking to you, boss, but I'd much rather talk about books and barbecued chicken, if it's all the same."

With my focus locked on the folder, I nodded. "I'll grab it closer to my lunch break. That way, I can stick it in my backpack."

Bishop clutched the folder to his chest and was about to turn away when I found my voice again. "And Bishop?"

He waited.

"I like talking to you too."

I was rewarded with a slip of a smile as he turned to his bed and set the folder down. Desperate to hold onto our moment, I shoved all questions and thoughts of his case aside and remained by his window, wanting—*needing*—more. "Tell me about your family. About your old neighborhood and these drawings on the walls. Please?"

He didn't return to the window, and my chest grew heavy with regret. Instead, he lowered himself to his bed and rested his elbows on his knees. Regarding me, that teasing smile returned. "I'll tell you about my family, you tell me about yours."

The walls of privacy I kept in place around inmates no longer existed with Bishop. Without thought, I returned his smile. "Deal."

A small part of me was alarmed at how easily I agreed, how willing I was to let him in, but I followed my gut, and my gut told me Bishop was safe. Bishop wouldn't hurt me. Bishop was as intrigued and taken with me as I was with him.

"What do you want to know first?" he asked.

"Your family?"

"Okay." He rubbed a hand over his jaw. "Jalen and I were raised by my granddaddy and Maw Maw. I was six when Jalen was born. Our mother died less than a week after giving birth to my brother. She had a cesarean section for both of us, but after they discharged her, she didn't take it easy like she was supposed to, lifting the baby, running around to do chores, up and down the stairs.

"I was out with Maw Maw, and she was home alone with Jalen. Her stitches opened up, and she wasn't able to get to the phone to call for help. Maw Maw didn't bring me home until that evening. She found my mother in the bathroom. Her insides all slipping outside her body. I didn't see it myself, but I was told about it when I was older. Maw Maw, she called the emergency number, and they came, took my mother to the hospital. She was there for a few days but ended up with a terrible infection and died."

"Oh my God. I'm so sorry. That's horrible. I didn't even know stuff like that could happen."

"Me neither. I don't remember her much. Little pictures in my head here and there. The smell of her perfume."

"Where was your father?"

"He was some drifter, drug-dealing, gang-type who Maw Maw and Granddaddy never liked, I guess. He came around a bit when I was little and Jalen was a baby, but then one day, he stopped coming. Maw Maw figured he got himself killed or locked up. He didn't have any interest in raising two boys, anyhow. We were better off with Maw Maw."

"I never knew my father. He took off before I was born."

"And your mother?"

"She raised me by herself. Gave me the best she could and has always loved me unconditionally. Even when…" I darted my gaze down the row in both directions.

"Don't say it," Bishop warned. "You never know who's listening."

"She taught me to love the written word."

"Maw Maw did that for me too."

"I'm from Michigan," I admitted, feeling an urgency to pull Bishop into my circle. "Grew up in a town called Grand Rapids. I moved to Portland, Michigan when I got a job at Ionia. Mom hated it because she wanted me close, and Portland was almost an hour away."

"And now you're in Texas? She can't be too pleased with that."

I laughed, hearing her worried voice in my head. "She's not. She hates that I ran this far. She worries. Doesn't like that I'm working death row. Doesn't like that I'm still working in prisons, period."

Bishop went silent, and I clamped my mouth shut, realizing what I'd said. His eyes narrowed, and he tipped his head to the side. "Something happened to you at Ionia." It wasn't a question. He was smart and observant.

"Yes. I'd tell you, but it's not wise for me to discuss all the details here. The walls have ears." I quirked a brow, beseeching him to understand.

He did. Rising from the bed, he came closer, examining my person as much as he could through a window, like he was looking for evidence or answers. "They hurt you?" he asked, his voice hushed.

Instead of answering, I ensured no eyes were on us, then untucked the edge of my uniform and revealed the scar along my side, still pink and raised. Then I unbuttoned the cuff of my shirt and pulled my sleeve high enough to show him the mark on my forearm. The only remaining evidence of my attack.

"Spent a few weeks in the hospital. Had surgery." I tapped my abdomen wound. "It wasn't safe for me to go back to work there. Prisoners had too much knowledge of my personal life."

Bishop's lips twitched and firmed. His dark eyes blazed as he focused on the wound on my abdomen. I covered it, tucked my shirt in, and straightened my uniform.

"They wanted you dead."

"I think so, but they failed their mission. I wasn't going back to give them another shot, that's for sure. The transfer was my best option. I hated leaving Mom, but I had to get away."

A heavy weight settled between us with the implication of why I'd been attacked. Bishop's anger sat on the surface, his jaw ticking.

"How far did you get in that book?" Changing the subject seemed like the best option. "Did you get much read today?"

Bishop blinked, and his discontent vanished with my question. He glanced toward his bed where the book I'd given him sat. "Savoring it, boss. Don't rush me. I'll tell you when I'm done."

The mood lightened after that, and we chatted books again until I had to leave and do my count. Before I was scheduled to go for my lunch break, I collected Bishop's case folder from him, accepting it as he passed it through the chute.

I tucked it under my arm, and when the officer came to relive me, I chatted good-naturedly, and he didn't notice or question the folder. It went snug into my backpack for another time.

Chapter Twelve

THANKS TO THE SHIFT switches I'd managed, I worked two solid weeks of nights on Bishop's row. Which meant two solid weeks of nightly chats and sharing where I learned a great deal about the big man inside the cell. Once he'd finished reading *1984*, we spent an entire night discussing the plot and debating every little part of the book until we exhausted ourselves. I got the sense he liked to disagree with me for the sake of it because I was passionate when I discussed books, and he enjoyed getting a rise out of me.

Bishop's reservation lessened, and he laughed and chatted more freely than he'd ever done before. I returned his trust tenfold and shared all kinds of things about myself I hadn't shared with any other person in my life—even Travis.

I no longer shied away from telling Bishop about the world outside the prison. Almost twenty years behind bars—fifteen on death row and the handful of years he'd spent in general population before his sentencing—had brought a lot of changes he wasn't aware of, and he listened attentively when I spoke of technological advancements and politics. He loved when I mentioned familiar places or items he could connect with his past. The movies, for example, or the smell of sunshine and roses, the taste of barbecued corn on the cob, or the feel of raindrops on my face when I'd come to work during a thunderstorm one evening.

He absorbed, listened, and smiled.

Every time I was gifted his wide, tooth-bearing grin, my heart skipped and ached and yearned.

Every morning, I walked away feeling more and more tethered to that man inside cell B21.

When I went home, instead of sleeping or running or watching TV or listening to music, I poured over his case. I read every sheet of paper stuffed into that file folder. The police reports, the affidavits, the appeals, the recorded testimonies, and the entire trial breakdown as it had been transcribed. When I came to the end, I read it again and again, making my own notes and stewing over every word.

It was later into the second week when I realized I hadn't made plans to trade any more shifts. Pulling up the schedule on my laptop, I noted who was where and placed a call to one of the guys scheduled for the night rotation in Bishop's row.

"Sorry, man, no can do."

"No problem, thanks."

I didn't have any better luck with the second officer either. It was a flat-out no from him too. With a scan of the schedule, I checked to see who was on the morning and afternoon rotation in that section next week. It was my next best option. Javier's name caught my eye.

"Piece of cake."

I shot Javier a text, asking him to call me on his lunch break.

It was closer to one when my phone rang. I was deep into studying Bishop's case again and hadn't realized how late in the day it was.

"Don't you ever sleep?" Javier said in lieu of a hello.

"I'll sleep when I'm dead. I have a favor to ask."

"What's up?"

"Can you switch me your rotation next week?"

There was a pregnant pause where I imagined Javier mentally pulling up his schedule in his head.

"You want to switch? Yeah, I can't see— Wait a minute. No fucking way. That's *his* section. What are you doing, man? You're gonna get your ass in trouble."

"How? Why? What difference does it make?"

"Anson." His voice dropped. "Whatever it is you think you're doing, stop it. Nothing can happen. He's inside, you're outside. Get that through your head. He's on death row. That ain't ever gonna change, brother. He's not getting out. This isn't some Hallmark movie or daytime soap. You aren't going to ride off into the sunset and have a happy little romance. He's going to die. Deal with it before you get your ass in trouble."

"You're a real dick, you know that? I'm not delusional. I'm not an idiot. I know the stakes. All I'm asking is for you to switch some shifts with me. Let me deal with it. It's my business, not yours."

A full thirty seconds of breathing came through the line before, "You really like him, don't you? It's not some infatuation or curiosity about his crimes. He's dug under your skin and got to you."

I didn't respond. How could I? Admitting my growing feelings for Bishop, even to myself, had been difficult. Saying them out loud was impossible.

"Anson? Look, I'm your friend. I'm worried this is a big mistake."

"I've been reading his case files. All of them. There isn't a doubt in my mind he's an innocent man. It's a classic case of race, economic status, and politics all rolled into one and working against him. He never stood a chance. The best he's had is a public defender, and you know how hard they fight and how much they care. They're overworked and underpaid. They don't give a shit. And you're right, if something doesn't change, he *is* going to die." I paused and let that information absorb before I whispered, "And I'm not sure what that will do to me."

Javier didn't say anything. His leveled inhales and exhales were all the noise that passed between us.

"Can you help me out? Just ... let me spend time with him. Don't judge me for it."

A long sigh of resignation came through the phone. "It's going to be suspicious. It will be the third week you've ensured to work his row. They notice stuff like that." Javier paused. "Switch with someone on escorting. You'll still see him, but it won't ping their radar."

I hadn't thought of that. Escorting wasn't ideal, but it was better than nothing.

"Okay, I will. Thanks."

"And, Anson?"

"Yeah."

"We're hanging out this weekend. Beers. Barbecue. Do some guy stuff. Get your mind outta that place for a bit."

"Sounds good."
"I'm serious."
"I know."

"YOU HAVE NO IDEA HOW glad I am to see you. When I saw the schedule, I was worried. I've heard rumors about that guy. Do you know him? Is he as much of a prick as they say he is?"

Derrick followed close on my heels like an abandoned puppy vying for attention as we passed through the crash gates, heading to our next transfer. It was a trip to medical for a guy who was recovering from a serious bout of pneumonia that had almost taken him out.

"I've had some run-ins with him." *Ezra.* "I don't like to judge, but his methods are unorthodox, and he's not my favorite person."

"You're so diplomatic. 'His methods are unorthodox,'" he parroted and laughed. "He's a prick, just say it."

"Fine, he's a prick. Happy?"

Derrick smacked my shoulder and snorted. I'd managed to persuade Ezra to trade me his week escorting. It was either that or trade with Derrick, which meant working *beside* Ezra for a week. I wasn't sure I'd survive a week of his shit, so I'd battled it out with him on the phone until I'd convinced him of the trade.

Derrick was decent company, but he was a talker and more than a decade younger than me, so I'd been suffering with his girl problems and drinking stories for half the morning. He was also a gossip—like half the other men at the prison.

"I heard he's walking a tight rope right now. Ray's gonna suspend his ass if he so much as sneezes the wrong way. Did you hear about what happened during a shakedown a few weeks ago?"

"I was there."

"No shit! Did you see him get spit on? I heard he sprayed the guy, and it was unwarranted."

"Have you never been spit on?" I quirked a brow with a wide grin as we climbed the stairs to the second level of section D.

"Nope. Never. I was only in GP for a month before I moved over here. Graduated from college in the spring."

"So fresh."

"Is it common? Have you been spit on?"

"More times than I can count. It's a rite of passage when you work in prisons, my friend. Give it time."

"Fuck, that's gross."

We arrived at our transfer cage and met up with the officers on duty before checking in with command again to go ahead with the transfer. Derrick walked the inmate through the steps of his strip search—he liked taking control, and I didn't care one way or the other.

I checked the man's jumpsuit, and once he was set, we cuffed him and guided him toward the infirmary.

The inmate coughed many times through closed lips, his chest rattling loud enough I could guess his pneumonia wasn't cleared up—and I was the furthest thing from a doctor. He was pale and lethargic, stumbling a few times in his ankle cuffs and slowing us down.

"You feeling all right there, buddy?" I asked when we had to pause so he could get through a rough patch of coughing.

He was bent in half, working up a lung, but we had to remain vigilant because prisoners had been known to pull fast ones and use situations to their advantage if they thought our guard was down.

"Feel like shit. Maybe if they didn't wait so goddamn long to give me medication, I wouldn't be this bad."

It wasn't uncommon for complaints of illnesses to be ignored. More than a few had played the system to get an unnecessary trip to the infirmary. More often, it took a prisoner to be on death's door before they were heard and taken to see the doctor. Another glitch in the system. Another example of the poor treatment of the men behind bars.

More than a few had died from untreated illnesses like pneumonia or cancer when they could have been helped.

We continued along, delivering our patient to the doctor and standing guard while he ran a few tests and fussed over the chained man. The expectation was that we were to deliver him back to his cell once the exam was over.

"I'm going to have to keep him here a bit, gentlemen. He needs IV antibiotics at this point."

We assisted the transfer to the secured ward for the infirm and chained our transfer patient to his bed. His gray complexion and sallow cheeks took away from the danger surrounding him, but even with physical evidence of his weakened state, we stayed alert.

The infirmary had its own unit of security, so once the man was moved and chained, we left him in their care.

Derrick radioed in the completed transfer and our location. We waited outside the infirmary for our next set of orders.

"Where'd you go to school? Michigan, right? Do they have a good college out there?"

"Yeah. It wasn't bad. Nothing special."

"It's cold there, isn't it. In the winter. You get tons of snow. I've never been to Michigan. Never been anywhere, to be honest. I met this girl in college, and she wanted to travel the world. Said I should go with her. Almost did, but it would have rendered my schooling obsolete, ya know? I liked her. Damn, she was hot in bed." He chuckled and shook his head, grinning like a fool. "Oh, the sacrifices we make."

"Yeah." What the hell was I supposed to say to that?

"Oh well, plenty more fish in the sea. Don't want to tie myself down yet, anyhow. Sew my wild oats. Spread the love." Derrick thrust his hips and wiggled his brow. "Am I right? Are you married? Girlfriend?"

"No. Neither."

"Better to roam free, isn't it?"

The radio on my shoulder chirped, and I thanked God for the interruption. "Transfer team one, we have a string of visitors signing in. We're gonna get you and team three on them as quickly as possible. Move your charges in, and then you can break for lunch. We'll suspend anyone going to rec until you're finished.

"Roger. Where do you need us first?"

"I have a section B, B21, and a section C, B40. If you guys want to take care of those two, I'll distribute the rest."

My heart jolted, and I depressed the button on my radio without further thought. "Roger that. We'll take B40 down first. B21 will follow. Heading that way."

"Dude, B21 is closer," Derrick said with a frown once I'd ended communication.

"Doesn't matter. Killing time. Come on."

I'd been waiting for this moment, and there was no way I'd pass it up.

By the time we'd moved B40 to the visitation room and returned to B-Pod, my hands were clammy with anticipation. My skin buzzed with every step closer to Bishop's cell. The minute we entered the row, Javier caught my eye. A warning passed through his eyes, a *be careful* and *don't be stupid.*

"We've got a visitor for B21, Ndi..." Derrick stumbled over Bishop's last name and passed me a desperate glance, looking for me to save him.

"Ndiaye."

"Yeah, him." Derrick thumbed over his shoulder at me.

Javier held my gaze and pursed his lips. "Yup. We got the call. Have at 'er."

Derrick, not picking up on the tension at all, skipped over to Bishop's cell and pounded on the steel door. "Visitor. Prepare for transfer."

I shared a long, silent moment with Javier. His worry sat on the surface as he eyed Derrick over my shoulder. "You best go help him out."

"Yeah."

We'd had a long talk about everything over the weekend. Javier listened and did his best to understand. I knew doubt lingered, but he'd accepted everything I'd shared and had stopped trying to convince me to back down. Whatever feelings for Bishop were growing inside me, they weren't hidden. Javier saw them all.

When it came to Bishop's innocence, he wasn't as easily swayed and warned me again about blind trust.

I joined Derrick at the window and caught Bishop as he removed his sweatpants. It wasn't until he stood naked in the middle of his cell that he noticed me looking in. Our connection burned hotter than ever. Flames simmered behind his onyx eyes, and my stomach grew tight, seeing him on full display.

It'd been weeks since I'd done a transfer with him. Weeks since I'd witnessed the polished beauty of his tall, dark frame. My control slipped—how could it not? Saliva pooled in my mouth as I roamed my gaze over the miles of smooth brown skin, caressing every inch of his body with my eyes.

My blood boiled, skin tingled, and had I been Derrick's age, the evidence of my desire would have shown in the form of a steely erection in my pants. Somehow, I managed to convince my soldier to stand down.

The draw to reach out and touch all that beautiful skin and map every inch of him was profound. My fingers twitched at my sides as my heart raced. In the distance, I heard Derrick instruct Bishop through the strip search, and only then did I realize Bishop was as stuck in a trance, watching my reactions as I was.

The power behind our locked stare was telling, and I darted my gaze elsewhere without turning my head. If I didn't garner some control, my secrets would be out in the open. It could be devastating for both of us.

Derrick took the reins as I'd been allowing him to do all morning. I forced my mind back on the job, refusing to notice how long and heavy Bishop's cock was as it rested against his thigh. My brain conjured fantasies of being intimate with that man, grinding our naked, sweaty bodies together, touching him, pleasuring him, and letting him pin me down and fill me.

I shuddered, and my breathing hitched.

"Dude, you all right?"

"What?"

"You're off in la-la land. I told you to unlock the chute and check his jumpsuit."

"Oh. Right. Sorry."

Slamming the door closed on my active imagination, I focused on my task. With fumbling fingers, I found the right key and jimmied it into the lock. When Bishop passed his clothing through, our fingers brushed. I lifted my head and caught the warning returned to me. *I see your desire,* it said. *I know what you're thinking.*

Forcing myself to remain in control, I checked his jumpsuit before returning it. "Clear."

Bishop dressed and offered his hands through the chute when instructed. I had my cuffs already off my belt, wanting to be the one to bind his hands. Derrick's confusion over our swapped roles showed, but he went with it, stepping back while I fixed them in place—hands in front for a visitation. The weight of Bishop's attention soaked through my pores.

Before stepping back, I chanced meeting his eyes. He blinked, long and slow, and the action said more than words ever could.

Out of his cell, I pressed a hand between his shoulders as he faced the wall, leaning in more than usual, taking the moment to absorb the feel and strength of him beneath me. Flashes of more fantasies tickled the front of my brain. I pictured gripping his chin and pulling his face around so I could taste his mouth and run my tongue along his plump lower lip. I imagined holding him to the wall and pressing inside him, feeling the surrender of his body under me.

I pinched my eyes closed and shoved my budding desires into a sealed box. My hand near Bishop's nape twitched, and I moved my fingers the smallest fraction, a tiny caress against his exposed skin. A tease.

Derrick worked Bishop's ankle cuffs in place and slapped my arm when he was ready to go. The fog that surrounded me gave the whole experience dream-like qualities.

As we aimed to guide Bishop off the row, Javier caught my sleeve and leaned in close, whispering in my ear, "You better take it down a notch."

I shoved him away, ignoring his warning, and we kept going. Derrick chatted away like Bishop wasn't a six-and-a-half-foot solid wall between us, and the way he acted like he didn't exist bothered me more than I could say.

"You like football, Miller? I'm a huge Cowboys fan. Can't wait for the season to start. I have a good feeling about this year. Cowboys are gonna win it. I suppose you're a Lions fan, aren't you?"

"Don't follow a lot of football, to be honest. If the game's on, I'll watch it, but I'm not hardcore."

"Damn. That's too bad. I was thinking of starting a betting pool here with the guys working The Row. Would you do stuff like that? Join in? I think you should. I might even host some Sunday game days at my pad, if my roommate is cool with it. I'll ask him."

Derrick kept talking, but I only half paid attention while I carded us through to the secluded visitation rooms used for guys on The Row.

Once Bishop was secured to a chair by a viewing window, I turned to Derrick and straightened to my full height, puffing my chest out and adding a touch of authority to my tone. I wasn't a higher-ranking officer than him, but I didn't need or want him second-guessing me if I gave him an order.

"All right. We're set here. How about you take off for a quick lunch. I'll do the same." It wasn't a question.

"Oh, yeah. I'm starving. Where should we meet up with after?"

"Radio me."

"Sure. All right. Are you eating in the staffroom? We could walk down together."

"I have to take care of some things first, but maybe I'll see you there in a few."

"Oh, okay."

He headed to the door of the secured visitation room, and I followed on his heels. I waited while he took off down the hallway and disappeared around the corner before turning back to Bishop. He was bound to the floor, still in a four-point restraint, but he had a crooked, shit-eating grin on his face.

"What?"

"You have a very dirty mind, boss."

I scanned the room and fought back my own amusement. "I have no idea what you're talking about."

"I don't believe that for a minute. You had a distinct reaction to whatever it was you were thinking back there. I felt it when you touched me too." His smile dissolved, and a wistful longing took its place. "You make me want things I can't ever have. It's torture. No one's ever looked at me the way you do."

Keeping my feet rooted in place, I swayed, fighting the pull to walk toward him. Close the distance. Touch him.

Since that one time Ezra had left me in the visitation room alone, I'd learned it was against protocol. Unless two officers were present, we were required to stand on the outside regardless of Bishop's cuffs, despite the chain attached to the floor. We were never to be alone in a room with an inmate from 12-Building.

Ever.

When Derrick had taken off, I was supposed to have left the room. Locked it. Waited on the outside if I needed to stick around. Those protocols and rules all turned fuzzy and non-descript whenever I was around Bishop.

My feet ignored my protests. My mind rebelled. I stepped closer, one measured pace at a time until I was close enough to reach out and touch him.

Hunger bloomed behind his eyes as he watched me, peering up with that steady gaze. He shifted his hands to his knees, the chains jingling in the quiet room. He was right there in front of me. No one was around. All it would take was for me to reach out and—

Bishop lifted his hands—together because he had no choice—and I reacted without thought, knowing only the burning desire to feel his warm skin against mine.

Our fingers brushed.

My heart stuttered with anticipation.

Palm to palm.

No reinforced window between us.

Our connection was light. Hesitant.

Dangerous.

Instinctively, our fingers weaved together, clinging, holding. Both of us watching the other. Neither of us daring to speak.

I shuffled closer yet. Our knees bumped.

Movement on the other side of the window caught us both off guard, and I launched away so fast I almost tripped on my feet and fell. Our link broke as a guard guided Bishop's aging grandmother into the room.

My lapse in judgment was brief, but it had serious implications if I was caught.

A flash of understanding crossed Bishop's face as I retreated to the door, letting myself out and locking it behind me, my heart bruising my ribs. For the following few minutes, I leaned against the wall with my eyes closed. Javier was right. I was being careless, and if I wasn't wiser, this would all blow up in my face.

I pushed off the wall and rounded to the window which gave me a view of Bishop's visitation room. He spoke with his grandmother, that peaceful kindness spilling from his core as he smiled and shared.

I knew I should go take a lunch break, get away from him while I could, but there wasn't a single part of me that wanted to. So I stood and watched, noting all his facial expressions and mannerisms. He gave his grandmother his undivided attention, talking and sharing and smiling a special smile that belonged to her alone. His love radiated through the room, dispelling the darkness of the prison and shining with a purity you had to see to understand.

When he was in this room, sharing time with this woman, all his troubles disappeared. They could have been chatting anywhere. A patio, a park, the local coffee shop. These weekly visits gave Bishop something to look forward to, an ounce of joy in an otherwise miserable existence.

I'd learned about his relationship with his Maw Maw, how she'd raised him and his brother. I knew how important she was in his life. Bishop didn't talk much about Jalen. He may have absolved Ayanna of blame when it came to his incarceration, but he hadn't forgiven his brother.

A thought struck, and I realized, the old woman visiting him hadn't come alone. Jalen would be waiting in the parking lot or be returning once the two hours was up.

Leaving Bishop to his visit, I decided I did, in fact, have something to do on my lunch hour.

Chapter Thirteen

DERRICK'S FACE LIT UP when I flew into the staffroom. He kicked the chair out across from him and waved me over. "Didn't think you were coming. Sit. I could use the company."

"I'd love to, but I have to meet up with someone. It might not take long, so keep it warm for me."

I grabbed my backpack, figuring if I didn't find Bishop's brother in the parking lot, I'd eat lunch in my Jeep—there was only so much of Derrick's young mind and energy I could take.

Curiosity made me walk fast. Adrenaline flowed through my veins as I considered what I might say to Jalen if I found him. I didn't know why I was chasing him down, I only knew I felt a sudden urge to seek out another connection to Bishop. Learn more.

In the parking lot, I shielded my eyes against the midday sun as I scanned the cars and trucks, looking for an occupied vehicle. I didn't know what Jalen looked like, but I wasn't shy, so even if I approached the wrong person, it wouldn't bother me. If he was here, I wanted to find him.

Sweat gathered under my heavy uniform and dampened the hair at my temples as I walked between rows of parked vehicles. Fanning my shirt, I was about to give up, surrender to the summer heatwave and go somewhere cooler when I caught sight of movement at the far side of the lot along the fence. A man leaned against a four-door, burgundy Pontiac Grand Prix.

His back was to me, but his dark skin and build were comparable to Bishop's. His black hair was buzzed short, and his shoulders were broad. As I neared, I noted he wore a charcoal gray tank top, a beat-up pair of Levis, and brown, steel-toed work-boots with the laces undone and tucked in the tops like he was too lazy or in too much of a hurry to do them up.

His head was bent to a smartphone, and he tapped away with both thumbs, a grin on his face that matched Bishop's perfectly.

"Jalen?" I called out when I was within earshot.

He startled and snapped his head up, brows drawing together as his smile disappeared. Confusion settled in. "Yeah? That's me." He peered toward the prison gates by the guardhouse and back. "Something the matter?"

He was slimmer than his brother but with enough muscles I guessed he worked a labor-intensive job. We were about the same age, but he had the air of someone younger.

I offered my hand and a friendly smile. "Anson Miller."

He shook, but the question on his face remained. "Jalen Ndiaye, but you knew that. Do you need me to come in or something? I told her I'd help her with the paperwork, but she doesn't listen."

I assumed he was talking about his grandmother, so I waved it off and stuck my hands in my pockets, aiming for casual.

"No, everything is fine. She's visiting right now. I'm a corrections officer. A guard in your brother's section. I thought you might be out here."

His body stiffened, and he tucked his phone into his pocket before crossing his arms. "Yeah? Here I am. What is it you wanted?"

"Yeah. I… He's mentioned you a few times. I thought"—I had no idea what I was thinking—"maybe we could talk."

He rattled his head like I was making no sense. "Talk about what?"

"Your brother."

If I'd thought Bishop's piercing glare was unsettling, it was nothing compared to Jalen's. He tipped his head to the side in the same fashion I'd seen Bishop do many times. His frowned deepened. "I'm not sure I understand why a corrections officer"—he waved a hand up and down my uniform—"wants to discuss my brother. If he's done something wrong or isn't complying with some sort of rules, then I'm pretty sure there are procedures to follow, and they don't include chasing down a family member in the parking lot. Am I right?"

My spine stiffened, and my relaxed demeanor shifted to a more defensive stance. Not that I sensed any violent intentions, but Jalen's bitterness poured off him in waves. It was reflexive to go on guard when someone grew indignant—too many years on the job to prevent the reaction.

"Bishop hasn't done anything wrong. I'm here as a frie—"

"Pretty sure two counts of capital murder is classified as *wrong doing*, Officer." He used air quotes for emphasis. "That's why he's here, ain't it?"

"Do you honestly believe he's guilty of those crimes?"

I met his unwavering stare with my own. Challenged him, dared him to lie to my face. It was brief, but his cheek twitched, and his gaze shifted away and back. No matter what Jalen claimed, the truth was right there.

"Doesn't matter what I think."

"Wrong. It matters a great deal. To him." I waved a hand at the concrete building housing his brother.

Jalen said nothing. He chewed the inside of his cheek, scowling, and pulled out his phone again, all-out dismissing me as he texted. He may have been in his thirties, but he was nothing more than a punk-ass kid in my books.

"Do you have any idea what it's like living on death row?" Jalen didn't lift his head, but I continued, knowing he could hear me fine. "It's brutal. You're confined to a cell that is smaller than most people's bathrooms. The bed they issue doesn't fit a six-and-a-half-foot frame like your brother's. The mattress is two inches thick at best. It's damp and musty and hot. The only window you get is a tiny slit by the ceiling that offers no light. You eat and shit and sleep in that room. There are zero luxuries. The only time you get out is to shower and go to your allotted rec time."

He continued to ignore me, so I stormed up to him and tore his phone from his hand, tossing it on the roof of the car so he'd pay attention. Then I got right in his face. "Are you listening to me?"

Jalen glared, jaw locked, nostrils flaring.

How could he not care?

I jammed a finger against his chest, unable to hold back my rage. "These men go nowhere without being strip-searched. They have no dignity. No privacy. Nothing. They go from one cage to another. They eat when we tell them, they sleep when we tell them, they breathe when we tell them. Now imagine living like that for fifteen fucking years, and imagine again being an innocent man who's been wrongfully accused. Think about that for five fucking seconds, you little shit. Remember it when you go home to your house, and your takeout food, and your comfy bed, and your phone, and your TV, and your freedom. That's your brother in there, rotting away in a cell. Does he deserve that?"

Jalen shoved my chest, and I stumbled back a few steps before catching myself. "I didn't put him there! What the fuck is your problem?"

"You're his family, yet you've abandoned him. You testified against your own brother? How could you do that?"

"I didn't have a choice! They subpoenaed me. They made me take the stand. I was sixteen, for fuck's sake. They asked me questions, I answered them. I didn't know they were going for the death penalty. All I knew was my brother got tangled in some love triangle and was in constant fistfights. His girlfriend wore bruises everywhere she went, and he yelled at her a lot. What the hell else am I supposed to think?"

"You told the court he uttered death threats."

"Because I heard them with my own ears."

"We're those threats made to Ayanna?"

"I don't remember. It's been almost twenty years."

"Think!"

"Why are you doing this? Why are you out here? You aren't a lawyer. You're a piece-of-shit guard. What do you care?"

"I do care. More than you. Bishop is a friend, and right now, outside your grandmother, I'm the only person he's got."

The anger leached from Jalen's body, and he turned, scrubbing a hand over his face and across his shaved head as he peered at the prison beyond the high fence. "Look, I've tried to make amends with him. I've tried to apologize for making him look bad on the stand. It wasn't my fault. I was a scared kid who thought if I didn't cooperate, they'd put me in jail beside him. They twisted everything I said. I know they did. I was there, but no matter how many times I tried to fix it, they shut me down. He got fucked over big-time. Don't think I don't know it."

Jalen turned around and stared at me through squinted eyes. "I don't know who you are or why you care about my brother, but coming out here and yelling at me isn't going to change a damn thing. I know he didn't kill them, and I'd give anything to tell him that to his face, but he won't see me."

"Maybe I can convince him to change his mind."

Jalen studied me, that familiar deep analysis stripping me bare. "Who are you to him? Why do you know about his case? About me? Why the hell do you care so much?"

"I told you, I'm a friend." It wasn't a lie. Jalen didn't need to know my feelings went far deeper than friendship. "We talk a lot. He gave me his case files. I've read it all. I know everything that happened that day and the years leading up to it. I believe your brother is innocent, but I'm scared," I admitted.

Jalen waited. Listened.

"They denied hearing his last appeal, Jalen. Do you understand what that means?"

He wet his lips as his thoughts turned inward. He nodded. "Means they're gonna set his date soon."

"Yes."

"I don't know what you want me to do about that. Nothing in my testimony was a lie. No matter what the truth was behind all those things I heard him say, he *did* say them. I didn't commit perjury. I'm his brother, and there isn't anything I can do to make them look at his case differently."

"I know, but there are a ton of things that got buried in that trial. Things they didn't follow up with. Things they dismissed. I'm a nobody and I can see the glaring holes from a mile away. He needs a real lawyer, not one of these dime-a-dozen, bullshit, court-appointed losers who aren't fighting for him. There is no way he should have been found guilty of those murders. There is no way Isaiah should have walked away that easily."

Jalen laughed, but there was no humor behind it. "And who's paying for this fancy lawyer?"

And there was the barrier. I didn't know how to help Bishop. This was beyond me. The only thing that might help at this point was a seasoned lawyer who dealt in hardcore criminal law, one who'd find a loophole or ask the right questions. One who'd stand their ground when push came to shove and fight back against the injustices.

But lawyers of that stature didn't work for the city. They worked for big firms and could easily incur costs greater than my yearly salary.

"Did you say your name is Anson?"

"Yeah. Anson Miller."

"Look, Anson, the system doesn't work for men like us." He didn't need to say it for me to understand he was talking about his race and social status. "The system works against us, in case you didn't know. If I could help my brother, I would. If not for him, for Maw Maw. Him being behind bars is killing her. I don't know if Bishop has any idea. For as long as I can remember, she eats, sleeps, and breathes for him alone. She talks about him non-stop, collects pictures for him every week, tells her lady friends and the doctors at her appointments about her grandson who's coming home soon. She's never accepted that he's there for good. Now her memory is slipping. Every day she asks me if it's time to see Bishop. Is today the day they let him come home? Every day, I have to explain it. She cries like the day they sentenced him. Do you know what that does to me? To her? He is her whole world, and it's me who's taken care of her for the last twenty years. Believe me, if I could get him outta this place, I would have a long time ago."

"I'm sorry. I had no idea."

"No, you didn't. She's sick. Dementia is setting in, and she's developed a lot of heart issues this past year. High blood pressure and some arrhythmia thing. They have her on medications, but getting her to take them is like pulling teeth."

This would kill Bishop if he knew.

"Does she live with you?"

"Yeah. We don't have money for home care or a nursing facility. I have to leave her when I work. And I'm gone long hours. I have a friend who stays a few nights a week who helps me, but otherwise, she's by herself."

"Shit." I kicked at a pebble and paced. Even if this family had money for a better lawyer, there were other places to spend it. "I'm going to try to find someone to take his case. Someone who knows what they're doing."

"How are you going to do that without a retainer? Are you paying for a hotshot lawyer?"

I didn't have money for that either.

"I don't know. I'll figure something out. Will you consider visiting your brother?"

"He doesn't want to see me."

"What if I could change his mind? He needs his family. You. If I can't stop this forward momentum, then he's ... coming close to the end." The words hurt and pinched in my chest. "Do you never want to see your brother again?"

"I'll think about it."

"I appreciate that." I held out my hand to shake. A peace offering since I'd come at him like a bull.

He accepted the offer, holding my gaze the entire time. "For what it's worth, I'm glad he has a friend."

Jalen pulled his phone off the roof of the car, and I dug mine from my pocket to check the time. I was late. My lunch had run fifteen minutes over. Why hadn't Derrick contacted me?

I gave Jalen a wave and headed back toward the gate, scanning my ID and pulling my radio from the holster as I went inside.

"D, where are you at?"

A crackle of static broke through before Derrick's voice cleared it away. "Staffroom. Waiting for you. Where are you at?"

"On my way."

In the staffroom, I found Derrick chatting with Ray and knew right away I was busted.

Ray's pale skin was sun-reddened, which made his freckles pop. I hadn't seen him since he'd returned from his camping trip, but it looked like he'd spent a good deal of time in the sun.

"There he is," Ray said, an edge to his voice that told me he wasn't altogether pleased with my tardiness.

"Sorry, lost track of time."

"Come walk with me, Miller. I wanted to chat about some things. Derrick, let them know your team is on hold for the moment."

"Yes, sir."

Ray patted Derrick on the shoulder and waved a hand at the door, gesturing for me to go ahead. This couldn't be good. Had that guard observed Bishop and me earlier when he'd brought Mrs. Ndiaye into the visitation room? A wave of guilt and nerves washed over me, but I followed Ray to his office, hoping it wasn't anything serious.

Ray's office wasn't too different from Warden Oberc's, minus the dying plant and crooked diplomas hanging on the walls. He took a seat behind an old, steel-framed desk and waved for me to sit across from him.

"How are things going?" he asked, leaning forward on his creaking chair, arms balanced on his desk. "You've been here a little while now. Are you fitting in okay?"

"Yeah, no problems. I butted heads a bit with Ezra, but you knew about that."

"Yeah, most guys butt heads with him once or twice. He makes his own trouble. How about harassment? Are these guys giving you problems?"

"How do you mean?"

"I read your file."

Heat swamped my veins. I knew Ionia had sent over all that information about the incident back home, but I was hoping Ray wouldn't find time to read it. This meant he knew about the attack back at I-Max and the reason behind it. He knew I was gay.

"Look, your personal business is your own. I'm not here to judge you or tell you how to live your life, but I know why you took the transfer, and I know what went down at your old job. As your supervising officer, it is my duty to ensure things are kosher with you here. We don't want a repeat, and this is a tough industry to work in if you're gay."

"Believe me, I know. I'm not open about it at work. Only one guy here knows. He's a friend."

"So you haven't encountered any harassment?"

"No, sir. I haven't had any problems. The biggest mistake I made back home was being forthright about my personal life. I won't let that happen again."

Ray shuffled and sat up straighter, his hands spread wide and gripping the desk's edge. "Anson, the reason I'm asking is because I noticed a lot of frequent shift changes with you. I went away and left a schedule, and when I came back, I saw you didn't work a single shift I assigned you. I'm not a stickler, and I encourage shift changes if there are legitimate reasons for them. Being harassed by inmates or other staff *is* a legitimate reason, but I have to know if it's happening so I can take action to stop it or build a plan to ensure you're safe so we don't end up with a repeat of what happened at Ionia. Why did you feel the need to re-write my schedule?"

Fortifying myself so the truth wouldn't show, I scrambled for a viable answer. "I'm a creature of habit, I guess. This whole move has thrown me off-balance a bit. It's a lot of new stuff to absorb and process all at once. Working a repeating shift in a familiar location helps. Takes the stress down a few notches. I didn't realize it wasn't acceptable. I apologize. I found myself comfortable with the nightshift and that section, so I switched with a few guys to keep it going."

"And your switch to escorting this week?"

"The night guys wouldn't trade-off with me. Escorting was the next most comfortable place to work."

I was lying to Ray like an idiot, but it was the best I could come up with on no notice. It painted me in a bad light, giving him a reason to question my mental health and whether I was indeed okay to be back at work since the incident at I-Max.

"I know this is a personal question, but I have to ask. Are you still seeing a therapist? In your paperwork, it shows Ionia covered your medical costs and was footing your therapy bills."

They were also fighting my case in court since I was across the country, and the three men responsible were being charged with assault for what they'd done to me.

"I haven't seen anyone since I left Michigan, but I didn't feel it was necessary anymore. I thought I was doing all right."

Ray shuffled a printout of the schedule around to show me and tapped his finger over my name, inserted into two night rotations in a row in the same area. Shifts I hadn't been scheduled. "This tells me differently. This tells me you're still a little uncomfortable."

I didn't know what to say to that. He was right. Evidence suggested I was anxious about working in different areas. My lies compounded it.

"It's not unusual for men to be nervous working with these guys in twelve. Their crimes speak for themselves. You've had firsthand experience of what kind of brutality can be thrown our way if we aren't careful. I get it. I don't judge you or blame you, but I am willing to put a call in to I-Max and get your therapy extended to cover you now that you're here. They don't get to forget about one of their own because he was shipped off elsewhere."

"I appreciate it."

Part of me thought I'd left therapy too soon, so it wouldn't be a bad thing to have someone here to talk to. The nightmares had stopped, but my restlessness and anxiety hadn't settled in the least. I ran daily and pushed my body to exhaustion so I could sleep at night and not think.

"All right. I'll get that done for you. In the meantime, do you have any outright objections to being scheduled in certain areas?"

"No, sir."

"If that changes, you come find me." He pushed back from his desk and extended a hand.

I stood and shook, hating the sinking feeling in my stomach, knowing my time with Bishop would be left to chance now.

My conversation with Jalen rang loud in my ears.

"If I can't stop this forward momentum, then he's ... coming close to the end."

"And who's paying for this fancy lawyer?"

Fuck if I had answers or knew what to do. My heart was in a vice, and every day someone wound the crank, and the pain grew. It was becoming unbearable.

Chapter Fourteen

THE FOLLOWING DAY, Javier informed me, Jeffery had been executed. His death rippled through the walls of B-Pod and left a foreboding presence in its wake. Every man in a cell knew their fate would be no different. One day, their number would be up too.

My nightmares returned full force that night, but instead of being chased by armed inmates through the endless halls of an abandoned prison, I stood by and watched as Bishop was marched off to the execution chamber. A silent observer in my dream, I was impotent as they strapped him to the stainless steel table and ran the IV that would be the port of injection that would end his life.

I'd never witnessed an execution firsthand, so whether my dream had any basis in reality or not, I didn't know. But the feelings and emotions it incited were as real as real could be. I woke up in a cold sweat with my heart racing, the images of doctors plunging needles ripe on the brain.

Every night.

Over and over again.

I had bits and pieces of time with Bishop that week, but nothing private. We'd been unable to talk or share more than a fleeting smile.

The following three weeks, I worked in different rows and didn't try to switch shifts with anyone, acknowledging Ray's warnings for what they were.

My research into Bishop's case was unending. I educated myself in criminal law and was put in my place more times than not when I phoned top-end lawyers and requested free-consultations on behalf of

Bishop. One guy laughed me out of his office the minute I asked if he'd be willing to take a contingency fee.

Late one night, when I wasn't sleeping, I joined a chatroom and talked privately with a law student who was more forthcoming and honest than anyone had been to date. We talked in hypotheticals—at her suggestion—since she explained she couldn't legally council me on a real case. I explained Bishop's circumstances—using a different name to protect his identity—and talked about all the things I'd read in his file that didn't line up—or at least to an amateur like me.

My untrained eye questioned the dismissed parentage of Keon, the apparent incomplete collection of evidence, the lack of follow-up when it came to Bishop's obvious defensive wounds that had needed to be treated in a hospital, and the testimony of a neighbor that seemed filled with holes. Lastly, the whole vibe that Bishop's attorney didn't fight for him.

She listened and asked her own questions. When I finished laying out all there was to know, she told me she had no doubt the right lawyer could turn this whole *hypothetical* case on its head. In her opinion, there was enough evidence of probable legal error and omission of evidence to make an appeal, but it would take some smooth talking to get a judge to listen considering being an eggplant attorney, as she put it, or someone who did jack shit to help their client could still be considered effective counsel.

So, I was back at square one. Bishop's best bet was finding a good lawyer who wasn't afraid to go up against years of potential secrets and lies. One who was willing to uproot all the mistakes from his previous trial while also shining a light on a public defender who may or may not have ignored or possibly concealed evidence that could have helped Bishop.

Perfect. Excellent. No problem.

Fuck my life.

It was the first week of September before I was scheduled back on Bishop's row. In the interim, I took advantage of the mail system. I revisited the used bookstore and bought Bishop more reading material—more classics and a bunch of my personal favorites I wasn't sure if he'd read. When I shipped them off, I included a small letter that revealed nothing about who I was to the team who went through the mail but would let Bishop know he was on my mind.

Bishop,
This is my way of taking you on vacation.
Getting you out of that dark hole for a little while.
There is much adventure to be had in the world. Someday, perhaps, we can explore it together.
You're always on my mind.

My scheduled shift was an afternoon rotation. I arrived early and paced the staffroom as I waited for our debriefing. Once it was over, I didn't waste time getting to the floor. When I arrived, Angelo gave me a rundown of the morning, explaining who was still at rec and visitations and any other imperative pieces of information I needed for my shift.

I was working with a guy named Sonny, who I'd met a few times before. He was the oldest officer on the team and had been working The Row for twenty years. I guessed him to be in his mid to late fifties. Not too far from retiring. His once dark hair was snowy white, and his eyebrows reminded me of Groucho Marx. He had a jovial laugh and a habit of sucking his teeth when he thought. I didn't mind working beside him but knew a twenty-year veteran might be a stickler for rules, so I had to be careful.

Bishop was having rec time when I arrived, so I set about orienting myself and performing checks that were required each time we started a shift. Jeffery's cell was occupied by a new man named Léon Kizer. He was of mixed heritage, pencil-thin, and a certified psychopath, according to Angelo.

During counts, I saw exactly why he'd made that analysis. Léon had the cold, emotionless expression of a killer. Dead eyes with an impassive, blank stare. Eerie stillness and a calm demeanor that gave him an aura of unpredictability. And there was something about his lanky frame and posture that threw up red flags.

He was always watching.

When I left his window, suppressing a shudder, Sonny chuckled at whatever expression was on my face. "That's an accurate reaction, my friend. Two weeks back, I worked a string of nights here. Watched that man pick a spider off his wall and eat it. No word of a lie. Wiggling and squirming legs and all. The man didn't flinch. And you know how big those spiders get 'round here."

"I should be surprised by that, but I'm not."

"We have an incoming transfer returning from rec."

"Cell?"

"Twenty-one."

"All right. On it."

I headed that way and unlocked the cell so it was ready for Bishop's return. The whole while, I hoped my eagerness wasn't as readable on my face as my reaction to Léon had been.

When the call came that the escort team was entering the block, I straightened and waited, glancing down the hall as they came around the corner. Mason and Jin had Bishop between them, guiding him by his upper arms. Chin down, he watched his feet as he shuffled along, so he didn't see me right away. When he was within a few feet of the door, he lifted his head and visibly flinched at my presence.

They brought him to his cell and pressed him against the wall beside it as they removed his ankle restraints. The entire time, his hot gaze remained sealed on mine. Once locked inside, they opened the chute and eliminated the wrist cuffs before closing it again and turning toward Sonny, who stood closer.

"We have one more coming up for this row from rec. Got a call that B16 has been granted longer visitation rights due to an upcoming trial he and his lawyer are working on," Mason explained.

"Sounds good. Let us know when you're coming, and we'll be ready with bells on."

Mason and Jin took off, and Sonny checked his watch. "Supper is gonna be coming down any time. I'll go wait by the doors and bring it in."

The dinner hour was ridiculously early for the guys on The Row. Three-thirty in the afternoon. It was a big reason why most of them bought extra food and snacks from commissary. The meals weren't sustaining, and there were long stretches of time when they did without. Like the twelve hours between supper and breakfast.

The instant Sonny was gone, I turned and was greeted by a familiar onyx gaze peering out of the window of B21.

"Wasn't sure you were ever coming back to this row."

I approached and kept my voice low, knowing everyone was awake and anyone could listen in. "Schedule is random, and my repeat visits didn't go unnoticed."

"Did you get in trouble?"

"Nah, it's all good." I glanced down the line of cells and back. "Did you get my mail?"

Bishop's smile grew. "I did. You spoil me, boss."

If only I could show Bishop the true meaning of spoiling someone. A few books I'd collected from a secondhand shop hardly counted.

"I want to talk to you, but I'm not sure how to fit it in without getting myself in trouble. I've been talking to lawyers, trying to see if anyone would be willing to take you on for a contingency fee. You have a strong case. There is no way you should have been sitting here for fifteen years. Those appeals your lawyer made in the past were bullshit. It's no wonder they didn't go anywhere."

Bishop shook his head and licked his lips as his eyes shifted back and forth between mine. I knew I was heaping on a pile of information, but there wasn't time for me to approach this topic delicately. I needed to jump in with both feet and hope he wasn't angry I'd gone over his head.

"You've talked to lawyers? Why would you… I can't afford—"

"I know. Don't be offended. I can't sit by and do nothing. This woman you have representing you right now is shit."

"Nancy. I know. She has about a hundred and one other cases on her plate. I'm the least of her concerns. My appeals go nowhere fast, and she doesn't see the point in wasting time and resources on a lost cause."

"I hope those are your words and not hers because I'll be having something to say about that otherwise."

"Calm down, boss. Those are my feelings."

"Are you upset I've been talking to people?"

He took a long minute to consider. "No. But I hate to think you're wasting your time fighting something that won't go anywhere. You have a life out there. Don't let mine suck you down the drain. I ain't worth it."

"I disagree."

The clatter of a lunch cart sounded from down the hall. To cover my ass, I slapped a hand on Bishop's cell door and called out, "Supper time," as Sonny came around the corner with the stacked cart of dinner trays.

"We'll talk more later," I said with my back to Sonny. "I met your brother a few weeks back while you were visiting with your grandmother. I wanted to ask you some things about him."

Bishop frowned but didn't question me, knowing our time was up. He stepped back from the door as Sonny wheeled the cart closer, poised as any other prisoner waiting for his dinner.

Sonny removed a tray and held it out as I performed the routine task of supper delivery—unlocking the chute and passing the tray through the slot. Bishop took it and nodded his thanks before returning to his bed and sitting with his meal.

It was later in the evening before I managed to steal more time with him. Sonny had taken his lunch break, and the guy replacing him for the hour chatted at random with a few inmates on the bottom level. I took it as a chance to do the same.

Bishop was reclined, reading one of the new books I'd sent him. I squinted at the cover, trying to read the title, and grinned. "I can't believe they don't have *Lord of the Flies* in the library here. I read that one in high school."

Bishop's attention flashed to the window, and his own smile climbed up his cheeks. "Me too. I remember how stunned I was they'd given us a book with such graphic depictions of violence." He closed the book and studied the cover. "Of course, that was before I'd read much worse. It's a good one to revisit. It's been a long time."

"Bishop, why won't you let Jalen visit you?" No sense beating around the bush. I was on a time restraint. Once Sonny was back, the chances of us getting to visit were slim.

Bishop's smile vanished as he set his book aside and stared at his hands. He didn't respond.

"He was subpoenaed, you know that. The questions they asked him were beyond his control. He was a scared kid and told them the exact truth, even when he knew it implicated you. He knows you're innocent. Why are you cutting him out of your life when you have such little family left?"

Bishop's large shoulders rose and fell with his breathing. The deep channels on his forehead remained. "I can't let it go." He shook his head. "I want to, but I can't. Hearing him tell the jury and the courtroom that I threatened to end someone's life haunts me. Hearing him throw my words back in my face, knowing how twisted around they were and how they made me look even more guilty, I just…" He trailed off.

"Bishop, you know he didn't lie. Yes, it was misconstrued, and yes, it was used against you, but he was a kid."

"That's just it. He didn't lie. I said those things, and what if… Some days I wonder… would I have killed Isaiah if he'd stuck around? I know I wanted to for months after. Maybe I'm no better than him or any of the guys sitting on The Row. If given the chance, would I have made him pay for what he did to Ayanna and Keon?"

"No, you wouldn't have because you're a better man than that. You aren't a monster. You're not like them."

"How can you be so sure?" He lifted his gaze to mine, pleading, imploring.

I brought a hand to my chest, placing it over my heart, and patted. "I feel it here. I know."

For a long time, we did nothing more than watch each other. Bishop with a mountain of guilt anyone with eyes could see, and me with a constant ache in my chest for the man on the other side of the locked door.

Bishop left his bed and met me at the window. He leaned his forehead on the glass like he'd done many times before. I wanted to copy the action, but the risks involved were too high, so I left my palm on the glass instead—reaching out, yearning for that contact.

"I wish, for one day, I could be out of this here cell. Just one day," he whispered.

"What would you do with that day?"

His fingers hovered over mine, sliding along the reinforced glass and curling as though to grab on to me. "I'd explore whatever this is between us."

I wanted that too. More than anything. Wherever these feelings came from, they were impossible to ignore. The draw toward Bishop was so intense I was willing to risk my job over and over again to be near him.

"I want to touch you," he admitted, the words almost lost against the barrier between us.

"Me too. Let me fight for you. Let me try to get someone to take your case. Someone better. I have no idea what I'm doing, but I'll do everything I can. Whatever it takes."

He chuckled and shook his head, his forehead sliding on the window with the action. "It's a lost cause, boss. My days are numbered. We need to accept that. There isn't a judge out there who'd be willing to look into the funhouse mirror and see the truth beyond."

"There is. I refuse to lie down and give up. You *are not* a lost cause. I'll find someone. Please hold on for me. Don't give up the fight yet."

He didn't respond, and my anger boiled because I knew he was already submitting to his fate. He had been for a while. I slammed my hand on the glass and spoke through gritted teeth. "Fight with me, goddammit. You get your lawyer to find something, *anything* that can be brought before the appeals court. Give me time. Please. You know as well as I do if they don't have something in the works, they will set you a date. Bishop—"

Giving up on appearances, I brought my forehead to his, our eyes locked with only a few inches of glass between us. "Please," I mouthed. "Please don't give up."

I didn't hear his response, but when his lips moved, I understood. "For you," he said. "I'll do it for you."

I'd drawn attention to myself. There were murmurs and people stirring. Voices calling out to me from other cells. Knowing I had to back away or risk problems, I left Bishop's window, realizing after, I still hadn't convinced him to talk with his brother. I'd save that problem for another day.

That week consisted of nothing more than passing moments of shared time and stolen conversations when no one was looking. It wasn't that officers didn't talk to the men behind bars, but it was hard to keep our conversations generic. We'd long since moved past that. When I wanted to watched Bishop create art with a small chunk of charcoal, I couldn't. When the urge to ask how his grandmother was doing arose, I tamped it down and walked away. When he read out loud from the books I'd gifted him, there was nowhere else I'd have rather been than propped up on the wall beside his door, listening.

He was right there, yet the distance between us was more vast every day.

The following week, I was once again in another area. Nights in section D. Javier was on morning shift in Bishop's row, but I knew asking him to trade with me wasn't possible. Because my sleeping habits were shit, I'd invited Javier over after he was done with his shift and offered to grill some steaks for dinner if he brought some beers. He jumped at the chance.

The daytime highs were still stifling, but the afternoon shade in my backyard provided some relief. A breeze rustled the leaves in the trees and cooled the sweat on my nape as I lit the barbecue and cleaned the grill.

"Hello?"

"Out back," I called through the screen door.

There was a clatter as Javier put beers in the fridge before joining me on the deck. He offered me an open bottle before tipping his own to his mouth and guzzling multiple long pulls. Chin in the air, he closed his eyes and sighed. "That breeze feels good. Fuck, it's hot."

"You should have changed before coming over."

He was still in his uniform, minus his utility belt and radio.

"I have stuff in the car. I will. Let me down this bad boy first. It's been a hell of a day."

"What do you mean?"

Javier chuckled and dropped onto an Adirondack chair, kicking his feet out wide as he slumped and scanned the backyard. "Relax, your boy is always well-behaved. You know that."

"He's not my boy. And that's not what I was asking."

"Bullshit. Yes it is. I imply a rough day, and your shoulders fly to your ears in a panic because you know I'm working his row."

I didn't bother with a response because he was right, and he knew it. Focusing on my beer, I adjusted the temperature on the barbecue and found a seat beside him.

"I was referring to the new guy."

My eyes widened, and I sat forward. "Jesus, he's a scary-ass freak, isn't he?"

"Right? Man, he thought he'd pull a fast one when we were taking him to the showers today. Got his leg hooked around Marx's and took him down. My grip on his arm was lax because I wasn't expecting it, and he slipped outta my hand before I could stop him. The guy headbutted Marx in the face at least three good blows before I managed to get Léon off. I pinned the fucker down and had Marx call in CERT."

"Shit. Is Marx okay?"

"Gave the guy a bloody nose but didn't break bones. He'll have some nasty bruises, that's for sure."

"What the hell was he trying to prove?"

"No idea. Some of these guys, it's a power trip. They do it to prove they can. I have a feeling that row just went from the cozy location to the shit show."

"Great."

I hopped up to get the steaks, leaving my half-empty beer on the arm of the chair. "Why don't you go change, and I'll throw these bad boys on."

I brought the seasoned steaks outside and set them on the hot grill, enjoying the sizzle and the hint of spices as they drifted on the air. While Javier was inside, I watched them cook and thought of Bishop, sitting in his cell. Alone. Always alone.

A guys' night of barbecued steaks and beers was something he'd never experience if things didn't turn around. All the small things I did on a daily basis stood out. From the wind ruffling my hair to seeing an airplane as it traveled across the sky. Choosing what I wanted to cook every night for dinner, closing the bathroom door when I had to shit, or kicking back with mindless sitcoms while curled up on a comfy couch when I needed to relax.

I didn't have to wash my underwear in a toilet or deal with one temperature of water when I showered. Nothing went unnoticed anymore. Everything was a luxury Bishop didn't have.

I hated it.

"Hey, remember that guy Melanie wanted to set you up with? The nurse?"

I startled and flipped around to find Javier leaning against the patio door frame, dressed in cargo shorts and a plain white T-shirt, shades covering his eyes.

"What about him?"

"Why don't you go out with him? See what he's like? Melanie can set it up. Apparently he's cute—her words, not mine."

"No thanks." I returned my attention to the steaks.

"Anson, this, whatever it is with Bishop, it's not healthy. It won't go anywhere. It's an infatuation. I think you should let it go."

"I'm meeting with a big-wig lawyer this week. Cynthia Bellows. She agreed to a consultation. If she feels the case is strong enough, she might consider a contingency fee. Apparently, innocent men who sit on death row for more than a dozen years like Bishop are entitled to a huge compensation if they are exonerated. So a win for her would pay out big-time. She's the first person I've convinced to at least look at it. I meet with her Thursday morning."

Javier sighed and came back outside, cracking a second beer as he lowered himself onto his seat again.

"And if she reads it over and won't take it?"

"I don't know. I'm still working on it."

"Anson—"

"Don't. I know how it looks. I know how it all sounds, but right now, I can't sit back and do nothing. Even if I can't fix it. Even if he ends up getting a date and… I want to know I've done all I can."

"And what if he's guilty? For real. What if this is all a lie for your benefit and he deserves this fate?"

"He's not. It isn't."

"Anson, you don't know."

"I do!" I snapped, my insides trembling. "I know you think I've lost my mind, but I haven't. Have you ever…? Shit, I don't know how to describe it. Have you ever felt like you were wandering lost and didn't know where your life was headed or what direction you were supposed to go?"

"I think we've all been there at some point."

"Well, Bishop brought me out of that fog. We have a connection. I think we're tied together, him and I. Somehow. For the first time, my future seems clear. Except, in the same breath, it's hanging on by a thread. If that thread breaks, not only will I lose him, but I'll lose what we were meant to have. I'll lose the one path I was supposed to follow. The future that once seemed impossible."

I glanced at Javier to see if he understood. The man's lips were pinched together, and the minute we made eye contact, he snorted, spraying beer across the deck as he laughed.

"I'm sorry. Oh my God, I'm so sorry." He kept laughing as he wiped a hand down his damp shirt and over his mouth.

"Fuck you." I couldn't help but laugh with him as I crossed my arms in defiance. "You're a dick."

"Dude, that was some deep, romantic shit you just spewed. It was poetic. I can't even…" He kept laughing, unable to contain it.

"I hope you snorted beer up your nose."

"We're tied together. I love him. If he dies, I die."

I kicked Javier in the leg and turned my attention to the steaks, laughing all the while. "I didn't say I loved him. God, you make me sound all sappy and sentimental."

"Dude, you made yourself sound all sappy and sentimental."

"I'm burning your steak."

"Aw man, don't wreck good food. If I can't tease you, who can? Fine, you've got all them gooey feelings for our brooding, silent giant. To each his own. I don't foresee this ending well."

Him and me both, but I couldn't admit that out loud.

"You wanna grab me another beer?" I asked.

The Adirondack chair creaked as Javier lifted off it. He slapped my shoulder and stood beside me a moment, both of us watching the food cook. "I know you're shutting down and don't want to talk about it anymore. You do what you have to do. I'll stop trying to talk you out of it, okay?"

"I made a pasta salad too. You wanna grab it? And plates?"

Javier sighed and gave my shoulder a squeeze before heading into the house.

Chapter Fifteen

THURSDAY, EVERYTHING WENT TO SHIT.

I drove the hour and a half to Houston to meet with Cynthia Bellows for our 8:30 a.m. appointment. I was dead on my feet by the time I pulled into the parking lot of Bellows, McNally, and Price Law Firm. My nightshifts and constant lack of sleep were catching up with me.

I was a few minutes early, so I sat in the Jeep and finished the takeout coffee I'd grabbed for the drive. It was lukewarm, and I cringed when the last mouthful was full of grounds. Popping the lid, I spat into the cup, scraping loose grit off my tongue and spitting again.

"Fuck. Way to ruin a coffee."

Before I got out, I checked myself in the rearview mirror to ensure I didn't look as tired as I felt. The dark bruises under my eyes were becoming a permanent fixture. I blinked a few times and patted my cheeks, urging color to the surface and waking myself up in the process.

I pulled my phone out to ensure it was shut off for my meeting and saw a text from Javier. He'd sent it right before he started work, and I hadn't noticed because I'd flown out the door in a hurry to get to my meeting.

Javier: This week needs to fucking end. I swear if we have more problems with 19 today, I'm cashing in all my vaca time and fucking off outta here.

I chuckled. And he thought I was a drama queen. I didn't have time to respond. It was twenty-five after eight, so I silenced my phone and tucked it in my pocket. Grabbing the thick file of information Bishop had given me, I headed inside.

Cynthia Bellows was a tall woman in her late forties or early fifties with a thick mane of brown curls that was dispersed with a heavy amount of silver. It was tied back in a low knot at her nape. She had yellow-green eyes that didn't miss a thing and seemed to judge every move I made, along with a sharp nose and severe cheekbones. She carried herself like a woman who knew she was that good, and she gave the impression no one pushed her around.

It wasn't often a person on the outside had the power to intimidate me, but Cynthia Bellows gave me chills the minute I met her. Her suit was tailor-made and fit her long, curvy form like a glove. Her lipstick was the same intense burgundy as her blouse, and her office displayed the characteristics of someone with severe OCD. Not a single item was out of place. Everything was neatly arranged and in perfect order, from the diplomas on the walls to her pens stacked in a holder.

"Mr. Miller. Nice to meet you."

Her handshake was firm and unyielding, her voice tight.

"Thank you for meeting with me." I sat on the chair in front of her desk and tried to look composed and comfortable.

She referred to her watch before threading her fingers together and resting them on her desk, pinning me with intense eyes. "We have thirty minutes, and then I have to run. No need to go over what we discussed on the phone. My understanding, we're talking about a fifteen-year-old death row sentence of a Mr.—"

"Ndiaye."

"Ndiaye, thank you. Your arguments are that there is possible indication that Mr. Ndiaye's constitutional rights were violated and that, to the best of your knowledge, exculpatory evidence is shown to be missing or was not followed up with in the proper manner during his trial. Is that correct?"

"Yes?" I didn't know what exculpatory meant, but I assumed it had something to do with my claim that evidence was missing or buried that could have helped Bishop.

Waving a hand, she urged me to give up the file. She plunked it on her desk and opened it, flipping through pages one at a time but too fast for a thorough inspection of facts.

My shoulders dropped. This woman was humoring me. She was going to take a quick glance, then turn me away like all the rest. I was never going to catch a break.

She paused a moment and frowned, gaze flitting over the page, then she kept going, flipping another and another. Without taking her eyes off the stack of information in the folder, she reached inside the top drawer of her desk and pulled out a single sheet of paper before sliding it toward me.

"I'll need that signed."

She flipped again. Squinted. Read a few parts and kept right on flipping. One after another. Flip, flip, flip.

I took the form and scanned the top. Consent for Release of Information.

"Legally, you and I can chitchat about this case all we want, but if I take it on, I prefer to get permission in advance before allowing an outside party to become too involved. If I should meet and discuss matters with Mr. Ndiaye, those conversations would be subject to client-attorney privilege, and I wouldn't be able to divulge that information to you without one of these." She flicked the form.

"I understand."

"Will you be able to obtain a signature?"

"Shouldn't be a problem."

"All right." She closed the file but kept her hand on top. "This is a lot of information for me to go over. Tell me in point form the specific areas where you and Mr. Ndiaye feel I should focus my attention."

Before I could open my mouth to reply, she held up a hand to stop me.

"So we're clear, this isn't me agreeing to take this case. This is me willingly setting aside a portion of my personal time to review it. *If* we have a viable and strong foundation for an appeal based on possible suppression of evidence or misconduct and *if* I feel there is a strong chance the appellate court will reverse and remand the final order, I will consider some varying methods of payment, including a *partial* contingency fee. But I warn you, that's a mighty big *if*."

I nodded, sitting forward, trying hard not to get excited. "I understand."

"Go." She checked her watch again. "Ten minutes."

No pressure.

I gave Cynthia a rundown of the key points I'd noted when reviewing Bishop's file. One of the areas that gave me pause and had me second-guessing included a less than complete forensic analysis. The pathologist's report talked about a lot of things I didn't understand, but there seemed to be scant follow-up questions by his lawyer that could have helped clear up Bishop's involvement. Why weren't they addressed? Why didn't a trained professional ask simple things my untrained eye observed? Also, the same was true with various neighbors' testimonies. The prosecution had a hand in making Bishop look guilty, but the defensive follow-up was once again lacking. It was like the woman had shrugged and laid down her cards, submitting without a fight.

The whole time I spoke, Cynthia took notes on a legal pad, her chicken scratch illegible from where I sat. Not once did she interrupt me or ask questions. When I finished, she scanned her notes and dropped her pen, pushing back from her desk.

"Okay. I'll review what you gave me and be in touch. In the meantime, get that form signed and ensure Mr. Ndiaye is prepared to go over this with me in full. *If* we move forward, *if* what you are presenting is accurate, it will be a long process for me to build a solid enough appeal the board won't dismiss it outright. They like to do that with these older cases, especially if they've done it once before. Which, I see here they have. That's not on Mr. Ndiaye's side."

She had an incredible way of making me feel hopeful and discouraged at the same time. I didn't know how to take her or where I stood. We shook hands again, and I followed her out into the lobby.

"We'll talk soon, Mr. Miller." Then, without further ado, she addressed her secretary with a few hushed words and hightailed it down a separate hallway, back ramrod straight and heels clicking in her wake. Then, she was gone.

I stood for a minute in the empty lobby, soft music from hidden speakers in the ceiling surrounding me, offering a false sense of contentment I didn't feel. If this was a fraction of what Bishop felt when he dealt with the legal end of things, I couldn't fathom how he'd stood strong for all these years without losing his mind. I was lost. Encouraged, yet sinking into despair at the same time. Was this meeting positive or negative? I had no idea.

Out in the parking lot, I started the Jeep and let it run for a few minutes while I waited for the air conditioning to leach the strangling heat from the cab. I mopped my brow with the bottom of my T-shirt, no longer concerned over appearances, before pulling my phone from my pocket. I'd missed two texts from Javier. Both had been sent while he was on his fifteen minute break.

Javier: Your boy has gone over the edge like I've never seen. You should rethink this love affair. No joke.

Javier: There were 4 guys trying to calm him the fuck down when I left for break. If I have to call CERT and do more goddamn paperwork, I'm kicking yer ass.

My blood turned to ice. No amount of Texas heat could warm me. Bishop? A call to CERT? Four guys trying to calm him? What the hell was happening?

I hit call even though I knew Javier's break was long over and he wasn't near his phone. It immediately went to voicemail.

"Fuck!"

My head raced. With a few quick keystrokes, I pulled up the prison's administrative line and called it. When the receptionist answered, I requested to be transferred to the emergency landline on Bishop's row. Those phones were rarely used and only in place for specific purposes. This wasn't one of those purposes, and I knew I'd take shit for calling it.

While it rang, I threw the Jeep in gear and burned rubber out of the parking lot. I was over an hour from the prison. Too far away to make any kind of difference. Too far away to talk Bishop down and try to help before excessive force got involved.

Dammit!

Someone who wasn't Javier answered on the fifth ring. I didn't recognize their voice over the phone, so I barked, "Put Javier on the line. Now!"

Commotion, yelling, clanging, and cursing came through the line in the background. I knew those noises. The CERT team was handling a full cell invasion and takedown. Bishop hollered like I'd never heard before, his voice broken and raw like he'd been screaming for hours and his vocal cords were reaching their limit.

"What?" Javier shouted over the chaos.

"What's happening?"

"Who the fuck is this?"

"It's Anson. What is going on?"

"Anson? What the fuck— You can't call this line! What is the matter with—"

"Answer the goddamn question. What the hell is going on? Why is he like that?"

"I wish I fucking knew. Seriously, I can't talk right now. Do you not hear the shit going down? Let me get this under control. I'll call you later, if I can. Do not call this line again, asshole. You want to get fired?"

"Wait—"

But he'd already hung up. I threw my phone on the seat beside me and pressed the gas to the floor. The US-69 was congested with traffic, but I weaved lanes and cut people off, refusing to reduce my speed. My head raced with questions I had no answers to. What was going on? Why had Bishop gone over the edge? If CERT had been called, it was bad. He'd either attempted or threatened suicide or gotten in a violent altercation with the guards during a transfer. Neither sounded like something Bishop would do. Not without a reason.

I tore into the Polunsky parking lot an hour later, glad I hadn't been pulled over for speeding, and thankful I'd managed to cut time off my trip. I dug my badge out of the glove compartment and ran for the gate. I wasn't in uniform, but I kept a spare in my locker. It was required on the floor, so I had to race to the staffroom first and change.

By the time I passed through the second crash gate that led to section B, an eerie silence had pierced the air. During the daytime, the echoing dissonance of 12-Building strained the air. It was never quiet. Men shouted, argued, and banged around. Such stillness at this hour worried me. It meant the CERT team's presence had struck fear into the neighboring cells, and the men had shrunk back to avoid being drawn into the mess.

I jogged the short distance down the lower level until I made it to the steel staircase at the end and ascended them two at a time. My boots hitting each stair and echoing off the walls told everyone in that row someone was coming.

Four officers occupied the hallway outside Bishop's cell. Javier and Marx among them, plus two remaining guys from the CERT team, still wearing their riot gear and holding their full-face helmets in their hands. Hearing my approach, the group turned around.

"What the hell are you doing here?" Javier asked, brow furrowed.

"What happened?"

Javier broke away from the group and planted a hand on my chest, guiding me backward and away from everyone else.

"What the fuck?" he hissed. "You can't show up here when you aren't on duty. What the fuck are you thinking?"

Ignoring him, I glared down the hallway, pressing into the hand holding me in place. "Let me see him."

"No."

"Don't fucking tell me no," I snarled. "What did they do to him?"

"They restrained him because he was losing his fucking mind. He made attempts on his life, and by the time the team got here, he was about this close to being successful." Javier held two fingers about a sliver's distance apart.

"Did they hit him? Hurt him? Did they spray him?"

"They had to."

"Fuck," I growled. I shoved away from Javier and laid a good kick to the opposite wall. Then a second for good measure.

"We're taking off, man," one of the CERT guys called. "Make sure to sign off on those forms. We'll take care of the other paperwork and make sure his possessions get stored."

"Thanks." Javier waved them off and waited until they were out of sight before facing me again.

"You can't be here. You're going to be in a mountain of trouble if anyone finds out why you came."

"I'm not leaving until I see him. He doesn't do shit like this. There has to be a reason."

"There was."

I searched Javier's face, waiting for him to explain.

Sighing, he rubbed his jaw and pinched his lips before reaching into a pouch on his belt and pulling out a piece of paper. It was folded but showed evidence that it'd been crumpled up at one time.

Peering back at Marx, he hesitated, then shoved the paper against my chest. "This whole thing happened right after mail delivery. This is why."

I unfolded the paper and smoothed out the wrinkles the best I could. My gaze dropped to the bottom of the page first to find out who it was from.

Jalen.

With my heart in my throat, I started at the top and read.

Bishop,

I know I'm the last person you want to hear from, but there isn't anyone else to deliver this news. On Monday, after I brought Maw Maw home from her visit with you, she went to her room for a nap, as was typical. The long trips in the car and the visits always make her tired.

Later, when she hadn't gotten up, I went to check on her. Something was wrong. She was incoherent and uncoordinated, and she wasn't communicating with me what was wrong, like she couldn't make the words. I took her to the hospital, and they informed me she'd had a stroke.

I'm not sure how to tell you this, but Maw Maw passed away Tuesday morning. I'm sorry. I didn't want you sitting around waiting for her to come visit you next week and her not show up.

I'll take care of her funeral and be sure she is put to rest properly.

Jalen

My hand dropped. The letter dangled in my fingers, threatening to fall. My entire being went numb. Outside noises grew muffled, and the beating of my own heart taunted me.

"Fuck," I whispered, more to myself than to Javier. Then a burst of rage broke through the fog, and I slammed my boot against the wall again, hard, crumpling the letter in my fist as I kicked. "Fuck!"

"Relax." Javier placed a hand on my shoulder, but I shooed it off and barreled past him. I didn't care what Marx thought. If he didn't like what he saw, he could take a walk.

Marx saw my fury and chose to back away, disappearing down the hall and leaving my unhinged ass to Javier. Wise choice.

At Bishop's cell, I peered in the window. The big man, the man whose sheer size and presence was so captivating and dominating, was curled up on his thin mattress, palms pressed to his eyes in the most vulnerable position I'd seen him to date.

My heart broke. The one person who'd helped him keep his feet on the ground all these years, his counterweight, his reason for fighting was gone. There wasn't anything I could say that would fix it. Knowing the way he'd reacted, the hoarse screams, the threats of ending his life, the attempt, I understood.

He appeared to be asleep. Every now and then, his big body shuddered with a hitched breath as though he'd been crying, and his body was still working through residual spasms. His skin was mottled, his cheeks damp under his palms, his jumpsuit twisted and sitting awkward on his body.

There was nothing in his cell. No books, no art supplies, no excess anything.

He'd been stripped to a level two, and all his possessions had been confiscated.

I leaned my forehead against the cold, reinforced glass and watched him as he slept. The urge to reach out and comfort him was almost more than I could take. He needed it now more than ever. But his solitary living didn't allow for personal touch of any kind.

"Go home, Anson. There isn't anything you can do for him."

I knew Javier was right. I wouldn't wake him. Not when his world had been destroyed. At least in sleep, maybe he could find peace.

Still, I couldn't convince my feet to move.

"Anson?" Javier tried again.

"I know. In a minute."

He sighed but let me be.

I experienced a raw moment of self-realization as I watched Bishop from the window. The entire course of my life played out like an old home movie inside my head, showing me every right and wrong decision that had brought me to this precise moment. Growing up with only my mom to guide me, my schooling, my initial confusion about being gay. Pride that came after when I decided I didn't want to be bound by other people's opinions or judgments when it came to my sexuality. Pride which initiated my leap out of the closet when I was in my first year of college. My first job, my first love, and the first time I'd had my heart stomped on. All the mistakes I'd made, and all the things I'd tried to do right.

Even the mess at I-Max that had launched me toward Texas and Bishop.

It felt like the driving forces in my life left me destined to find him. Destined to lose my heart to him even when I knew it wasn't a safe or wise bet.

Such was the nature of life. It was unpredictable and often threw us curveballs, but we rolled with it, knowing we were on this path for a reason, knowing, somehow, it would all work out in the end.

Except, with Bishop, I didn't have any guarantees.

I left 12-Building without a word to Javier. On my way to my Jeep, I texted the guy on nights in that section, begging him for a trade-off for this one night. He agreed, and the relief that rushed through me was palpable. Perhaps there would be consequences, but I'd deal with them when and if they arose.

THE DEBRIEFING BEFORE OUR shift included a rundown of the incident with Bishop—of course, they never once used his name. He was an ID number and a cell location. Nothing that gave him humanity of any kind.

I gritted my teeth as the CERT teams' intervention was explained and broken down, and I bit my tongue when they skipped over the reason why he'd become upset in the first place. When I relieved the afternoon officer in my section, he shared that Bishop had been subdued since the incident, but they were watching him closely for signs of potential self-harm. Despite a cell being stripped bare, the inmates always managed to find a way to off themselves if they were determined enough. He'd been given a sedative in the late afternoon and had been sleeping on and off ever since.

The afternoon shift cleared out. Doug and I remained; the night crew for section A/B.

"I'm not sure we should split up tonight. B21 sounds like he might need extra eyes."

"He'll be all right. If there's a problem, I can call for help."

I wanted time alone with Bishop. When he woke up, I wanted to ensure he knew I was there for him in whatever capacity he needed. Doug sticking around would hinder that.

"You sure?"

"He's knocked out good. I doubt he says boo tonight. He'll sleep that shit off, and if anything, he'll cause trouble for the morning staff when he wakes."

"Okay. Let's touch base more frequently, though. Don't be a hero."

"Sounds good. I won't."

We knocked fists, and Doug headed down the stairs, his boots echoing and fading as he went.

So I didn't get distracted, I did a count and checked in with the other men before focusing my attention on Bishop. Like that morning, he was curled up in a ball. He faced the wall, and the only sign he was alive was the steady rise and fall of his large frame under the thin, prison-issued sheet.

Unable to take my eyes off him, I stood by his window for a long time, wishing there was something more I could do. Not for the first time, I tried to put myself in Bishop's shoes. I wasn't sure I'd have survived this long if it was me behind bars, in solitary. It scared me when I considered what losing his grandmother might do to him long-term. Jalen was officially the only family he had—that I knew of—and I didn't know if they would ever repair their relationship.

Bishop slept for many hours.

Working through my nightly duties, I couldn't seem to shake the crippling grief surrounding me. My own sadness and pain for what Bishop was going through clouded my thinking and leached my energy. My processing and reaction times were cut in half—which was never good on the floor.

I hated our restrictions. I hated that I couldn't support him the way I wanted to. I hated the barriers between us the most and denying him basic human contact when he needed it.

All night, I checked in on him. Each time, he slept on.

It was nearing three in the morning, forty-five minutes before breakfast when I passed by his window for the umpteenth time and faltered in my step. All night he'd been curled in the same unmoving ball. He was in a similar position, but this time, a hand rested on the concrete wall beside his bed, fingers splayed over the portrait he'd drawn of his grandmother.

I paused, waiting for more signs he was awake.

After a minute, those thick fingers of his moved, caressing the cold concrete like he used to do to the viewing window in the visitation room. The blankets hitched with a shuddered breath, but I couldn't see his face because of how high they were drawn.

"I'm here." My voice croaked, and I knew the two words weren't audible enough to penetrate the door. I tried again. "I'm here."

His fingers stilled. There was a pause. He rolled to his back and lowered the blanket enough for me to see his face. Bloodshot, swollen eyes anchored onto mine—sore both from crying and the assault of pepper spray. So much sorrow and pain reflected back at me. My chest ached and pulled toward him.

I planted my hand on the window, rested my forehead on the glass, and implored him with nothing more than the beating of my heart to stay strong for me.

"I'm here." I had no other words. Nothing more to offer. *I'm sorry* wasn't enough.

My eyes stung, and I swallowed away the tightness in my throat, beseeching him to join me at the window, knowing he needed the closeness as much as I did. I was so helpless. So impotent. So heartsore.

He covered his face with both hands and remained on the bed, his chest rising and falling. He needed time. I waited. When he'd composed himself, he tried to sit up, the residual effect of the sedative giving him the shakes as he worked at finding his footing.

This giant, this titan of a man emitted such misery and grief it radiated outward, and anyone nearby couldn't help but feel it too.

At the door, he leaned heavily. With effort, he raised a trembling hand, and it joined mine on the window. Our foreheads connected in the only way they could. He closed his eyes, chin wobbling once before he tightened his jaw to stop it.

"I'm here," I said again. "You aren't alone."

"I can't do this no more." The handful of words left his lips on a choked sob before he once again fought to control himself. "I'm done. They can kill me now. Give me a goddamn date and put me out of my misery."

"Stop it. You promised. I'm not letting you go down without a proper fight."

He slammed a fist on the door, and I jumped back, startled by his sudden burst of anger. He did it again as he roared, "There is no fight, Anson. They don't care about me. They never have. I'm as good as dead to them, and I have been since the day they locked me up. I will *never* win this, you understand?" He slapped his palm against the door once more and turned away, pacing, body vibrating.

I glanced over my shoulder, knowing how far that kind of racket would carry.

"Calm down, or they'll be forced to sedate you again. Do you want the team called back?"

He whipped around and pinned me with raw anguish. "I don't care anymore. They can come and beat me into submission all they want, and I will fight them so it hurts more. They can spray me and kick me and stick me with whatever drugs they can find. I'm done, do you hear me? *Done.* They best give me a date soon, or I'll do it myself."

I needed him to lower his voice, or Doug was sure to hear and come running. So far, all was still quiet around me. A few murmured, "Shut the fuck ups," came from adjoining cells.

Thinking on my toes, the drum and ache in my chest trumping my good sense, I unhooked my keys from my belt and worked the right one into the lock on his chute. Bishop was back to pacing, too tormented to hear what I was doing. He scrubbed his head and mumbled to himself.

Once I'd slid the chute open, I called out, "Come here," as I presented one hand to him through the small opening.

Bishop halted and studied the offering before fixing me with an injured, confused expression. "Boss, you'll get yourself in trouble."

"I don't give a shit. *Come. Here.*" I put authority in my tone and refused to give in.

Bishop's breathing came faster as he approached. The instant our hands connected, another sob escaped him. He fell against the door and whimpered as his hold on me tightened. Tears escaped his eyes and left wet trails down his dark cheeks.

I clung to him, caressing my thumb along his hand. "Don't give up on me."

We explored one another's fingers and palms, savoring the connection for what it was, knowing it might be all we ever got. His hands were always warmer than mine, a little more roughened on the fingertips and firmer.

"This can't be anything. All this will do is hurt you in the end. I'm not meant for this world, and I'm not gonna be here much longer. Why can't you accept that, boss?"

"Because I can't. I won't." *Because there are things in my heart that I can't explain, and I refuse to leave them unexplored.* "I know you're hurting. I know this whole thing feels utterly hopeless. You loved her, but I know she would never want you to give up. She believed you were innocent. She waited every day for you to be released. Are you going to lie down and submit because she's gone?"

At the mention of his grandmother, more tears tracked down his face to his chin. He took my one hand in both of his, and his desperation for contact showed. He mapped every inch of my skin, his urgency expanding as he took his time touching me, holding me.

Bishop dropped to his knees and placed my hand on his face. The angle was awkward, so I crouched enough I could still see in the window but also have enough room to explore. I felt his damp cheek under my palm, his warm skin. Touched his lips with the tips of my fingers. They were chapped and dry. His nose. One eye, then the other—his lashes fluttering when I passed over them. Then he bent his head and encouraged me to run my hand over his shorn hair to his nape. I memorized all of it.

When I finished my journey, I rested my hand back on his cheek and tipped his face so he'd look up into the window.

"Don't give up on me. Let me be your strength. Let me be the one you lean on now."

His hand came up and covered my own, pressing my palm harder to his face, holding me there like he feared I'd let go.

No more words were shared. He needed this comfort, and I refused to pull away. When much time passed, Bishop turned his face to my hand and planted a kiss to the center of my palm. *"I'm with you,"* it said.

I closed and locked the chute without incident. Bishop found a seat on his bed because his legs wouldn't hold him up any longer. He stared at his drawing, lost in thought.

"I always looked forward to our visits."

"I know you did."

"She kept me connected to the outside world in her own way. With those pictures. Her stories."

"What if Jalen came now? Would you see him?"

"He won't come."

"If he did?"

"He won't."

There was no arguing with him, so I changed the subject.

"I saw a lawyer today. A good one. She's willing to look at your case with new eyes and see if there's ground for another appeal. A proper appeal."

He didn't respond, his mind lost in the past as he continued to examine the sketch on the wall.

"She might work for a contingency fee, if the case is strong enough."

"Why? Getting me outta here won't pay her bill."

"If she can get you a new trial and then wins, having you exonerated, she can also fight for compensation. Being wrongfully accused and imprisoned for almost twenty years makes you eligible for a huge lawsuit. You'd be entitled to a lot of money, and she knows it. That's how she'd get paid."

"I don't care about money or compensation or whatever you call it; I want out of here."

"I know, and she might be willing to fight for you. Get you out. You'd be a free man if she won."

He dropped his chin, breaking eye contact with the drawing, and turned to face me. "You'll forgive me, boss, if I don't get excited."

"I understand."

I withdrew the folded consent form from my pocket and listened again for Doug. Breakfast would be there any minute, and I knew that would be it for our time.

Unlocking the chute, I waved Bishop over. "I need you to sign this. It allows us to discuss you and your case. She said if she takes it on, she will be here to meet with you and go over everything."

He returned to the door and took the paper, scanning it once before nodding. "I don't have a pen anymore. They took everything."

I found one on my belt and passed it through the door. Bishop signed the paper and gave it back. With the chute closed and locked again, I tucked the form back into my pocket.

"I know you're trying, boss. I thank you. There aren't many people who would give a rat's ass about someone like me."

"They don't know you like I do."

A faint smile turned the corner of his mouth, but it disappeared almost as fast. "You make me dream things I have no business dreaming."

"You have every business dreaming them. I'll do all I can to make them come true, but I need you to trust me and not give up."

"I'll try."

That was the best I was going to get. I checked the time and sighed. "Breakfast will be here any minute. I gotta go. Think you can stay out of trouble?"

He nodded and glanced around his empty cell. "I'll try."

"Good. I'm not sure when I'll see you again. This isn't my rotation, but I'll see what I can do."

Chapter Sixteen

THE BEER TASTED SOUR—which was a direct reflection of my mood—and the music pounded in time with my headache. A steady, thumping bass beat from some new-age punk band I'd never heard of. The Friday night crowd at The Barrel was thick, and Javier and I had been lucky enough to grab the last available booth when we arrived.

"Quit looking so miserable." He shoved my arm, catching my attention. I didn't realize I'd been scowling into my beer.

"I'm not miserable. I have a headache and this"—I waved a hand through the air, indicating the music—"isn't helping."

We'd chosen this popular bar and grill in Livingston because Javier had been raving about it for weeks. We were both working the morning shift, so we'd shown up around five in the evening, hoping to eat and be gone before the rowdy college kids started their Friday night rounds.

"You have a headache because you aren't sleeping."

"I know. Too much on my mind."

Javier sipped his beer and eyed me, a look of consideration on his face.

"What?" I snapped when he didn't spit it out fast enough.

"There's been talk going around."

"Talk of what?"

"You. Bishop."

"What are they saying?"

"That you spend a good deal of time lingering at his cell. That you whisper back and forth a lot."

How would anyone know that? I'd been careful to ensure no other officers were around when Bishop and I engaged in long conversations.

"Inmates talk, you know. They listen. They see. They share. You aren't as sneaky as you think."

I guzzled my sour beer, refusing to acknowledge his statement.

"Word will get back to Ray, and you'll be in his office again if you're not careful."

"I don't care."

"You should. Maybe they don't know the truth about why you and he talk so much, but their suspicions can go in an entirely different direction, which could be damaging for you in a whole other way."

"How so?" I glanced toward the bar, wondering where our food was and what was taking so long.

"We've had officers in the past who've been suspected of trying to assist prisoners in escaping or smuggling stuff in they shouldn't have. There are records of it happening in other places. Do you realize how your actions look? You're so concerned about people figuring out you're gay, but you're ignoring the other vibes you're putting out. Equally damaging vibes, I might add. Career ending."

"That's ridiculous. They see us talk. They can't prove shit because that isn't happening."

A server weaved through the crowd with a loaded tray, aiming for our table. She set down Javier's burger and fries and my loaded nachos before unloading two fresh beers onto the middle of the table.

Once she was gone, I spent a minute dispersing the extra side of jalapenos I'd ordered all over the mountain of nachos. Javier bit into his burger and chewed as he observed me. Once he swallowed, he wiped his mouth on a napkin and sat back.

"So what's your plan?"

I picked at a hunk of ground beef and popped it into my mouth. "I don't know yet. I'm working on it."

Javier leaned forward, looking ready to launch into more invasive questions when my phone rang. Thankful for the interruption, I dug it from my pocket and checked the screen. It was Cynthia Bellows' office. It'd been a week since our meeting, and I'd been waiting for this call.

I waved the phone at Javier as I rose from our booth. "I have to take this. Be right back."

I aimed for the front doors and exited onto the quieter street. The evening heat slapped me in the face, an assault after having been in the air-conditioned building for so long.

I tapped to accept the call and paced to the corner near a lamppost, away from prying ears coming and going from the restaurant. "Hello?"

"Yes, I'm looking to speak with an Anson Miller."

"This is him."

"Anson, Cynthia Bellows."

"It's good to hear from you. I've been hoping you'd call soon."

"I've reviewed the file you brought me for Bishop Ndiaye. I must say, what I've read astounds me. I'm thoroughly baffled if this is considered a complete compilation of his trial. It feels like there are a lot of missing pieces, and that leaves me with a number of questions and a lot of speculation with regards to certain aspects of his case."

"Is there anything I can help with?"

"No." It was easy to picture the woman on the other line. Her straightforwardness and sharp tone were in line with the person I'd met a week ago. She wasn't one to beat around a bush. "I'll need to meet with Mr. Ndiaye and review the areas in question before I can make a proper conclusion."

"Okay."

"Here's the thing. I have what appears to be a strong case of due-process violations unless this file you gave me is missing a slew of pertinent information. Which it could be. Here's my offer to you. Based on what I read, I'm willing to meet with Bishop one time to help me fill in a few blanks. Should I still feel as confident afterward, I'm willing to consider a mixed bargain."

"And what would that entail?"

"I'd require a retainer of ten thousand dollars before accepting the case. I know that sounds high. Ordinarily, I'd ask for about half that. However, hear me out. Once that money has been exhausted—which I assure you, in a case like this, it will not take long—my firm will absorb the remaining fees based on a twenty-five percent contingency fee should we win. Remember, we are looking at multiple processes here. An appeal hearing, a full retrial, and then we'd have to file a civil suit to get an expunction which would wipe his record clean before the final goal of obtaining sufficient compensation for years unjustly served. Ideally, if this all goes as planned, I'd recommend filing a suit against his previous representation as well. This is no small case, Mr. Miller. We are talking about the potential for a large sum of money should the judge overturn the ruling. Twenty-five percent is a significant drop from my usual forty. Should we lose, my firm absorbs all costs above the ten thousand retainer."

Ouch. As much as I could see it was a reasonable deal, it was far steeper than I expected. I didn't have ten thousand dollars kicking around, and neither did Bishop. Jalen didn't strike me as the kind of person who would either, and if he did, the likelihood of him using it to help his brother would be slim.

"So, let me make sure I understand this." I pinched the bridge of my nose, staving off the steady throb behind my eyes. "Before you'll even consider this as a potential deal, you have to meet with Bishop first?"

"Correct. I'll absorb the cost of that visit provided you are serious about moving forward. For the record, I wouldn't be doing this much if I didn't have an inkling we were talking about a strong case."

"I understand. I am serious. I'll need to sort out that retainer, but I'll find a way to make it happen. When can you meet him?"

"I'll contact the necessary people and ensure I'm included on his visitation list, then I'll make an effort to stop in sometime in the next two weeks."

"Did you get the consent form I faxed to your office?"

"I did. After my meeting with Mr. Ndiaye, I will connect with you again, and we'll go from there."

"Okay. Sounds good."

"Something to note. These processes take a lot of time. I sense you're anxious to move things along quickly. There is no such thing in cases like this."

"I understand."

"I'll be in touch."

The line went dead, and I pocketed my phone, staring unseeing across the road for a few minutes while I tried to process our conversation. I wanted to be hopeful, but it felt too risky at this point.

Besides, if I couldn't shit out ten thousand big ones in a couple of weeks, this would go nowhere."

In a distant part of my brain, it occurred to me, I hadn't even flinched at the idea that if I had that kind of money, I'd use it without question to help Bishop. Maybe I'd lost my mind, but I couldn't ignore the connection between us.

If he disappeared from my life tomorrow, I knew without a doubt, I'd be devastated.

Back in the restaurant, I found Javier texting his girl with a grin on his face, his burger half gone in front of him, beer empty. I waved down our waitress to get another round and plopped onto the seat across from him.

He tucked his phone away and raised his brows. "All good?"

"Yeah. That was the lawyer I met with. She might take his case. She's going to meet with him in the next week or so to fill in some blanks before deciding, but it sounded positive."

"Pro bono?"

I laughed. "No. Are you kidding? Do lawyers really do that? I swear that only happens in the movies. She is considering a mixed retainer and contingency fee."

"How much?"

"Twenty-five percent."

"No, the retainer."

I picked at my nachos, delaying.

"Don't fuck around, tell me."

The waitress came and deposited a couple more beers on the table. I still had a full one, so I had some catching up to do. I grabbed a mug and swallowed a few long pulls.

When I set it down again, Javier's attention hadn't drifted.

"Ten thousand."

Silence.

Javier blinked, his brows sat so high on his forehead, his skin wrinkled. "Say again?"

"Ten thousand. Then twenty-five percent."

"You should have offered to sleep with her. Cut that cost right in half. You're a nice-looking dude. She might have considered. Wouldn't sleeping with a woman hurt less than forking up ten big ones?"

"What is wrong with you?"

"What is wrong with you? Are you considering fronting that money to pay for his lawyer?"

"Maybe."

"Do I have to tell you—"

"No, you don't. I know how it looks. Anyhow, let's say I do and she gets him out of there with a decent compensation for years served, he could pay me back."

"*If.*"

"I wouldn't be doing this if I didn't believe it was possible."

"Anson—"

"Eat your burger and shut up. I don't want to talk about it anymore."

IT WAS THE FIRST WEEK of October before I was on rotation in Bishop's section. It'd been three weeks since he'd received that letter from Jalen about his grandmother's passing and two since I'd spoken to Cynthia outside the bar. I'd heard nothing from her office and could only assume she hadn't been to visit with Bishop yet.

I was on afternoons with delightful young Derrick. How I managed to end up with him all the time, I had no idea. The one positive: he was easy to manipulate and order around. He acted as though I was of some kind of superior rank to him and ran around doing my bidding like I was going to reward him with biscuits or belly rubs. He was a good kid when he gave his mouth and lungs a break and he wasn't telling me about his latest *score* with the ladies.

By afternoon shift, showers were complete, but rec time was still being distributed. We had a few people off for visits and one down in the infirmary. Bishop was confined to his cell due to his behavioral restrictions—his rec and shower time were reduced by half for ninety days. I didn't have to see him to know he was miserable.

We had thirty minutes before dinner arrived, so we did our rounds, radioed in our counts, and confirmed a returning transfer.

I stopped by Bishop's cell after asking Derrick to run ahead and get the cage below open for the inmate coming back from rec. Bishop lay on his bed, hands behind his head, staring at the ceiling.

"Bored out of your skull yet?"

He didn't move. His gaze remained fixed in place. "You should try it sometime. After a few days, you're convinced you're going mad. You start hearing things inside your head. This is why I read. It stops the madness from coming."

"I'm sorry. It was a bad joke."

He tipped his chin forward and eyed me at the window. "Are you working here this week?"

"I am. Working with Tigger himself. Should be fun, fun, fun, fun, fun!" I sang the last bit in the same fashion the cartoon tiger always sang it in his song on *Winnie the Pooh*.

Bishop chuckled but didn't get up, his attention drifting back to the ceiling.

"Did the lawyer come and meet with you yet?" I asked, understanding he wasn't in a mood to be entertained.

"Nope. They told me about her. Requested permission to add her to my visitation list but informed me she couldn't come until this week due to my restrictions."

I hadn't considered that. "I have a good feeling about her."

He didn't respond.

Derrick yelled from the lower level, calling my name.

"I gotta run. I'll pop in here and there."

"Sure thing, boss."

I hesitated before moving away from his door. His entire demeanor had changed. He exhibited little energy or motivation, and I was disappointed he wasn't more excited at the prospects of a new lawyer. The truth was, I didn't know what it was like to stare at a ceiling for three weeks straight with nothing to entertain you.

SERVING FOOD COULD GO well or it could present challenges if an inmate decided they were feeling feisty or rebellious. Trouble was mostly reserved for F-Pod and the Ad Seg guys who liked to cause problems, but there was always a black sheep in the flock who surprised us when we least expected it.

Léon was determined to be that sheep. I'd been hearing plenty of rumors about the guy, and none of them were pleasant.

Derrick pulled Léon's dinner tray off the cart and waited as I went to open the chute. Before I got the lock disengaged, Léon lurched forward and slammed his body against his door, leering out the window like a predator sensing his prey.

I didn't step back or give him the pleasure of knowing he'd startled me, even when my heart lurched at the suddenness of his attack.

"Back the fuck off, Léon. You wanna eat?"

"I'll eat the meat right off your fucking bones, big shot. Go ahead. Open the chute." He licked his lips, eyes gleaming in the low light of his cell, wild and crazy.

I refused to entertain his taunts. "Back up or this chute isn't opening, and you'll go hungry."

He did the opposite. He pressed his face against the glass, licking the pane, eyes bulging from his gaunt face as he stared at me with a look of pure insanity.

"I guess he's not hungry," Derrick pointed out.

Léon slammed his body against the door again, never taking his eyes off me. "I know about you, *bosssss*. I hear things." He grabbed his head with both hands and hollered, "Like fucking maggots crawling in my brain. Disgusting. Awful. Putrid things."

With effort, I tamped down a reaction, the bubbling fear that Léon knew more about me than I wanted anyone here to know.

"He's nuts. What do we do?" Derrick asked.

Léon punched the reinforced window over and over. "*Boss. Boss. Bosssss. No! No!* You'll get in trouble. This. Can't. Be. Anything!" Léon screamed the last bit at the top of his lungs.

Then he went still. His eyes wide and lost in his mania but fixed on me. He dropped his voice, whispering, "But you want it, don't you? Don't you, *boss, boss, boss, boss*. You opened it. You opened it. Opened it. Opened it. *Opened and touched!* I know." He slapped his ears over and over, screaming again, "I heard it! I heard it!"

Léon kept yelling broken, incomprehensible words that made one hundred percent more sense to me than they did to Derrick. But his knowledge, no matter how hysterical and incriminating, meant nothing when spoken in cryptic code. The ambiguity painted him insane.

I slapped my hand on his door, yelling equally loud to break his raving chants. "Shut the fuck up and move away from your door if you want to eat. This is your last warning."

Léon's mouth slammed closed. His twitching gaze flitted over my face. Whereas I might have recognized that as a sign of drugs in other inmates, I didn't feel it applied to Léon. The man needed an institution, not a prison cell. I was no doctor, but this guy was certifiably insane, if you asked me.

Hands opening and closing, Léon backed up, a tick in his neck making his head jerk to the side at sporadic intervals. When he'd moved away to a safe distance, I brought my voice back to a normal level and spoke. "Now. I'm going to open your chute and pass you your tray. If I have *one* issue. One. I will not hesitate to call CERT. Do you understand me?"

"I know. I know. I know I know I know! But I have a secret. *I know!*"

My old stab wound burned, and I resisted clutching my side. His secret was my secret, and it was my worst fear realized. A guy like Léon was crazy enough to be a threat. Even without a weapon handy, I could envision him tearing my throat out with his teeth if he ever got the upper hand.

I shoved away the image, shivering on the inside.

When I reached for the key still dangling in the lock, Derrick tensed.

"Are you gonna open it?"

"Yes. He's been given a warning. It's up to him. Relax, kid, there's a steel door between us. The worse that can happen is we wear this tray of food."

"Great."

I opened the chute and took the offered tray from Derrick's hand, sliding it halfway through the opening and balancing it on the small ledge the lowered door created.

"Come and take your tray, Léon. No funny business."

He shot forward and snapped the tray from the hole with enough force, he slopped his soup everywhere and almost lost his drink. Not my problem. Once the tray was gone, I locked the chute and followed Derrick, who was making a quick retreat.

A faint singing from Léon's cell followed us. It was the nursery rhyme "Three Blind Mice," but he'd adapted the lyrics to parallel the growing relationship between Bishop and me. There were two mice, and instead of tails, he spoke of chopping off dicks and frying them up in a frying pan. It was unsettling, to say the least.

"That guy is not normal." Derrick couldn't take his eyes off Léon's cell. "I heard he killed over fifteen people. Locked them in his basement and mutilated them while they were still alive. Mason heard he always made a feast on the day he killed them. Ate his victims for dinner after he fucked their dead bodies."

"Don't believe everything you hear."

"You don't believe it?"

"I'm not saying he didn't. I'm saying, people around here like to embellish stories. It may not be accurate."

"Fuck that. You saw him. He'd do it. I have no trouble imagining it. What do you think he was talking about? He was taunting you, but it didn't make any sense."

"He's rambling. The guy isn't right in the head." It was my one saving grace. If people *did* listen to Léon's nonsense, it could be dismissed without causing me real damage.

I hoped.

What scared me was Léon knowing anything about me and Bishop. If he suspected I was gay or Bishop was gay, it could be catastrophic.

"You all right? Got pains or something?"

I frowned, realizing I was unconsciously rubbing my side. "Old wound. Aches sometimes." Like now. Although the residual discomfort was inside my head, it served as a warning, reminding me to be more careful.

Bishop took his dinner tray without a word or a glance in my direction. His movements were sluggish, and it took prompting to get him to retrieve it before I'd have had no choice but to keep it and let him stay hungry.

This wasn't the same man I'd come to know.

Dinner finished, we collected trays and received the rest of the guys back from rec, visits, and the like. Those men ate cold food once they returned. The evening was settling in, and our frantic duties were calming down. Derrick took his lunch break, and the guy relieving him wasn't too social. He volunteered to cover the lower half and abandoned me to the upper. No skin off my back.

I went to Bishop's cell.

He was exactly as he'd been when I came on shift. On his back, eyes glued to the ceiling.

He couldn't read. He couldn't do his art. He couldn't listen to the radio. Nothing. All he could do was lie there.

He refused to acknowledge my presence, but not for one second did I believe he didn't sense me standing there. He was too keen. Too aware.

Depression was a common symptom among inmates. We saw it all the time, along with a slew of other mental health issues associated with long-term imprisonment. Until this point, I hadn't seen a great deal of them present in Bishop. Today, he was despondent, lacking any spark of life.

I hated it.

Scrambling for something, anything that might help revive the man I'd come to know, I dug through my brain for a poem or a short story I could recite from memory. If I had a book—

I slapped over my pockets out of habit, looking for my phone. It was in my locker. *Shit.*

If I had it, I could have pulled up my Kindle app and found a book to read out loud. I was an avid hardcover collector, but I had a few I'd purchased in digital format that would have worked. But of course, prison regulations didn't allow me the luxury of a phone on shift. I'd never cared to this point, but today I was frustrated.

There had to be something. How many times had I read and reread certain pieces of writing? Then it struck me. Edgar Allan Poe. Bishop and I shared a passion for his work, and I didn't require assistance to recite one of the great writer's more popular pieces. "The Raven." I knew it by heart.

I admired the troubled man who I'd become fond of over the past few months and cleared my throat.

"Once upon a midnight dreary, while I pondered, weak and weary,
  Over many a quaint and curious volume of forgotten lore—"

Something in Bishop's demeanor changed. He hadn't outwardly reacted, but I knew I was having an effect. It was in the tension of his muscles or maybe the rigidity in his face. It lessened.

I continued.

"While I nodded, nearly napping, suddenly there came a tapping,"

"As of some one gently rapping"—he took over, his soft baritone floating through the air, warming my heart—*"rapping at my chamber door."*

We continued together, reciting each line and every word without pause, both of us having long ago taken this classic poem into our hearts, absorbed it into our skin. If one of us tripped or fumbled over a section, the other picked it up and kept us going. We worked well together, but I always knew we would.

With each verse, Bishop came more alive.

By the last quarter, he lifted his head off the bed, and we finished while staring deep into each other's eyes.

Once the last line was spoken, silence slipped in around us. My chest tightened with all the emotions swirling in Bishop's eyes and across his face. I had a thousand things I wanted to say to him but didn't know how.

"If you're trying to cheer me up, boss, maybe you should choose a less morbid poet."

"You like Poe, and they aren't all morbid." I chuckled and enjoyed the hint of a smile that stole Bishop's melancholy for a fleeting moment. It was something—better than the lifeless soul who looked ready to give up. "Besides, I was scrambling. As many times as I've read some books, I don't memorize things often. 'The Raven' is one I know well." I tapped my temple and winked.

"Me too." Bishop dropped his head, and he went back to staring at the ceiling. I was going to lose him again.

"Talk to me."

"I'm so lonely, boss. She's never coming to see me again. Every week for near on twenty years, I cherished our visits. It was the one bright moment in this miserable life. But that's gone now, and the hole in my heart is eating me alive. How many more years am I going to have to endure? Don't get me wrong, I hear you when you tell me this lawyer woman is good, but … I can't find it in me to hope. Not anymore. I eat. I pray. And I think. That's it."

If I could convince Jalen to come, maybe it would help, but Bishop wouldn't hear of it. What could I do? It dawned on me. It wasn't a solution, but it had the potential to cheer him up. What I didn't know was if it was permittable. Plus, his current restrictions put a small kink in my plan.

I wouldn't let any of it stop me.

As the old saying went, *"It's better to ask for forgiveness than to ask for permission."*

Javier was going to kick my ass.

Chapter Seventeen

I CHUGGED MY FIRST BOTTLE OF water dry and tossed it into the pail before snagging a second from the fridge and leaning against the counter to drink it too. My tank top was soaked and stuck to my back. Sweat trickled down my temple. I'd just gotten in from an after-work, hour-long run and was catching my breath when my phone rang.

I placed my water on the counter and dug it out from the pocket of my running shorts. It was after five in the evening, office hours were closed, but it was the lawyer's number. Cynthia. I swiped my damp hair off my forehead and answered.

"Hello?"

"Anson Miller?"

"Yeah." Too exhausted to stand, I tugged a chair out from the table and dropped down on it. "How are you?"

"I have a question for you." I wasn't surprised Cynthia did away with pleasantries. "I met with Mr. Ndiaye this week and gathered a full rundown of events, however, it wasn't until I got back to my office and was sorting through my notes that I noticed something peculiar about the consent form he signed."

Confused, I waited for her to go on.

"Are you aware if Mr. Ndiaye is right- or left-handed."

I scrubbed my face and squinted into the near distance as I thought. Did I know? His art. I'd seen him drawing many times. I pulled up an image of Bishop using his charcoal to sketch his grandmother's portrait on the wall. Recalled the few times I'd cuffed him and seen black residue on his hands.

"Um ... left. He's left-handed. I think."

"It makes a big difference. I need you to be certain. Mr. Ndiaye is on tight restrictions right now—which I'll be honest doesn't bode well for him and makes me more hesitant to accept his case—and he can't receive calls for me to ask him directly. Think, Mr. Miller."

I closed my eyes and pinched the bridge of my nose. He'd sat on his bed, facing the wall. It was the arm facing away from me he'd used to draw. That was his left.

"I'm sure. He's left-handed. Why?"

"And which palm carries the scar that is allegedly a defensive wound?"

"Same. Left."

"Perfect. I have a strong feeling we may have found our edge. Okay, here's the deal. After reviewing everything and speaking to Mr. Ndiaye, I'm willing to follow through with our previously discussed arrangement. Ten thousand down and twenty-five-percent contingency."

"This means you think he's innocent and can get him out?"

"This means he has a strong case for an appeal on the grounds of due-process violations—which it's up to me to prove. There are far too many gray areas in his previous trial. For example, the forensic analysis is incomplete. Whether it's missing information on purpose or was poorly done, I don't know, but I want to look into it and get a second opinion. For whatever reason, the full report is not filed, and I want to know why no one questioned it. I have my suspicions."

"Which are?"

Hell, if I was going to cough up ten thousand dollars—somehow—to pay this woman, it'd be nice to know what angle she was working.

"Which means this case could be as simple as knowing what hand the attacker used to wield the knife which isn't in the report."

"But that seems too easy a solution."

"It does. And it likely won't be that simple. There is much to be argued with regard to handedness. However, left-handed people make up a small percentage of the population. I want to say ten percent, but I'm pulling numbers out of the air. If the analysis proves a right-handed person wielded the knife, the state will say it doesn't exclude Bishop, necessarily. In my opinion, it does. True, I've seen arguable cases where an assailant intentionally used their less dominant hand in their crime, but the likelihood of that being the case is slim to nil. However, this omission on the pathologist's report does cast suspicion and gives an appellate court grounds to remand his case. Also, the fact that this information is missing makes me skeptical about a lot of things. How many more things are missing or incomplete, and why didn't his legal representation take action in this regard?"

"Is this all you have?"

"Heavens no. I have a list of about eight items I want to look into further. The main focus right now is to get the appeal heard and the case remanded so we can go back to a courtroom with this. The more things I can unearth for the appellate court, the better his chances of being granted a new trial."

"And you think you can get the appeal approved or remanded or whatever you called it?"

"Yes. But again, it won't happen overnight. If we want to ensure they reverse the initial court's decision and let us have a new trial, I need to bring concrete evidence forward. Such as this failure to provide favorable material evidence."

I absorbed it all, rolling it around my head, still unsure where I was getting the money to move forward.

"Do we have a deal, Mr. Miller?"

"We do. I'll need some time to come up with the retainer. Is that okay?"

"That's fine. I have a lot on my plate right now. I'll put Mr. Ndiaye's file on hold, and once we have a written agreement signed and a retainer in hand, we'll start moving on this."

"Thank you. You'll hear from me soon. I promise."

I hung up and sank back on the kitchen chair, dropping my head back and groaning as I stared at the ceiling fan that was doing little to cool my overheated body. What the hell was I going to do?

I'd picked up two extra shifts this week, which left me without a day off in sight. My best bet—and the only thing I could think of—was to touch base with Jalen to see if he'd be willing to help out. If he cared about his brother, then maybe between the two of us, we could work something out. It'd be much easier to come up with five grand than ten.

If he slammed the door in my face, I'd have to resort to plan B—which I didn't have at the present moment.

I shoved those thoughts aside and dragged myself upstairs for a cold shower.

TWO WEEKS PASSED BEFORE I managed to get a free day to drive to Georgetown and hunt down Jalen. Two weeks with minimal contact with Bishop. I wasn't in his area, but I'd snagged an overtime shift doing escorts and a morning shift in his section on the weekend, so we'd had a few stolen moments. Not near enough.

He was sinking lower and lower every day. Ninety days at a level two was a long time with nothing to entertain him but his own spiraling mind, which was also why I'd made plans to surprise him with something. The plan I'd thought up a couple of weeks back. Once this visit with Jalen was done and over with, hopefully, I'd have positive news to share and could bring a smile to his face.

Georgetown boasted a population of fifty thousand. I drove through the downtown's historic district, admiring the old buildings. I'd set my GPS to take me to the address I'd found for a Jalen Ndiaye. The five o'clock sun was low in the sky, a clear indication we'd changed seasons and fall was in full swing. We lost more and more daylight every day.

Ten minutes later, I pulled up in front of a small, pale-bricked, single floor home with an attached garage on the side of the house, and an overgrown garden that looked like it'd been neglected for a long time. There was a path that went to the front door from the sidewalk and a second that led around to the backyard, which was gated and surrounded by a six-foot-tall fence. A few sparse trees sat on the property, but they weren't big enough to offer much privacy or shade.

There was a white Tacoma in the driveway. Its tailgate was missing, and there was a large, unfortunate dent in the passenger side door. Beside it was the same burgundy Pontiac Grand Prix I'd seen at Polunsky the day I'd sought Jalen in the parking lot.

I got out of my Jeep and scanned the neighborhood. Was this where Bishop had grown up? The houses were set far apart, and the landscape was sparse and desolate. None of the dwellings were new. They'd all been built in the fifties or sixties, if I had to guess, and were in various stages of disrepair. It was a bit beat-up and rough looking compared to the neighborhoods I'd driven through to get here, but it wasn't like some of the places I'd seen back in Michigan as a teen. Every city had a place where the people with lower incomes gathered—I knew because I'd lived in one growing up. Those type of people made the best out of what they had. I had the feeling, this was that neighborhood.

Scanning Jalen's house, I emptied my lungs and drew in a cleansing breath, praying this wouldn't be a catastrophe.

At the front door, I knocked with a closed fist, ensuring the sound traveled since there didn't seem to be a bell.

When the door swung open, I was greeted by a man I didn't recognize. He was younger than Jalen, late-twenties, if I had to guess. He had a warm smile, light brown skin, and piercing green eyes. His black hair was spiked with gel, and he wore faded skinny jeans and a red T-shirt that formed to his body. He was thin but tall. Question filled his face as he scanned me.

"Hi. Can I help you?"

"Maybe. I'm looking for Jalen Ndiaye. Does he live here?"

"Yeah. Hang on." He held the door with his barefoot as he called into the back of the house. "J-bay, the door's for you."

"Who is it?"

"I don't know. Get your butt in here."

The man turned back and scanned me before noting my Jeep out on the side of the road. "You got a name?"

"Anson." Because it felt like the right thing to do, I offered my hand to shake.

"Drake. Nice to meet you. How do you know J?"

"I don't. Not well. We met once. I'm a corrections officer at Polunsky."

"Oh. Right. He told me about you." Something changed in his eyes. Speculation arose, and the way he scanned me a second time made me wonder if Jalen had figured out on his own how close Bishop and I were and shared it with this man.

As far as I understood, no one knew Bishop was gay. Not even his family. The way he talked, I got the feeling even Ayanna had been in the dark about his sexuality. He'd been young when he was arrested, at an age where he'd probably still been questioning it himself.

Jalen appeared from another room and stalled. "What are you doing here?"

"I was hoping we could talk."

"About?"

"Your brother."

"I believe we exhausted that conversation already."

"Things have changed. Do you have a few minutes?"

"Of course he does." Drake waved me inside, but I didn't take the invitation since Jalen had crossed his arms and looked ready to throw me out on my ass. Drake noticed his reluctance and rolled his eyes, a gesture that caught my attention because he'd done it with a dramatic flair that tripped my gaydar. Not that straight guys didn't roll their eyes with impatience from time to time, but it was his method of delivery and the way he dropped one hip to the side while perching his hands on his waist.

Jalen caught it too, and his jaw tightened. "Can you give us a minute?" he asked Drake.

"Sure." He slipped around Jalen, disappearing into the house, but he called out as he retreated. "When should I take the rice off?"

"Now's fine." Jalen wouldn't meet my eyes. A beat passed. Then another. "He's a friend. He's helping me go through Maw Maw's stuff." The defensive tone of his voice was all too familiar.

"I didn't ask."

"Whatever. What do you want?"

"Are you going to invite me in, or are we going to stand in the front hallway and chat?"

"I'm good here."

"All right." I hadn't expected an easy conversation. I shoved my hands in my pockets. "Look, I'm sorry for your loss."

"Thank you."

"Your brother didn't take the news well."

Expressionless eyes waited for me to go on, but I got the sense it was a ruse. Jalen was hurting inside but didn't want me to know.

"He's had a rough go," I said.

"That's nice. He didn't live with her and take care of her for the last twenty years, so you'll excuse me if I don't feel more sympathetic to my brother's *rough go*."

"She was no less a mother to him than she was to you. His heart is broken too. Unlike you, he doesn't have any outside joys. She was it."

"So, what? You came here to tell me to go visit my brother, is that it? I thought we already discussed this."

"That's not why I'm here."

"Well, spit it out. My dinner's getting cold."

Drake poked his head around the corner, surprising us both. "Talk, bay, we can nuke it later." Then he squeezed Jalen's arm once, and the man went stiff as a board. Drake retreated, and Jalen lost three shades of color.

I wanted to tell him I didn't give a shit if he was gay, but I'd learned over the years with deeply closeted men never to draw attention to their secret, no matter how transparent it was. The last thing they wanted was for their sexuality to be acknowledged by anyone outside their tiny bubble of reality. It was best to pretend to be oblivious.

To obliterate his unease, I jumped in with my true purpose. "I found a lawyer willing to represent your brother. She's the real deal. Top of the line. Amazing success rate. She feels confident she can have his case sent back to court. I don't know all the technical terms but something about winning an appeal and showing that his other lawyer was deficient."

"Okay. Good for him."

"I managed to swing a good deal with her, but—"

"Here we go."

"But I need your help. We need a ten-thousand-dollar retainer, but that's it. All costs over and above, she will take care of. If she wins, she'll take a contingency fee. If she doesn't, it's her firm that's out."

Jalen laughed. It was dry and sarcastic. "Ten thousand? And you're here because you think I can help? Buddy, we talked about this."

"I know, but this is your brother's life. This is the best and probably only chance he has of ever seeing the outside of a cell again. I'm not here asking you for all of that sum, I'm asking for whatever you can manage. I'll get the rest on my own. I'll take a loan if I have to."

If my personal assault case back in Michigan ever saw the inside of a courtroom, it would help. But they'd told me it could be a long time yet.

Jalen studied me. I could see he wanted to ask why I was so willing to help his brother, but he refrained. Bringing my bond with Bishop into the conversation would nag at his own insecurities, especially if I hinted at a possible building relationship. He'd know I was gay. He'd have to acknowledge his brother's sexuality, too, but at the cost of too much inner turmoil.

So he avoided that question.

"Jalen, you know he's innocent. You said so yourself. How fair is it to let him rot away in a cell when we have this chance to help him?"

"You say that like I have some secret stash of cash and nothing to do with it. Buddy, I work construction. Do you know what that pays? Let me tell you. It pays shit. If this house wasn't already paid for, I'd never be able to stay here. Thank God for small things. But I'm telling you, after I fork out money for utilities and my car and food, I have pocket change. The end. Where am I getting money for my brother?"

"J-bay?" Drake poked his head around the corner again and gave me a sympathetic smile. "What about the insurance?"

Jalen's body went tight again, and he wouldn't look at his friend. "Whatever, and house insurance. The guy doesn't need a list a mile long of all our—*my*—expenses."

Oops. Didn't mean to slip that out, did you, Jalen?

"Not that. Maw Maw's life insurance. Remember?"

Jalen grew quiet, his gaze shifted sideways like he was thinking, then he mumbled, "I forgot about that."

"Isn't it technically half Bishop's?"

"Drake!"

"Sorry, just trying to help." He brushed his fingers against Jalen's and ducked away again. It was meant as a subtle gesture, but I didn't miss the connection—or Jalen's reaction. The guy was sweating inside. Poor Drake was going to get an earful when I left.

It took a minute, but the tension fell from Jalen's shoulders, and he risked meeting my gaze. "He's right. Apparently, there was a life insurance policy. I've been dealing with a lot of shit—the funeral and closing her accounts and such. Tying up loose ends." He scrubbed a hand over his face, and I saw his weariness on display for the first time. "I forgot about it."

"And would Bishop technically be entitled to half?"

"I have no idea, seeing as he's in prison. I'll have to figure it out. They told me there was a bunch of paperwork I had to fill out to process it all, but I haven't had five minutes to go down there and see them."

"It would be helpful."

Jalen leaned against the wall and pinched the bridge of his nose. "I don't think we're talking about a lot of money, so you know. Maw Maw and Granddaddy didn't live too far above the poverty line. They got by."

"I'm willing to find half if you can."

For the second time, Jalen's gaze pierced me, that unspoken question on the tip of his tongue. Why? Why was I so willing to help his brother?

"Can I give you my number?" I asked, rerouting our conversation again. "You can call me when you've learned more. I have the lawyer on hold for now, but the sooner we can move on this, the better."

"Yeah. Okay."

He pulled out his phone, and we exchanged phone numbers.

"If..." Jalen hesitated. "If Bishop isn't entitled to anything because he's in prison, I'll still give you the money. Maw Maw would have wanted that. I wasn't trying to be a dick earlier, it's just—"

"I know. I appreciate any help you can give. He would too."

Jalen shuffled and glanced into the other room before facing me again. "You said he's not doing well?"

"He's depressed. Your letter was a gut punch, and he didn't take it well. Ended up getting dinged on behavior and is on a ninety-day restriction. Between that and his grief, he's sinking low."

"Will you see him soon?"

I smiled. "Yeah. I'm planning to visit him tomorrow. Properly visit, as in, use one of his slots since your grandmother isn't coming anymore."

Jalen cocked a brow. "You allowed to do that?"

"No idea. I'm going to anyway. I took some pictures with my phone and had them printed. Of my own neighborhood, my house, my poorly constructed meals, and such." I chuckled. "I know he always liked it when she shared the outside world with him. I was hoping to bring back his smile."

That look was back. Jalen shuffled. He knew the truth, and it made him uncomfortable. "Do you have a minute?"

"Yeah."

He held up a finger. "Hang on. I'll be back."

Jalen disappeared into the house. A moment later, Drake appeared, a wide grin on his face. "So you and Bishop, huh?"

I cracked a smile. I liked this kid. "I think we're supposed to be feigning ignorance."

Drake did the eye-roll thing again and waved it off. "Riiight."

"So, you and *J-bay*, huh?"

"I'm sure I have no idea what you're talking about."

"Of course."

"He's not doing great either. He tries to hide it, but losing Maw has been hard on him."

"I bet. She sounds like she was a wonderful woman."

"She was. I'll keep on his ass about the insurance policy. He's overwhelmed right now, but I won't let him drag his feet."

"I appreciate it."

Drake winked and slipped away when we heard Jalen returning. It was obvious how much he cared for Jalen.

Jalen returned, carrying a shoebox. He popped the lid as he came into the front hall, examining its contents. "I found these with some of Maw Maw's stuff the other day." He pulled out a stack of pictures an inch thick and balanced the box on his hip so he could thumb through them. "There are a lot here Granddaddy took when we were kids and some when we were older. There's even one in here of our mom, and a few random ones with our school friends." He held them out. "Take them. I'm sure he'd love to see them, but if you don't mind, I'd like them back."

I accepted the pictures and browsed a few on the top of the pile. My heart squeezed, imagining the look on Bishop's face when he saw them. "Thank you. But maybe you should take them and show him. Go visit. Coming from his brother would mean a whole lot more."

A shadow passed through Jalen's eyes. "He doesn't want me there," he whispered. "You take them. You... sound like you're close."

"We are." I conceded, knowing I wouldn't win. "Please keep me posted. Once we can get this retainer to the lawyer, she can get started."

"I'll figure it out."

We shook hands, and I took my leave.

Chapter Eighteen

"PUT YOUR KEYS, PHONE, BELT, loose change, wallet, basically all you have on you, in the bin and pass through the scanner." Blair, the officer in charge of signing visitors in and out, shook his head with a smirk. "You know the drill, Miller. Why am I telling you?"

Grinning, I emptied my pockets and dropped everything into the plastic bin before waiting for him to wave me through the scanner.

On the other side, he pushed paperwork my way, and I filled out all the information they required before I could go into the visitation room.

Unbeknownst to Bishop, I'd added myself to his visitor list and told them to tell him it was his lawyer visiting him today. It was supposed to be a surprise. I couldn't wait to see the look on his face.

"Did you get permission for this?"

"Do I need it?"

"No clue, man. Never had an officer come visit an inmate before unless they're family."

"Can I take these in?" I picked up a plastic baggie with a stack of photos inside.

Blair took them and turned them over in his hand. "Yup, no problem." He handed them back. "You get one hour maximum since he's on a restricted list."

"I understand."

"Through this door, remain seated the entire time, and use the phone receiver located on your right. Any excess volume, yelling, or arguing will result in a shortened visit."

I nodded as Blair opened the door for me to enter. It was odd being on this side of things. The room was small and stuffy. Air circulation in the entire building was poor. Bishop was waiting on the other side of the plexiglass window, head down as he toyed with his hands, chains linked around his wrists. His escort had already left.

My entrance made him lift his head, and he flinched, his eyes widening when I walked closer and took my seat across from him. I lifted the receiver off the wall and gestured for him to do the same. He was stunned immobile and hadn't moved.

With two hands together, he reached for the handset and tucked it between his ear and shoulder, tipping his head to the side so he could keep it there and have his hands free. "Boss?"

"I think maybe you should start calling me Anson."

"What are you doing here?"

"Visiting a friend. Objections?"

"No, no. Not at all. I'm surprised."

"Good. That was the idea."

He peered around, noting the cameras before looking back.

"Same as everywhere else. They record, but no one watches them unless there is a need."

"I know, but you being here can't be wise, boss. They'll hear of it and want to know what's going on. They'll pull these up and watch them. Listen."

"I thought of that. I don't care. We *are* friends, aren't we? There are no rules saying I can't be your friend."

We both knew it was more. How much more was the question. We hadn't discussed our feelings, nor could we without risks.

"How've you been?" I asked.

"It's been hard. Lonely. How about you?"

"I'm doing all right. Work too much, don't sleep enough, story of my life."

A smile teased his mouth. I liked it and wanted more.

"I have something to show you." I patted the baggie I'd laid on the table in front of the window. "Wanna see?"

He eyed the package of photographs. "What'd you bring?"

I pulled the stack of pictures out and held them so they faced me and not him. "Don't be upset, but I went and saw Jalen. I had some stuff to discuss with him. About the lawyer. Anyhow, he gave me these to bring to you. He thought you might enjoy them."

A few mixed emotions passed through Bishop, but his curiosity won, and he nodded at the bundle in my hands. "Show me."

"Okay, but you'll have to help me out because I want as many details and as much story as you can give me."

I picked the one off the top. It depicted the two brothers sitting on a low stone wall that rounded a garden, bursting with color. It was summertime, and they both wore elastic-topped beige shorts and plain T-shirts. Both grinned wide at the person taking the picture. Bishop was about ten, and Jalen looked to be around four years old.

I turned it around and held it to the window like I'd seen his grandmother do on past visits.

Bishop's eyes roamed the picture for a minute, his lips parted, gaze lost in the past. "That's the butterfly garden. Granddaddy used to take us there on weekends when we were little. Get us outta Maw Maw's hair for a while. It cost pennies to walk around, and when we were done, he'd take us to this huge park across the street. It had the most amazing twirling slide." He lifted his chained hands and touched it through the plexiglass. "We're so little."

"You were a cute kid."

Bishop chuckled, but his eyes never left the photograph. "I was a bully. Never stopped pushing Jalen around. He pestered me to no end. Always tried to copy me and followed me everywhere I went. Made me crazy."

"He admired his big brother."

"I guess. I don't know why."

I set the picture down and picked the second off the pile. Two boys again, this time with their faces painted, both like Spiderman. They wore costumes and held pillowcases in their hands.

"Halloween," Bishop said, eyes shining as he took it in. "I was thirteen in that picture. I remember. Maw Maw told me if I wanted to go out trick-or-treating that year, I had to take my brother. Jalen was seven. If I refused, I wasn't allowed to go because boys of thirteen were too old for that. So I agreed."

"And of course, Jalen wanted the same costume as you?"

"Yup. I pretended to be annoyed with him all night, but in truth, we had a lot of fun. The house on the corner was giving out full-sized candy bars. We were so ecstatic we hid behind the neighbor's car and ate them before going home again. Maw Maw would have had a cow if she knew. She was a stickler for inspecting our candy. And Granddaddy used to take the good stuff and tell us it was poisoned and only he could eat it because he was immune."

I laughed. "And you believed him?"

"Hell no, that man was a thief with a wicked sweet tooth."

The next picture was the two boys and an older man. They sat on a couch, Bishop to the man's left while Jalen sat on the old man's lap. The boys were in pajamas, and the man was reading them a story.

Bishop's eyes softened, and he traced a finger over the three people. "That's my granddaddy. He read to us before bed sometimes when Maw Maw needed a break. Mostly it was all Dr. Seuss because that was what Jalen chose, but after Maw Maw put Jalen to bed, we shared the more grown-up books, taking turns reading out loud."

He tapped the glass over the picture. "I'm about twelve here. We read all kinds of chapter books and made the pictures in our heads. That's when I read *Treasure Island* for the first time."

"My mom used to read with me too. Not every night, but sometimes."

We went through each picture one at a time, and Bishop shared more and more about his past. The weight of his confinement left him, his eyes shone, and he smiled more. The somber tone in his voice disappeared. It may have been a simple gesture, bringing pictures, but it was everything to him. It took him away for a little while. Allowed him to be free.

A few times, I caught myself admiring Bishop and soaking up the tone of his voice, missing the details of the tales he told. He was captivating and handsome. Distracting when he smiled. It pulled in my chest and warmed my blood.

Three-quarters of the way through the stack of pictures, we came across a teenaged Bishop, all arms and legs and sitting on top of a picnic table beside a girl with curly dark hair that fell past her shoulders. The way she looked at him left no question as to who the teenaged girl was.

"That's Ayanna," he said, his voice near a whisper. A furrow appeared in his brow, and he retracted his hands from the plexiglass like he was afraid to touch her.

"She's beautiful." It wasn't a lie. She was a pretty thing.

"That was before Keon. Before…"

Before she was raped, I thought, finishing his sentence in my head when he couldn't. It was before Bishop's life took a drastic turn.

"We were dating then. I'd invited her over for dinner. Maw Maw said I should because that's what boyfriends did. That picnic table was where we were sitting when she first kissed me. Not that day, a different day, but I damn near fell off the end of it when it happened. Didn't see it coming and jerked away in surprise. Boy, was she angry with me for ruining our first kiss." He chuckled, but it was filled with sadness.

Sensing he didn't want to linger on memories of Ayanna, I skipped through a few pictures, setting them aside. Bishop didn't argue. He had enough darkness in his life. The mood had been light and happy, and I wanted to bring us back on track.

Once I'd exhausted all the pictures Jalen had given me, I came to the few I'd taken on my own. They seemed trivial in comparison, and I was about to shove them away when Bishop asked, "What's those ones?"

Warmth climbed up my neck and over my ears. I shuffled on my seat, readjusting the receiver and scrambling for an explanation. "Um… They're a few I took. Before I went to see Jalen, I thought I'd collect pictures of my neighborhood and daily life, like your grandmother did, so I could show you. They're stupid. Don't worry about them."

"Can I see them?"

"Oh. Yeah. Okay. Sure."

There were only twelve in total. I showed Bishop one at a time, explaining each.

"This is my house. It was a shithole when I bought it. Rundown and falling apart. I've been working on making it nice. I've painted, done some work in the kitchen and a bit in the bathroom upstairs. It needs a lot more love. New windows. Floors." There were seven pictures that gave him a modified tour. Two were of the outside, and the rest depicted the interior. The front of the house from the street, the living room, kitchen, front hallway, backyard deck with the barbecue, my creaky old staircase, and—

"Is that your bedroom?"

Butterflies danced in my stomach. "Yeah." I didn't tell him I'd tidied and smoothed the covers over the bed and made sure it looked appealing before snapping the shot. How neurotic. And why was I concerned about what he thought of my bedroom?

His attention was rapt, so I held it to the glass longer as he mapped out every square inch. Once, his tongue poked out and wet his lips. My nerves mounted with each passing second.

How many times had I envisioned having Bishop in my room, on my bed? How many times had I jerked off with him in mind as I imagined him pressing me into the mattress and claiming me from behind?

His pupils were more blown than before, and I wondered if he'd thought the same things. The vision of him masturbating was never far from my mind, and I'd used it to get off more times than I could count. It hadn't happened again, but a small part of me wouldn't be sad if I stumbled upon the scene a second time.

"You have a nice bookshelf. Lots of books."

"Yeah." My voice croaked, and I cleared my throat. Books. We were going to focus on the books. Right. Yes. I could do that.

"Been collecting for a long time."

"I'd love to gander your library."

"I'd love to show you."

He lingered another minute on the picture before his focus turned to one I'd put down. "Have you fired up that grill lately?"

"I haven't. I'll have to do that soon. Been hankering for a nice steak."

Bishop licked his lips again, this time like he was tasting the flavors. "You tell me all about it when you do."

"I will."

There was silence between us as I tucked the pictures back inside the plastic bag. Our time was running out, but I hoped to come back in a couple of weeks for another uninterrupted session where we could chat and visit and not have to worry about other people as much.

"Anson?"

I set the pictures aside. "Yeah?"

"Where will I go? What will I do? I mean ... if they do let me out of here, I don't have a place in the world anymore. I don't belong out there. I wouldn't know where to begin. Or how."

It was the first time he'd talked about hope for the future. I studied his face and leaned closer to the glass. Knowing there was a high probability our session would be reviewed, I didn't want to shed light on our deeper bond. As much as I wanted to touch the glass, seek his fingers, and have them close to mine, I refrained.

"You'd come home with me, if you wanted. You're welcome at my house. There is a spare room. I'd do all I could to help you readjust. I'd help you find work, if you wanted, or a place to stay that was your own. Help you get back on your feet."

It was a future he struggled to picture. The proof was written all over his face. He couldn't imagine a day that would ever happen. The world I spoke of was an illusion.

He didn't respond.

"Look, I didn't want to talk technicalities, but I want you to know, Jalen is going to work with me on securing this lawyer. She's good, Bishop. These might be nothing more than fantasies to you, but if I have my say, they will be your reality. You'll see. Have faith. I'll do everything in my power to get you out."

Bishop frowned as he absorbed my words. "What all did you tell Jalen? About ... you and me."

"That we're friends. Whatever assumptions he draws from that are nothing more than that. Assumptions."

I didn't tell Bishop I suspected Jalen knew, but I also didn't tell him his brother was deep in his own closet either. It was between them to work it out.

"Will you hide who you are when you get out?" I asked.

"If. *If* I get out."

"Will you?"

"I don't know. It's hard to imagine another life. In here, there is no doubt that secrets will save your ass. On the outside ... it's different. I'd like to think I'd take my freedom on every level if it was given to me."

"Something to consider."

But it was too abstract for him; I could see it in his eyes.

A pounding on the door behind me was followed by Blair poking his head in. "Time's up. Say your goodbyes."

At the same moment, two officers came through on Bishop's side to collect him. Jin and Sonny. We got the expected odd looks, but neither man said a thing.

There was no intimate goodbye. No words of longing that were on the tips of both our tongues. Our silent exchange said all we couldn't. Bishop did that long blink thing I'd seen before, and it was full of affection. I returned it, letting him know I understood.

I hung up the receiver on my end. Bishop was relieved of his receiver, and the men in charge unchained him from the floor.

Then, he was gone.

Was it stupid to hope? Maybe. But I had no other choice. I wasn't about to give up.

"DID YOU EVER THINK MAYBE it's the thrill of him being inaccessible that turns your crank? You like the secret fantasy of fucking a killer? Or maybe you have a fetish of being overpowered and made to comply with a violent man's standards. Or maybe—"

I threw a pillow at Javier's head, shutting him up and making him almost spill his beer. He laughed.

"Shut up and watch the game. He's not a killer, and I don't have fetishes." I paused. "That I'm willing to share."

"Oh! Nice. Spill."

"No." I chuckled into my drink as I took a swig.

It was a Sunday, and the Dallas Cowboys were playing Philly. Javier had insisted I come over to watch the game since we both had a day off. Melanie was in the kitchen with a friend from work since she wasn't a football fan.

It was November. The cooler weather had moved in—or so Javier kept telling me. Midsixties was luxurious, in my opinion. Back home, there was always a huge possibility of snow this time of year, so I was impervious to Texas' version of cool weather.

Jalen had touched base with me twice since I'd been to see him, and he'd told me he'd filled in all the paperwork to claim his grandmother's insurance, but it would take time since there were a number of hoops to jump through. There was a snag when it came to Bishop's imprisonment, so they were working out the details. I'd volunteered to drive down a few times to collect papers for Bishop to sign. We hoped it would all be taken care of by December.

So the lawyer was still on hold.

I'd had one more visit with Bishop in that time and worked another rotation in his section. Four times I'd picked up random overtime shifts to be near him. As of yet, no one had said a thing. Rumors had spread, and I felt lingering eyes on my back on occasion and encountered a handful of abruptly ended conversations when I'd entered the staffroom.

Suspicions were bleeding through the officers. Javier said there hadn't been a single mention of my sexuality. *Yet.* Their speculation surrounded my motives, so far. But he warned me every day how that would soon change. All it would take was one person to suggest the idea that I was gay, and it would blow up.

I was playing with fire. Late at night when I couldn't sleep, my side ached, reminding me why I'd abandoned my old life in the first place.

"Did you guys want me to order pizza?" Melanie called from the kitchen.

"That'd be great, doll. What do you like on your pizza?" Javier asked me.

"I'm easy."

"I bet you are, but that doesn't answer my question."

"I'm running out of pillows to throw at you."

"Meat Lovers okay?"

"Yeah. But no pineapple. That's all kinds of wrong."

Javier tipped his head and yelled to his girlfriend. "Meat Lovers and extra pineapple, babe."

I launched my last missile, but he was waiting for it and blocked the attack, laughing.

Melanie poked her head in the living room. "Ew, Anson, are you serious? Pineapple doesn't belong on pizza."

"No pineapple. Your man's being a dick."

"Javier, behave. You guys want wings too?"

"Yes please," we both rhymed together.

For the following thirty minutes, we were absorbed in the game. I hadn't been fully converted to a Cowboys fan, but Javier had bought me a hat and insisted I wore it for every game we watched together.

When the pizza arrived, we headed to the kitchen to fill our plates. Melanie handed out napkins. When Javier reached for a slice, I stayed his hand.

"One second. Let me take a picture of this." I pulled out my phone and squared up the shot, moving the box of wings closer so I could get it all together.

"What are you doing? You're not one of those people who post all their meals on social media, are you?"

"No." I chuckled. "It's something else." I hadn't shared details about my visits with Bishop. They were private, and Javier had proved time and time again, he didn't understand.

We landed back on the couch and pigged out on pizza and wings while the game played out. It was during the fourth quarter when my phone buzzed with an incoming text. I pulled it out and frowned, an icy chill running through my veins.

"What's wrong?"

"Ray wants me to come in a half an hour before my shift tomorrow so he can talk to me."

Javier shook his head. "I told you this shit would bite you in the ass."

"There is no policy that says I can't visit an inmate. I looked it up."

"Yeah, but your behavior is suspicious as hell. People are talking, and God only knows what Ray has heard."

I typed a response, telling him I'd be there and repocketed my phone.

"I'll figure it out."

"Dude, he's messaging you on a Sunday. That man isn't happy, I'll tell you that much."

I couldn't worry about it now. I'd deal with it tomorrow and hope I wasn't in too much trouble.

Chapter Nineteen

I SAT AT THE TABLE IN THE staffroom, knee bouncing, fingers tapping on my thigh, insides jittery. Ray had texted me that morning and told me to wait for him here. I was on afternoons this week and had arrived earlier than he'd asked so I could have time to pull my shit together. It was a joke. I was a bigger mess now than when I'd been pacing my floors at home.

I constructed worst-case scenarios in my head, and the reality scared me. Could I be suspended? Fired? Written up? I had no clue. Would they pull the videos of my past shifts to see what I'd been up to while working in Bishop's section? Would they see the handful of times I'd opened his chute for nothing more than to make physical contact and comfort him?

"Miller." Ray's voice at the door startled me, and I jumped up, tugging my uniform straight as I steeled myself for our meeting.

"Hey."

He gestured at the door. "Come on."

His face was unreadable. I followed him down a tangle of hallways to his office and found a seat once the door closed behind us. Ray didn't sit. He perched on the corner of his desk and kicked his legs out, arms crossed over his chest.

"Do you know why I asked you to come in?"

Did I feign ignorance or go with the truth? How much did he know or suspect?

"I have my guesses."

"Care to share with the class?"

"I assume this has something to do with my reoccurring visits with a prisoner."

"Correct. We can do this two ways. You can tell me everything that's going on, full disclosure, or I can use my working theory and evidence and go from there. What will it be?"

My side ached. Throbbed. I rubbed the old scar, unable to stop myself. Ray already knew I was gay. I didn't know how badly the truth would hurt my career, but his assumptions could be devastating in comparison.

"Anson?"

"Full disclosure."

"Good. Talk."

"I…" Where did I start? "I've developed a friendship with Bishop Ndiaye. More than a friendship. I … have strong feelings for him, which I believe are returned. On many occasions while working his row, we've chatted and shared about our lives. We've grown close."

"And is he the reason you were switching off your shifts a few months back?"

"Yes, sir."

"And the visitations?"

I stared at my hands and tried not to fidget. "Because I stopped switching my shifts, like you advised, we didn't see much of each other. He's on a level-two restriction right now, as you know. He's been depressed, and I thought I could help cheer him up by visiting. His grandmother, the only person who ever came to see him outside his lawyer, passed away. He's lonely." I looked at Ray. "I didn't read anywhere that officers couldn't visit inmates."

Ray pursed his lips. "You're putting me in a very difficult position. I have concerns about the safety of my other officers, you, and the way the choices you make on the floor might be compromised since you've developed feelings toward this man. A convict."

"I don't let it affect my job."

That was a lie. I did. I had.

"And if I chose to review the videos of your shifts working his section, I would see an officer performing his duties without bias or bending the rules?"

Shit. Had he already?

My delay in answering was all the proof he needed. He nodded as though I'd admitted my faults, and he rubbed a hand over his jaw.

"What are your intentions down the line when it comes to this prisoner? What is your end goal? Where do you foresee this going? He's more than a lifer, Anson. He's on death row."

"I know. He has a new lawyer fighting for him." Or would when Jalen and I could sort things out. "I believe he's innocent, and I hope she can set the record straight and give him a shot at life."

"You realize how far-fetched that dream is, don't you? Men don't walk away from a death sentence that often."

"I know."

"So what's the draw to him? Why? Aren't there plenty of other fish in the sea? I'm not gay, but I sure as hell know there are other choices for you out there. Why him?"

"I don't know. We're alike. We get along. Talking to him is easy and comfortable. Maybe this is all it will ever be. I'll take what I can get."

Ray pushed away from the desk and rounded it, sitting on his chair and drawing one ankle over his knee. "This takes me to my second concern. Rumors are running wild through my officers. I have to settle them somehow. I fear they will make the connection soon, and your sexuality will come front and center into this mess." He held up a hand, placating. "Again, your private life is your own, and I don't judge you for your choice of bedpartners. None of my business. However, as you've seen before, that kind of information getting leaked around a maximum-security prison puts your safety at high risk. We can be as all-inclusive as we want to be around here. I can discipline any officer who thinks to take issue or discriminate against you, but there isn't shit I can do if an inmate gets the upper hand and decides to fuck you up or stick another blade in your kidney. We have every measure in place to keep people safe, but so did I-Max, and you know how that turned out."

"I know."

"So what do I do?"

I shook my head. I didn't have a clue because any solution would compromise my time with Bishop, and the idea of not seeing him hurt too much to consider.

Ray dropped his foot and pulled closer to his desk. "You will no longer be scheduled in his section, and you will no longer pick up shifts in his section. I am officially forbidding you to work with him, do you understand me?"

My stomach sank.

"So long as you and this inmate are in what you might classify as a relationship of any kind, I can't have you working with him." I opened my mouth to object, but Ray held up a finger, silencing me. "However, your personal time is yours. You're right, there are no concrete rules stating you can't visit an inmate. So feel free to develop whatever relationship you want on your own time. So far as the other officers are concerned, you're friends. I suggest you use an element of discretion when you visit. Rumors could affect your wellbeing."

I was torn. Part of me knew he was cutting me some slack and this could have gone far worse than it had, but it hurt. Deep in my bones and heart, it hurt.

"I understand."

"And Anson?" I met his hardened glare. "If I *ever* find you or hear of you being in his section, there will be disciplinary action taken."

"Yes, sir."

I was dismissed and wandered back to the staffroom with my gut in a knot. Bishop had another handful of weeks before his restrictions were lifted. Come December, I could visit him once a week for two-hour time blocks. In the meantime, I would keep up with his bi-monthly allotment at a reduced length of one hour.

Since Ray told me my free time was mine, I decided there was nothing stopping me from writing to him more often or sending him more books once he could receive them.

I'd become an official prison groupie in my own way. It was a well-known fact that some women wrote to and sought out incarcerated men because they were fascinated with the dangerous side of their personalities. They developed unhealthy attachments or fell in love with those men.

Was that what I'd become? Was Javier right?

Except, I knew Bishop wasn't dangerous.

He was innocent. I'd bet my life on it.

THE NEW ARRANGEMENT WASN'T horrible. December came, and Bishop's restrictions were lifted. We visited weekly, and I took pictures with me every time, like his grandmother used to. We chatted about everything and nothing. He smiled more and shared how much he looked forward to seeing me every week.

Javier reported Bishop was doing better during the time in between our visits as well. Javier was my eyes on the inside. When I couldn't be in that section, he kept me in the loop.

"Your brother messaged me yesterday. Whatever mess there was with that policy has been worked out. He arranged for your share of the money to be put in an account for safekeeping rather than have it put here in your prison holdings. They take a huge cut of your money if we do that. Jalen is co-signer on the account and he's going to sort out with the bank the retainer for your lawyer. There is enough for the whole amount. I'll probably have to bring you papers or something to approve the withdrawal, but I'll take care of it."

Bishop listened, absorbing the details. I'd kept him up to date about what was going on. When he'd disagreed about me putting forward half the retainer, we'd argued. As it stood, I wouldn't have to. I'd saved money over the past few weeks and had accumulated a healthy sum, but I could tuck that away now and enjoy the extra cushion.

"So what happens after she gets her money?"

"Then she is going to put together your appeal. It will be rock solid. She will ensure there is no way it's denied."

He nodded. "Okay."

"It will take time, she told me. Be patient."

"Got nothing but time, boss." I cocked a brow, and he grinned, correcting himself. "Anson."

It'd been a tough habit for him to break. I teased him and corrected him, but in truth, I didn't mind the nickname. It was ours. He didn't think of me as superior or above him in any way, and it was nothing more than an affectionate term that had lingered between us.

"How's Jalen?" he asked, studying his hands.

"He seems to be healing. It's a lot to take care of when someone dies."

"Is he alone? Does he have a girlfriend or someone to lean on?"

I scraped my teeth along my lower lip, hesitating. "He has support. It'd be good for him to have family too."

Bishop shook his head, shutting down the idea as quickly as I suggested it. Every time. He was adamant. I wish I knew why. These two brothers needed each other more than ever, and I couldn't make either of them see it.

"Did you take any more pictures of pizza?" Bishop asked.

I smiled and pulled open the little baggie I'd brought. "No pizza this time, but I was out running the other day in the evening, and the whole town was shining with Christmas lights, so I took some pictures of that. Thought you'd like to see some holiday cheer."

I showed him all the images of small-town Christmas in Onalaska. Lampposts wrapped with lights, hanging wreaths on doors, and store shop windows with gorgeous wintery displays. I'd decided to put up a tree in my house this year, something I'd never done as a single man. I'd done it for Bishop, so I could take a piece of Christmas to him and show him what life could be like if he ever got out.

His eyes turned glassy as I placed them one at a time on the plexiglass window. He touched them, memorized them. He'd told me how he sketched the images on his walls like he'd done with the pictures his grandmother used to bring.

When I'd exhausted the dozen snapshots, I returned them to their baggie and stared at him through the window. Our magnetism was stronger than ever. The pull was hard to resist. Until then, we'd been careful. No officers were in the room, but they could look through the viewing window on Bishop's side at any moment. It was private, but not.

Bishop placed his hand on the glass and whispered into the receiver, "I want to touch you. I miss that connection."

Unable to deny him, I covered his hand with my own. "Me too."

"I think of you every night when I close my eyes. I read your letters over and over. They carry a hint of your scent. Did you know that? I look ridiculous because I smell them all and close my eyes, pretending you're near me. Pretending your right there on the bed beside me."

My gorge tightened, and I fought the sting in my eyes. "Would you want that? To lie in bed beside me?"

"More than anything."

"Me too."

"Can I admit something to you?"

"You can tell me anything."

He leaned closer to the window, even though it made little difference in our communication. His voice remained low and deep. "I dream about kissing you. Tasting you. Lying with you like that, like how two men do."

My skin prickled, and I shuddered. "Me too," I croaked. "All the time."

"If I never get out of here, I want you to know, you mean something to me. You've made all the difference in my life, and I care for you. A lot. I've never been given a chance to explore things as they are with me, but if there was ever a person who I'd want to share those experiences with, it would be you."

My chest ached. "Bishop, you *will* get out of here. We *will* explore all those things, if that's what you want. I want them too."

"We gotta hope, right, boss?"

"Yes. We have to hope."

HOPE RAN OUT THE WEEK BEFORE CHRISTMAS.

It was the twentieth of December. I'd collected bank papers from Jalen the previous week and had Bishop sign them. Jalen would have the money for the lawyer before the holiday—or so he'd promised.

Everything was finally moving forward. I felt positive Bishop's case was going to see the attention it deserved.

I'd gotten off the phone with my mother, who was not happy about my decision to remain in Texas over the holidays, when my phone rang.

Lounging back on my bed, wearing nothing but boxers and an old T-shirt for sleeping, I frowned at Javier's number on the screen, wondering why he was calling instead of texting. I was working midnights this week, and he was on mornings. He knew I tried to crash out after a run, so I was confused by his midmorning call.

"What's up? Aren't you working?" I asked, checking the time on my digital clock beside my bed. It was shy of ten in the morning.

"I'm on break. Where are you?"

"At home. What's wrong?" There was a quality to his voice that put me on edge.

"Sit down."

"I'm in bed. What the hell?"

Silence screamed in my ear, and I shuffled out of my covers, on alert. Something wasn't right.

"Anson, I ... don't know how to say this."

"Just say it. What the fuck? You're freaking me out."

"The District Court Judge signed his Warrant of Execution. Bishop's been given a date, and they moved him to deathwatch this morning."

My whole body went cold. I was going to be sick. Panic shot through my veins, and all outside noise except for the racing of my own heart disappeared. I couldn't find words.

"Anson?"

"I'm here. That can't be right. You're joking. Tell me you're joking."

"I wish I was. I thought you'd want to know."

I stood up, but my world spun, and I had to catch myself on the wall so I wouldn't fall over. This couldn't be happening. Not now. Not when we were this close to getting an appeal.

"Anson. Breathe."

"I ... I gotta go."

Javier protested in the background, but I disconnected the call. My vision was hazy, and my ears rang as I fumbled down the hallway to the bathroom. I splashed cold water on my face over and over, trying to dispel the mushrooming cloud of anxiety growing inside me.

It didn't work.

I heaved and caught myself on the edge of the counter as convulsions shook me. My eyes burned, and before I could stop them, tears streamed down my cheeks.

"Fuck. This isn't happening. It's a bad dream again. It's not real. Wake up." I squeezed my eyes closed as tight as possible and did all I could to pull myself from this nightmare. "Wake up. Wake up. *Wake up!*" I slammed my fist against the counter, and pain zipped up my arm.

It wasn't a bad dream. It was happening. It was too late.

I darted from the bathroom and almost fell as I took the stairs two at a time. I didn't know what to do, but I had to move. I had to think, but I couldn't. It was a jumble inside my head, and the apprehension over Bishop's situation that I'd been managing all these months overwhelmed me.

I collapsed on the kitchen floor and clutched my chest.

Think!

I tugged my phone from my pocket and pulled up Jalen's number with trembling fingers. Hitting Call, I put the phone to my ear and closed my eyes, sucking in air and blowing it out again in as measured a pace as I could manage while I waited for him to answer.

"I'm working. This isn't a good time." Beeping and loud machinery sliced through the phone, Jalen's voice fighting for dominance over the noise.

"We need that money now. Yesterday. You need to leave work and go get it. I'm coming to you."

"What the fuck is wrong with you? I'm working. I told you I'd have it before Christmas. My schedule has been shit. I'm doing overtime all week and won't be off early enough to hit the bank until Thursday."

"We need it now!" I yelled.

Filling my lungs, I worked to steady my panic, knowing anger wouldn't get me results. Jalen would grow defensive, and I couldn't afford him hanging up on me. "Jalen, they moved him. The judge signed his Warrant of Execution. They've given him a date, and that date will be one month from now, give or take. Do you understand me? They're going to execute him."

The only sound was of the construction site in the distance. Jalen didn't respond for a long time. When he did, his voice was thick. "You serious?"

"I'm not about to joke about something like this. I'm on my way to your house. Your brother's life is worth a missed day of work, I should think. Get that money."

"O-okay." He sounded far younger than his thirty-four years. And frightened. "Okay, I'm going now."

"I'll be at your house in about three hours."

I hung up and pivoted, unsure of my next step. Clothes. I needed to get dressed. After rushing up the stairs, I pulled on a pair of jeans and a hoodie. I crammed my wallet in one pocket and my phone in another before racing back downstairs and fetching my keys.

The whole while, all I could hear was Cynthia's voice in my head telling me it would be a slow process. It would take time.

We didn't have time.

I was on the road for an hour when my phone rang. I connected the call through the Bluetooth without checking who it was.

"Yeah," I snapped, unable to hide the tension from my voice.

"Where are you?" It was Javier.

"Driving."

"I'm at your house."

"Why? Shouldn't you be working?"

"Yes, but I requested to leave early because my best friend is a fucking mess right now, and I didn't want him to be alone. So where are you?"

"Driving to Georgetown."

"Why?"

"Because Jalen has the retainer for the lawyer, and I need to collect it and bring it to her so she can move her ass on this and get his fucking appeal heard before he dies."

"Anson."

"No!" I slammed my fist on the steering wheel as the sting returned to my eyes. "Do not fucking tell me it's too late. I am not giving up. Don't tell me I've lost my mind either because I will hang up this fucking phone right now."

"Anson, take a breath."

I tried but it hitched in my throat and my vision blurred with tears I could no longer fight.

"I'm here for you, man. Put your head together so you don't have an accident."

"I'm fine."

"Bullshit. What can I do? Anything."

I batted my eyes with the back of my hand and clenched my jaw, staring at the road ahead. "Request deathwatch. Tell Ray you'll work it. You know he prefers taking requests for those shifts."

"Okay. Done. Do you want me to take Bishop a message?"

"No. I want you to give me your shifts when you get them."

"Anson."

"Not all of them. Two or three, and preferably on a weekend so Ray isn't wiser until Monday."

"You'll get your ass fired."

"You know what? I don't care anymore. I'm not his family, so I won't be permitted to visit him now that he's on watch. If this is it, if I can't work a fucking miracle, you'd better damn well know I'm going to do all I can to see him and at least say goodbye."

Javier didn't say anything. I knew he disagreed, but it was my life and my career. He wouldn't be the one in trouble, I would be.

"Javi, please. I'm begging you."

"Okay. Okay. Let me work it out."

"Thank you."

"Call me when you get home."

"I will."

The rest of my drive passed in a blur. My hands ached when I pulled up front of Jalen's house, thanks to my death grip on the steering wheel over the last couple of hours. I'd developed an internal shake I couldn't seem to shed. My teeth chattered if I didn't keep my jaw clenched, and I was cold.

Jalen's car was in the driveway, and when I hopped out of the Jeep, the front door opened. Jalen hugged himself, paler than I'd ever seen him. I hoped Drake was around because he needed someone to lean on right now.

"Did you get it?"

Jalen nodded and unfolded his arms, holding out a crumpled envelope. "She'll be able to stop this, right?"

"I don't know." It was the truth, but saying it out loud made me sick. "I'm taking this to her office right now. I'll beg and plead and do anything I can to get her moving on this."

"W-when? When are they gonna execute him?"

"I don't know. A buddy of mine called to tell me, but I didn't ask for specifics. A month. No more."

Jalen nodded and looked at his feet, his arms pulled tighter around his body, and he shivered.

"When an inmate is moved to deathwatch, they are only permitted visits from family members. This might be your last chance, Jalen."

He lifted his head, eyes bloodshot and filled with sorrow. "They won't let you visit?"

"No."

"But you work there, right? You can go talk to him anytime."

"No. That's not how it works." There was no way I was explaining the whole story.

"I… I don't know if I can go. I mean… What if he tells them no?"

I couldn't guarantee he wouldn't. Bishop had been stubborn when it came to Jalen.

"All you can do is try."

"I don't know. Maybe."

"I have to go." I waved the envelope and thumbed over my shoulder. "This close to the holidays, I have no idea what this lawyer's office hours will be, and I have another three hours to drive to get there."

"Will you keep me posted?"

"Of course."

I was halfway to my Jeep when Jalen called, "Anson?"

I turned and was met with so much heartache my throat tightened.

"I can't lose them both. I know Bishop and I haven't been close, but he's still my brother."

"I'll do everything in my power to help."

"Thank you."

"Go call Drake." His eyes widened. "You need a friend right now. You shouldn't be alone."

THE OFFICE OF BELLOWS, MCNALLY, AND PRICE was only open until five. I pulled in the lot at twenty to and burst through the front doors, my dread and fear on the surface, hoping Cynthia was available and not gone for the day or in court.

The receptionist startled at my unexpected entrance, her hand landing on her chest. "Oh crap on a cracker. You scared the bejesus out of me. Can I help you?"

"Cynthia. I need to talk to her. Is she available? It's important."

The woman flipped a page in a day planner, scanning before looking up. "Do you have an appointment?"

"No. I was hoping to have a minute of her time. She's working on a case for me. Or she will be. I need to give her this retainer and explain a few things."

"Oh, I can help you with that." She held out her hand, but I kept a tight grip on the envelope.

"I'd really like to talk to her. Something came up, and it's time-sensitive. An emergency."

"I can make you an appointment, if you'd like? Being the holidays, however, she doesn't have any availability until January. Does that work for you?"

"No. That will be too late. If I could talk to her. Is she in? I only need a few minutes."

The receptionist peered down the hallway toward Cynthia's office and pinched her lips, drawing them to the side. "She is, but I'm not sure—"

"Can you ask? Tell her it's Anson Miller. I have her retainer, but there is an urgent matter attached to the case that she needs to know about."

The receptionist hesitated but reached for her phone. "I'll tell her."

She tapped an extension and waited. "I'm sorry to bother you. I know you asked me to hold your calls, but I have an Anson Miller here, and he's a tad frantic. He says he has a retainer for you but also urgent information regarding the case that can't wait." She stopped speaking and looked up at me while she listened. "Uh-huh... Yes. Okay."

She hung up and gestured to the hallway. "She said to go on back."

I was off like a shot, unable to contain my nervous energy any longer. My canting heart hadn't settled since I'd received the call from Javier that morning. Being mobile and actively doing something was the only thing keeping me from breaking down.

Cynthia sat behind her desk, glasses perched on her nose as she studied her computer screen, a mess of folders and papers spread out in front of her. "Mr. Miller," she said without lifting her gaze.

"Thank you for seeing me."

"Appointments are the best way to ensure we have time to talk. I haven't heard from you in a while. I assumed you no longer required my services." She tipped her chin down and peered at me from over the top of her glasses.

"I'm sorry. Ten thousand isn't pocket change for me. It took time to acquire." I slid the envelope across the desk and sat on the chair opposite her. "A cashier's check for ten grand. But there is a problem."

She focused again on her computer, typing and squinting at her screen like I wasn't in the middle of a crisis. My legs jumped, and I almost shot off my seat to pace when she took off her glasses and spun her chair to look at me.

"Talk. Condense as much as possible, please. I'm swamped with cases right now, and with the holidays, I tend to fall behind. Remind me what case this is."

I wiped my palms on my jeans. "Death row. Bishop Ndiaye. Two counts of capital murder. You said there was potential—"

"Suppressed evidence. That's right. Okay, go on."

"They've given him a date. If he doesn't get an appeal hearing in the next month, they're executing him."

Cynthia's lashes fluttered in a succession of many quick blinks. "One month?"

"Yes. I know—"

"Impossible."

"No! It can't be. Please."

She was already dismissing the idea, shaking her head and regarding me like I'd lost my mind. "First, it's the worst time of year to move any case along *quickly*. Second, I told you, to guarantee the appellate procedure is a success, I need to present an impenetrable case, which means gathering as much evidence as I can, prove the previous trial had too many holes, and that my client's sentence is unjust. I can't do that in a month. And at Christmas time? Impossible."

"We're talking about a man's life. I know I'm asking a lot. I know you're busy, and I have no right. If there was time, I'd wait, but there isn't. He's innocent. You agreed when you read his file. How can we let an innocent man die without trying? Please. I'm begging you." My vision blurred again, but I blinked a few times to clear it, refusing to break down in front of this woman.

"Rushing an appeal jeopardizes the chances of having it heard, never mind winning."

"Doing nothing guarantees his death."

She pushed a long exhale through her nose, hardened eyes analyzing my face.

"Look," I continued. "Ten thousand is more than you required to pull together an appeal. That was quoted based on a full retrial with an added contingency fee if you won and other stuff. You yourself told me it was a much higher retainer than you normally requested. If they turn it down, if they deny him again, then you aren't out any money because he'll die. There won't be any more chances to rework or refile. That will be it. The end. One shot. I know it's the holidays and you are loaded with work, but this man's life is on the line. You are the only hope he's got."

She closed her eyes and dipped her head, removing her glasses and pinching the bridge of her nose. "Let me see what I can do. I'll pull together the best appeal I can in the time frame we have, but I make you no promises. This isn't how I work. I'm a stickler for details and assuring there are no holes in my cases. You aren't giving me much time. I don't know that I can get the proof I need to make the appeal I want in time. I don't have time to request anything excess or to investigate certain leads."

"I know."

"Also, there is no guarantee I can get the court to even look at this in that time frame. Ordinarily, there would be a waiting period of several months before the appellate court would even consider hearing my case. We're now asking them to rush. They could tell us forget it. You've narrowed the chances of success by half, or more."

"Half is better than nothing."

She sighed. "I'll be in touch. I'll need the date on his warrant so I know how long I have."

"I'll call it in. I have to find out what it is."

"You better cross your fingers, Mr. Miller. You're asking me to work a miracle."

With Cynthia's services arranged, I left the office, no less distressed over the news about Bishop, no more settled in my heart. Numbness enveloped me. My drive home happened in a fog. More than anything, I wanted to see him, reassure him everything would be all right.

Except, I didn't know if it would. A sinking feeling in the pit of my stomach told me I was going to lose Bishop. All we had was all we were ever going to get.

Chapter Twenty

JAVIER MANAGED TO SECURE TWO weeks of shift rotations on deathwatch. One for midnights over Christmas and the week following on afternoons. With no less than a dozen warnings and pleading with me to reconsider, he gave up three nightshifts in a row that covered a Friday, Saturday, and Sunday. Christmas Eve and Christmas Day were included in those nights, and it was the best hope I had at deceiving Ray. He'd taken extra time off over the holidays to be with his family, so by the time he realized what I'd done, I would have had some days with Bishop.

They'd be my only days. I wasn't delusional. This stunt would get me fired. Suspended, if I was lucky and Ray was feeling generous.

The knot in my stomach hadn't left me in days, and when I arrived on shift the first night, I was a sweating, trembling ball of nerves.

Newbie Derrick happened to be one of the other three guards working with me. The other two were from other pods, and I didn't know them. Peter and Malcomb were their names. They took one row, while Derrick and I paired off in the other.

"Did Javier want time with his girlfriend? Is that why you're here?" Derrick asked.

"Yeah," I lied, scanning the cells, unsure which contained Bishop. All I knew was that he was on this level.

"Okay, no. I lied." Because my life was already upside down and inside out, I tugged Derrick aside and pinned him with a hard glare. "Listen. I need to tell you something, and you need to go with it."

"What's up, man?"

I cleared my throat and glanced around to ensure the other guys weren't around. "You're young. Please tell me you were raised with open-minded parents."

Derrick frowned. "Sure. They're all right. Why?"

"I'm here for a reason, and I'm not supposed to be. Ray has forbidden me from working with a certain prisoner. I need you to turn a blind eye for the next three nights. Can you do that?"

Derrick's eyes grew wide. "Dude, you ain't gonna bust someone outta here, are you?"

I swatted him across the back of the head. "Christ, no! You watch too much TV. Do you think that's even possible?"

"No. Not with this kind of security. What's up then? Why am I turning a blind eye? Why are you forbidden? Who aren't you allowed to work with?"

"Prisoner Bishop Ndiaye. You know who I'm talking about?"

"The big guy? Scary fucker? Never says much, but he stares at you with those crazy eyes? Yeah, I know him. I heard you've visited him a few times. What's up with that? You know him from the outside?"

"No, but we're friends." I hesitated. "More than friends. Are you following?"

Derrick frowned, then his brow shot to his hairline. "Dude, are you gay?" he hissed.

"Yes, but it's better no one knows because it could be dangerous for me." I hiked up my uniform shirt, exposing my scar. "See this? Back in Michigan where I used to work, the guys on the inside found out. They attacked me, beat the fuck out of me, and stabbed me. I could have been killed. They tried."

"Holy shit."

"So you tell no one, understand?"

He couldn't nod fast enough. "Yeah, man. I get it. I won't tell. And I'm all cool with the gay thing too, so you know. I ain't biased."

"Good. Thank you."

I wasn't an idiot. Derrick was a gossip, and this was big-time juice. He'd spread the word the minute he was able, but I figured it didn't matter since I had three days before Ray canned my ass for going against his orders. I was done here, regardless.

"Now listen. Bishop is here in this row. They are going to execute him, and these three days are all I get. You need to give me some free rein and turn your back. I'm not going to be stupid and open his cell or anything, but I need to talk to him. Spend time at his cell. Can you be cool for three days?"

Derrick's gaze drifted down the row. "That big fucker is gay?"

"Derrick, pay attention. Can you help a bro out?"

He slapped my shoulder and gave it a shake. "I gotcha. No worries, my friend. You do what you have to, and I've got your back."

"Thank you. You're a good kid."

"So how's that work? He's inside, you're outside. I ain't gonna see you get all sexy at the window and yank yourself, am I?"

"Derrick—"

"Sorry. It's weird."

"We'll be talking. Nothing more." This was not the time for *yanking*. I had bigger things to worry about.

With my first order of business out of the way, I paced down the row of cells, glancing in each to determine who was inside. The Warrants of Execution always came in chunks. We could have no guys in this row, then get twenty warrants and fill it up overnight.

My gut churned as I passed man after man whose clocks were ticking down to their final hours. No matter what they'd done, it had to be a scary time for them. Alone in a cell. Nothing to do but think about the dwindling time passing you by and whatever it was you'd done that had put you there.

I found Bishop, two cells from the end of the row. The moment I laid eyes on him, my stomach clenched and tears burned to the surface. I didn't want him to see me like this, so I took a minute to compose myself before approaching his window. The shadow my body cast across his cell made him lift his head from where he sat perched on the side of his bed, stewing.

Our eyes locked, and the emotions that poured from his surface almost made my knees buckle. He rose, and I didn't miss the tremors rocking his big frame as he crossed to the window.

Without words, he rested his forehead on the glass and closed his eyes. I copied. We stood there, connected but for a thick slab of a reinforced barrier.

"You aren't supposed to be here," he whispered after a time.

"I couldn't stay away. I needed to see you."

"You'll get fired."

"I don't care."

"You should. In a month, when I'm gone, you'll regret this."

"I will never regret this," I hissed, slapping my hand to the door. "And I will fight this until you take your last breath."

"There is no more fight, boss. It's over."

"No. The lawyer has her money. She's racing the clock to make your appeal. It *will* happen. I have to believe that. You aren't going to die here." A lump rose in my throat. "I won't allow it."

Bishop opened his eyes and regarded me with such longing, such heartache. "It's time you let that go. It's time you face the truth." He placed his hand on the window. "You've fought for me like no one ever has. You believed in me when I was sure there wasn't a soul alive who was listening. I can't thank you enough for what you've given me, but it's time to accept the truth, Anson. This is it."

I covered his hand with mine and got lost in his dark eyes. "I don't want to argue it. Know this, there are people fighting for you on this side. People who care and know you aren't meant to be here. I have three days on this row. After, I won't be back, but don't for a second think I'm not fighting still."

He grabbed at the glass, fingers seeking that connection we couldn't have. "Thank you," he whispered.

We remained like that for a long time. I had duties I couldn't neglect, but leaving his window was a struggle.

"I'm scared." Bishop's words were faint. A whisper that threatened to get lost in the air. "I've spent fifteen years preparing for this, but I'm scared, Anson. I'm so scared."

His eyes shone with unshed tears and mine filled, hating the physical barrier between us. "I know. Me too."

"Distract me, boss. Please. It's all I can think about, and I don't want to think no more."

With a pinch in my chest, I tried to push my own anguish aside and give him what he requested, but my mind drew a blank.

"What do you want to talk about?"

"Anything. Books. Food. About your Christmas plans."

"These are my Christmas plans. I'm not going home. I'm staying right here with you."

"No turkey or apple pie?"

I chuckled as the first tear escaped and trickled down my cheek. "No pie. I might make a turkey sandwich with cold cuts, but that's the extent of my dinner plans."

"Do you like mustard on your sandwich?"

"A little. And mayo."

"How about tomatoes and lettuce?"

"Both. Maybe I'll crisp up some bacon in the frying pan and add it too. Kinda make a Christmas clubhouse to celebrate."

"My Maw Maw used to add cranberry sauce to mayo during the holidays. She said it gave it a nice zip."

"I've never done that."

"You should try it."

I sighed and nodded. We were talking about sandwiches. It was bizarre yet necessary. It was simple and safe and distracting. We both grasped hold of such a trivial conversation and rode the wave for all it was worth. The alternative was unspeakable.

"My mom used to make hot turkey sandwiches with the leftover feast when I was a kid. They were open-faced. Loaded with turkey and stuffing and smothered with gravy. I think I liked them more than the turkey dinner itself, but don't tell her I said that."

"Your secret is safe with me."

We talked about desserts and traditions. We shared about the special toys we'd received growing up. Over time, our conversation died off, and we stood there, watching each other. There were a million things I wanted to say. A hundred other meaningless conversations I wanted to have. Time was not on our side, and the thought that we'd never get to indulge in such simple pleasures or traditions as a couple slayed me.

Reluctantly, after a time, I left to perform other duties and talked with other men who needed an ear, but my thoughts and my heart were with Bishop the whole time.

Three night shifts passed much faster than I liked.

On the final evening, I couldn't ignore the nausea filling my gut. I'd been unable to eat much for two days, knowing this was the last time I'd see Bishop unless Cynthia worked a miracle.

That night, I brought a book on the floor with me. A pocket-sized paperback copy of *1984* I'd had for years. It'd since been replaced by a hardback copy in my collection, but I'd never gotten rid of this smaller, well-worn version. I shoved it in my belt before leaving the staffroom.

Words had failed us the day before, and I knew today would be worse. So I'd come prepared with something familiar we could share together. It'd been the subject of many of our debates, so I hoped Bishop would appreciate the distraction.

I wasn't wrong. He leaned against the door of his cell, listening while I read. When I'd gone so far, he requested jumping ahead to parts he liked, and I obliged him. Over the course of the night, I read, and he listened.

"You won't forget me, will you?" he asked after Winston in the story had explained how people ceased to exist in his world. In the flesh and in people's minds.

"Never."

"Do you think we parallel Winston and Julia a bit?"

I stared at the book in my hands and leafed through the pages as I thought. We'd discussed this before. Many times. "In some ways. Like them, we're denied a chance to freely explore what we have because society put you in there, and I'm stuck out here. We aren't allowed to be together. Also, we've stolen secret moments we know we weren't supposed to have, like they did."

He nodded, a furrow in his brow as he thought. "But we're not the same."

"Not really."

"I'd never betray you."

I smiled and moved my hand to the window to grab his attention so he'd look up. When he caught my eye, I said, "And I'd never betray you."

He chuckled, but it was filled with sadness. "Will you keep reading?"

"Of course. Where from?"

"Go back to the part where they're hidden away in the clearing. The first time they come together."

I found the spot and read.

When the end of my shift loomed in the near distance, I left Derrick to the count and lingered again near Bishop's cell. I'd been there half the night. It was time to say goodbye before the shift change made us busy and I missed my chance.

But I didn't know how to say goodbye. I didn't want to give thought to the possibility that this was it. I wanted to cling to hope.

But if I was wrong, and this was all we got, I needed to make it count.

At his cell, I unlocked his chute as he stood on the other side, watching. Waiting. I lowered the door and held out my hand. He took it, and I closed my eyes at the warmth of his skin wrapped around me. His grip was tight and full of all the anxiety I had running through my veins. We touched, moved fingers over palms, and fingers over wrists. We clung and squeezed.

Bishop dropped to his knees and placed my hand on his cheek. It was wet with tears, and I stroked his face, cradled his head in my hand, warming when his lips made contact with my palm.

He kissed each finger and guided my touch all over his face and head and neck. Lips. Eyes. Nose. I memorized it all. It was everything and not enough.

"Dude, I don't mean to interrupt, but the shift change is gonna be here soon." Derrick stood a distance away, shifting between his feet and struggling to meet my eyes.

"Okay. Thanks."

"I'm sorry. I thought you'd want to know."

He walked away, and Bishop stood. Our foreheads met and gazes locked. I closed the chute without looking, secured it, and placed my hand over his on the glass. "This isn't over," I whispered. "I have to believe this lawyer can work a miracle."

"Thank you ... Anson. For everything."

"Hang tight. We'll see each other again ... one way or another."

He brought his fingers to his lips and kissed them before laying them on the window. I did the same, my heart wanting to collapse with the sheer volume of pain and duress it was going through.

"Goodbye," I said. "For now."

"For now."

I SAT IN RAY'S OFFICE, the ticking of the clock on the wall the only sound between us. He'd done nothing more than sit on his office chair, fingers steepled and bouncing against his puckered lips as he stared at me with a deep frown.

I could have tried to defend my actions, but there was no point. The minute I'd told Javier to take deathwatch and switch off a few shifts with me, I'd accepted the consequences. All I could do was wait Ray out and hope for the best.

My heart had been in my throat since I'd left Bishop early Monday morning. I hadn't slept, and the amount of food I'd consumed all weekend was pitiful. Ray's message that I should be in his office Tuesday morning at seven sharp came through five hours after I'd left work. Midday. A handful of hours after Ray would have found out what I'd done.

So there we sat. Staring at one another. The clock a steady reminder of passing time. With Bishop on deathwatch and a date lingering closer and closer, the lost minutes stabbed in my chest.

"What the hell am I going to do with you?" Ray spat, slapping his desk and scowling. "You deliberately defied my order."

I stayed quiet.

"I should fire your ass."

He scrubbed a hand over his head and pushed out of his chair so he could pace. "What a completely idiotic and stupid thing to do. What is wrong with you? Do you have anything to say for yourself?"

"No, sir."

"Nothing?"

"No. I defied your order. I knew when I did it, you wouldn't be happy."

"You're damn right I'm not happy. What the hell were you thinking?"

"I was thinking that a man I care deeply for has been given a date of execution, and because I'm not family, I'll never see him again. So I did what I had to in order to say goodbye."

"So you aren't regretful for your actions? Is that what you're saying?"

"No, sir, I'm not."

Ray stopped pacing and bent over his desk, hands planted wide as he lowered his face to my level to pin me with a hostile glare. "Have you lost your mind, Miller? You think this convict is worth your job?"

I couldn't look him in the eye. I stared into middle space and gritted my teeth. "Do you love your wife, sir?"

His frown deepened. "Of course I do. What the hell does that have to do with anything?"

"If you were in my shoes and she was in Bishop's, would you not break every rule and do all you could, if only to say goodbye?"

When he didn't respond, I blinked away the storm in my head and met his glare, waiting.

Ray squinted. "Are you telling me you're in love with this man?"

I considered, dropping my focus to my hands and fidgeting. "I don't know what I feel. Love is complex, and to be honest, we haven't had a chance to explore what's between us properly. I know he's important to me. I know I get tight in the chest whenever I'm around him. I know the thought of him dying floods me with panic and makes me feel like I'm going to be sick. I don't know if I love him, but I know I *could* if given time. But we aren't going to get that time. So yes, I broke some rules and defied your orders. I'd do it again."

Ray heaved a heavy sigh and dropped onto his chair. He scrubbed his face with both hands before tipping his head to the ceiling. "What the hell am I supposed to do with that?"

"You do what you think is right, sir. I was prepared for this, and I'll take the consequences, whatever they may be."

Ray snagged a folder on his desk and opened it. He rooted through the pages inside until he found what he was looking for. He scanned before slapping the sheet back down and sitting forward. "You're suspended without pay until January nineteenth."

Bishop's date of execution.

"I can't have you here so long as I can't trust you. You're a good officer. Tough and fair. But your judgment is skewed by this man. I don't want to fire you, but I promise, if this behavior continues when you come back, I will not hesitate to do so."

"I understand. Thank you, sir."

"Get outta here."

I hustled out of his office and made my way to the staffroom. I emptied my locker, stuffing the extras I kept inside into my backpack. After I left the building, I shot Javier a text, telling him the results of my meeting.

In the parking lot, I sat for a long time in my Jeep, examining the concrete walls and high razor-topped fences of Polunsky. He was in there. Alone. Frightened.

I felt so helpless. No amount of nagging would make Cynthia move faster on the appeal. No amount of hoping and wishing would make this nightmare go away.

I fought off another wave of panic and pulled out my phone. Then I called the sole person who would support and love me no matter what.

"Hi, Mom?"

"Sweetheart, what's wrong? You don't sound all right."

"I'm not. Mom, I'm scared…"

Then, I told her everything.

Chapter Twenty-One

TIME BOTH DRAGGED AND RACED during the weeks following Christmas. My suspension gave me too much free time, and there was only so much pacing and running I could endure as I waited for updates from Cynthia.

I'd taken up Ray's previous offer of seeing a local therapist and had word-vomited my entire situation during our last appointment. She'd cleared me two spots a week while I struggled with my growing anxiety surrounding Bishop's execution.

At the same time, my days flew by, and time disappeared faster than I could grasp. Too fast. I worried we'd never get the appeal in on time. I worried they'd deny it. I worried that January nineteenth would arrive, and my world would be destroyed.

Jalen and I spoke a few times on the phone. I had no updates to share, but our mutual concern over Bishop gave us a companionable bond. I'd never admitted to being more than a friend with his brother, but Jalen knew. He also spoke often about Drake, and I thought, as much as he held his secret close to his heart, he suspected I knew his truth as well.

He was a long way from admitting it though.

He still wouldn't go see his brother.

"It's admitting defeat," he'd told me on the phone. "If I go, I'm declaring his death inevitable."

We argued. He put his foot down.

There was nothing I could do.

January fourteenth, a shade after eight in the morning, my ringing phone tore me from a nightmare-laden sleep. I awoke, tangled in my blankets and disoriented, unable to process the sound filling the once quiet room.

When I located the cause, I fumbled to answer, instant panic choking me when I saw the law office's number.

"Hello," I croaked, my voice scratchy from sleep.

"Anson Miller?"

"This is."

"Cynthia Bellows." My spine stiffened, and I sat up. "I wanted you to know, I've submitted the appeal. They understand the urgency of the case, and it will be pushed to the front and processed first before others, if possible."

"And how do you feel about it?"

There was a pause, and my insides turned to liquid.

"I've done my best. I've presented a strong argument and played on the time restriction to hopefully gain an edge of pity. I'm relying on my reputation to hopefully get us through to the next phase."

"Okay. How soon will we know?"

"Two or three days. They will call me in when they're ready to hear it—*if* they'll hear it. The state won't be happy at this time restriction. They'll try to shut us down on the grounds that they haven't had time to prepare."

That was cutting it close. Three days took us to the seventeenth. They'd be preparing to take him to Huntsville and the death house by that time.

"And if they will hear it, how long will it take for a decision?"

"In this case, we will try to wrap it up in one session and get the judge to rule. Two sessions, at the most, provided the state doesn't try to block us."

"Okay."

"When I know, you'll know, Mr. Miller."

"Thank you. For everything. I know you didn't have to do this, but I appreciate it more than you'll ever know."

"Thank me when I win the appeal. I'll be in touch." She hung up without saying goodbye.

Cynthia was a woman who hated losing, and it showed. Asking her to take on a case where the end result wasn't guaranteed was devastating for her. She was wound as tight as me.

I flopped back on my bed and stared at the ceiling. I had to call Jalen and let him know, but first, I needed Javier to take a message to Bishop.

I called his number.

"I hate you," came a muffled voice through the phone.

"Did I wake you?"

"Yes."

"The appeal's been sent in. They're rushing it so we can get answers."

Javier was silent.

"Can you tell him?" I asked.

"I'll tell him. How are you doing?"

"Not great."

"Figured. Are you eating?"

"Yeah."

"Melanie said you looked skinnier last time she saw you. She said you're full of shit and are lying to me."

"Tell Melanie I appreciate her concern, but I'm fine. When do you work?"

"Afternoon. Don't worry, I'll tell him."

"Thank you."

The silence stretched, but Javier knew me too well. "What else do you want me to say to him?"

"Um…" I couldn't unload my heart through a third party. It wasn't fair. "Tell him he's not alone. Tell him … to believe in hope because that's all we have right now."

"You're a sap."

"Fuck you. Give him the message."

"I will. Why don't you come over for breakfast? You sound like you need company."

"Yeah. Okay. Thanks. What time?"

"Ten. I ain't getting up yet."

I smiled, but it was strained. "Okay. Ten it is."

I'D THROWN UP MY BREAKFAST and then the glass of water I'd drunk afterward to wash away the bad taste from my mouth. My morning run had lasted two hours because stopping meant thinking and thinking meant crippling anxiety and anxiety landed me in the bathroom, barfing.

It had been three days, and there was no word about Bishop's appeal.

Nothing.

Ear-raping silence.

Cynthia informed me there was nothing she could do on her end, and poking them at this point would be in bad taste. They knew about our deadline. We'd get answers when they were ready to give them.

It was the seventeenth. The following day, Bishop was being moved to Huntsville. I'd begged and pleaded for Javier to volunteer for the escort, but he'd refused.

"It's too much. I've done that once before, and I can't do it again, man. Especially when I know the guy is close to one of my best friends."

I clung to the bathroom sink and stared at the dark circles under my eyes. Rinsing with mouthwash, I started the shower. I cranked the volume on my phone, determined not to miss the call when it came, before hopping under the cold spray.

I shivered and washed, wishing it would alleviate the toxic soup flooding my veins and making me ill. It didn't.

Once I finished, I pulled on sweatpants and a hoodie before crawling into bed with my phone. All I could do was stare at the screen and wait. Sleep found me. I wasn't surprised. I'd been sleeping like shit for weeks. Nightmares plagued me every time I closed my eyes, and I woke up more tired than I was when I went to bed.

It was evening when my phone woke me. I darted up, scrambling to answer as fast as I could, my stomach pitching and heart squeezing at what this call meant. I answered without bothering to check the caller ID.

"Any word?"

Javier.

I collapsed on my pillow. "No. Nothing."

"I'm sorry."

"What time is it?"

"Six. Were you asleep? You sound like shit."

"I guess I was. I laid down around lunch. Are you working?"

"Yeah, but I'm on break. Thought I'd check in."

"It's too late for word today, isn't it? They aren't calling."

"Yeah. I would think so."

"Shit. They move him tomorrow."

Silence.

"I don't know what to say, man. It could happen. You might hear still. I've never seen it on—"

My call waiting beeped, and I choked on air as I sputtered, "Shit, I have to let you go. I have another call."

"Go, go. Maybe this is it."

"Fuck."

"Breathe, and call me back."

I hung up on Javier and clicked to accept the incoming call. "Hello?" My voice cracked.

"Anson?"

"Cynthia?" My heart lodged in my throat. "You heard? Will they hear his appeal?" She had answers, I could feel it.

"They already have." She was too calm, too unreadable.

"Jesus, tell me!" I didn't mean to yell, but my nerves were shot.

"I was called into court this morning. It was lengthy and, as I suspected, the state played every card against us. They fought hard to shut this down. I'll read the final statement made by the Court of Appeals for you."

I held my breath as she read.

"'After reviewing the substantial amount of evidence presented to the court, we find that serious questions exist as to whether or not Mr. Ndiaye received a fair and just trial as mandated by the Constitution. Therefore, it is recommended by this Court of Appeals that Mr. Ndiaye's case be remanded and that he receive a new trial.'"

I broke. Sobbed. Weeks of being strung out and worried all came to a head with this news, and I couldn't do anything but cry and thank her.

"We have a lot of work ahead of us, Mr. Miller, but now we have the time to do it properly. So you're aware, they might have remanded, but they have stated quite clearly that Mr. Ndiaye will remain in custody during the duration of his trial."

"I understand. Thank you."

"Take a deep breath, Anson." There was a smile in her voice for the first time.

I wiped my eyes, and curled forward, tucking my head between my knees. "Thank you. Thank you so much. You have no idea. Thank you."

"I've been informed my client is being relocated to his former cell. I suggest you plan a visit. You both need it, I'm sure."

I'd never mentioned the depth of my relationship with Bishop, but Cynthia wasn't a stupid woman.

I thanked her again and got off the phone. Sitting for a few minutes, absorbing the news, I took several satisfying breaths to cleanse the turmoil that had poisoned my insides for weeks. There was hope. Hope I'd almost given up on five minutes ago.

I called Javier back and shared the news. He informed me they'd received a call almost at the same time as me that Bishop was being brought back to his cell.

"What's gonna happen with you now?" Javier asked. "Ray didn't foresee this?"

It was true. Ray had assumed when I came back to work, Bishop would be gone. "I guess I'll find out."

"Maybe now you can get some proper fucking sleep, yeah?"

"God, I need it."

"I know. I'm gonna pass by his area when I'm done with my shift. Do you want me to tell him anything?"

"Tell him I'll be there for a visit at the first chance I get."

"Done. Congratulations, Anson. I hope this works out."

It had to. We were on the right track. A new trial with an amazing lawyer was what Bishop needed.

RAY MOVED ME TO D-POD. I wasn't surprised. But with the move came a final warning. I was restricted to my pod, no ifs, ands, or buts. If I tried to pull a fast one, I'd be shown the door. Like before, I was free to visit Bishop on my own time or correspond through mail, but that was to be the extent of my contact with him.

I was okay with that. He was alive.

The trial hadn't started yet, and Cynthia had informed us both it would take some time. These things never happened fast. She was building a rock-solid case in the meantime, and in doing so, she'd unearthed a startling number of things that had been buried or ignored during Bishop's first trial that cast significant doubt on his public defender's efficiency. The mounting evidence pointed at possible persuasion from the opposing party, and if proven, it could end in his old lawyer being charged and disbarred.

One huge discovery was a new witness. While following up with previous witnesses, a young man of twenty-eight named Henrick, the child of one of Ayanna's old neighbors, had come forward with new information. At the time of the crime, he'd been eight years old. But he'd been a friend of Keon's, and they'd played together plenty at Ayanna's apartment. As a young boy, he'd witnessed a great deal.

Henrick's mother hadn't allowed her young son to talk to the police during the time of the investigation, but Henrick remembered Isaiah's presence at Ayanna's apartment all the time. He also recalled the physical abuse because he'd seen it firsthand. He shared that he was afraid when Isaiah used to come by during playdates, and he'd run home and tell his mother—a woman who'd done nothing to help poor Ayanna. On more than one occasion, Henrick heard Isaiah make promises to shut Ayanna up permanently if she didn't cooperate.

In the same breath, Henrick remembered Bishop being at the apartment, too, because Bishop was always telling Ayanna to call the police on Isaiah, and Henrick had agreed, unable to understand in his little eight-year-old brain why she wouldn't listen. Everyone was scared of Isaiah.

Henrick's testimony could be vital in helping clear Bishop's name. Although, Cynthia warned that the prosecution would do everything in their power to discredit Henrick's testimony based on his age at the time he'd witnessed everything.

It was still something.

Winter turned to spring.

Spring turned to summer.

Summer turned to fall, and still, we waited.

It was midwinter again before Bishop's trial was given a court date. There was a new jury selection process, and additional professionals brought in for evidence analysis since Cynthia no longer trusted the old findings and wanted new eyes on everything.

She was a predator in the courtroom and left no leaf unturned. I pitied anyone who stood in her way. She was ruthless and determined. I liked her more and more every day.

Trials were slow-moving. Everything happened at a snail's pace. They could spend hours—*days*—discussing the smallest details, but I didn't care. I booked off all shifts possible so I could be there to support Bishop and hear how everything was going firsthand.

Jalen wouldn't come. Refused. It was excuse after excuse, but the truth was, his and Bishop's relationship was damaged. Until they talked it out, tension would always exist between them.

Jalen was relieved to know his brother was getting a second chance, but his guilt was profound and tainted all his willingness to clear the air. When I asked Cynthia if Jalen would be taking the stand again, she told me it was possible, if only to clarify his first statement all those years ago.

It was a chilly day in April when I sat in the back of the courtroom and listened to a forensic pathologist by the name of Dr. Montgomery go over Ayanna and Keon's autopsy report while giving a complete etiology of how the weapon was used to kill the pair based on his findings.

"It's clear by the angle of the wounds that the attacker was right-handed or wielding the knife with his right hand when he or she stabbed the victims. The weapon was found to be an eight-inch long chef's knife taken from a block in the victim's kitchen. That corresponds with my findings. A chef's knife is a single-edged blade, sharp on one side for cutting, and squared off on the other. As you can see here." He indicated to a slide. "These marks show a clear distinction of that pattern. One edge of the wound shows the blunter edge while the other is much sharper in appearance. As you see, the blunt edge is on the top, and there is significant trauma from impact here, which tells me the attacker used a downward thrust when stabbing this victim." The doctor made a motion to show the court.

"Is there any way of knowing how tall the attacker might have been based on these wounds?"

"The victim, Ayanna, was five feet ten inches tall. Based on the angle of penetration on the first few wounds before she went down, her attacker would likely be taller than her."

"How much taller?"

"Hard to determine."

"Over six feet? Under? Can you ballpark me a guess?"

"No more than six feet. Any taller and the angle of the wounds would have been more drastic unless the man was crouching or lost his footing and was not attacking from his full height, which is not consistent with my findings."

"Thank you. Please continue with your analysis."

Dr. Montgomery checked his notes and adjusted his glasses. "Right. The size of the wounds found on the surface of the body directly correspond with the depth of penetration." He flipped the slide until another gruesome photograph was on display. "Here, here, here, here, and here." He pointed from one wound to another on the photograph. "The wounds measure the full width of the knife which tells me the attacker's hits were made with full strength and without hesitation, ensuring to embed the weapon as deeply as it would go. The impact marks you see here and here and here show where the hilt of the knife punched against her flesh, marking her skin. Full penetration. One hundred percent force."

Cynthia held up a finger, stopping the man.

"I'm sorry, I'd like to take us back a step. You indicated there were no signs of hesitation on the victim."

"No, ma'am."

"And how likely is it that the attacker, if using his less dominant hand, would have had the strength and stamina to fully impale the victim this many times in a row without showing signs of weakening or awkwardness?"

Dr. Montgomery made a face as he thought. "Not impossible, but certainly not likely. Wounds to this degree, and this many, would eventually show indications of sloppiness or weakness if the attacker was using his less dominant hand. The depth of penetration would likely be less, and there would be signs of awkwardness in the strikes, like you mention. The person would tire much faster. Have you ever tried to write with the wrong hand or eat or brush your teeth with the wrong hand? It'd be like that. Hypothetically, it's not impossible, but like I said, it would be highly unlikely this was done by a left-handed individual. Considering this attack and violence shows an extreme act of passion, the attacker would have had to consciously have made a decision to go against what felt natural if he or she used their less dominant hand. In the heat of the moment, most individuals wouldn't have the capacity to forethink something like that."

"Thank you. Continue."

The back and forth went on and on, but I zoned out and found Bishop up front.

He was fully chained, hands and feet, and was made to sit a small distance away from Cynthia. Four officers from Polunsky flanked him, two of whom I recognized. Sonny and Mason. Bishop's expression was unreadable but attentive. He absorbed every word and sat rigid as though waiting for the ball to drop. Waiting for the lies to swallow him whole once again.

They didn't.

Everything Cynthia brought forward was solid. Every question she asked was concise and well thought out. When the prosecutor tried to gain an edge, she was like a viper, striking before there was a moment of doubt in the jury's mind. Everything she brought forward cast doubt on Bishop's old lawyer and his old trial. It was terrifying to hear and see. She was brilliant.

Knowing who Isaiah was and who his father was, I couldn't help but wonder if they'd paid people off to keep their mouths shut during the original trial. To steer evidence away from Isaiah and onto Bishop. It sounded ridiculous. Those things only happened in the movies, right?

But maybe they didn't.

Or maybe nobody fought too hard the first time around because they were convinced they had their man.

When Cynthia called the original pathologist to the stand, he was green and sweating, unable to give a proper answer to why his report from years ago was full of holes.

Maybe Bishop had sat on death row for all this time because one man held enough power and money to protect his son and had used it to put away an innocent man.

It made me sick to consider.

In June, Henrick gave his testimony, as did his mother and a few other neighbors who'd lived in the building at the time. It was funny how much more elaborate their memories were this time around when someone asked the right questions.

The day they called Jalen to the stand, I felt the tension wafting off Bishop all the way across the room. He wouldn't look at his brother. With his head bowed, Bishop stared at his hands the entire time.

"Did you ever see your brother raise a hand to Ayanna?"

"No." Jalen was pale under the fluorescent lights of the courtroom, and he wouldn't look Cynthia in the eyes.

"Did you ever see him raise a hand to Keon?"

"No."

"Was Keon Bishop's son?"

We all knew he wasn't. The court knew he wasn't. Paternity testing had proven Keon belonged to Isaiah.

"No."

"Can you describe the relationship between Bishop and Ayanna?"

"They were close friends. They dated in high school for a bit, but then they broke up. I don't know why because they got along well enough. She disappeared for a while, but then she was around again. Pregnant. She had a kid, and Bishop saw them all the time. She came over for dinner. He helped her out. She leaned on him. I thought maybe they'd patched up their differences and he wanted to date her again but wouldn't tell us."

"Tell me about the time you claim to have overheard Bishop say he was going to kill her."

"He didn't say that," Jalen snapped.

"But that's what it says here in your previous testimony."

"That's incorrect. Bishop never said he was going to kill her. They turned my words around. She came to our house one night, and he snuck her into his room. I heard her crying and them talking. He got angrier and angrier. Then, he was really upset and punched the wall. That's when I went into the hallway to listen. What I heard sounded like he found out she was cheating or something. He was angry at this other guy and said when he found out who it was, he was going to kill him." Jalen shrank back on his seat, hearing his own words as they floated through the room. Again, it pinned Bishop as violent. "He wouldn't hurt anyone. I know my brother. Ayanna spent the night that night. Maw Maw was pissed because he had a girl in his room, but she wouldn't have stayed if he was threatening her, right?"

Bishop scowled at his hands and wrung them in his lap. His knee bounced, his jaw ticked, and I wanted to scream at Jalen to shut up.

But Cynthia didn't flinch. She wanted the whole truth out there. Even the uttered threats Bishop had cast toward Isaiah.

"So you were under the impression your brother was dating Ayanna again."

"Yeah, and that she'd cheated." Jalen shrugged. "They could've got back together. That's what I assumed."

"My client claims Ayanna came to him in anguish that evening because she'd been abused. She sought him out for comfort because she was afraid. Is it possible what you heard could have been an outburst aimed at her abuser?"

"Objection. Leading the witness."

Cynthia raised a hand. "I withdraw my question, Your Honor." She paced in front of the witness stand, focusing on Jalen. "Did you see Ayanna the following morning?"

"Yes."

"And how did she look?"

"Rough. Bruised."

"And how was she acting toward your brother."

Jalen shifted on his seat. "She wouldn't leave his arms. He held her and held her, and she cried. She said she didn't want to go back to school because she was afraid."

Cynthia had a miraculous way of flipping Jalen's testimony in the exact opposite way it'd been presented before. Even the state's cross-examination was tame. When he was allowed to step down, his gaze lingered on his brother, who still wouldn't meet his eyes.

Defeated, Jalen hung his head and left the courtroom.

DURING THE MONTHS of Bishop's trial, I continued with my weekly visits at Polunsky.

"You look good," I said one Monday morning in August. "You don't look as beat-up as you did a few months ago."

He smiled, a sight that warmed me inside and out. "I've never felt hope like this before. Things feel good right now. The trial feels good. I don't feel like they're kicking me down every time I try to stand."

"I feel good about it too. We're closing in on the end."

He nodded and picked at his fingers. "I still can't picture it, you know? Being outside this prison. They take me to the courthouse, but

I'm so locked up in the van, and there's no windows and open space, I can't hardly imagine what it'd be like to get out."

"You'll see. Where is the first place you want to go when you get out?"

Bishop laughed and shook his head. "Nah, I don't wanna play that game. That's dangerous."

"Are you superstitious?"

"No, but it still feels like tempting fate. I don't wanna do that."

"Fair enough."

"Wait. Maybe one thing."

I grinned and watched the light shine in his eyes. It'd been absent for a while, but it was back and beautiful to behold. "What's that?"

"Not somewhere to go, but I'd sure love to have a barbecued steak."

"Medium-rare, right?" I winked, teasing him, knowing his true preference.

"You best not put bloody meat on my plate, Anson."

"Medium-well. I remember."

"With potato salad?"

"You know it. Do you want crispy bacon bits in the salad?"

"I do."

"I make amazing veggie skewers, if you'd like."

"Damn. That's got to be better than the mushy canned vegetable slop they give us in here. For the record, I never want to eat creamed corn again."

"If you get out of here, I promise, I will never feed you that again."

We fell silent, humbled by the path of conversation we'd chosen to take because there was still a lot pending Bishop's release. The case seemed to be going well and strong, but anything could happen.

"How are your renovations going?" Bishop asked, steering our conversation into safer territory.

"Good. I finished painting the guest room." I didn't tell him my focus on the guest room was because of his potential release. I wanted him to have somewhere to go without putting pressure on him to stay with me in my room. I didn't know how soon he'd be ready to jump into a physical relationship if he was released. "I'm getting new windows installed too. Next week. Mom is coming to visit for a few days, so I wanted them in before she showed up."

"You'll have to take pictures."

"I always do."

Chapter Twenty-two

OCTOBER SECOND WAS THE DAY my life would change. It would either begin or end with the jury's verdict. I'd arrived at the courthouse early. Javier had come with me, and he watched, hands shoved in the pockets of his trousers as I paced back and forth in front of the concrete stairs leading to the entrance.

The wind was warm, but I shivered regardless, chilled on the inside and unable to stop the tremors rocking through my body.

"Breathe, man, before you pass out."

I messed a hand through my hair, trying to find an even rhythm but failing. "How can I be sweating and freezing at the same time?"

"You're stressing out. Stop wearing your shoes out, and let's go inside."

I stared down at the ground beneath my runners, kicking pebbles and grinding my teeth. "Okay. Okay, let's do this."

As I turned to the stairs, a familiar face caught my eye. Jalen was approaching the courthouse from the street, his shoulders hunched, and his body language screaming anguish. He looked like he wasn't sure he should be there.

I halted Javier with a touch on his shoulder. "Hang on. Give me a minute."

I approached Jalen, who'd stopped walking when he spotted me. "I had to come."

"I'm glad you did. Bishop needs you here. You're family."

He shrugged, not buying it. "He might hate me forever, but I wanted to be here to support him."

I gestured to the front doors. "Come on. You can sit with us. Is Drake here?"

Jalen flinched and scowled, shaking his head fast like I'd asked a stupid question. Of course he wouldn't let him come. People might see or suspect.

We entered the courtroom to a steady buzz of people all standing around, waiting for the proceedings to begin. There were reporters of all kinds who'd taken an interest in Bishop's trial over the past few months, so I wasn't surprised to see a roomful waiting to hear the verdict. His case was hot news. It wasn't often a man on death row stood a chance of getting exonerated.

Bishop wasn't there yet, but I kept an eye on the door where they'd bring him in and waited.

Javier introduced himself and struck up a conversation with Jalen. I was too distracted to pay attention.

It was ten minutes later when Bishop was brought in, hands bound in front, legs cuffed, and a chain connecting them both. He scanned and found me in the crowd. Our eyes locked, and I could see the worry lines making grooves in his forehead. I gave him a nod, reassuring him despite carrying as much concern on my shoulders.

Derrick was one of his escorts today, along with Jin and two guys I didn't know. Off-premises escorts always required a double team. Oddly enough, Derrick hadn't spilled the beans about my sexuality to everyone and their mothers. I respected him a lot more for that.

Derrick caught my eye and winked, a grin splitting his face. I forced a smile to my lips and turned away.

It was another few minutes before the room settled and the judge came in. There were some technical things to cover before the judge asked the jury if they'd reached a verdict. The presiding juror stood and addressed the bench.

"We have, Your Honor."

"We'll hear it."

You could hear a pin drop in the room. All the air was sucked from my lungs. I fidgeted, staring at the man who held Bishop's life in his hands. Dizzy, nauseous, and cold inside and out, I waited.

"With regards to the murder of twenty-one-year-old Ayanna Williams on April 13th, 2001, how does the jury find Mr. Bishop Ndiaye?"

"The jury finds him to be not guilty."

The air left my lungs in a great burst, and I collapsed against Jalen, clinging to his arm. Tears filled my eyes, and I barely heard the second half.

"With regards to the murder of five-year-old Keon Williams on April 13th, 2001, how does the jury find Mr. Bishop Ndiaye?"

"The jury finds him to be not guilty."

The room erupted into chaos. The judge called for order and closed the proceedings with a few quick words. Clapping and murmured chatter filled my ears. Jalen turned to me, and I caught him in a tight hug that went on and on. Javier patted my back and whispered congratulations in my ear.

But it was Bishop I needed to see. Batting the tears from my eyes, I straightened my shirt and searched through the sudden throng of bodies. Without thought or care, I shoved my way toward the aisle and battled through the crush of people to get to the front. Cynthia was surrounded and accepting congratulations from people she must have known. I scanned but didn't see Bishop.

"They removed him so he wouldn't get mobbed," Cynthia said, catching my arm.

She held out her hand to shake with a beaming smile on her face, but I smacked her hand away and grabbed her, hauling her into a tight hug. "You are the best. I can't thank you enough."

She patted my back but didn't pull away. She held me close and whispered in my ear. "I approached Nancy Petty, Bishop's old representation, earlier this morning. The woman is sweating in her high heels because she knows I've discredited her with this trial. I informed her there would be a civil suit filed for malpractice. She's prepared to make a statement. My guess is she's fishing for leniency because she knows she's done wrong and is about to lose her license. She claims she has information that could be of great value with regards to Isaiah and his father, Terry Gordon. This is far from over, Anson. You tell Bishop, Ayanna's case will be reopened, and justice will be served one way or another."

My heart clenched, and I squeezed Cynthia tighter in my arms as more tears surfaced. There were no words I could offer to express my gratitude. "I'll tell him. Thank you so much."

Cynthia pulled out of my arms and clutched my shoulders, a rarely seen smile glowed up at me. "One more step down, still many more to go. Now, we get Bishop's record wiped clean and fight for compensation. Twenty years in prison for no reason? They will pay up if I have anything to say about it." She patted my chest and smoothed my wrinkled shirt. "But that's enough for one day. Head through there, and they'll let you know where he is."

I took her hands in mine. "Thank you. From the bottom of my heart."

"You're welcome, Anson. Now go."

I ran. Through the door was a long corridor, and I stood, lost, glancing from door to door. They were all closed.

When Derrick stepped out of a room at the end of the hall, I picked up my pace.

"Through here, lover boy."

I burst through the doors and ground to a halt. There he was. And free. No more prisons. No more restrictions. No more plexiglass barriers.

"Take his fucking chains off," I barked when I noticed they were all still in place.

Bishop turned at the sound of my voice, his eyes lit up with his smile.

"No can do just yet," one of the officers I didn't know said. "It all has to be processed yet. We need signed paperwork and confirmation before we can do that. He'll go back to Polunsky, but I assure you, it will be worked out."

"It's okay, boss. It's a few more days or hours."

"It's not okay. Leave us," I snapped.

The same man was about to protest when Derrick spoke up. "He's an officer, Bruce, the same as us. Cut him some slack. We'll be right outside the door," Derrick informed me.

They left, and when the door clicked behind me, I found my feet and moved forward. He was there. In front of me. In the flesh.

The moment was so huge, so devastating neither of us could move.

"You did it, boss. I'm a free man." He shook his head. "I didn't ever think I'd see this day." His eyes pooled, and a single tear spilled over, tracking down his face.

I reached out, caught it with my thumb, then cupped his warm cheek in my palm. His gaze roamed my face, and when he reached out to touch me, his binds stopped him.

"Dammit. I want to touch you."

With a hitch in my chest, I pulled him against me, wrapped my arms around him, and hugged him with all I had. Burying my face in his neck, I inhaled, taking his scent into my lungs and shuddering with the reality of what had happened.

Bishop leaned against me, unable to hold me in return, but taking the embrace and soaking it in.

We stood like that for a long time, absorbing one another, unable to move, unable to find the strength to let go now that we were in each other's arms.

After a time, I inched away and took his face in my hands. He was a lot taller than me, but he tipped his chin down and connected his forehead to mine. No window. Flesh to flesh.

"Boss?"

"Anson."

He chuckled. "Anson?"

"Yeah?"

"I've never kissed a man before, but I've been dying to kiss you for more than a year."

I didn't need any more permission than that. I tipped my head up and found his lips with mine, brushing them together with a feathering touch before moving closer and taking the kiss.

His breathing hitched, and he pressed against me, sighing when I traced my tongue along the seam of his lips. In a flash, they parted, and our connection deepened.

My heart was going to explode at this rate. I'd longed for this moment. Dreamed, prayed, and wished for it more times than I could count. It was everything.

Our tears mingled, and still, we couldn't break apart. It was new and necessary.

When we came up for air, neither of us moved. Bishop vibrated in my arms, his breathing labored and shallow.

"You okay?" I asked.

"Nervous. Excited. Scared."

"And free."

"And free. God, I wish Maw Maw was around to see this day."

"She'd be so proud of you."

There was a knock on the door, so I stepped away and wiped at my mouth as though Bishop's kiss lingered there for others to see. He smiled and put more distance between us.

"Yeah," I called out.

Derrick poked his head in but looked at Bishop. "There is someone else to see you."

Bishop's brow dipped before he nodded and checked with me.

I knew who it was, but I didn't think Bishop knew he was here.

Jalen walked in the door a minute later, his gaze seeking Bishop, his feet stalling the minute they made eye contact.

I felt more than saw Bishop stiffen, but he remained silent.

"Congratulations," Jalen said. "I know you don't want to see me, and I'll stay out of your life, but I wanted you to know how happy I am for you. You may not believe me, but I always knew you were innocent."

When Jalen stopped talking, silence seeped in from all sides. There was a standoff, and it was painful to watch.

Jalen gave in first and dropped his chin. "I'm gonna go. Anson has my number, if you ever want to talk."

He backed out, but before the door shut, Bishop stepped forward. "Jalen?"

When Jalen turned, there was desperation in his eyes. He was still that little boy who wanted nothing more than his big brother's love.

"Thank you," Bishop said. "Anson told me how you helped. I appreciate it more than you know."

A sad smile came and went on Jalen's face before he nodded and left.

Derrick was about to come back in the room, but I gave a pleading look that begged for one more minute.

When we were alone again, I reached for Bishop's hands, holding them both and running my thumbs along the cuffs that bound them together. "You have your life ahead of you now. I wanted you to know, there is no pressure from me. There will be a lot to take in, and figuring us out on top of it all might be too much. But I've cleared out my guest room, and it's yours, if you want to come and stay with me.

Cynthia still has a fight ahead of her to get you some type of compensation, but you aren't homeless, and you have a friend."

Bishop squeezed my hands. "More than a friend. I've been wanting to explore this for a long time, and now I can."

I smiled. "You can."

"Will you kiss me again, boss?"

"Will you stop calling me that and use my name?"

His joy was blinding. "Anson, will you please kiss me again?"

"Try and stop me."

We came together with more certainty than the first time. Our breaths mingling, our tongues testing this new connection, our hearts beating together.

It was the start of a whole new life for Bishop. For me.

I was under no delusions that it would be easy. Twenty years of confinement would have severe consequences. I knew that much, but we'd figure it out.

He was done living the life of a convict. Bishop was an innocent and free man now.

It was time to step outside and see the world again.

The End

Join Bishop and Anson as they explore their brand-new relationship in *Outside (Death Row Chronicles Vol. 2)*. It won't be easy. Bishop's struggles are far worse than either of them expected as he learns to adapt to a life outside of Polunsky and death row.

OTHER TITLES BY NICKY JAMES

Standalone Contemporary
Trusting Tanner
Twinkle Star
Love Me Whole (available in audio)
Rocky Mountain Refuge
The Christmas I Know
Long Way Home

Trials of Fear
Owl's Slumber (available in audio)
Shades of Darkness (coming soon in audio)
Touch of Love
Fearless (A companion novel)
Lost in a Moment
Cravings of the Heart
Heal With You
A Very Merry Krewmas (Trials of Fear Special)

Fear Niblets
Rigger's Decision

Healing Hearts Series
No Regrets (available in audio)
New Beginnings: Abel's Journey (available in audio)
The Escape: Soren's Saga
Lost Soul: AJ's Burden

Taboo
Sinfully Mine
Secrets & Lies

Historical
Until the End of Time
Steel My Heart

Tales from Edovia Series
Something from Nothing
Buried Truths
Secrets Best Untold

Printed in Great Britain
by Amazon